The Blessed

Titles by Lisa T. Bergren

৬ ৬ ৬

Novels of the Gifted

THE BEGOTTEN
THE BETRAYED
THE BLESSED

৬ ৬ ৬

THE BRIDGE
CHRISTMAS EVERY MORNING
THE CAPTAIN'S BRIDE
DEEP HARBOR
MIDNIGHT SUN

The Blessed

A Novel of the Gifted

LISA T. BERGREN

B

BERKLEY BOOKS, NEW YORK

THE BERKLEY PUBLISHING GROUP
Published by the Penguin Group
Penguin Group (USA) Inc.
375 Hudson Street, New York, New York 10014, USA
Penguin Group (Canada), 90 Eglinton Avenue East, Suite 700, Toronto, Ontario M4P 2Y3, Canada
(a division of Pearson Penguin Canada Inc.)
Penguin Books Ltd., 80 Strand, London WC2R 0RL, England
Penguin Group Ireland, 25 St. Stephen's Green, Dublin 2, Ireland (a division of Penguin Books Ltd.)
Penguin Group (Australia), 250 Camberwell Road, Camberwell, Victoria 3124, Australia
(a division of Pearson Australia Group Pty. Ltd.)
Penguin Books India Pvt. Ltd., 11 Community Centre, Panchsheel Park, New Delhi—110 017, India
Penguin Group (NZ), 67 Apollo Drive, Rosedale, North Shore 0632, New Zealand
(a division of Pearson New Zealand Ltd.)
Penguin Books (South Africa) (Pty.) Ltd., 24 Sturdee Avenue, Rosebank, Johannesburg 2196,
South Africa

Penguin Books Ltd., Registered Offices: 80 Strand, London WC2R 0RL, England

This book is an original publication of The Berkley Publishing Group.

This is a work of fiction. Names, characters, places, and incidents either are the product of the author's imagination or are used fictitiously, and any resemblance to actual persons, living or dead, business establishments, events, or locales is entirely coincidental. The publisher does not have any control over and does not assume any responsibility for author or third-party websites or their content.

FIRST EDITION: September 2008

Library of Congress Cataloging-in-Publication Data

Bergren, Lisa Tawn.
   The blessed / Lisa T. Bergren.—1st ed.
      p. cm.
   ISBN 978-0-425-22342-0
   1. Aristocracy (Social class)—Fiction. 2. France—History—14th century—Fiction. 3. Provence (France)—Fiction 4. Good and evil—Fiction.   I. Title.

PS3552.E71938B55 2008
813'.54—dc22   2008023601

PRINTED IN THE UNITED STATES OF AMERICA

10 9 8 7 6 5 4 3 2 1

To Roy and Jane,
battered but not broken, beloved, blessed.
Keep watch in the night!

ACKNOWLEDGMENTS

Special thanks to my editor, Denise Silvestro, her assistant, Meredith Giordan, and the incomparable copyeditor, Amy Schneider, who kept track of me from start to finish on the Gifted series. Collectively, they saved me from making many grave errors; any that remain are my own. I'm in debt to Stephen Rice, who edited my Latin, provided some translation, and set me straight on a few other linguistic matters. *Post tenebras, lux.* Thanks also to Joel Fotinos, Leslie Gelbman, Lara Robbins, Craig Burke, Chris Mosley, as well as Norman Lidofsky, William Bauers, and the rest of the sales force, and everyone on the Berkley team.

VISCONTI FAMILY

PATRIARCHATE OF TRENT

DELLA SCALA FAMILY

Lyon

COUNTS OF SAVOY

PATRIARCHATE OF AQUILEIA

Verona

REPUBLIC OF VENICE

Venezia

VIENNE

Milano

Genova

GONZAGA FAMILY

ESTENSE FAMILY

FRANCE

REPUBLIC OF GENOA

REPUBLIC OF FLORENCE

PROVENCE

Avignon

Marseille

REPUBLIC OF PISA

Pirenze

PAPAL STATES

CORSICA

Siena

REPUBLIC OF SIENA

Roma

ITALIA C. 1340

Napoli

KINGDOM OF NAPLES

KINGDOM OF SICILY

BEYOND THE MOAT

Provence

CHAPTER ONE

February, the Year of Our Lord 1340

OUTNUMBERED and surrounded, they were lost before it began.

Daria d'Angelo, unable to sleep upon the wet, rocky ground that seeped its chill into her bones, heard their stealthy approach. She removed the twill covering—an attempt to ward off the constant rain—and found her knight, Gianni, already beside her, face taut with tension. Grimly she took his hand and rose, joining the group beside the fire, faces betraying weariness and worry.

Daria's knights had only just drawn their swords and formed a line around the group when the intruders shoved Vito, bound and bleeding at the lip, into their circle. Gianni and Ugo narrowly swung their swords away, barely missing him. The knights held the line around their people, swords drawn. But for each man, three others were before him.

Ugo untied Vito and both brothers stared up in fury at their captors, itching for an order from Gianni to strike out.

"Be at peace," said the opposition's leader, from atop a fine Spanish mount. "We mean you no harm."

"Could've fooled me," Vito said, wiping away the blood of his lip with the back of his hand.

"If you speak the truth, advise your men to sheathe their swords and stand down," Ugo added.

Gianni edged forward, in front of the brothers. "I am Sir Gianni de Capezzana, and this is my lady, Daria d'Angelo. We seek safe passage to Avignon. We believed this to be a public road."

The captain dismounted and neared the campfire light. He nodded, regally, at Gianni, but his eyes quickly moved on to Daria, who tried to calm her white falcon, Bormeo, screeching in alarm. "You are on a public road, but one we watch closely. I am Sir Lucien Gisserot," he said with a nod and a courtly arm outstretched as he bowed in her direction. When he rose, he smiled at her and then turned his attention back to Gianni. His cape fell into place behind him, and Daria's eyes widened.

"I know your coat of arms," Daria said, studying the white sixteen-pointed star on a bed of red. "You are of Les Baux."

"Just as Les Baux knows the peacock," said the knight, tossing her a grin and turning to face her again. "Come, Duchess. Les Baux would very much like to welcome you and be your protectors while you abide in these lands. You are tracked by a group of men, not half a day's ride from here. From what my lord knows, they intend to do you and yours harm."

Gianni appraised her, confusion rife in his eyes.

She would have to explain later. She nodded at Gianni, telling him this was a good choice, trusting Les Baux, and her captain immediately turned and gave the order to pack and mount up. They were on the move within a few minutes, with six of the knights carrying lanterns to ward off the dark of night. All told, the Gifted were thirteen in number, including five knights, one lady, her maidservant, a priest, an artist, a fisherman, and three children.

Daria looked over her shoulder, beyond the last knights of Les Baux and into the dark forest, even more menacing since she knew who it was that tracked them. Why? Why track them here? And how could Les Baux know that other travelers upon this road—of which they were few of many—might be chasing them at all?

"You know the lord of Les Baux," Vito said dryly, riding up beside her. He still dabbed blood from the corner of his lip. Gianni was up ahead, talking to Lucien. "You so enjoy a night of drizzling rain that you could not have mentioned a warm castle ahead?"

"My father established a good cloth trade here with the people of Les Baux when I was but a child. They weave a fine, strong, smooth cotton. Even now, I suppose that Baron del Buco still sees to the trade—he did when I left Siena."

Vito considered her words. "Could it then be a trap? Might Les Baux be waylaying us, to allow del Buco and Amidei to catch us?"

" 'Tis my greatest fear. But I saw little choice other than to accept a night's hospitality. Did you?"

Vito looked out from under his hood at the rain and the men-at-arms.

Father Piero rode up beside them, catching the last of their conversation. "Amidei and del Buco are bound to be holed up for the night, even if they are those who track us. We shall pray for an exit from Les Baux if it is not the protection we seek."

He rode on to speak to Gianni, leaving Daria to her thoughts. When she was a child, there had been talk that she and the future count of Les Baux, Armand, might be a good match. Her father was in strong position to take the seat of one of the Nine, his wealth and properties growing, and he had but one heir, a daughter in need of a strong husband. She supposed it was why her mother had brought in a tutor to teach her French, with the twists that made it uniquely Provençal.

Armand was but three years her senior, the same age as Gianni, and handsome, even as a boy. But the thought of leaving Toscana for the foreign lands to the north had made both Daria and her parents ill at ease. And from an early age, her heart had been tied to Marco Adimari. It did not take long for Giulio d'Angelo to tell Count Rieu de Baux that his daughter would remain in Toscana.

It had not interrupted trade between the family and the people of Les Baux. And gradually the count's letters had become Armand's letters, always addressed to Daria d'Angelo, never Baron del Buco. It had irked Vincenzo, but he understood family ties. From their formal tone, Daria knew that Armand considered her still handfasted to Adimari. But there was always one line to his letters that was friendly, familial, words that spoke to her, reached out to her.

Daria sighed. What would happen when the lord of Les Baux and her newfound love, Gianni de Capezzana, met? She did not know if Armand was yet married himself. She had received no invitation nor announcement, which would have been customary among trade associates. She knew of his reputation; he loved courtly conduct, courtship, adopting the ways of the Franks in wholehearted fashion. Gianni struggled with jealousy, always present at her side. And yet nothing was declared, established between them. Aboard ship, she had made it clear how she felt about him. He had kissed her, made it clear he had deep feelings for her, but weeks later, nothing more had been said, nothing more had transpired.

She sighed. It would be what it would be. It was out of her hands. With one word, the count could be cut off, should he begin to pursue her. *Barren.* After all, he would be in as high a need of an heir as Marco Adimari had once been. She looked to Gianni again, able to see nothing but the outline of his form under a hooded cape, drawn close against the steadily beating rain. Two men at the front carried lanterns, holding them aloft to find the path and lead the way.

Did Gianni truly not care if he had a child of his own? He held no lands nor title beyond that of a knight. But did not every man wish to pass along his blood to the next generation? Was this what kept them apart? Why he had drawn away?

Gianni and Sir Lucien fell back, awaiting her, then rode alongside her. "You shall find," Lucien said, "that Lord Armand Rieu is a good man, a valiant protector. He had gained word from Conte Morassi that you might be en route to Avignon through Provence."

Daria lifted her head and shared a long look with Gianni. She turned her head back toward Lucien. "Conte Morassi de Venezia?"

"One and the same," he said, his blue eyes clearly taking in her wonder. "Conte Morassi and Lord Armand have long been as close as brothers. Their forefathers served together in the wars against the infidels."

Crusaders. So the ancestors of both Lord Rieu and Conte Morassi had been crusaders. She had saved the Morassis' twin children in Venezia, turning them in their mother's womb when many a midwife had bid them lost. It was one of many miraculous healing stories . . . and only part of the Gifted's journey together. Clearly God was leading them ever onward.

cb cb cb

GIANNI turned in his saddle to eye Tessa, who was able to discern light from dark, good from evil, within others. The girl raised her eyebrows in response, giving her head a little shake as if to say she sensed no ill portents. His gaze moved on to the priest, Father Piero, gifted in wisdom, who lifted his small shoulders. He seemed to accept that they might already be in the company of friends.

Gianni missed Hasani's presence. The tall African had been abducted in Venezia, and one of the Gifted's many goals was to find him again. He was their seer, the one who could envision what was to come, often drawing elaborate pictures that had been so vital in leading them forward on this mad course. Where was he? Had he drawn these men or the lord of Les Baux?

He had drawn Daria, chained in Amidei's dungeon, and Piero, taking Amidei's arrow to the chest, arms outstretched. Gianni's jaw muscles worked as he studied the Provençal knight on the other side of Daria, still trying to decide if they should take their chances and try to break away.

Daria placed a reassuring hand on his forearm, sensing his unease.

He ignored Lucien's curious glance and stared back into her wide, long-lashed olive eyes, so regal, his lady, with her dark brown hair coiling in ringlets along her neck in the damp, cold air. The bruises on her neck were long gone, but Gianni was more wary than ever when it came to safeguarding her. Unfortunately the Gifted's call seemed to continually place them into the lair of their enemy. Mayhap Daria was right; Lord Armand's castle would be a respite, a place to gain intelligence on the pope and his court, plan their entry into Avignon. Still, he hesitated.

"Sir de Capezzana," said Lucien, "you knew of the knights that trail you?"

"Nay. We were not aware of it," he allowed. "Simply another group of pilgrims?"

The knight smiled and glanced at Daria. "Come, now. It is plain that neither of you has a pilgrimage in mind."

Gianni paused. "You are certain that they follow us?"

"Indeed. They have matched your pace since you departed Marseilles."

"I take it that you, then, have as well."

Lucien smiled again. "My lord, after receiving Count Morassi's letter, was most insistent we find and protect you."

Only one group would be following them into Provence. He could feel Tessa edge closer.

"They merely are as slow as we," he tried tiredly.

"Not with the horseflesh and manpower they boast. They follow you. Be they friend or foe?"

"Foe," Gianni grit out. "Lord Abramo Amidei, I'd wager. Baron Vincenzo del Buco. And their entourage."

Sir Lucien eyed one of his scouts. "Off with you, then. Go and see if it is Amidei or del Buco and report to us at Les Baux." The man disappeared immediately into the shadows. They all could hear the beating of the horse's hooves as the man and his mount departed into the night. "Come, my friends. You are road weary and plainly battle scarred. I can see it on your faces. Cease your ideas of fleeing, accept my lord's favor and protection, and face your foe in the light of day."

ॐ ॐ ॐ

VINCENZO del Buco laid back tiredly on his cot. The straw tick was musty and the cloth that covered it rough, but at least they were in an inn, not out in the woods as the Gifted were this night. His shoulder ached and he felt a dull hunger in his belly, but no real desire to go and seek food. On the far side of the room was Abramo Amidei, his lord and master, who had elected to avoid women this night and rest. In fact, Vincenzo had not seen him partake of the women since that fatal night on the isle, when the Gifted had so narrowly escaped them.

Abramo's hand covered his patched eye as if it hurt him. Only Vincenzo and a doctor had been allowed to see the deep and angry wound, where Daria had dared to slice him from brow to cheekbone. The doctor had removed the eviscerated and infected eyeball as Abramo screamed, screamed until he mercifully passed out. He slept then, through the doctor's cleansing and stitching of the wound, through the night and through the next day. And when he woke, he had one thing on his mind—to track down the Gifted.

Vincenzo sighed and rolled over. He longed for his dry Siena, a crackling fire of Toscana oak in the hearth. He could almost smell it. Winter in these lands was harsh and cold, the damp entering his bones until he felt every year of his life. Memories of traveling with Tatiana in their hopeless search for a cure flooded through his mind. Tatiana . . . Daria . . . all the women he had loved and lost before them. Until Amidei, his grief over them had raged in his mind like an infection. Only his lord's endless stream of female companionship had assuaged the illness of memory. And alongside Abramo, he had experienced wonders he had not dreamed possible. . . .

Until the Gifted gained strength and threatened all they had built. Daria, Gianni, the priest, Piero. Hasani. The child. The fisherman. He and Abramo had nearly decimated them . . . tearing them apart in an effort to rule them. Taking them nigh unto death, to show them the true vitality of life. But had they seen the path to victory? Joined them in the quest for power? Strength?

Nay. Stubborn were they, doggedly traveling forward as if driven by the hounds of hell. Vincenzo laughed under his breath.

"You cannot sleep?" Abramo asked from across the room.

"Nay."

"What amuses you?"

"Tell me, Abramo. Are we but the hounds of hell?"

"Better the hounds of hell than heaven's henchmen."

Vincenzo considered that a moment. "Do you not fear hell, Abramo?"

"I fear nothing." He sat up and lit a candle on the table by his bed, then leaned against the wall, drawing one leg up to the bed and resting an arm across it. Shadows danced across his handsome, scarred face, a long dark furrow undercutting the patch over his left eye. "This is all there is, Vincenzo," he said, gesturing around. "This. If we do not take it all now, here, we have nothing. And if we do not kill our enemies, we may well be glad to find ourselves in such humble surroundings, night after night. Gone will be our day of glory."

"Mayhap there is still a way of vanquishing our enemies, turning them, utilizing their power."

"The Gifted must be eradicated. They cannot be turned and therefore threaten everything we wish to accomplish. So they must die, every one of them. We will use the Church to kill them, or do it ourselves. But it ends here. The hounds of hell will seem like puppies in a pen beside us. The Gifted will know sorrow. Will know fear. Will know defeat."

Vincenzo said nothing. After a while, Abramo blew out the candle, and in seconds his breathing was slow and sure.

Daria, Daria. Once a niece to him. Once a business partner, co-consul of the guild in Siena. Once beloved. And now she was to die.

Vincenzo stared to the dark ceiling, longing to give in to slumber as his master had. But it eluded him.

Avignon

CARDINAL Boeri hated this city. For all the political intrigue and dangers of Roma, it was far cleaner and well organized than this cesspool above the Rhône. Avignon was ill prepared for the growth that came with housing the pope and his minions. Moving the offices of the pope to Avignon brought more than a thousand people to the city of old. And the impact of those thousand people brought thousands upon thousands more: people to sell food and supplies, sew garments, clean and cook, herd in animals, and haul refuse away—not that the refuse haulers were doing well at their task—essentially, those who made life in a city comfortable. And the pope, for all his famous fortitude and strivings to rein in the abuses of the cardinals and lesser priests, still enjoyed his comfort.

As did Cardinal Boeri. It was with relief that he made it to the bishop's mansion, ate, bathed, and then gratefully sank into the luxurious sheets in his quarters, a stone's throw from the Palais de le Pape. Bitter gall rose in his throat, even as he drew the feather-stuffed coverlet over his shoulders and leaned deeper into a feather pillow. He would do well to bring a set of this bedding home to Roma, when he went. Yes, quality bedding and the papacy both where God deigned them to be—Roma. This was his call, this was his duty, to serve the Church by showing her the way home.

The Gifted were making their way to Avignon, just as he knew they would. They were following the clues in the letter, as well as the glass map of which the doge had spoken. It was all part of Providence's plan, this, and Boeri would facilitate it. The Gifted would seek an audience with the pope; he would help them gain entry. The Gifted would want their own Hasani back among them; he would deliver the man to them. The Gifted would not fail to display their God-given glories, and he would be the one to showcase them. Through and through, he and the Gifted would become solidified in their partnership. This was why God had granted him a portion of their precious letter. Holy allies is what they were. Holy allies.

He sank a little deeper into the featherbed, closed his eyes, and smiled. The spies had told him they had docked in Marseilles, and even now traveled northward. *Come, my friends, come. The hour is drawing near for God's perfect plan to come together at last.*

CHAPTER TWO

2 *February*
Les Baux, Provence

THEY entered through the guarded castle gates in the dark watches of the night, but a feast was still keeping the castle alight. Piero searched his mind for holy holidays—in the chaos of their travels and days that became nights, he had fallen short of his priestly duties. It was February, the beginning of February. *Candlemas.* Terce and the candle vigil were long over, but Les Baux was still celebrating. Clearly, this Count des Baux enjoyed his feasts.

Piero's people were weary, from Daria to little Tessa, Gianni to young Roberto, but still they kept their chins up, eyes aware. He was proud of this troop, God's Gifted, heady in the knowledge that each one had been brought to them for God's own purposes. They were not the heavenly army that some might have wished for, but they were his army. So like his God, to bring such a disparate group together for his own good purposes. And what was this? A powerful lord, friend of Conte Morassi, sent to them as if he were God's own angel, protecting them from the dark? Swooping in to save them as Amidei's own men prepared to pounce? Piero shivered and glanced up with a prayer of gratitude.

They were all shown to the guest quarters, walking long passages hewn from the gray limestone cliffs on which the castle had been built. They had climbed and climbed, their horses and donkeys laboring under their weight, and Piero knew that the castle was likely to be high atop a bluff. He could hardly wait for daybreak to view their surroundings. Music and the aroma of roast duck floated down the hallway, twining as if in a bell pull that drew them forward, out of their muddy travel cloaks and into clean robes that would make them presentable in a count's court.

He was changed in moments and joined Sir Lucien in the hallway, who waited to show them the way, along with Gianni, Ambrogio, Gaspare, and the knights: Vito and Ugo, Basilio and Rune. They could have found their own way, given the promising aromas of feastings and a delicate, angelic singing now floating down the torch-lit hallway. The women and children were obviously still changing, and Lucien said he'd send back a servant to fetch them. They set off down the hallway, entranced by the song. It became louder the closer they came, and they emerged into a massive hall, with an arched roof and intersecting ribs high above them. They paused to take in their new surroundings.

Ambrogio whistled lowly and leaned toward Gianni. "This place could keep a painter employed for years."

Beautifully dressed ladies hovered in groups about the edges of the room. Knights, equally dressed in finery, sat in other groups or cavorted with the women in courtly fashion. Elaborate fixtures—that would keep a chandler working all year above his cauldrons of tallow—lit the room with a warm glow. A woman, the songbird, stood on a dais before the lord, singing such a heavenly, sweet tune that her immediate audience closed their eyes in plea-sure. Indeed, the singer also kept her eyes closed, her small chin raised as if toward God, her long, blond hair pinned in coils over the nape of her neck, above a royal blue dress with gold ribbons at the seam.

When she was finished, she slowly opened her eyes, as did the men be-fore her. Slowly the young, handsome lord grinned and then began to clap in appreciation, as did the others around the room. Gianni and the knights ap-plauded as well. Piero merely smiled in satisfaction. The singer gave a deep, regal curtsey and then sat down.

All attention moved to them, the group newly entered upon the hall. Sir Lucien led them forward and bowed before the lord, sitting in a center chair; the singer, who now sat beside him; and an older gentleman, mayhap the lord's steward. "Lord Rieu, may I present these men of Siena, who have recently traveled from Venezia?"

The slender but strong man, as blond and as blue-eyed as the singer, plainly his sister, accepted them into his court with all the regal ceremony of a king. Gianni eyed Piero. They had heard that north of Provence, in France, and may-hap now in Provence, courtly conduct had been developed into an art form, which in turn had influenced the papacy itself. The Gifted would need to learn how to flow through such finery and fluff and use it to their advantage.

"You are welcome to abide here, fellows, for as long as you feel necessary. We have a great deal to discuss. But first, my sister and I must meet your lady."

"She is weary from the road and may well have chosen a decent bed and coverlet over any feast," Gianni said.

"Nonsense. I must meet her, this night. We have been awaiting your arrival for nigh unto a week, now. After Conte Morassi's letter reached me, I've thought of little else." He rubbed his hands together with glee. A ruddy blush was at his jawline. This was a man who was used to getting what he wanted, when he wanted it. Gianni swallowed hard, weighing the words in his mouth. They needed allies in this land. But was this lord of Les Baux simply another danger to Daria? To them all?

"I will see what is keeping her," Father Piero said. He met Gianni's glance with a reassuring look and set off down the dark hallway. Fortunately he met up with Daria, Agata and the children in tow, partway to the guest quarters and merely had to turn and escort them back.

Lord Armand Rieu of Les Baux stopped midsentence when he saw Daria and stepped down off the dais to meet her halfway across the room, Gianni right behind him. Armand paused before her and bowed regally, taking her hand and kissing it for an unconscionably long moment. Her eyes met Gianni's, searching for reassurance, but the lord was already on the move, studying Daria with the intensity of a painter, slowly circling her. A quick bath and clean gown had done wonders. "M'lady, at last you have returned. Welcome to my humble castle. I feel as if an old friend has been regained. And look at you! As lovely as they say!"

Gianni stepped beside Daria, so the lord of Les Baux was forced to go around them both as he completed his turn. His eyes crinkled at the corners in glee, and he clapped his hands together. "Ahh, a worthy knight for his lady, protecting her. You will find, Sir Gianni, that we of Les Baux prize nothing more than courtly love. But beware," he said, leaning closer to the taller knight, "there is something within our limestone that seems to sow love deeper and higher and wider than anything else you have ever experienced. Right, Anette?" He turned to eye his sister.

The young woman flushed prettily at the neck and gave her brother a small nod. But was there an air of sorrow in her expression?

"Lady Daria, you see from my sister and many of the fine women in this room that you will be one of many lovely females to grace my castle.

Undoubtedly you are well used to being the only beauty in the room, given your uncommon countenance." He eyed Gianni knowingly and then looked again to Daria. "But when it comes to Les Baux, beautiful women and their entourage are always welcome. And when they are friends of our family and arrive on the recommendation of a favored friend . . . well, there is no higher pleasure in my life." He bowed again, a hand splayed to his right.

"Please, m'lord," Daria said. "There is no need for such ceremony on our—"

"No need? No need!" He scoffed, but it was delight that shone through his eyes. He gesticulated with exuberance, lending weight and drama to every phrase. "This is what we are known for, m'lady. Pomp. Ceremony. Here in Les Baux, we are teaching the world how to properly conduct courtly life in a castle. Do you not remember us?"

Daria smiled. "It has been some time, m'lord."

He grinned back at her. "Come now. It has only been a couple of decades. I do not pardon ignorance because of youth."

"I was no older than two."

"And I was five. Surely you recall our time together." He reached for her hand and brought it to his chest, smiling mischievously at Gianni. "I believe it involved mud."

Daria pulled her hand gently from his, and Armand's grin faded. He was at once sober, responsible, and inquisitive. "My father often spoke of your family with reverence. He considered Giulio d'Angelo a fine and honorable man."

"What of your father, m'lord? M'lady?" Daria asked. "Is he well?"

"The count has been abed for some time," Armand said, clearly not wishing to speak of it. "I enjoyed our occasional letter exchange. Trade between Les Baux and your woolen guild has not been . . . the *same* since you left your position as co-consul."

"Yes. But please know I had little choice in the matter." She frowned, thinking of all she had lost, and what might be happening to her beloved guild. "I am sorry to hear that things are not well . . ."

"Armand," Anette said.

Armand glanced back her and then frowned as well. "M'lady, I forget myself," he said with a slight bow. "Speaking of business when it is time for feastings and frivolity. We shall speak further of the fabled Duchess d'Angelo, mysteriously the former co-consul of Siena's woolen guild, now intriguing healer of the masses . . . and deliverer of children. But not until after we dine." He waggled his eyebrows, blue eyes twinkling, and then gestured toward a table and chairs for them to sit, off the side of the dais. The others around the room, taking the lord's cue, resumed their conversations, affording them some privacy. But what had been shared already? Piero thought. The lord's knowledge already ran deep. Were they well past any semblance of secrecy? What was left to protect?

As the young lord and lady, Armand's steward, Daria, Gianni, and Piero sat down, servants set heaping trenchers of food before them and poured goblets full of wine. Vito and Basilio stood guard nearby, ready to come to their aid if necessary. The others moved off to gain a plate of food themselves.

"Please, you must be famished," Armand said. "You eat and I will talk. Given your status, I am certain you are eager to know what I know. Rest assured, I will demand to know more." His sister walked up behind him and rested a delicate hand on his shoulder. He put a hand atop hers. "Anette fears I will pry too deeply. But my friends, please know that while I was born with a curious mind, I was also born with a loyal heart. You have nothing to fear in my keep."

ᚦ ᚦ ᚦ

As he talked, Daria bit into a tender slice of duck, roasted to perfection with a delicate plum sauce on its crust. He was a charmer, this young lord, clearly used to having exactly what he wanted. His tendency toward courtly romance, chivalry, seemed silly to her, but harmless enough. And yet she battled against memories of Abramo Amidei, how he ruled his own court and had once tried to rule her. She and the Gifted had narrowly escaped his clutches. All men who wielded power were dangerous, in some measure. They would need to tread carefully.

But Father Piero had said that Armand Rieu of Les Baux might well be God's own provision, an ally in a foreign land, desperately needed, highly coveted. And her father had known his father, been in this place with her. . . . They intended to enter Avignon and take on the papacy itself. This was where their letter, the clues, the glass map all led. Avignon. And if they were to address the pope himself, any noble support they could garner would be a blessing.

She watched him as he spoke. Three years her senior, but not yet married. He met her bold gaze and studied her, then looked in deference to

Gianni. There was clearly no secret that he could not decipher. Within moments upon her entry, it was plain to him that she and Gianni were in love. He was a student of human nature, the best of a nobleman's skills. For if a lord could decipher how people thought, moved, acted, loved, made decisions, then he could most effectively rule.

Daria shivered. Once again, it reminded her of Abramo Amidei, how he wormed his way through any crack—

"M'lady, have you caught a chill?" Armand asked, narrowing his eyes in her direction, while waving a servant to fetch a blanket.

"Nay, m'lord," she said, trying to shake off his attentions. "I am merely weary."

"M'lady," he said, leaning forward. "By the end of this night, I trust every one of you will call me friend. Therefore, let us begin by using my Christian name."

"Very well, Armand."

"We shall speak further of the guild on the morrow. But tell me what you must this night, Daria, about you." He waved toward the others. "And your troop. Conte Morassi was dreadfully sketchy in his details of you. He's obviously protecting you. But you are in need of aid. I am able to provide that."

Daria hesitated. Armand coughed and turned languid eyes back to her. He gentled his tone. "It does not take a great intellect to put the stories of Siena's healer and the healer of lepers in Venezia together with you. She is one and the same?"

Daria eyed Piero and Gianni. Piero gave her a slight nod. Tessa had given her a squeeze to the hand when they entered, telling her she sensed no danger in the man. Mayhap Piero was right; mayhap the lords of Les Baux were exactly the allies they needed. "I am the healer," she said, looking to Armand. "Once a lady of some wealth, now but a humble servant of my Lord."

"As are we all," said Piero, leaning forward. "You must know you harbor the hunted, m'lord."

"Hunted?" He waved a hand dismissively. "By Lord Amidei? The baron? They boast nothing Les Baux cannot ward off."

"By them, and soon by the Church, I'd wager."

"You are a priest who wagers?"

"Figuratively speaking, of course."

"Do you speak of the Inquisition? Papal auditors? Because of your lady?"

Piero pursed his lips and sat forward. "Because of all of us. Because of an ancient prophecy. Because it has been known for some time that we would gather, and our goal would be change."

"Change?"

"Change, on a level that may well shake the Church to its roots."

"You are one of those who wishes for the papacy to return to Roma?"

"That matters not to me. I am one who wishes for the papacy to return to its Christian ideals. To confess sin and attempt to live exemplary lives. To honor love of neighbor and love of God above all else. To shake off its cloak of wealth and give to the poor instead. To drive out the evil that exists within its walls and fill the world with light, light that others can emulate. To allow the masses to read the Holy Writ for themselves. To allow them to pray directly to their God, without aid of priestly intervention. To practice the faith of Jesus Christ of Nazareth, rather than the faith of man."

Armand sat back and studied the priest. And then he began to laugh, laugh so hard that tears rolled down his cheeks. "You are quite the mad little priest, are you not?" he said, wiping his cheek with the back of his hand. He sobered some when Piero made no response. "You do realize they will tear you limb from limb."

"They will try," Piero said, eyeing Daria and Gianni. "But we have already weathered many storms the enemy has sent our way. Our God goes before us. We can do no other thing than to honor his call."

Armand smiled and nodded his head. "I believe you mean what you say, priest. So tell me, tell me all of it."

Piero hesitated and glanced about at all the people.

"Your days of secrecy are over, priest. I am not the only one who knows of your presence and your powers. Morassi's letter merely confirmed what was already common court gossip. I wager even the courts of England know of you. Your only hope now is to take on your enemies with courage and intelligence." Still, Armand ordered many to leave with but a wave of his hand, shooing them out the door. Half the hall cleared, leaving only his sister, steward, and most trusted knights behind.

Piero took a swig from his goblet and dived into the story—of how they had been brought together by the prophetic letter, possibly penned by Saint Paul or his friend, Apollos. He pulled the leather pouch from his robes and gently took the sheets from within. After gathering Abramo's pages, they now had six in total. Armand whistled when he saw the likeness of Daria and Piero on the first, and listened intently as they told of the other clues God had given them, all leading them here. The boys brought the small chest that held the glass blocks. On the floor of the hall, they put them together, a glass map of amber and turquoise, outlining the boot of Italia and the curve of Provence's southern coast. A gold line traced their path from Roma, to Siena, to Venezia, to Avignon.

"We came by sea, rather than overland, of course," said Piero.

The lord's eyebrows shot up in mild surprise. "It would've been foolhardy to take on our mountains in the midst of winter. The sea is dangerous enough." He leaned forward and moved the pages of the letter until those depicting Daria, Piero, and Gianni battling the sea monster were in view. "Who is the monster?"

"Abramo Amidei," Piero said.

"Ah yes, Amidei. We have confirmed that it is he who tracks them?" His eyes went to his captain, Lucien.

"We have a scout out now, m'lord, to verify that."

Armand's eyes returned to the Gifted and shifted to Anette. "We know him well. A fearsome adversary." Daria could feel Armand's eyes hover upon her. "He nearly had you then, Daria? If he is the dragon and you are the peacock?"

"Nearly." It was enough, their scant reference.

"And you swore never to let him get close to your lady again," Armand said to Gianni.

"Indeed."

The young lord nodded approvingly. "Yet you cannot shake him. He still tracks your every move. His goal is still to capture the lady?"

"Given our last exchange, I think he would prefer to kill me," Daria said, leveling a gaze at him.

"Kill you? What did you do besides refuse his advances?"

"Maimed him. Took an eye."

Armand nodded, barely concealing his immediate fear for her. "There is little Amidei prizes above his wealth and power. His own physical beauty might be one. Why does the baron travel with him? Was he not once a loyal friend to the house of d'Angelo?"

"Once," Daria said. "Far has he fallen."

"I believe they wish us all dead," Piero put in. "Amidei had in his possession a portion of this letter. Well he knows what our intent might be—to be agents of change within the Church, to bring light where there is darkness. This is antithetical to his goals. If he cannot control us, use us, he will try to destroy us."

Armand rose and paced, back and forth, fingers steepled before him, eyes shifting back and forth, deep in thought. "So Amidei wanted you to turn to him so that he might make use of your powers, your *gifting*, as the priest calls it. He framed your knights for a crime they did not commit, kidnapped another, and stole Daria to his dark isle."

"Yes. He believed separation would weaken us, leave us vulnerable. It did for a time," Daria allowed. "But he did not count on God's own power undergirding us all. He did not understand that for all the drama of my own gift of healing, Gianni's faith, Father Piero's wisdom, Hasani's visions, Tessa's discernment, Gaspare's powers—that God himself wishes us to be together, remain together. Together, we are mightiest of all."

"You are all of the Body," Armand mused. "One an arm, another a leg, another a hand. Together, you are of the most use."

"Well said," Father Piero said, appreciating the nobleman's obvious knowledge of Saint Paul's writings to the Corinthians. "Amidei wished to tear us apart, take Daria because her gifting is the most public, the most useful to him."

Armand cocked an eye at Daria and then looked to the priest. "I beg your pardon, Father, but I doubt it was only Daria's gifting that drew Amidei's attention. Your lady is famed for her beauty and clearly harbors an intellect to rival any man's. If he is after her, there shall be no dissuading him."

Daria sighed impatiently. "We shall not fail one another nor our God. We shall never bow to Amidei. Despite your chivalry and hospitality, we shall never bow to you."

The young lord blinked slowly in her direction and gave her a patronizing smile. "I see, m'lady, that while you are beautiful and intelligent, you still have much to learn in the art of courtly conduct."

Daria frowned. They hadn't time for such trifling. "M'lord, please understand. We have been brought together by God's hand. We live to serve him in his call, alone. Nothing must get in our way."

Armand became as still and focused as she. "Even at further threat to your lives?"

"If necessary. Obviously we prefer to live. But no matter the cost, we are committed to this call and this cause. We can do no other."

Armand shared a slow smile with Anette, then looked to the others. "You are aware that you are in a castle that has long housed true believers."

"Speak plainly," Gianni said.

"We are descendants of Balthazar," Armand said, rising. He walked to a nearby wall and tapped on the family crest on a massive tapestry, hung from rings atop a bar.

"The star of Bethlehem," Daria whispered.

"You are a descendant of a king who worshipped at the feet of the one true King?" Piero said, rising. His voice was tight, full of wonder.

"Indeed," said Armand. "We have long risen when our Lord beckons. To his birthplace. On crusade to the Holy Lands. And in light of that, I have something to show you." He walked to the edge of the tapestry with the family crest and drew it backward, showing an aged and badly damaged fresco of six knights on horseback, the flag of the crusaders high above them, an Oriental castle before them.

The Gifted rose from the table and stumbled closer, seeing now the family crest across each knight's chest. "Our great-great-grandfather," Armand said, tapping the man on the first horse, a star of Bethlehem across his armored chest plate. "Morassi's great-great-grandfather," he said, touching the next man. They all could see the other family crests on the following four horses.

The peacock of the d'Angelos. The dragon of the Amideis. A lion, paws outstretched. A fox, as if on the prowl.

Daria's hand went to her mouth. "How long has this been here? Our ancestors . . . they were all together in the Holy Land?"

Armand shook his head. "I do not believe they made it there. This fresco was done soon after the castle was rebuilt around eleven eighty. I believe this depicts the Fourth Crusade—see Constantinople in the background? They intended to enter the Holy Land through Egypt, but lacked the funds to pay for the provisions and fleet contracted from Venezia, so they sacked Constantinople instead."

Daria gaped at the wall. "I never knew a d'Angelo as a crusader."

"But as I understand it, your ancestors arrived in Siena with some wealth to their name, *oui*?"

Daria blinked slowly. "Yes. They did."

"Men of the Fourth Crusade plundered Constantinople. They came home wealthy, if not victorious for the faith."

"Hardly something my family would wish to remember."

"But they put the money to good use, did they not? They invested in Toscana, in the woolen guild, and imported inks, dyes, and parchment for the neighboring scribes. Yes?"

"Yes," she said, still searching her memory for any word from her father or grandfather about a crusading ancestor. Her eyes went back to the fresco. "And Amidei . . ." Her voice trailed off.

"The Amideis tend to be either the best of men or the very worst. They have enjoyed power for some time, in any region they enter. It is logical that they had a family member on this crusade. Your family did well with the money, redeemed it. Amidei's family used it for more base desires, building, always building, but corrupt."

He moved in front of Daria. "You see, Duchess, why I have known of you for some time," he said, gesturing toward the fresco. "As a boy, I longed to go on crusade, and begged my grandfather to tell me all he knew of the great battles. He knew of your family, knew they had settled in Toscana. He even knew of a lovely young daughter, a promising beauty who might have been a good match for me, but she had been promised to another in Siena—"

"And these others?" Gianni interrupted. "What families do these two represent?" he asked, waving toward the knights with the family heralds of lion and fox.

Armand dragged his eyes from Daria, and waved toward the lion. "The herald of Lord Blanchette, of Uzes, and this," he eyed Daria again after pointing to the fox, "is the herald of the Richardieus, of Villeneuve-des-Avignon. Both are longtime friends of Les Baux."

Piero sighed. "Just one more clue, in a long line of clues. God knew we would need allies, and here they appear to be." He turned to Armand. "We are on God's own path, m'lord. Surely you see that."

"Indeed I do. And I aim to aid and protect you, if necessary. I will do all I can to assist others in pursuit of the King and his cause. If I cannot go on crusade," he said, waggling a brow toward Daria, "this is a close second." He reached out a hand to Daria and led her back to a chair. "You are in the abode of a friend, m'lady. You shall stay with us as long as you see fit. And we shall aid you in any way possible."

Chapter Three

"Where is your father?" Daria asked Armand as they finished breaking their fast with a hot, delicious gruel laced with dried fruits and nuts.

"He is ailing, as he has for some time. For the past six months, he has not been able to rise from his bed."

"You must take me to him."

"As you wish, m'lady," he said with a smile, and Daria blushed, realizing that she had no place in ordering a future count of Les Baux about. He lifted his arm and ushered her away from the main room. Daria met Gianni's eyes for a moment, and his brows were lowered in consternation. She brushed off the look in irritation. If he was not going to formalize his claim upon her heart, she owed him no explanation.

Vito and Ugo fell into step behind them, a silent guard she allowed. Armand ignored them.

The lord led her down a stair and through a hall. He cleared his throat. "How is it that you do not travel with Marco Adimari?"

Daria shifted, suddenly more aware of Vito and Ugo's presence. But this was no time for secrets. "Marco broke our handfast."

"What? Why? Your love was fabled. We have sung of it in our own courts. My mother told me you loved one another as children. That you were destined to be man and wife."

Daria smiled a little. "It was a grand love. But unable to surpass what men of power need most. An heir." She paused. It was best to be out with it and get beyond it. Soon enough, if the lord thought her mysterious and intriguing enough to try to pull her from Gianni, he would need to know it as well. After all, Vito and Ugo already knew of it. "I proved barren," she said.

It had been some time since she had felt the impact of how her womb had failed her. She despised herself for dropping her eyes.

Lord Armand drew her to a pause by a torch and slowly, tentatively reached out to lift her chin. Daria was acutely aware of her men's presence, but she could not keep her eyes from slowly lifting to meet the handsome noble's.

"Daria d'Angelo, you are a fine woman, a prize, regardless of the heartache you have suffered. You are serving our God where you live and breathe, and his angels must be singing in the heavens because of what you have done already, to say nothing of what you shall do ahead." He shook his head and dropped his hand, his eyes rife with wonder. "A healer. You are a healer," he said. " 'Tis a remarkable, enviable gift. Never forget that you have value and might as a daughter of God and daughter of Toscana, regardless of what your womb produces."

He resumed their walk, and Daria could hear Vito and Ugo breathe a sigh of relief. She could feel Armand take a step away from her within, as well as without. He did not wish to take a barren bride. But it was just as well—she could no longer imagine being with anyone but Gianni, if even that was to be. She appreciated Armand's friendship, his encouragement of her and the task ahead. In the lord's eyes, she still had value, merit, even though Marco had abandoned her.

"I fear my father is beyond healing. He merely waits for something, day in and day out. The physicians have come and gone, all claiming old age will take him at any moment."

"Mayhap," Daria said, climbing a narrow stair behind Armand. "Yet I should still pay my respects to a kindly count who once welcomed a daughter of Toscana as potentially one of his own."

Armand smiled down at her and gestured inward. "Prepare thyself," he whispered.

Daria stepped forward, hesitated, and had to fight against the urge to step back. The smell of decay and urine was overwhelming. A young maid rose from the corner of the dark room.

"Saints in heaven," muttered Daria, bringing a hand to her nose. "Does your noble patient have no vessel in which to move his bowels?" she whispered.

The girl looked confused and whispered back, "Nay, m'lady. We simply change the bedding twice a day."

Daria frowned. "Vito, please go and fetch my medicinal trunk." She turned to the maid. "Go and fetch four more maids, two with fresh linens, two of you with a new featherbed. This one needs to be burned. Bring along three large kettles of boiling water and clean cloths. This room is to be scrubbed, top to bottom."

She went to the window and opened the shutters, letting fresh cool winter air into the room, ignoring the rain that spattered in with it. Then she turned to the bed and slowly approached the count.

Armand was on the other side, watching her.

She knelt at the old man's side. His face was covered in a long, scraggly beard. He was terribly thin, and each breath did indeed sound like a death rattle.

"Count Rieu," she said softly. He did not open his eyes or move at the sound of her voice. "Count Rieu," she said again, covering his hand with her own. "I am Daria d'Angelo de Siena."

The count moved a bit and moaned, then coughed, a pitiful, gurgling sound. It made Daria wish she could cough for the old man, force the blockages that kept his lungs from full, free breaths. She stood and carefully folded back the blankets that covered him, taking in the sight of a once hale and hearty man, who now weighed little more than Nico or Roberto. She leaned down and laid her ear against his chest, listening to him breathe, then stood straight again, covered him, and laid two fingers on his neck.

Armand looked at her hopefully. Did he think she might heal this aged man now, here before him? She gave him a small smile. "It is as the doctors have told you, Armand. Your father is soon to move on to the next life. But we can certainly make him more comfortable in the meantime."

The silent hope in Armand's eyes died down again, like flames turning to embers, but he was grateful. He lifted a weary hand to his head. "It has gone on so long . . . I suppose Anette and I have grown weary from the effort."

"I understand," she said. "How long has he been like this?"

"More than two years."

"What does he eat?"

"The maids manage a thin gruel and water, spooned down his throat."

"Good." She could well imagine the enormity of such a task. It likely took a good part of their day. "He is in a fine robe, but let us put him in something softer. Do you have any of the smoothest silk, from the Orient?"

Armand smiled at her. "Spoken like a merchantess of cloth. I shall see what we can muster."

"We also need something highly absorbent, like the thick cotton that mothers use to cover their babes. We shall use it to protect the new bedding and keep your father more comfortable."

Armand paused, hesitating over the emasculating dishonor of it all. "The servants are bound to have some of it. If not, I will send one to fetch a bolt of it."

"And a barber. A noble should be freshly shaven, should he not?"

"My father always wore his beard long."

Daria turned to the count and ran her fingers across his forehead. "But it no longer looks well upon his face. Let us shave it closer to his cheeks, and cut his hair, so that we might easily wash and dry it. It is not seemly for him to be in such disarray."

Armand nodded. "It shall be so."

Vito arrived, out of breath after his run through the rabbit warren of halls to fetch Daria's trunk. She went to him and set to work, pulling out small boxes and her mortar and pestle, to create a poultice that might ease the count's breathing.

ॐ ॐ ॐ

"The count has roused," said the servant excitedly, the following day at noon meal.

Armand and Anette both leapt to their feet. "He has spoken?"

"In a whisper, but yes," she said, nodding repeatedly, a grin across her face. "He knew my name! After all this time!" Her eyes moved to Daria. "He has asked to see you both . . . and Lady d'Angelo."

They rushed toward the door, but Daria drew them up short. "My friends," she warned, "it is common for the old and infirm to rally, but then soon give in to death. It is as if God gives them one last window upon this world. Make the most of this time. Say what you must as if it is the last you shall share with your father."

Armand frowned, and Anette's wide eyes filled with tears. And then they disappeared into the dark hallway, Daria directly behind them. Gianni caught up with them, silently echoing her steps. He paused outside the door, standing guard, she supposed. Looking in, but not intruding.

The count's room was so different than when she had first arrived. The fire still crackled in the hearth, but it had been built up to produce a constant and maximum heat, to counterbalance the open window, which allowed fresh, cold air from the valley floor. The room had been scrubbed from top to bottom with lime, and Daria could smell the acidic clean scent of it still in the room.

The count had been bathed as well, prepared for his new bedding, and shaved. His beard was now but an inch from his withered cheeks, and his hair in back was no longer than his shoulders. Armand and Anette went immediately to him, sitting on either side of him, each taking a hand. Daria smiled over the scene. These were children who had been loved by their parents, and who loved them as well. It made her miss her own father and mother, now gone for years.

"Father?" Armand asked.

The count's eyes moved beneath blue-tinged, paper-thin lids and then fluttered open. He stared at the wooden ceiling a moment, as if trying to focus, and then turned his head to smile upon his son. "Armand. Where is thy sister?" he asked, voice cracking.

"Right here, Father," Anette said, and the count turned to give her a weak smile as well.

Daria went to a pitcher and poured the count some water. "Please, friends, help your father to rise a bit, so we might give him some water."

They helped him rise, and the count studied her over the rim of his goblet as he drank. They eased him back to the pillows.

"You, m'lady," he said, raising a finger to Daria, "are the mirror image of your mother. Even more beautiful, if it is possible."

Daria smiled. "I see how your son has come by his gift of flattery."

"Bah. Flattery is false. I speak the truth."

"Thank you, m'lord."

The count eyed Armand and then looked back to Daria. "You know, your father and I once spoke of arranging a marriage between you and my son."

"Yes, m'lord. Armand and I have already addressed it."

His face fell a bit. "Ah. Then you have been promised to another."

"She may as well be," Armand put in. "Her heart, alas, can never be mine because she loves another."

"Phh. Love is one thing. A good union even better."

Daria shifted uncomfortably and glanced at Gianni. He smiled back at her with a soft look in his eyes.

"Who is there?" asked the count, following her gaze out the door.

Armand waved Gianni inward. "This is Captain Gianni de Capezzana, Father, the lady's knight."

The count sank back into his pillows and stared at Gianni as if he were a vision. His mouth fell open as his eyes flitted back and forth between them in the slow manner of the aged.

"M'lord?" Daria asked in concern.

He lifted a hand to stop her from nearing him and then rested his hand on his chest. "The old prophecies are true . . ."

Gianni frowned and leaned forward. "My lord. Tell us what you must. You plainly recognize us."

"I thought . . . I thought the resemblance to Daria's mother was coincidence. But I see that . . . it was Lady Daria all along. And you . . ."

"Father?" Anette asked, seeing him pale.

"The . . . chapel. An . . . entrance . . ." His breathing was becoming labored again.

"Quickly, lay some more horehound upon the fire," Daria said to Gianni, motioning to the stack beside the hearth.

The count reached for his daughter's hand and his son's with the other, pulling both to his chest as he fought for breath. "I have loved you . . . both. Remember that. Serve our people. And my children . . ." He pulled them closer. "Serve these two with us . . . with your very lives. It is . . . important . . . for reasons I cannot . . . begin to share."

"We shall, Father," Armand pledged, seeing the urgency in his face.

"We shall," repeated Anette.

The old man's face eased into relief.

When Daria turned back from her medicinal chest she saw the still death mask upon the count. Anette leaned down to place her face on his chest, her shoulders shaking with sorrow.

Chapter Four

Days later, they had seen the wondrous castle of Les Baux in the golden light of sunset, the lavender light of dusk, and the russet tones of sunrise. Whatever light God cast upon his earth, the castle's stones seemed to absorb, giving Daria the protective feeling of a cloak, as if she might be invisible to the naked eye. But that was a falsehood, of course.

Vigil had been observed over the last few days for the count of Les Baux, and a sennight after their arrival, against a dim and gray winter sky, they burned his body in the manner of ancient kings, a Les Baux tradition. Afterward, they processed toward the castle, all eager to escape the cold northern winds that now nipped at the bluff.

Daria, Gianni, Armand, and Anette exchanged solemn condolences. Piero neared and talked of their hope in heaven, of freedom from pain, of unspeakable joy ahead. "It is for this reason we wish to speak to the people, wherever we go," he said. "To tell them the hope we have in heaven, and the hope we have here, on earth. But there are many who wish to dissuade us."

"He is there, your enemy, among those rocks you see in the distance," Armand said, pulling the group to a stop and pointing across the valley. He seemed eager to switch the subject from his father to the new battle at hand.

Daria shivered. Whereas the rocks of Les Baux were mostly weather-worn and rounded, the rocks the count pointed to looked as if they had been hewn from the earth that morning and set at precarious angles.

"Hell's Keep," Anette mused.

"I beg your pardon?"

"From Dante's *Divine Comedy*? The poet rested here for a fortnight, and it is said that he took that valley there as his inspiration for his vision of hell."

"Then it is apropos that Amidei shelters there," Gianni said.

"Rest assured, my men will keep him from crossing the valley floor between us."

"You shall make an enemy of him," Daria warned.

"I believe I became his enemy the moment my men brought you here to shelter for the night," Armand said with a rakish grin, a bit of himself coming back, away from grief's covering. "It matters not. Your enemy is mine as well."

"I fervently hope we shall not bring your castle down behind us. They will stop at nothing, Armand," she said, turning to lay a hand upon his arm in forewarning. "Nothing. They murdered my servants, captured my friends, burned my mansions to the ground, ousted me from the Mercanzia, even managed to disassociate me from my bank accounts. It is all gone, save my friends and my faith." Her eyes shifted to Gianni, and she abruptly dropped her hand from the count's arm. "Do you understand what this may cost you?"

Armand looked her in the eye, his admiration for her obviously growing by the day. "Daria, I understand. Les Baux stands beside you. It is clear that the Lord is moving among you. That we are to walk this path with you, as your protectors in a foreign land. We shall not fail you, no matter the cost."

His eyes wandered over her shoulder, where his father's remains now were mere smoldering ashes. "It was Father's dying wish." His blue eyes returned to search her own. "No matter the cost," he said resolutely.

Daria shook her head a little. The cost. The cost had already been dear. Nearly everything, she thought. It was one thing to cast herself into such a chasm of loss. Was it fair to ask this man to endanger everything he had as well? His loved ones? His livelihood?

"Cease your fretting," he said, taking her hand and placing it on his arm, strolling along the castle guard walk. He cast an eye back at Gianni to make sure he was not overly agitating the knight. Gianni clumsily offered his arm to the countess, seconds too late. "You forget I am now a count of this region, held in high regard by many. My reach is long and strong."

They strolled for a while in silence, lost to their own thoughts. Daria paused as they neared the northeast corner, turned, and pulled her hand from Armand's arm to stare back toward the mountains. Gianni came to her other side, rested a hand at her lower back, and leaned close. "What is it?"

"What is up in that direction?" she asked.

"Why, that is the road that leads to the Pont du Gard," Anette said, her voice soft.

Gianni was already shaking his head. "No, Daria. We must not tarry. We do not have time for this." He could read it, then, from the look on her face. He did not say the words that came next, but Daria could feel every syllable. *Amidei is right here. He watches our every move.*

"Along that road. There is a man? A man who is in need of healing from a cancer?"

Anette gasped and pulled a hand to her mouth, her blue eyes wide. "Why, yes. Lord Devenue."

Daria studied her. The young woman's tone was odd. "Who is he to you, Anette?"

Anette glanced at Armand and then back to Daria. "Once . . . once he was to be my husband. But he has ailed these last years. The cancer, the tumors have distorted his face and head. The doctors believed he would die right away. But he lives on, cursed, mad with the pain. Waiting every hour of the day for the Lord to come and free him."

"He believes, then."

"Oh yes. It was the only thing that sustained him . . . for a time."

Daria studied the girl, so delicate, so lovely. She was most likely widely sought as a bride, given her beauty, name, and wealth. And yet she was nearing the age of spinsterhood. "Anette, why did you not marry him? It is common enough for ailing nobles . . . to attempt to leave an heir. You obviously care for him."

A slow, deep blush climbed Anette's neck and face. "He ended our fathers' agreement the day the doctors told him what he already knew to be true. He cast me out, refused me entry."

"How long ago?"

"Two years and three months . . . past."

The girl avoided the additional days that obviously loomed large in her mind. She knew exactly how long ago her love affair had ended. Daria, remembering Marco, felt something stir deep within her.

"She has refused all other suitors," Armand said, wrapping an arm around his sister's shoulders. "I could force her to marry, but I must confess, I envy her devotion to the man. I cannot bear to end it." Daria knew by now that Armand prized the idea of courtly love above everything else short of his faith in his Savior. He spent a good deal of every day encouraging others to pursue love, even going as far as to ask Gianni when he planned on marrying Daria, but then the next day extolling the virtues of unrequited love to him, and how it might be better to always pine in a heavenly manner for his lady rather than knowing the fleshly comforts of earthly love. He flirted and teased her, taunting Gianni, delighting in the game. No doubt the romantic, albeit tragic, elements of his sister's love affair with Lord Devenue appealed to him.

"We shall go to Lord Devenue. I believe I am to heal him."

Anette gasped.

"Nay, Daria," Gianni said. "Every step away from this castle puts us closer to the enemy at our gates." He nodded to the eerie rocks. "It is not even in the direction of Avignon!"

"He shall not dare to come near," Armand said, leaping upon the opportunity for an excursion. "Amidei travels with but ten men and two women. With your own men alongside my own, I shall ensure we outnumber them three to one."

"Counting women and children," Gianni ground out.

"Come now, Sir de Capezzana," Armand said with a good-natured frown. "Your women and children are extraordinary, are they not? To a one, they exhibit valor and faith. Give me but the females and the small ones, and I shall take on any foe myself." He waved his arm in the air as if waving a sword.

Gianni sighed. "If we go, God goes with us, that is true. But our Lord also asks us to be wise as well as faithful. We shall consult the priest. If he deems it wise, and only if he deems it so, we shall go. We must keep our eyes on the prize, Daria, our mission with the Church, our calling to Avignon."

Daria's eyes went to the northern horizon. God had never called her to heal another and then failed to make a way. Piero would deem it wise, a part of their Lord's plan forward; Gianni would faithfully walk beside them, protecting them as best he could. Lord Devenue, once young Anette's betrothed, would find healing and hope again.

Her mind went to Marco Adimari, the man she had once loved, once believed she would stand beside forever. By now, his wife would be heavy with their child. Marco had been a part of her capture in Venezia, but Daria believed he had been an innocent pawn in it all. He had loved her still, mayhap might always love her. Amidei and Vincenzo had simply played upon his emotions for their best use, to aid their cause. She hadn't seen Marco after she had been squired away to Amidei's dark lair, making her confident that he was not culpable. Thoughts of Marco, as long and as lithe and elegant as Count Armand, made her mildly melancholy. But she was clearly free of the dull ache and sorrow that had plagued her. Her heart, more and more, belonged to the towering knight, Gianni, glowering in his concern for her. Regardless of whether he would confirm his declarations of love, she knew where her heart now belonged. With Gianni, with the Gifted, with God.

Gianni stared over at her as if he knew what she was thinking, remembering, but allowing it. He loved her but did not seek to control her as so many would. He simply wanted her safe. God knew what he was doing, entwining their two hearts. For Daria's presence undoubtedly demanded that Gianni search his heart daily for his gifting of faith, just as Gianni's presence encouraged her to go where God led, knowing she was never alone, never unguarded, and where he failed, her God stood in the gap.

ↁↁ ↁↁ ↁↁ

"THEY prepare to go, master."

"Where?"

"I know not. We are trying to gain word."

"Leave me." Abramo stood in the space between two oddly shaped rocks, a hand on each as if he was strong enough to push them apart. He stared out, across the valley at the impregnable castle, Les Baux, watching as a dull sunset changed her colors to a pale gold. Why did the Gifted delay here? Was not Avignon their goal? It mattered little. Given the chance, he would kill them outside the pope's gates. Whenever there was an opening, he would rush through. What had Vincenzo called them? The hounds of hell. Abramo smiled. He liked that very much.

Daria d'Angelo had dared to deny him, thwarting his every advance. That last night in Venezia, what had been meant to be the culmination of his work in the vast lagoon, had been devastating, casting doubt among many of his followers in the wake of the Gifted's escape. And his eye . . . she had dared to slice open his face and eye, leaving a long scar from cheek to brow, the eye broken and withered within its socket. He could still smell the stench of his rotting wound every hour of every day.

"Draw strength from it," his dark lord said, from deep within the rock's shadows. He hovered, Abramo feeling the sheer force of him, his words. "The woman shall pay for her error in judgment. And it shall be a glorious day when it comes."

"Yes, yes, m'lord." He moaned, seeing it ahead of him, as if he could reach out and grab hold of it. Whatever the master told Abramo to do, he would do it. His lord had drawn closer these last weeks, even honoring his servant by taking form. "Delve into the depths of it; seek out the hatred and spite that lingers there, Abramo. It shall strengthen you."

"They believe they can escape us," Abramo said.

"They are fools on the edge of being vanquished. We trail them at every step, and our opportunity will come. We simply rest and wait upon them to take a misstep. And then we pounce." He circled Abramo, and Abramo drew in his scent of power as if he were feeding upon it. "Yes, take me within you, brother. You shall know victory, soon. You shall take the woman upon our altar. You shall sacrifice them all to me, one at a time. You shall drink the priest's blood. Your women shall read the child's entrails and discover the next glorious chapter of your lives within them."

"Yes, yes, master. It shall be as you say."

"Yes," said the dark lord, receding again into the shadows as Vincenzo approached, moving into the crevice of two great boulders.

And when Abramo looked the master's way again, he was gone.

ᚥ ᚥ ᚥ

TESSA stood at the castle window as the Gifted conferred about their journey on the morrow. Roberto and Nico stood on either side of her, staring at her with concern and fear. She trembled, her teeth chattering, until Vito came to stand behind her and stare out with her. The night was now fully upon them, but there was something much darker than the night's shadows, something much colder than the bitter north winds. "It's as if he can see us, even in the dark of night," the girl whispered.

"Well, we've hardly been in hiding," the knight said. "We're in the biggest castle within miles, the torches all about us." He studied the child and then waved Piero over. " 'A city on a hill cannot be hidden.' "

The small priest came and stared outward in silence. The others gathered at other windows, all looking across the valley to where they knew the odd caverns and rocks lay. "What is it you sense, Tessa?" the priest asked softly.

"It is Amidei, and Baron del Buco," she said, trying to be brave, trying to still the quiver in her voice. "But there is more. There is greater evil among those rocks than any I have yet sensed."

"Greater than the isle outside Venezia?" Piero asked lowly.

"Much greater."

They all stood in silence for some time.

"Can the count's men not drive them out?" Tessa asked. Her voice held a tinge of hysteria.

"They have tried, but that valley is riddled with tunnels and caves. They disappear as soon as they see the count's men approach, and then resume their watch as soon as the men return to the castle."

Gianni shook his head. "Like the catacombs. They favor the places of bats and other vermin, places deep in shadow and damp chill. Places that resonate with death."

"Like it or not, they shall follow our every step until our battle is over," Piero said. "And with every step we take that draws us closer to the Lord's desires for us, greater will our opposition be. We may as well accept them as our shadow, only escapable when the Light is directly above us. We must concentrate on staying on his path, following his lead. Rest assured, he shall keep his enemy at bay." He gave Tessa's shoulder a squeeze.

He turned away from the window and beckoned them away as well, into a circle. "Although we cannot see them, our Lord's warriors are all about us. We must don our own spiritual armor and trust our God to see us through. He has not brought us this far to see us die here, as pleasant as Les Baux might be." He gave them a wry grin. It had been a long while since they all had eaten and slept as well as they had in these last days at the castle.

"If God has called our lady to heal another noble, there will be a harvest gained from following his call. We shall go on the morn, as planned, and we shall go under the protection of God and his angel armies. *We shall not submit to fear.* Our enemy trades in fear. We shall only submit to love, to light, to hope. Understood?"

He eyed each of the twelve, and each one nodded back. "If God is for us . . ." he said, reaching a hand into the center of their circle.

"Who can be against us?" the rest returned.

Avignon

"IT is our most fervent hope that you arrive on an errand of good faith rather than your old quest to return the papacy to Roma," said Cardinal Saucille of Avignon, walking beside Cardinal Boeri.

Cardinal Boeri pursed his lips and tucked his hands behind him as they walked. He studiously ignored the flirtatious glances of several women as they passed by. Was it as bad as he had heard, with cardinals housing mistresses and children within the palace? Surely it could not be. "My dear friend, I have come to a place of peace about the matter," he said. "Although I confess that I will always believe the papacy deserves to reside in Saint Peter's city, I understand that the dangers at hand keep us from even considering it."

"Ahh. Good, very good. So what brings you to travel such a far distance, Your Grace? We did not expect you until summer."

"I have come on urgent court business. After discussing it at length with the doge de Venezia, we decided I must come at once. There is a group that will approach the pope in due time, an uncommon group."

"Are they a menace to His Holiness?"

"Nay. Not to his person. But I believe they threaten the Church at large."

Cardinal Saucille stopped and reached out a hand to stay Cardinal Boeri. "Speak plainly. Be they Cathars?"

"Nay, not Cathars. But similar in that their convictions are far from our own. They preach about the need to love, God and man."

"That is nothing outside the Gospel."

"It is as you say," Cardinal Boeri said, walking again, drawing the other beside him, completely captivated by his story by now. "But I have it on good authority that they baptize and commune and confess as they so desire."

The other cardinal gaped at him. "Without a priest?"

"There is a priest among them. But he is the worst, leading them in unholy ways."

"Which priest? Do I know of him?"

"I doubt it. He is Father Piero de Roma, and crossed paths with a woman who had come on pilgrimage." He paused, drawing the other to an abrupt stop like a duck seeking a portion of bread. "There is more, m'lord Cardinal. We could easily set them straight by calling in the Lord's Commissioner, were it not for . . ."

"Please. Rest assured that I will not share anything about our discussion."

He lied. Cardinal Boeri had known him for twenty years; never had he been able to keep a confidence. It was precisely for this reason that he had gone to the man first. He nodded as if in appreciation of the confidence, and drew him to one side of the hall. "This group would be best corralled and utilized by us. We can harness their momentum, their strength, for His Holiness's own gain."

Cardinal Saucille's eyes sparked with interest. "How so?"

"You see, I already am in good stead with them. They have obtained an ancient letter, a letter that appears to prophesy their arrival. So they believe that God himself has brought them together. But you see, Your Grace, I have a portion of that letter they seek."

"You?" The man practically quivered in anticipation. Anything that stirred intrigue and drama within the Palais de le Pape was in favor with those of the court. "You have it on your person?"

"Indeed. And that is just the beginning, Your Grace. There is much, much more to share before they arrive."

"They are in transit now? They journey here, to Avignon?"

"Indeed. If they tarry longer than a fortnight, I would be surprised."

CHAPTER FIVE

THEY set off at daybreak, with Bormeo set free and flying high overhead. And for the first time, they were afforded a perspective of Les Baux they could not see when they approached in the dead of night. They wove down a steep rock road paved with rounded limestone and lined with wild figs and black cypress. There was even a lotus tree or two, heavy with the many branches that boasted of age. Daria glanced back to admire the castle before it disappeared around the bend in the road, like a red ruby atop the cliffs, absorbing morning's glow. Inside, she knew Ambrogio, Ugo, and Nico still rested, each needing more time to heal or gain strength for the journey ahead.

Nearby, the spiny Les Alpilles mountains climbed to rim the lustrous valley, named Les Fontaine for its celebrated springs. Vast olive groves and fields covered the belly of the valley. Avignon was but a day's ride to their north.

Anette had told her they would spend the day traveling northwest, to the south of St. Remy and her ancient Roman ruins of Gaul, across Le Rhône via ferry at Tarascon by the old castle and traveling up the Gardon river to the Pont du Gard. There on the tributary's banks, they would encounter the castle of Lord Devenue.

Her eyes flicked to the oddly pockmarked and shaped rocks above the canyon beyond Les Baux. Undoubtedly Amidei and his men would follow their every move. But in the light of day, they would not dare to attack their number. All they had to do was make Lord Devenue's manor by nightfall and set up a perimeter. Father Piero's words echoed in her mind.

She would not give in to fear. She would not. But still, she could not resist searching the eerie hills once more for signs of the enemy giving chase. Too many nights in Lord Amidei's dungeon, too many lashings across her back, too near to despair . . . how could she banish the memories? She would not give in to fear, no, but how did one battle *memory*?

Gianni, so handsome on his steed beside her, searched her face as if reading the memories there, and she tried to smile at him. It had been weeks since he had stolen a kiss, and she had wondered if his interest was fading. But what she saw in his eyes was no lack of care. He loved her. He had seemed to love her from the moment that God had used her to pull him from the brink of death, at once furious with her for taking him from heaven's door and thankful that he had been brought back and into her life. As soon as he had been on his feet, he had pledged his loyalty, so sure, so very sure that his place was with her. Even at the expense of leaving his post as captain of the Knights de Vaticana de Roma, Cardinal Boeri's most senior guard for years.

Cardinal Boeri had been in Venezia . . . were their paths destined to cross again here? He had been on the hunt for Amidei; undoubtedly it was what had led him to Venezia. If his sources were good, it could lead him to Avignon. Was he an ally, or another enemy of which they need be wary? Was Gianni's history with him, his abandonment of his post, a detriment for which they all would pay?

"What troubles you, m'lady?" Gianni asked.

She smiled again. "Too many thoughts. My mind works on so many fronts that I grow unbalanced from the effort."

"Then cease. Give in to this lovely countryside, the first day without rain in a week, and my company," he said.

Daria laughed softly. "You are learning to speak in the courtly manner of our count."

Gianni raised his eyebrows and grinned at her. "I am yet humble enough to remain a student in arenas I have yet to learn. Our count is the master in this regard."

"Indeed." She eyed the count and countess, riding ahead of them, in front of Vito and Ugo. They all rode, two by two, down the winding road that eventually met up with a straight Roman road. To either bank of them, scouts rode, on the lookout for Amidei's deadly archers. Behind her were the rest of the Gifted—aside from Ambrogio, who had been left in the castle chapel to paint—and at the end were Basilio and Rune and a portion of the count's own men. "Do you trust them, Gianni?"

"Our lord and lady? I do."

"I miss Hasani." In all her years, she could not remember being without her tall, black friend and guard, a slave child her father had freed and raised as her playmate, even going as far as to educate him alongside Daria. "He might be able to confirm that we are right in our beliefs." What visions might he have had in his days since the slavers took him from the cell in Amidei's dungeon? What traps might he allow them to avoid? Moreover, was he ill, beaten, lost? Even dead?

"He is well, Daria, and strong. We will find him, as soon as this is over."

"I cannot help thinking that we ought to have gone after him before taking on this task before us. We are stronger together."

"It would have taken months, tracking the slavers to Constantinople and beyond."

"But what if the trail is long cold by the time we get back to it?"

Gianni was silent for a while. "God has called us here, to this path. You know it as well as I. And as for Hasani, the fact that he is not with us . . . does not mean God has abandoned him, Daria. He is a follower of the Christ, one of us. His path will not be dark for long."

"I pray you are right," Daria said. "And I pray that he will forgive us for pursuing this over his slavers."

"It will be well. When this is over, you and I will not rest until we find our friend and free him again."

Daria shared a long look with him. His words washed over her like balm on a fiery wound. So he did think of being with her beyond this mission before them. Was his love one that would lead them to marriage? Or more of a courtly devotion like Armand lauded as the highest of the loves, most perfect when it was unrequited?

She swallowed hard. The thought of their love remaining unresolved, unrequited, left a hollow ache beneath her breastbone. What was the hesitation she sensed within her captain, ever since they had landed upon this shore? Did he fear his lack of lands or means? Did he really think she thought of anything of that order, a woman without any sort of dowry? Or was it her barren state that troubled him? Mayhap he did not wish to be with a woman who could not bear him an heir, landed gentry or not. Mayhap he thought her less of a woman because Marco had left their handfasting for another. Mayhap he did not wish to take a bride who had lain with another. Daria sighed.

"What is it?" Gianni asked, reaching across to lift her chin. "Daria, what troubles you?"

"Amidei," she lied. "He cannot be far behind."

And Gianni, ever vigilant and on guard, believed her, immediately sinking into their shared concern.

♧ ♧ ♧

THEY made it to Lord Devenue's crumbling manor as the early-winter sun made its way over the far hills, casting meager light upon their path. The building sat on a road that hugged one hillside, the sprawling, blue-sparkling Gardon river meandering its way down below. On the far side, a dense forest covered the land. Farther upriver, Count Armand said, were the ancient remains of the Pont du Gard, the massive Roman aqueduct that had once carried water to the city of Nimes.

Armand and Anette shared a long look, pausing at the front gates of Lord Devenue's dilapidated home. It was apparently as bad as they had heard or imagined. The entrance was unguarded. The towers and walls were in fearsome disrepair. Now Piero knew why they had two wagons of stones and mortar, and four masons, trailing them. The nobles of Les Baux knew well of the disintegrating state of Lord Devenue's estate. If Daria was to heal the lord, the count and countess would do their part in helping to aid the lowly country manor.

Generous, their count. For the hundredth time, Piero thanked the Lord that he had granted them a benefactor and guard. Who among the nobility would have dared to support a group of pilgrims who pledged to take on the Church itself? The Church and nobles wrangled far too often; one did not wish to invite oneself to a new battleground. To say nothing of facing Amidei and his men, who undoubtedly watched them even now. Only God could have orchestrated such a meeting, such an alliance.

But what was this they were about to discover? They marched into the courtyard, paved with the same limestone that seemed to dominate every structure in this part of Provence and beyond. They were more than forty in number, and still not one person had hailed them. Had the lord abandoned his property? Gone elsewhere? Mayhap left to seek out his own cure? Or worse . . . died?

"Stay where you are," growled a man from the top of a parapet walkway above them. He pulled back the string of his bow, aiming at the count. Ten of Armand's men, along with Basilio and Rune, immediately nocked an arrow and drew their own bows.

"Lord Devenue," Countess Anette said, pulling back her hood. "It is us. Be at peace."

The man on the parapet above them audibly drew in a breath, which seemed to reverberate around the stone courtyard. He lowered his bow a bit, his mouth slack. "Anette?"

"It is I, m'lord. Please. Come down and greet us."

The man lowered his bow and arrow but slowly shook his head. Even in the dim light of winter's dusk, Piero could see the massive tumor that distorted the man's head. It was as if he had sprouted yet another skull atop his own, the size of a child's head. "Nay. I am here alone. I have nothing for you or your people. Go on your way. You may not stay here."

Anette leapt down from her horse and straightened her skirts, at once every inch a noble lady. "Nay, Lord Devenue. We shall stay here. We have brought a healer. She says you are to be well."

The man laughed, softly at first, edging into a guttural guffaw. "Nonsense. I am to die. Here. Alone. We said our farewells more than two years past. Be on your way."

Count Armand dismounted and stood beside his sister. Immediately the rest of them did the same. All looked up to the man on the wall. "We are here until you see our healer," Armand said. "Only a fool would turn away God's own path out of hell."

"Call me a fool, then."

"Nay," Anette said. "I once called you my own. My beloved," she said softly, so softly that Piero wondered if the man could hear her. "Will you not see her? Our Lady Daria?"

She gestured back toward Daria and Gianni. Gianni tossed his cape backward in agitation, revealing the red peacock on the white background, as well as the hilt of his sword. In the dim light, the d'Angelo crest almost glowed, and Piero could feel the man's eyes drawn to it like moths to a flame. Of course. God had given him a sign, just as he had the Les Bauxs. Some key that would unlock the door to this man's hardened heart.

Lord Devenue leaned backward, as if against a wave of wind, eyes still upon Gianni's cape. And yet it was utterly still.

Piero whispered to Daria, "He knows your family crest. He has seen the peacock somehow, somewhere."

"Only the healer and her people. Even you, Anette. The rest will have to stay in my courtyard or the stables. The mansion is not suitable anyway." What he meant to say . . . *I am unsuitable* . . . remained unspoken.

"As you wish, brother," Count Armand said with a smile, as if the man had offered them his choice accommodations.

"I have no food," said the lord.

"We brought enough for all," said Armand.

And with that, Lord Devenue left the wall and came down to let them in.

༜ ༜ ༜

THE pain radiated off him like heat off a sun-baked stone. No doubt the massive tumors were causing him to lose balance, hunger, thought, memory, as well as forcing him to endure intolerable agony. Daria struggled not to gasp at the enormity of the two bulges atop his head. And the smell of him . . . the man reeked as if he had not bathed in months. Tessa leaned hard against her. "Oh, m'lady, he is in such pain," she said.

"I know, Tess," she said, studying the man. She took the torch from Gianni and slowly circled the man, who stood under a cobweb-covered chandelier and in front of a door that did not latch properly. The stairwell was covered in dust. Two chairs were in the corner, little more than a pile of splintered sticks. What impotent rage had this man suffered?

"Be at peace, m'lord, I have come to bring you the Lord's healing."

"Be that in heaven or on earth?" he asked, meeting her eye as she came before him again.

"I do not yet know. But your agony ends here, this night," she said.

"There have been others, others who have pledged the same."

"Then why allow me entry?"

"Because you are in the company of my one great love."

Daria paused and considered Piero's whispered words. "And something more. The peacock. You have been given a sign."

Lord Devenue looked away. His chin was strong, his eyes wide and clear, even if filled with pain and sorrow. But she was right. "For days now, I have not slept. And when I doze off, one thing has come to me in my dreams . . . a red peacock on a white background."

"Our Lord was preparing you, showing you that we were to come."

He did not answer. He feared believing. She had to awaken in him at least a tiny glimmer of hope.

"We are here, Lord Devenue, to heal you. God has used me to heal many in this past year, and you are to be the next. He is always very clear in his direction. I was at Les Baux when he spoke to me about you."

The young lord eyed her. "It was not Anette, or one of her maidservants, who spoke of me?"

"Nary a word. I knew not your name, but I knew where you were, and what ailed you."

"How?"

"I cannot explain it. I simply knew, as if someone had whispered to me in my own dreams."

Lord Devenue paused, studying her with eyes that bore the ravages of pain. "So come, then. What have I to lose? I have long embraced death, prayed for it. Do what you must, m'lady."

"I thank you, m'lord, for entrusting yourself to my care."

"What shall I call you? And why travel in such number?"

"We are on God's own errand, traveling to Avignon to await an audience with the pope. We are the Gifted, a group of believers whom God has drawn together for his good purposes. I have the gift of healing; Gianni, the captain of my guard, has the gift of faith; Father Piero, the gift of wisdom; little Tessa here, the gift of discernment."

"And the others?"

"Part of my adopted family or my guard. Necessary all."

"Very well. As I told the countess, I no longer have bedding or suitable accommodations for any of you. You shall have to find . . ." He wavered on his feet, as if about to fall. Gianni reached out an arm to his elbow, but the lord shook it off, turned on his heel, and walked up the stairs. "Come, healer. Do your worst and then be on your way."

❖ ❖ ❖

"To whom does this land belong? Why do they now tarry here?" Amidei asked Vincenzo.

"The scouts report that it belongs to a Lord Devenue, once a suitor of the Countess des Baux."

"Once?"

"Lord Devenue ails from the cancer and broke off their engagement some time ago. Many believed him already dead."

"No one knows if he is alive or dead?"

"Nay."

"They could have made Avignon in a day and found much more appealing accommodations. But instead they come here with masons, stone, and mortar. They knew they were to stay for a few days, mayhap even as long as a week. Lord Devenue may be near death's door, but I'd wager our Daria is about to change that."

Vincenzo said nothing.

"I want our men to be watching the Gifted night and day, armed and ready to seize them if any opportunity arises. And while we wait, I refuse to sit here and watch while they go about the task of our enemy. We shall go to town, spread word of a meeting here, in the hills, in two nights' time. It's time for us to draw our faithful in again. We shall have use for them at some point. The master calls and I aim to answer." He jutted his chin out, as if pointing with it to the mansion. "They'll feel us here. Know we're present. It may impede their progress."

"Do you truly anticipate trying to intercept them? Take them?"

"We will toy with them, remind them of who their enemies are. We cannot take them here, not now. Not with the manpower they boast, not at risk to the count and countess of Les Baux. If we wound one of them, our enemies will triple. Our only opportunity is if they enter the right road where we can separate the Gifted from the others. At that perfect moment, should it present itself, our goal shall be solitary."

"Kill them."

"Kill all the knights. Capture and sacrifice the others. Slowly." Abramo grinned. "If they won't make haste and get to Avignon where I can get the churchmen to do my work for me, then I must do it myself." He leaned closer. "But I must confess, brother, that I would not mind it at all, to feel the terror within that girl child. To see Daria broken. I believe I might give them the taste of me and our master tonight. Remind them of their weakness, the danger hovering nearby."

"You shall draw near? How?"

"They fear us. We simply play upon those fears. Come, we shall gather some of the village simpletons and tonight, I shall show you more of the master than you have ever known before."

૭ ૭ ૭

TESSA stood at the window with Anette, and Daria went to join them. Outside, the count and his men were already at work. They could hear men entering and exiting the rooms downstairs. The smell of cooking food roamed through the mansion. Two bonfires had been lit, and the men fed them with the broken furniture of Lord Devenue's mansion. Only his bed and the massive dining table had been spared, it seemed. Every other piece had been torn apart, broken apart, pulverized by the raging, lonely lord. Atop the fires were massive cauldrons, holding boiling water that would be used to clean the mansion from top to bottom . . . and warm the lord's bath.

Daria had done a cursory exam and then demanded he bathe, that the linens atop his bed, his blankets, all would be clean before she proceeded. He also accepted a bit of bread and cheese, the first meal he had taken in some time, by the look of him. Daria took his acceptance of her demands as the tiny glimmer of hope she had been praying for. If he believed God could heal him, even in this late hour, it would be done. God had revealed his plan to heal him, had he not? Or was it as the lord had said, the final step to usher him into heaven and ultimate healing there?

It mattered little. In heaven, Lord Devenue would know release, freedom, total peace. If that was how the Lord wished to heal him, she could abide by it. But as she glanced at the lovely countess's face, the glimmer of hope in her wide blue eyes, Daria fervently hoped for a miracle here on earth.

"They call him Devil Devenue," Anette said, staring outward and swallowing hard. "He was banished from court three years past, the other nobles fearing that somehow the cancer might be a contagion, a curse upon us all. But I believe it was mostly a desire to keep his disfigurement out of courts that preferred beauty."

"You left him as well?" Daria asked softly. There was no accusation in her voice.

"He banished me. Refused to see me. I could do nothing but leave."

"And yet you married no other in that time."

"Nay."

"You love him."

"Always. And forever. If you could've known him before, Daria . . . as he once was . . . He was a different man then. The cancer changed him. He was beset by rage. A fury like I had never seen before. It frightened me."

Daria nodded and wrapped an arm around the countess. "I understand. Let us see if God means to yet deliver him, here on earth. The cancer has moved in his head and affects him severely. I have seen it before. People change their ways, their manner of speech, even the way they see the world when they become so riddled with disease."

"Will he . . . if you heal him . . . What I mean to say . . ."

"Will he ever look as he once did?"

The countess nodded eagerly, hope alive in her eyes. "He was handsome, once."

"I know not. The cancer, it has moved bone, muscle, deformed in ways I've never seen before. Can you love him, even if he looks as he does?"

"If he loved me. If he were kind again. If we could walk, hand in hand, along the river . . ." Her eyes searched the far hills of the Gardon. "Mayhap it could be rediscovered." She looked to Daria, begging her to understand. "So much has transpired . . . I . . ."

"Pay it no further heed, Anette. Let us see where God leads us all, yes?"

The countess, eyes filled with mixed emotions of hope and confusion and fear and love, turned away, chin in hand. Daria watched her for a moment. Armand, with his love of the court and the drama that unfolded within it, would either reject such a notion out of hand or embrace it, relishing the sense of repulsion and the challenges that would present themselves in defending his brother-in-law. Daria hoped it would not come to that. And yet the lord's monstrous deformities . . . never had she seen anything like it.

Tessa took her hand. "Remember Old Woman Parmo, m'lady," she said, staring intently up at her mistress.

Daria smiled, remembering the old woman's legs, damaged from decades of rheumatism, becoming straight. Bones in her fingers doing the same. A back, long curved into the arch of a snail, once again in alignment. Muscles lengthening beneath her fingers to match. God had done it. God had done his miraculous work through her there, in Siena. He could do it again, here.

She leaned down and kissed the child on the cheek. "Thank you, Tess. I was giving in to doubt. You are absolutely correct. I must believe in the power of our Lord and his good intentions, then trust in his answer."

The child looked across the river to the densely wooded forest. "They are there. It is they that cast doubt and shadow in our direction."

"I know, Tess. We're well aware of the dark ones' presence. You are right—we must remain vigilant, standing against the pull of their dark ways."

"Who is there?" Anette asked. "Lord Amidei?"

"Indeed," Daria said. "And others. For every moment we spend in prayer to the God of light and hope, they spend another in prayer to those of darkness and despair. In him, they sow power. In him, they hope to thwart our good efforts here."

"Then we must summon the priest and get to prayer immediately. Especially as you do your work upon Lord Devenue. Our God is not one who cowers when threatened. Believe that, Daria. We all need to believe."

Chapter Six

Avignon

Cardinal Boeri hated to keep Hasani in chains. But twice he had tried to slip away, and the last time they had caught him at the city gates. If he had made it but fifty yards farther, to the docks, Hasani would have been long gone.

The cardinal would let Daria d'Angelo's man go, when it best suited him. The doge, after intercepting the Turkish slave ship, had given the freed man to him, to use him as he saw fit. Slavery was an accepted practice in Venezia, but the Turks had tried to slip the lagoon without paying the required taxes. God's own hand had delivered Hasani to the doge, and then to the cardinal. Once he was in their care, they had bound his wounds and nursed him back to health.

Cardinal Boeri had made the mistake of telling Hasani he planned to free him, when the time was right. Now the tall, black man followed his every move with his wide cocoa-colored eyes, saying nothing but bespeaking much. Rather than accepting Cardinal Boeri's promise of impending freedom as placation, a reason to trust the cardinal, he saw it instead as reason for doubt. It was if he knew the cardinal's plan without being told.

Cardinal Boeri went to the second-story portico to again see the man, pacing down below. He moved his hands as if talking to himself, but the cardinal had yet to hear him utter a word. The doge had said his tongue had been cut some time ago, a barbaric practice common in decades past. His sources told him the man had been educated alongside Daria d'Angelo, undoubtedly making the pair of them unique in all of Italia. Educating women was rare; educating freed slaves was unheard of. But in turn, Hasani had become one of the most vigilant of guards for Daria. No doubt she wondered where her trusted friend had been taken. No doubt Amidei had tried to use the event for his own devices.

The cardinal leaned down to rest his forearms on the guard rail of the portico, still staring down at the man as he paced. Hasani did not know that the cardinal had also purchased his long, curved sword back from the slavers. He was surprised it was still in their possession—that Amidei had thrown it into the deal and that it hadn't already been bartered off. It was back in his guest quarters, within the trunk, a fine specimen of weaponry with the ivory handle and precious, uncommonly sharp iron blade. When he freed the man, restored him to Daria and Gianni's side, the black man's worst fears would be assuaged. And when he handed the blade back to the man, he was confident all would be forgiven, trust in him restored and useful in persuading the Gifted to play their cards as he instructed.

Amidei had sliced the man's back to bloody ribbons. Had he forced Lady Daria to watch as he did so, hoping to turn her? Spies had told the doge she had been a prisoner, and the Gifted had freed her on the eve of the biggest storm to hit Venezia in decades. Tides had climbed and waves washed over walls and breakwaters until the whole city thought they would drown, as if God intended to wipe them all away. What had Amidei done to her in those weeks of imprisonment? Had he dared to whip the Duchess as he had her freed man and friend?

Hasani moved below him, the heavy chain links dragging behind him. Cardinal Boeri shifted in agitation. This was what chafed at him. If he objected to Amidei holding Hasani, using him to try to persuade Lady Daria to turn, was he any different in holding the man to try to use him to gain the Gifted's good graces?

He swallowed hard. Of course it was different. Of course. Not similar at all. Amidei had only evil intentions. All the cardinal wanted was good—for the Gifted, for the Church itself. A comparison was preposterous. Preposterous.

Provence

DARKNESS was upon them. Lord Devenue, long without tallow or wick, had lived in dark halls, dependent upon the sun to aid him with warmth and light. Fortunately Anette had packed a crate of candles of every size, as well as a good number of cloths to make torches. Daria rounded a corner, heading toward Lord Devenue's quarters, and walked down a long, narrow hallway, alight with three torches.

A cold draft, more than a wind, swept through, making the torches flicker until Daria wondered if they would be snuffed out entirely, and then it reached her, so bitterly cold it was as if it carried snow, stealing her very breath. She coughed and looked up.

And stared into the eyes of Abramo Amidei.

Amidei smiled, but made no move forward.

She screamed, and Gianni and Vito were beside her within three breaths, swords drawn.

"Daria? Daria, what is it?" Gianni asked, turning her toward him. Ugo and Basilio reached the top of the stairs, Tessa hard on their heels.

"He is here. The dark one," Tessa said, panting, eyes wide as they searched the hall.

"Inside?" Gianni shouted, shoving Daria behind him. "Where did you see him, Daria? Where?" he snapped back at her, moving forward.

"There," Daria whispered, backing up until the cold wall met her back. "He was down the hall, by Lord Devenue's room." The men moved forward as a group, leaving Tessa and Daria behind them.

"Not there, darling," whispered Amidei, lowly in her ear. Daria whirled and Tessa screamed. "Here, I am here," he whispered again, now in her other ear. Daria turned quickly and Gianni came running.

But Piero was already beside her. He placed small hands on her shoulders. "Daria," he said, shaking her slightly. "Daria!"

She glanced at him, eyes wild.

He pulled Tessa to him with one arm and then forced the child's face up to look at him. She was as crazed with fear as her mistress. "It is naught but an apparition. Amidei's dark magic, nothing more. He is not truly here!"

Vito arrived back at the end of the hall, Lord Devenue by his side. He shook his head at Gianni. *Nothing. No one.*

"He was here," Daria said, almost shouting. "I felt him."

"As did I! I was certain of it," Tessa said.

"I experienced something similar once," Gianni said, drawing Daria into his arms, cradling her head beneath his chin. "He is powerful, in his magic. I almost cut a man down, as I whirled upon Amidei. But he was naught but smoke."

"Listen to me," Piero said, still staring at woman and girl. "This mansion now houses more than twenty-five men who will do everything to keep you safe."

"But how does one stop a man who moves in smoke?" Daria whispered.

"He wants to interfere. He knows why we are now present here, at Lord Devenue's mansion. If he can stop you from healing the lord, he can consider a battle won. We beat him, Daria, sorely, on his own dark isle. We must beat him back here. Quickly, Daria. You go to the lord and be about your business of healing. Take whom you wish with you to feel safe. I will take the others, make certain we are all safe from invasion, and utilize the others in prayer. Be at peace, daughter." He reached out a hand and cradled her cheek. "We will inundate this house with prayer, with God's own light." A smile grew across his face. "And you, you shall see the greatest evidence of the Lord's power yet."

Piero turned to pace between them all. "The devil opposes those most when they are doing the greatest good for God. This is not the last time that we will encounter Lord Amidei and his minions. But we shall remain strong. And vigilant. We shall not cave to fear. We shall not give in. This region will know the Lord on High because he will work through us, right now, here in this mansion. And he will use that for his own good, his own purposes. We are blessed to be his humble servants. Let us go about serving him, shall we?"

Daria smiled. Her priest. Speaking as if he were more a warlord encouraging the troops than a theologian. But she loved him, every little bit of him. She glanced up at the ceiling, breathing a sigh of a prayer of thanks to her God. She would fill her mind and heart with thoughts of the Christ, rather than let it be taken over by thoughts of Amidei, memories . . . black memories. Nay, not those. That is what he counted upon, why he preyed upon her. She had suffered at his hands, suffered his ill intentions, his abuse. He counted on her remembering that. Remembering doubt, remembering fear. But nay, she would not consider that now.

She stepped forward. "Gianni, Vito, Tess, Anette, you four come with me. We shall go about our God's business, not Lord Amidei's." She eyed the man down the hall. "Lord Devenue, prepare yourself. We aim to enter your quarters and not leave until you are free. God has sent us here to heal you. Do you believe?"

"I . . . I wish to."

Daria took strides forward, galvanized now with the enemy's line so near. "Cease your wishing, m'lord. You must delve within you, deep within, like a drowning man searching his lungs for but one more half breath." She walked onward, until Lord Devenue was forced to take a step backward. "Lord Devenue, I must hear it from your own lips."

He retreated until his back was against the stone bricks.

Daria paused before him. He stared downward.

Slowly, gently, she raised her hands so that he could see them in his line of vision and continued until one hand was on either side of his misshapen head.

Lord Devenue gasped at the feel of her hands upon his head, half in fear at the sensation of touch, half in desperate grief that a lady dared to touch his deformities. His slow sigh made Daria's eyes well with tears. Such sorrow, such loss he had suffered. Holding his head, closing her eyes, she could sense the dearth within him, the wild, yawning chasm and the masses, dark and throbbing within him. She panted, connecting with him, knowing his illness from the inside as if she could see it, reaching out to silence the life within him.

"M'lady?" he asked, breaking her reverie.

Daria opened her eyes, tears streaming down her face now, and looked him in the eye. "Oh, m'lord. I am so sorry. So sorry for your pain. Your grief. I know it now. I feel it."

Lord Devenue slowly reached up his hands and covered her own, bringing them down to cover his chest in an oddly intimate moment that neither of them could stop. Tears slid down his face as well, such a handsome face beneath the odd bulges that deformed his forehead and skull. But in his eyes, although tears flowed, there was a spark of something else.

Daria smiled through her tears. "You know? You know now. I am here to help, m'lord, only help. God himself has sent me, us, to do his work within you. You are chosen. You are blessed. You shall be whole again. Healed."

Lord Devenue's wide lips split into a slow grin and he laughed silently. "Yes. Well I know it. While the dark lord dared to make an appearance, so did our Lord's angels. They are behind you still, Lady Daria. Behind you all. I believe. *I believe.*"

Daria turned with Gianni, Anette, Vito, and Tessa, and watched as rays of light, as if from a quickly receding sun, slid up the floors and walls and out the window.

Daria wiped her cheeks and turned back to Lord Devenue. "Countess Anette's men guard our walls. Our people are in unceasing prayer. God's own angels are here to keep out those of the dark. Let us be about our Lord's business without further failure or hesitation."

☙ ☙ ☙

"THEY grow stronger," Amidei growled. He leaned against the cave's walls and stared out through the tree branches that shielded their location but gave them a view of Lord Devenue's mansion, alight from every window. "I merely frightened her for a moment. But what I sense now . . . it is as if my action worked in their favor more than our own, master."

"Fool. For every move we make upon the Gifted, our enemy shall make a countermove. They are precious to him, these Gifted. He obviously intends to use them for something we must stop, at all costs."

"I have tried everything I can think of. Used everything you have taught me, master."

"Nay. Not everything."

His master's deep voice slipped into Abramo's ears, as if more liquid than sound, entering his head, his neck, his heart, warming all as it went. He closed his eyes, relishing the moment of communion, infiltration, oneness with his master. "Yes, yes," Abramo moaned. "I had wondered . . . considered . . . now I know." He opened his eyes and stared down at the red tiles of Devenue's roof. "She shall heal the sad, decrepit shell of a man. And then I shall take one of them. Tit for tat. It is only just."

The master laughed behind him, his laughter resonating in Abramo's own chest. "Yes, my good and faithful servant. It is only just."

Chapter Seven

"It is well with you that Countess Anette is present?" Daria asked. The countess hovered near the door, as if ready to flee, as Lord Devenue lay back upon his bed, following Daria's instructions.

"M'lady, if you are indeed about to heal me, no one more deserves to be present." His tone was intimate, his heart in his throat, but his focus was on Anette more than Daria. "The countess lost as much through my illness as I."

Tears threatened again as Daria looked from one to the other. So they both had truly known love once. Could it be again? What had Lord Devenue done to make Anette stay away? Could that, too, be healed? One glance into the countess's wide, blue eyes and the hope therein, and Daria knew that that rift, too, could be bridged.

Lord Devenue sat back, sinking into new feather-filled pillows covered in new linens. He smelled like a new babe, so fresh was his bath. He had even allowed Agata to cut his long, brown, unkempt curls, bringing them back to shoulder length, as was the current style, and trim his beard into something manageable.

Daria stood beside him, hands knit together, and stared at him. "The cancer. Do you believe it to be anywhere else in your body?"

Lord Devenue hesitated for a moment. "Of late, the pain has resonated here, in my chest," he said, gesturing toward his sternum, "and along my arms. But there is no deformity as one can see atop my head."

"You must remove your shirt," Daria said.

He sat up and did as she bid, revealing a thin but well-formed chest, almost entirely devoid of hair. She glanced at Gianni, wondering if he thought it improper, this view of a man's naked chest, but then looked away before he could meet her gaze. Thankfully, Lord Devenue's chest was devoid of any errant bulges.

But Daria knew that the cancer could dive deep, deep within bones and organs, destroying from within like the devil's best work. She had seen horrendous cases, as a child, alongside her mother . . . cancer like a weed among a dung heap, eating from within and then exploding outward, taking bone, muscle, tendon, anything it could within its wild, hungry wake.

"Forgive me, m'lord, but I must lay my hands upon you."

"There have been far worse things done to me, m'lady," he said, eyeing Anette with a grin. She could see that the man had once been skilled in the ways of courtly endeavors. Lord Devenue glanced to Gianni and his grin faded. He closed his eyes and leaned back. "Your love is plainly in the room with us, as is my own, Lady Daria. Be about your work, not as a woman, but as a healer."

"So be it," she murmured. She leaned down and again covered his head, feeling the angry heat that resonated there. She covered every inch of his head with her fingertips, then his neck, then his shoulders and arms. Finally his chest. Briefly, she hovered her hands over his legs, a mere inch from his leggings, but sensed nothing there. "Turn over, please," she instructed. Slowly, methodically, she moved her hands down his spine, out each rib, then lightly down his legs.

"You may rise, Lord Devenue, and turn."

He did so, and his expression was serene. "Give me thy worst," he said, staring into her eyes.

Daria hesitated but a moment. "M'lord, the cancer is deep within you. I can feel it within your chest, several ribs, even as far as your forearms. Moreover, I feel it within your belly. It is why you are distended, even after months of self-starvation."

Lord Devenue paused, his eyes clouding. "But you believe you can cure me? I shall still be healed?"

Daria nodded once.

"Then be about it. I wish not to tarry one moment longer in the realm of the dying when I have living yet to do." He reached out a hand to Anette, and she stepped across the room, taking his hand in her own, and then sank to the floor, weeping.

"Do not cry, my love," Lord Devenue said.

"She cries out of relief more than fear," Tessa said, from the corner of the room. "Can you not feel it, m'lord?"

"Yes, yes, I suppose I might," he said, in wonder.

Daria placed her hands atop Lord Devenue's head and closed her eyes. Deep in the mansion, she could feel the prayers of Father Piero and the others like a warm blanket, wrapping around their shoulders. Beneath her hands, she could feel Lord Devenue's heartbeat, longing to be set free, grow stronger, flourish. She smiled and opened her eyes.

"Countess Anette?"

"Yes?" The woman raised her head and looked to Daria.

"Please, dry your tears. Lord Devenue is about to be restored to you. I need one thing of you . . . to sing. Sing of our Lord on high. Sing of the Christ. Sing of light. Fill this room with a voice that you, yourself, have never heard before. Allow God to work within you and be present here, from *within*. Can you do that for us?"

Anette nodded tentatively and rose, hope alive in her eyes.

Daria turned to Gianni, Vito, and Tessa. "You three, please pray, incessantly. You knights I trust will be on guard, but even in such a state, the Lord on High shall hear your prayers for Lord Devenue. Every word out of my mouth, please echo silently, as if you were speaking to the Christ, here in the room. You understand?"

The men and child all nodded as one.

She turned back to Lord Devenue. "Before we begin, Lord Devenue. Before you know life again, a life purchased by your Lord God, to be celebrated and praised always, I shall have your Christian name."

He smiled. "It has been some time since I have heard it uttered by another," he said in little more than a whisper. "It is Dimitri. I am Dimitri Marciano Devenue."

"I am most pleased to be of your acquaintance," Daria said with a nod. "Let us now go about restoring you, Dimitri, once and forever."

֎ ֎ ֎

DARIA had never experienced anything like it. The more she dropped into the cascade of prayer, the more she could feel the Spirit draw near. Anette's voice, so high, so sweet, pulled her inward, closer to Dimitri. In her mind, she could see the depths of the cancer, wonder that he still lived at all. It was so vast, so strong . . . but in prayer, lost in Anette's song of praise to the God on high, she began to see past the cancer, past the degradation and dismemberment to what Dimitri's body would look like whole.

She prayed that God would begin his healing work now, cutting out each limb of the tumors, eviscerating them open, digging out the poison, capturing it, pulling it from the man's body, and knitting together his bones and muscles and sinew where there would be vast holes. Anette's voice came down low, and then slowly, steadily edged into the upper reaches of a perfect pitch that gave Daria chills up and down her arms as she worked.

Then suddenly, Anette stopped.

Daria opened her eyes and saw what had given the countess pause. The angels . . . at first it was as if a line of candles was casting a warm glow about the room. Eventually they took form, and Daria could see them as well as the others. Tessa stood in the corner of the room, eyes wide and tears running down her face.

They were taller and broader than Gianni, so brilliant in the clarity of their white that Daria could barely stand gazing upon them. At each window, an angel stood on guard, looking out into the dark night. They were safe, so safe in this room, even with forces of evil just steps away. Because God's own were here to protect them.

"Daria," Gianni said in a low whisper, eyes alight in awe.

"I see them, Gianni. Vito?"

"I see them, too, m'lady. 'Tis a pity the priest isn't here."

Daria smiled. "Oh, he knows that God's warriors are here, one and all."

Those angels on the inner circle, five in all, stood between and about Lord Devenue's bed. One looked to Daria, his face a marble masterpiece of frightful, fearsome beauty. She could barely tear her eyes from him, but he gestured forward, to Dimitri, wanting her to complete her work. Daria glanced to the others. They, too, stared at her and down to Lord Devenue, faces alive with anticipation.

"Lord Devenue . . ."

"If I didn't believe before, I most certainly do now."

"If you didn't believe before, this would not be transpiring." She closed her eyes again, calling upon the heavenly hosts, upon the Holy Spirit, to aid her in her cause. Her hands traced the mammoth tumor to the side of Lord Devenue's head, praying that God would take it from him, destroy it, bit by bit by bit . . .

Anette gasped and again, Daria opened her eyes. Dimitri was unconscious, but beneath her hands, it was as if her fingers were of a stone from the fire, and the tumor butter melting at her touch. She leaned closer to the man and could feel an angel on either side of her, leaning in, watching, almost as wondrous as she at what was transpiring. Daria pressed down on the apex of the largest portion of the tumor, and within minutes, it was flattened, Dimitri's skull again in proper proportion. She reached for the fingers of the tumors, slowly flattening each tendril, as if she were a potter and Dimitri's skull mere clay.

Anette laughed then, watching in wonder, crying incessantly. She tried to sing, but the tears caught in her throat. That was when they heard it. Heavenly realms picking up her note and carrying it to such heights that Daria thought it might kill her to listen to such perfect, majestic beauty. She prayed for several minutes over Dimitri's head, asking the Lord to eradicate it of illness, to cleanse him, to knit him back together, healthy and whole.

Then she moved to his torso and hovered over the areas that radiated angry heat, as if defying her presence, or the Lord's presence. It was as if the cancer wanted to stay, like an angry lion defending his dead prey as tomorrow's sustenance. But she stood her ground, leaning harder into the tumors there, sensing their exact dimensions again, as she had on Dimitri's head. She stood there and felt heat move from her fingertips, countering and then surpassing the cancer's heat until it succumbed and receded, slowly, ever so slowly.

Daria searched Dimitri's chest for any further sign of the illness, but could find no more. Could it be so simple, so quick? She opened her eyes with a smile of gratitude on her lips and gazed in wonder at the angels within Dimitri's room. But they were already disappearing, becoming a wave of warm light again until nothing was left but the flickering candles at each window.

She rose and walked after them as if she could capture them, contain them until she had enough of looking upon their holy visage. Their exit left her feeling breathless. But they were gone.

"I was not the only one who just witnessed that," Vito said flatly, hand on chest, face pale.

"Nay," Gianni said. "We all saw it. The Lord's own were here. Here in this room with us."

"Daria," Anette said in little more than a whisper.

Daria turned and looked back to the bed.

"They were here as witnesses," Anette said, stroking Lord Devenue's head and face. He still slept, but his head was once more in perfect proportion. The light of the Holy Spirit shone through Anette's eyes. "They were here to witness the miracle of healing. And sing of it in the heavens. Can you hear it, m'lady? Can you hear it?"

And in the distance, as if the tiniest sound at the threshold of human hearing, Daria could still hear the strains of a heavenly chorus.

Chapter Eight

Avignon

"Cardinal, Cardinal," the man said urgently, shaking Cardinal Boeri awake.

He sat up, head in hand. "What? What is it?"

"Your slave, Cardinal. He is mad, drawing with his own blood upon the walls! He screams as if bearing a demon. We fear he'll break his wrists, the way he pulls at his irons!"

Cardinal Boeri rose and hurriedly pulled on a robe. Bishop di Mino came into the room, already dressed, and met his gaze with equal concern, having overheard the whole conversation. Together, the men left the cardinal's guest quarters and hurried down to the stables, where Hasani was being held.

It was not screaming that met their ears but the deep, aching tones of grief. The big, black man sat in a corner, his robe torn as the men of old used to do in mourning, rocking back and forth, weeping. Cardinal Boeri ventured inward, shaking off the bishop's warning hand, raising his lantern high to see the walls, strewn with blood.

"I . . . I know this place." The Pont du Gard, an ancient Roman aqueduct that spanned the sprawling Gardon. It had once aided the Romans in bringing water to the city of Nimes, and in recent times it had been converted to a bridge.

His eyes scanned the other figures in the drawing. Even clumsily drawn in blood with the end of a stick, he could easily make out Daria d'Angelo, Gianni de Capezzana, the priest, and others in the company of the Gifted. He did not know two men and a woman beside them, but they looked oddly familiar. Who were they? Who—

Cardinal Boeri's eyes stopped at the figure on the end. This was a knight he knew. He had seen him more than once in the company of Gianni, Daria, and the rest. His face was distorted by the pain, an arrow in his chest.

The cardinal looked to Hasani, and the man stared back at him in agony. "So you are their seer," he said bluntly. "Honestly, man, I had no idea." He knelt down beside him, staring into Hasani's eyes. "How long until this transpires?" he asked, waving toward the bloody wall.

Hasani stared back at him, the whites of his eyes bloodshot from weariness? Or tears? For a long moment, Cardinal Boeri did not believe he would answer, confirm what he knew.

But then Hasani shrugged.

He beat his chest once and pointed, as if to say, *I must go, go now.*

Cardinal Boeri stared at him a moment longer. "It is not far, this place. I cannot depart on the morrow—I have an audience with the pope. But we can go the next day. At first light."

Hasani rose, regal and menacing even in chains, as if he meant to make them go within the hour.

"At first light," Cardinal Boeri said evenly. "You do not know whether this will transpire today or on the morrow or a month from now, correct?"

Hasani continued to watch beneath a furrowed brow, not answering. The cardinal took that as agreement.

"I am here on your behalf, Hasani. I am here to argue for the safe passage of your own Daria, my former captain, Gianni, and the rest. They head in our direction even now."

Hasani's eyes shifted, and he raised his chin, hope alight in his eyes.

"Yes, they escaped Amidei's isle and have followed the path of the glass map here, to Provence."

Hasani studied him, frowning. The cardinal could see him wondering how he knew of the map, how he knew so much of the Gifted.

"I know much of your group, Hasani. Of Daria being a healer. Gianni, your man of faith. Piero, with the gift of wisdom. Gaspare, the fisherman . . . he must have the gift of miraculous powers, right? I've heard tell that he commanded the skies to rain, and commanded them to cease, and nature heeded his call. Is that true?"

Hasani looked away, unwilling to betray his friends.

Cardinal Boeri began to pace. "I know of the healings throughout Toscana. I surmised that your lady must have healed Gianni himself, when all his men were killed. I know of the healing of the lepers off Venezia, the healings of others in the city herself."

Hasani rose, every muscle in his body tense, but the cardinal could not stanch the cascade of words from his mouth. The seer! Here! The Gifted were his!

"The doge told me of the legend of the glass map, how it came from Alexandria and was distributed among the seven main churches of Venezia. No one had seen them for several hundred years, but somehow the Gifted were given the clues to find them, yes? Hidden beneath a peacock in each church?" He let out a laugh of wonder. "As if Lady Daria's own family crest were in each church, right?"

Hasani leaned an arm against the stone wall and let his head droop.

"Did you think we of the Church would not notice your actions? Did you truly believe you could keep it covert? We know everything that transpires in our lands, keep close tabs on anything that might subvert our faithful. And the Gifted . . . I had been watching for you for some time."

Hasani looked up at him then, across his rippled bicep, so that the cardinal could see only his steady eyes.

"Oh yes," he said, pacing again. "I have a portion of your letter. The letter that may have been penned by Santo Paulo?"

Hasani's brow furrowed as he looked down at the cardinal.

"I purchased it from an antiques dealer in Constantinople, some thirty years past. I was a mere priest then, studying and serving in the old capital." He stepped closer to Hasani. "I would like to believe that the Lord brought it to me because we were to somehow serve together, Hasani. It could not be coincidence that would bring Gianni into my service for years, a man who would become a part of the Gifted, and I, the man with a portion of the letter that foretold of his coming—six hundred years before he was born. It cannot be a coincidence that I am a cardinal able to travel here to Avignon, now, to assist in the defense of the Gifted so that they might be allowed to do what the Lord has asked of them."

Hasani grunted and lifted a hand.

"Yes, they have already landed in Marseilles. Their intent is obviously to travel here and seek an audience with the pope. I am here to help them."

Hasani searched him intently.

"What do you think will happen if they march in here, unannounced, unaided? The Lord's Commissioner would be immediately summoned.

They would spend the next year on trial, harangued, interrogated, defending their actions without sanction of the Holy Church. They would be imprisoned, punished, mayhap even tortured by the civil authorities, of course, until they said the words the Commissioner wished to hear. Their only chance"—he raised a hand and stepped toward Hasani—"*their only chance* is if I help them make a way. I can tell of the wonders that transpired in Italia, their battle against the Sorcerer, a proven enemy of the Church and of Christians everywhere. I can introduce them so that their presence is not such a shock to His Holiness. I can make him see that the Gifted might be of assistance to the Church rather than a threat."

Hasani looked away, thinking over his words.

"Lady Daria suffered enough nights as a prisoner, don't you agree?"

Hasani frowned in his direction.

"The doge learned she was severely whipped."

Hasani moaned and looked to the ceiling.

"There is more, my friend. Amidei, our Sorcerer, already has inroads here in Avignon, forged years ago. Not only must I lay the groundwork to introduce the Gifted and win them support, I must also begin to dismantle Amidei's foundation so that we can take him down as well. Otherwise, the Gifted may be in as much danger in facing him with his increased influence as they are in facing the Church." He walked to the door of the prison cell. "So you see, I must have this meeting with the pope on the morrow. To give it up will hurt our cause in multiple ways." He glanced at Hasani's drawings on the wall. "If the knight is to die, he will die. Have you been able to change the winds of fate as of yet?"

Hasani stared at him and then hung his head and slowly shook it.

"Nay. I did not believe so. You can see the future, but you cannot change it, right? You are simply condemned to live through it."

Hasani looked up and then lifted his hand to his chest, gesturing toward the heavy silver cross hanging from Boeri's neck. "Pie-o," he tried, grimacing at the effort. He pointed again at the cross and said, "Fa' Pie-o . . ."

"Father Piero?"

Hasani nodded. "A-ay?"

"Alive? Is Piero alive? Why yes, I think so." He studied the man. A wave of relief swept over his face. Had he had a vision that the priest would die? *Ah yes, the arrows.* "The doge . . . he learned that in escaping the isle, the priest took several arrows to the chest. Is that what you saw?"

Hasani nodded slowly. It was good. He was beginning to trust Boeri. At least a little. "How horrible for you. You believed he would die?"

Again, the nod.

"He did not. He lived. Mayhap Daria healed him. But he is here, Hasani, here in Provence. Soon, you shall be reunited. I promise." He hesitated. "I would free you, man. But I cannot allow you to run. I know you want to go to the Gifted, go this night. But you must wait upon me. Together we will find them. And in the meantime, we shall pray for all the knights in the company of the Gifted."

Provence

"You need to rest," Anette said, pushing Dimitri Devenue back to his bed.

Dimitri threw back his head and laughed. He gestured out the window. "Do you see how glorious it is outside? How can we keep to the mansion? This valley has not seen such warmth in the midst of winter's keep in more than a decade. Come," he said, taking her hand in his, placing it on his chest. "Let us go to the river. I have not laid eyes on it for more than two years. I am a man freed. Would you keep me prisoner here?"

Anette cast a helpless look in Daria's direction.

Daria shook her head and drew closer. "He appears the picture of good health," she said. She smiled into Dimitri's eyes. "And I understand your desire to see the banks of your beloved Gardon once more. You are like a man reborn." She studied him for a moment longer. He was as dark and handsome as Anette was fair and beautiful. Both of them fairly glowed with love and joy. "But give it one more day of rest. If you still feel as well tomorrow, we shall see about going to the Pont du Gard. But you shall remain swaddled like a baby in the back of a wagon. Do you promise this?"

"I promise," he said dramatically, with all the flair of Count Armand. Was this the same man who was at death's door but two days past? Never had Daria been privy to such a dramatic healing, so quickly. Only Gianni's return from death's door and Old Woman Parmo, in Siena, measured near to it. Many had she seen healed, but mostly it was but the beginning of a long process. A jump forward, to be sure, but far from the end of the road. This man bore witness to a healing of biblical proportions.

"M'lady, do you think it wise?" Gaspare said, stepping forward. The tone of his voice gave her pause, and she studied his face. He had drawn her aside earlier, given her much to think about in terms of others recognizing a miracle. He had lived it, given his gift, known the good and the bad. He stood there beside Gianni, like two glowering big brothers. She knew that they had only her best interests at heart . . .

But one more glance to Dimitri and her decision was made. "We shall go and take our noon meal at the river's edge." She looked to Gianni and Gaspare, now with Piero at their side. "It is only a matter of time until word gets out about Lord Devenue's healing. Let us enjoy the day and capitalize upon the event. Clearly the Lord God wished us to come here, to heal this man. Do you really believe he would not bless our celebration with him before we depart for Avignon?"

Gianni stepped forward and took her arm. "Amidei and his men have not been seen for more than a day."

She pulled her arm from his grasp in irritation. "Very well. Mayhap they knew that God was present with us and they could never win. Mayhap they turned tail and ran."

"Mayhap it is all a ruse to persuade us to believe just that."

Daria squared her shoulders and looked up to the knight, then allowed her face to soften. "Please, Gianni. Would it not be good for us as well? To relax upon the banks of the river and bask in God's glory? For but an afternoon? It has been so taxing, so long, this journey. We do not go away from God's care. Surely his angels shall be as close to us in the midst of the wilds as they are in this mansion."

"Daria, I—"

"Please," she said again, resting a hand on his chest. "We'll give Amidei and Vincenzo another day to make an appearance or obtain confirmation they have indeed left."

He stared down at her, helplessness and frustration knitting his brow in wrinkles.

"If you are leaving soon for Avignon, we shall go with you," Dimitri said. "You shall need an introduction to His Holiness's court. Who better than I, your newest evidence of divine favor?"

Daria raised her eyebrows and looked to Piero. The priest shrugged his small shoulders. "It would help," he said. "Or we bring him in at an opportune moment."

"You shall need to know quite a bit before you enter the city," Count Armand broke in, moving from the window to the group beside Dimitri's bed.

"Such as?" Gianni said.

"Some courtly ritual, games, dances," the count said. "The pope's favorite gifts, his favored friends as well as his antagonists."

Piero frowned. "There is not gaming or dancing in the *papal* court."

"More so than any other," Armand returned. "I shall introduce you to my friend, a poet and a critic of Avignon, back in Les Baux. I fear there is much ahead of you that you are not yet prepared to face. Let us take our picnic on the morrow, then return to Les Baux to pick up the rest of your people and spend a few days in preparation. You must not enter this battle blind."

Daria angled a smile toward Gianni and he nodded, once. "Very well," she said. "Let us be about it then."

She departed in a swish of skirts and heard Lord Devenue laughing at Gianni in the room behind her. "You, my good knight, are as deeply in love as I find myself." His voice echoed down the hall. In the exuberance of his newfound life, Lord Devenue seemed to have lost all restraint and any sense of propriety. In her mind's eye, she could see him reaching for Anette. Ever since his healing, he had been unable to keep himself from touching her.

But if Gianni was as deeply in love with Daria as Dimitri was with Anette, why did he not reach for her at all? On the ship, en route to Marseilles, it had been different for them. It was as it once had been between her and Marco, falling in love, free and deliciously beguiling, consuming her nearly every thought. There were soft conversations and embraces, stolen kisses . . . but when they had set foot on land, he was once more the knight, she the lady, and it was as if a wall had risen between them.

ᛞ ᛞ ᛞ

HIGH on a hill, farther north in the valley of the river, Amidei received the spy and heard of Lord Devenue's miraculous healing, and their intended excursion to the Pont du Gard the following day. The Gifted believed Amidei and his people had departed, but knew not where they had gone. Reportedly they were still on alert, cautious that he hovered nearby, but understandably, they drew some comfort from the fact that he had not been seen for more than a day and a night.

Abramo had had the ceremony in the cave across from the mansion. But it had been lackluster. Few of the villagers had responded to their invitation. He found none of the women appealing. His master had awakened him the next morn, drawn him to the mouth of the cave in order to converse. "The enemy has gained strength this night, as we knew they would," the master said. "But send Vincenzo, my son. Send him to follow their every move and strike the moment he has opportunity. He shall draw blood among the Gifted. He will remind them that although they are watched over by the God who believes himself most high, they still live in a natural world. They are but human, still subject to pain and even death. If we maim many, surely the healer cannot get to them all before one or more dies."

"It will be so, master."

"We must remind them that although they worship the God of the heavens, I am the god of this world. And Vincenzo shall be more firmly tied to our ways than ever before. He is hesitant. We must force his hand now, before he weakens."

"Yes, it shall be so, my master."

"Have Vincenzo and the archers cut away their bloody robes and bring them to the next ceremony. Their blood shall feed you and yours, give you strength. Remind you of the power within your grasp."

"Yes, master." Abramo salivated at the thought of the coppery taste of his enemy's blood in his mouth. Daria's blood. Gianni's blood. Piero's blood. Tessa's blood. Surely it would be sweet. Savory. He closed his eyes.

Sustenance. To feed, to feed upon the Gifted. Glory. Glory. Glory!

He sank to his knees before his dark master, who now levitated before him. "What would you have me do, master?"

"We, my son, shall go to Avignon and prepare the way. The Gifted may be maimed, but not vanquished here, in the countryside. But we will use God's own to bring them down in Avignon. Once there, we shall begin laying a carefully crafted trap."

⚓ ⚓ ⚓

"You are torn, torn between being master, servant, lord to his lady," Piero said, staring at Gianni intently. "What keeps you from professing your love?" It was only Piero, Gaspare, and the knight, sitting on a wall outside the mansion that night.

Gianni lifted a shoulder, looking miserable. "I am her defender."

"Is not a husband a defender as well?" Gaspare ventured.

Gianni cast a sharp look in his direction. "I have no means, nothing to offer her."

"The lady is a fine woman," said Vito, joining their circle uninvited.

"But she is no longer a woman of means herself. I fear our days of drawing more than warm vittles in the pot as payment in her service are long over. But still we stay. Why? Because we are called to this place. Called to serve one another on this mad quest."

"He is right, Gianni," Piero said. "Wealth has little bearing at this point. If you love her, if you are called to serve as her husband as well as her captain, move, man. She is clearly confused. And remember Adimari . . . you must not scar her tender heart again. Give in to it, man. You are more in love with her than you thought possible."

Gianni sighed. " 'Tis the truth of it. And if I fool none of you," he said, looking from one to the next, "I doubt I fool our lady. But is it the way of wisdom, priest? Does it not make us somehow more vulnerable?"

Father Piero smiled. "Love always does, my man." He stared at him a moment longer. "I tell you this but once. I fear that your unspoken vows, your unrequited passion, as much as Count Armand celebrates it, makes us more vulnerable than anything. Better to find satisfaction and communion in each other's company. It shall give you both strength for what we face ahead."

Gianni eyed him. "So you would bless it, then? If she would have me?"

Count Armand stole up behind him and clasped him on the shoulder. "What is this of which you speak? Could you be planning a betrothal to the Duchess?" His eyes were alight with pleasure. He shook his head. "It must be in the air. I doubt my sister will last a sennight before she is married to Lord Devenue. We may not even get her home to Les Baux. It will take everything in me to persuade her to depart. Most likely I'll need bring Devenue with us back to the castle."

"The cardinal de Provence shall marry them, then," Piero said, his disappointment barely disguised.

"Ah, no. I doubt anyone but you shall do, Father Piero," Count Armand said. "Those two," he said, nodding in the mansion's direction, "are your two newest patrons, such as they are. You'll be happy to know that the countess brings a handsome dowry to the marriage. And what they cannot provide, I can. You and yours shall want for nothing while you travel in Provence."

"You are most gracious, Count Armand," Father Piero said, grinning. "But if the cardinal is not invited to preside over such a ceremony, there shall certainly be retribution."

Count Armand sat back and considered his words. "You know as well as I that if the cardinal gets in the middle of this now, we'll be embroiled in papal scrutiny as to Lord Devenue's healing. A marriage ceremony could be postponed indefinitely as the papal rats filled out forms and conducted interviews. Anette and Dimitri have waited for years for this chance. Love dawns. I say seize it now, before it disappears. Love, like life, is a fleeting opportunity. Hesitate, and it is gone." He stared at the mansion again, but his eyes swung back to Gianni and stayed upon him for a long moment.

He twisted off a garnet ring from his pinky, barely getting it off. "My grandmother's, worthy of any lady as a marriage band," he said, offering it to the knight.

"I cannot, m'lord."

"You can and you shall," the count said. "What do you fear? That she might deny you?"

"At least you can bury the dream if the lady says no, Captain," Vito said. "Better to have tried than—"

"Cease!" Gianni growled at Vito, grabbed the ring with mumbled thanks to the count, shoved off the wall, and stalked toward the stables, mumbling something about helping to get the horses ready.

"Where's he heading?" Basilio asked, just joining the group, with Rune at his side.

"Apparently to saddle some horses," Vito said. "I think you should go join him. Ask him about Lady Daria," he said with a laugh.

"Do no such thing," Piero warned, although his eyes danced. "The poor man is already in enough misery."

"Yes, it's exquisite, isn't it?" Armand asked. " 'Tis almost too perfect to ruin by a common marriage."

"I believe," Piero said, "a union between Lady Daria and Sir de Capezzana will be anything but common."

CHAPTER NINE

THE group spent the night at Lord Devenue's mansion, eating around a restored dining hall table, alight in the glow of fifty candles and loaded with feastings. Dimitri had summoned two dramatists from Nimes who made them laugh with their antics, so hard that tears streamed from their eyes. Even Gianni gave in to the laughter, relaxing for once from his constant guard, and eyeing Daria from across the room. Their eyes danced together through the evening, silently, one glancing at the other, the other holding a gaze, glancing away. Three musicians arrived quite late, just as Daria was considering retiring to bed and forcing her newly healed patient, Lord Devenue, to do the same. But Armand and Anette would hear nothing of ending the festivities then. It was too lovely to let it go. Dizzy with the glowing joy all about her, Daria felt herself powerless to resist.

The musicians began with a haunting, lovely tune native to Provence. After one verse, Anette began to sing, her eyes solely on Dimitri. It was a song of love found, and love lost, and as the words cascaded from her mouth, tears rolled down Dimitri's cheeks. He reached out for her, and abruptly her voice cracked, even as she smiled through her own tears. She went to him. The musicians finished the song as if nothing out of the ordinary had occurred, and Vito arrived with his flute. They conferred for a few moments, and then a more vivacious, joyful song emerged.

Anette stood beside Dimitri, still painfully thin but gloriously straight. He was a head taller than his lady, and he took the countess's hand and led her to the center of the room, where tables had been moved to the side. They faced each other and moved a step away, their hands meeting in the middle, their eyes never leaving their beloved's face. Daria brought a hand to her throat, a bit unbalanced by the intimacy of it. But they cared not. It was as if nothing else mattered than this rediscovered love affair. Her eyes went to Gianni, and he stared at her without wavering, eyes full of words he longed to share. But then Count Armand abruptly stepped between them, standing in front of Daria with hand extended. He leaned forward. "M'lady," he whispered. "Come and dance with me and we shall make your man mad with envy."

Daria looked up into his kind blue eyes, sparkling with mischief, and considered his invitation.

"Come, Daria, trust me," he said. He waggled his eyebrows. "We shall move the knight to declare what is upon his heart before the moon descends."

She took his hand and rose.

"You need to know this dance and several others anyway," he said, leaning to his right so that their heads were scandalously close. "The pope, his court, the nobles who entertain them, all enjoy dancing. You must learn the steps in case you are invited to one of their social occasions. We shall follow my sister and my future brother-in-law, if they can keep their minds on the music."

Anette smiled over her shoulder at them, hearing Armand's teasing, and followed Dimitri's lead. She took a handful of her skirt and swished it to the left for several steps and then to the right, moving her head in tandem with it and the beat of the music. It was as if she were floating about Dimitri.

Daria shook her head. Could she move in the same manner? She had grown up with the traditional dances of Italia, but this was something altogether different. Their dances had been in groups of four or eight, circles that intertwined and moved together and parted, breaking up on occasion in couples. This appeared to be a dance performed solely in couples and occasional, larger rings. A peasant's dance, at once intimate and showy. No wonder Piero had been dismayed to hear that the papal court enjoyed such a spectacle!

"You are thinking far too much," Armand said in her ear, moving to take her right hand in his left and placing his other hand at her waist. She dared not look Gianni's way. "Watch my feet for a moment. These are your steps, in time with the music. Follow along. One, two, three, one, two, three, one . . ."

Daria began to echo his steps and, shortly thereafter, to match them.

"Now keep doing that, Daria," he said soothingly. "Lighter on your toes, drifting, like a boat upon the ocean, as Anette is doing it. That's it. That's it, m'lady." He moved to the side, eyes upon her. "Keep looking at me, that's right. Don't let your gaze leave me," he said, half teaching, half daring her, smiling, obviously knowing how much Gianni must be despising this moment.

He turned to the musicians as they concluded their song. "Another, in a similar tempo," he instructed.

Dimitri and Anette began the dance again, alongside Armand and Daria. This time, Armand took his small steps, simply leading Daria about in a circle, then stepping forward to repeat the process three paces away.

"You are a vision, Daria," the count said. "Nay, do not look away. Eyes on me, 'tis part of the dance. It's the most daring part of it, right? It is called the Dance of the Eyes for a reason. Scandalous, is it not? We are barely touching, but there is much that transpires between two people in a gaze."

Daria returned his look, smiling slightly. She fought the urge to glance away, feeling a slow, red burn rise on her neck.

"I want you to hear it from me, m'lady. I know your heart belongs to the knight, and his to you. But know that you are a lady who deserves nothing but the truest of loves."

"What makes you believe I do not think the same?"

"Because I can see it in those big, olive eyes of yours. You have already loved, and lost. It is the same haunted look as I have seen in my sister."

At that point, one of his knights arrived beside them, keeping step, and then took a turn with Daria about the floor. A second arrived and then a third, as one tune melded into the next, all in the same tempo. Then a fourth and a fifth man came, all as well schooled in the art of the dance as their count, it seemed, and eager for a turn about the floor with the lady. None dared to approach the countess. Mayhap because her eyes were solely upon her beloved, mayhap because it wasn't seemly. Once again, Armand arrived and took her hand.

"How is it that you have not loved and lost, Armand?"

He waggled his eyebrows and continued to hold their gaze. "I have not yet found my lady. But I tell you this . . . if your knight hesitates much longer, I shall be forced to consider the opportunity before me, Duchess."

Daria let out a scoffing but friendly laugh. "Count Armand Rieu des Baux. You favor courtly flirtation so much, I doubt you shall ever settle down to but one woman."

"A woman such as the Duchess d'Angelo, healer of Toscana, called and gifted from on high, does not oft arrive in my realm. I would explore it with you further," he said, "but your man approaches, and it is he who has your heart. No, keep my eye; do not look away until the next man has your hand." He lifted his head, still staring at Daria, still keeping time with the beat and yet remaining beside Daria. "You wish to learn this dance, Sir de Capezzana?"

"It is in our best interest to all be prepared, is it not?" Gianni ground out, well aware that the count baited him.

" 'Tis the truth of it," Count Armand said, smiling a farewell to Daria and then looking to the knight at last. "Follow my steps." He counted it out for Gianni, showed him what to do with his hands. The music seamlessly flowed into a fifth song.

Dimitri and Anette left the dance floor, Dimitri suddenly fatigued. Daria knew she should feign exhaustion as well and demand they end the festivities, but Armand continued his instruction, even as more of their party disappeared into the shadows of the hall.

Gianni's gaze held her there anyway. His hand felt so right under hers, and the nearness of him made her feel as if she were indeed afloat about him. His green eyes studied her silently, but seemed to call to her. She found it easy to meet them, not to lower her gaze. This was the idea of the dance, she realized, to find the one from whom you could not look away.

They danced and danced about the room, reveling in their proximity, their silent conversation. The music seemed to envelop them, lead them, coax them onward, sometimes quiet, sometimes building.

At one point Daria dimly became aware of the music fading, leaving them. They were leaving, moving down the hallway, and Daria pulled her eyes from Gianni's to see that they were utterly alone in the dining hall, the music dying like the last embers in a hearth. In the end, it was silent but for their slow breaths and the sizzle of an occasional candle's wick, sputtering out in a pool of beeswax.

Gianni stopped but still held her hand. Slowly he lowered it and pulled her to the side, until she faced him. Daria's heart picked up a beat. He lifted both hands to cradle her face and gently tipped it upward. His mouth covered hers in a long, tender kiss, their eyes both closing at last. He smelled of cedar and peat, and she pulled him closer.

"Daria, Daria," he moaned, pulling her close, running his fingers through her hair. "You confuse me."

"I confuse you?" she said, pulling slightly away. "We had this, this on board the ship. What happened when we reached land?"

He sighed. "I love you, Daria. From the first moment I laid eyes on you, I have loved you. But I have nothing to offer you as husband."

"Nothing but love," she said, resting her chin on his chest to look up at him. "'Tis enough for me. I need not land or title from my man. Only love. And yet I have my own question for you."

"Speak plainly."

"Is love enough for you, from me? I have no means, either. No dowry. And after a broken handfast, I am neither virgin nor able to conceive. Can you tolerate that? Don't you long for an heir?"

Gianni ran his fingers through her hair and held her face again. "That another man has touched you is something that I will endeavor to forget, but can manage, as long as it is only I who touches you in the intimacy of a bedroom from here on out." He gave a small shrug. "It is what it is. Understandable. Common enough among nobles. And that you are barren bothers me . . . solely because you would be a fine and lovely mother and I would love to see our babe in your arms. But I do not need a child to find completion. I only need you, Daria. You. I tried to pull back, to exist beside you as only your captain, but you have my heart. Totally. Completely. I am yours, if you will have me."

He knelt down before her and looked up into her eyes. Daria remembered the first time he had done so, outside Roma. And again in Siena, when he had sworn fealty to her. It was then that she knew that something else existed between them, something growing and grand. "You have no man in your life to whom I my go to ask permission, so I ask it of you. Daria d'Angelo, I pledge to you my life and my heart. Would you do me the overwhelming honor of agreeing to be my bride?"

"Gianni de Capezzana," she said without hesitation, "it is as if I have waited my whole life to say these words. I would be honored to share your name and your life, forevermore."

Gianni smiled and leaned down to kiss her hands, over and over again, laughing breathlessly, and then rose to kiss her again on the mouth.

Applause behind them made them turn, and they grinned to see their friends arrive back in the hall, clearly never intent on sleeping after all. The musicians returned to their position in the corner and began playing, but the Gifted came to offer their congratulations, with Armand and Anette and Lord Devenue right behind them all. Piero smiled widely, wrapping a small arm around each of them. "Let us marry you now, here, my friends. You have been in love since that day in the grove. It is time you make your love official."

"Right now? Here?" Daria gasped. "Not in a church?"

"Right now, here. We are present, your friends. There is much ahead of us. Let us make your union official and you can begin the morrow without this on your mind. You need clear heads. Come, let it be done."

"Such a romantic, priest," Armand chided. "Can you make it any less appealing?"

"It *is* romantic," Anette said.

"Then let us be about it as well," Dimitri said. "Marry us at the same time, Father. This night. I cannot last another hour without Anette as my wife."

Piero stared hard at him and then glanced at Armand. "You are asking me to perform the marriage ceremony of the Countess des Baux? The cardinal would be deeply offended."

"The cardinal will have his due," Armand interceded. "Go about your business. Marry these two couples this night. We will see to political protocol later, and have the 'official' festivities the countess, and her cardinal, deserve. But love cannot wait a moment longer."

Daria smiled. She felt dizzy, as if she had drunk too much wine, and clung to Gianni's arm hoping the muscles beneath her fingertips might steady her head.

He turned to her. "Is it all right, Daria? A wedding, such as this? It is hardly what a girl dreams of."

She smiled. "Nay. It is more."

And as she said it, she was sure of it, the rightness of it, the full-circle completion of it. She had dreamed of the festivities of a church wedding, but that dream belonged to what she had once shared with Marco. All her time with Gianni had been in transition, it seemed, en route to follow God's call. And God was calling her now, here, to him. To this man before her, her knight, her soon-to-be husband. She glanced around at the smiling faces about them and found only confirmation. It mattered not where they were married. It only mattered that they were together, and never parted again.

CHAPTER TEN

Avignon

"Word has reached our ears of the Gifted," the pope said without preamble, studying Cardinal Boeri as he kissed his ring.

"Yes, Beatissimo Padre," he said, bowing.

"You may rise." The man sat on his hand-carved throne, on a dais, and steepled his fingers as if in thought, the tips touching the end of his drooping nose. He was a wiry, small man, wielding sharp intelligence and insight as well as renowned faith.

Cardinal Boeri stood at the base of the dais, patiently waiting.

"You know these people well?"

"Indeed I do, Holiness. The knight who leads them, Gianni de Capezzana, was once the captain of my guard at the Vaticana." His eyes moved to four knights of the *Honneur Gard*, those who protected the pope and his court.

"Ahh. And how did he become tied to this group?"

Cardinal Boeri paused, choosing his words carefully. What transpired now would set the tone for the rest of their conversation. "I believe they have been drawn together for God's own purposes, Holy Father. I know Gianni de Capezzana well, and he is truly one of the most devout in all of Christendom. The priest that travels alongside them, a Father Piero, was once an abbot outside Roma. He too, is highly regarded. And Daria d'Angelo—"

"The Duchess, they call her?"

"One and the same. An honorary title given to her by the people of Toscana. She is a healer, Holiness. Many of her healings have been authenticated, most recently a group of lepers in Venezia."

The pope's brow furrowed at the mention of the city on water. Much love had been lost between the reigning pope and the doge, duke of Venezia. He sighed and rose, moving down the steps of the dais in stately fashion to walk toward the window. Two bishops, his aides, trailed behind him, then Cardinal Boeri.

"A knight of the Church, a former priest-cum-chaplain, and a fabled Duchess who can heal. Hardly the makings of such legend."

"But there is more. While I was in Venezia, residing with the doge, he came into possession of a slave, a man named Hasani."

The pope eyed him from the side. "We have heard of Hasani. He moans as if the weight of the Holy Spirit is upon him, while walking the Court of Familiars in chains."

"Indeed. He is actually a freed, learned man educated alongside Daria d'Angelo by her father. And gifted with foresight."

The pope's eyes returned to his as he faced the cardinal in full. "Tell us, Cardinal. Do these Gifted carry with them any letter? Any papers they claim as prophecy?"

Cardinal Boeri took a deep breath, desperately trying not to take a step back from the shorter man. Had Saucille told him of it as planned? His tone echoed with older knowledge. He had to trust his Lord in this. "Indeed, Beatissimo Padre. They believe their coming was foretold."

"And what is their stated mission?"

"To bring the faith back to the people." He sighed, as if very concerned. "They are preaching, baptizing, even communing outside the Holy Church, insisting upon translating the Scriptures into the common tongue."

The pope glowered. "Why have they not already been arrested and brought to us?"

"They are en route to Avignon, intent upon an audience with Your Holiness."

The pope gave him a wry grin. "And they anticipate what? A blessing?"

He began to walk again and Boeri fell in step with him. "Mayhap. But this is what I wished to speak of. The Gifted have already won wide public support, from Toscana northward. Now in Provence, they continue to sow their seeds deep. They are on a poorly chosen path, to be certain, and need to be set straight. But Holy Father, given the Church's need for public support and tithes, would not the Gifted garner the perfect method? The masses love a good tale to tell, and the Gifted are giving them plenty to wag their tongues."

"We wish for the masses to speak of their Lord in such a manner, not of heretics."

"Agreed. The Gifted are . . . unorthodox in their methods, but I do not believe them to be heretical. Let me bring them here, to Your Holiness, to set them on the right road. Let us utilize their gifting for God's greater good. I am certain that if the masses learn of their story and hear of the miracles that transpire behind them, this court shall benefit greatly. Your treasury will have never seen the flood of gifts that are sure to come, without one papal bull or indulgence issued."

The pope drew to a pause. "You wish to be the Gifted's shepherd?"

"I do," Cardinal Boeri said, with a slight bow. "With your blessing."

"It is quite a gamble, Cardinal," the pope said with a cocked brow. "Should they prove unmanageable, unwieldy, or heretical after all, you shall find yourself a common priest in some God-forsaken location."

Cardinal Boeri returned his look with a small smile. "But if they do not . . ."

"Then, Cardinal," the pope said, placing a hand on his shoulder and resuming their walk, "you shall be in mighty stead indeed."

"There is more, Holiness. An evil lord preys upon the Gifted, seeking to destroy them. I believe he has designs upon your holy house as well. You must—"

"Be off at once, then, Cardinal," he said in dismissal, moving back to his throne. "We now wish to meet your Gifted. We charge their safe arrival to your care. Upon your return, we shall address your other concerns."

Provence

SHE awakened late the next morn, wrapped in Gianni's arms. His presence was warm and surprising, a welcome reprieve from morning's chill. Had she dreamed the night before? Now? Or was she truly now Lady de Capezzana?

Her husband was awake, but unmoving, simply staring at her in awe. He kissed her forehead as she moved. Daria rose onto one elbow, pushed her cascading hair over her shoulder, and rested her head on her hand. With the other, she covered his chest, broad and exquisitely muscled with a smattering of light brown hair. Her fingers found one long scar, still white, just above his right kidney. "Where did you obtain this?"

"South of Roma. Apprehending a highwayman."

"And this small one here?" Her fingers moved to his left shoulder, directly beneath the clavicle.

"North of Roma. A man stealing from a church."

"And this one?" she asked, tracing a red line down his arm.

He rolled to his side and pulled her close. "A battle I'd prefer to forget. Against a man I'd prefer to never see again. Can you help me forget him, wife?"

"I believe so, husband. But shouldn't we be getting to the others? Today is our outing to the Pont du Gard."

"The Pont can wait. It is not every day that a man awakens to find he has married the Duchess d'Angelo. I want to revel in this moment, and the fact that you are mine." He kissed her on the neck, slowly moving downward.

She smiled languidly. "No more than I want to know that you are mine as well, husband. But we need to break our fast."

"I will fetch us some food in time. But . . . not . . . yet . . ."

꒰ꗥ ꒰ꗥ ꒰ꗥ

THE group elected to make their picnic an afternoon event, given the late rising of the four newlyweds. A report came back that Amidei had been seen leaving the nearest town the night before, and Gianni visibly relaxed. If Amidei had left, then Vincenzo surely couldn't be far behind him. Still, he made sure that the knights of Les Baux planned to leave with full armor. If Amidei did not give them chase, then the townspeople might, given their first glimpse of Lord Devenue, once again restored.

They made their way down the country road and onto an old Roman road, paved with broad, flat stones. Within minutes the towering Pont du Gard, a Roman architectural marvel, came into view. It was a series of three levels of arches, the bottom made up of six massive arches that crossed the Gardon river. They were like the feet of a giant, capable of withstanding more than a thousand years of battering flood waters and rising fifteen paces—the height of three grown men—to the next level. The second level was a series of eleven arches, another thirteen paces in height, with narrower arches that gave the bridge an elegant feel. It was on this level that the road had also been erected, made from the original foot-traffic bridge by narrowing the arches at the base.

The third level was a series of thirty-five smaller arches, like the top of a queen's crown, the jewel of the bridge. But five of them had collapsed and others had been dismantled, the stones used in churches and other construction in the region, according to Dimitri. The aqueduct had lasted for only several hundred years before it ceased working and the Romans abandoned the project, finding alternative means to bring water to the thirsty city of Nimes.

Daria looked up to the holes in the face of the second level as they crossed to the other side.

"Where they inserted wood scaffolding to build or repair," Gianni explained, riding beside her.

She could see the curving adze marks of the quarrymen, men who were naught but drying and disintegrating bones in shallow graves by now. Such a testimony of the human spirit, this place was. It reminded her of the ruins outside St. Remy, and the Colosseum in Roma. Count Armand had told her there was something similar in Orange. If they had the opportunity, Daria thought she might like to see it.

She was about to say something to Gianni and looked in his direction, but his eyes were on the woods high above them. On either bank, dense, scrubby oaks and other trees covered the rocky hills. Below, limestone cliffs gave way to the water, providing lovely access to the river. Already, people gathered down below them, where Lord Devenue pointed. He gestured farther downstream, to an empty plateau that would give them a panoramic view of the bridge to their north and the valley to their south.

Gianni's frown deepened.

"Can you not rest and endeavor to enjoy this day, husband?"

"It is not my duty to rest. It is my duty to protect you, wife."

"What if your lady relieved you of such duties? You are a spouse now, as much as a captain-at-arms."

"Being your husband," he said, reaching to take her hand, "only makes me want to protect you more. Whether you like it or not." He gave her a small, tender smile. "I would rest easier if we knew where Amidei had gone."

"Mayhap he left, gave up on us. Look at us, Gianni. We have our men, and Count Armand has twenty more. They would be foolhardy to attack us here."

"Lord Devenue!" a woman cried as the lord passed. Dimitri and Anette were directly in front of Gianni and Daria, traveling behind Count Armand and his men. People had separated obediently to make a path for the nobleman, nodding or even bowing as he passed. Up to this point, no one had noticed Lord Devenue, their attention on either of the Rieus instead. The count and countess had not been seen in this region since the engagement between Lord Devenue and the Countess des Baux had been broken.

Dimitri turned in his saddle and smiled at the woman, tipping his hat. "Madame Emile," he said in greeting.

The woman lifted a hand to her gaping mouth, then a moment later shrieked and ran off, gesturing to three others.

"So much for keeping news of Lord Devenue's healing a secret," Vito said behind them.

"Let them come," Daria said. "If we are surrounded by the faithful, we are more protected than ever from those who hunt us, yes?"

Gianni smiled again and gave her a half nod, seeing the wisdom of her words. He looked over his shoulder, and Daria did too. Already, villagers were amassing and slowly following behind them on foot.

They spread blankets out across the rough rocks, and two servants laid out trenchers full of meats and cheeses and breads. There were dried apricots and peaches as well as a light red wine. They had all been served and had just begun eating when the first villagers dared to draw near.

"Lord Devenue?" called a man.

Dimitri turned and lifted an arm to a middle-aged man dressed in a woolen cloak to ward off the afternoon chill. He beckoned him closer.

The man, hat in hand, his wife beside him, drew closer. "M'lord, we . . . we believed you dead."

Dimitri rose and shook the other man's hand. "I believed it myself. It is good to see both of you."

Daria watched their interaction. Obviously acquaintances of old. Or servants once dismissed?

"How? How has this miracle transpired?" the woman asked, staring blatantly at Lord Devenue's head.

Dimitri smiled and glanced at Daria, then on to Piero. Piero nodded at him. "The priest brought to me a healer in his fold," he said carefully, intent upon this knowledge spreading the way it would benefit them the most—as a holy event, a Christian and priest-blessed event. "Three nights past, I was healed, completely healed."

The woman crossed herself and sank to her knees. "For so long, m'lord, for so long . . . we prayed that you should be healed. I confess to you now that I did not believe it possible."

"All things are possible when the Lord is present," Dimitri said, standing to reach down a hand and help the older woman to her feet. "Come. Let me introduce you to my new friend, Father Piero."

Piero rose and greeted the couple. "We shall hold a service of thanksgiving here, by the river, in but a few hours. Will you be so kind as to join us? Invite others?"

"Here? By the river, Father?" the man said. "Mayhap you'd like to come to our village chapel . . ."

"Nay, it shall be here," Lord Devenue said kindly. "Did not John the Baptist baptize new believers on the banks of the River Jordan?"

The couple departed, obviously confused but intrigued. Four others took their places, greeting Lord Devenue as a family member back from the dead, bowing in the countess's direction. As with the first two, Dimitri sent the four off to gather friends and family and return.

Daria glanced at Gianni. As expected, her husband's jaw worked in frustration. But could he not see this was right? The way of wisdom? If they could win the villages of Provence as supporters, their way might be easier in Avignon. With Les Baux and Lord Devenue as friends, surely this was God's own path. The pope might imprison them, separate them, even hand them over to civil authorities to be killed. Here in Provence, they needed all the support they could garner. This was why Piero had agreed to Devenue's plan to come to the river. This was why he had leaped at the opportunity. He knew that as soon as the people saw their Lord Devenue, long lost to them, they would flock to the Gifted. He had longed to preach for some time. Now would be his opportunity. And there was more, someone new to be healed . . . she could feel the first stirrings within her heart.

Dimitri turned to Piero and nodded, then looked to the rest of the Gifted and his own men. "They will come, then, in throngs. The village priest will be one of the first, to make sure we are not leading his people astray. But he is a good man, and he will recognize that the God on high is traveling among us." He again looked at each of them. "I have told

Father Piero I believe I was healed for two reasons—to be a testimony of the Lord's blessing upon the Gifted, and so that love might be requited at last." He smiled at Anette and bowed toward the count. "My thanks to the count who did not allow me to languish in the world of unrequited love any longer."

"Happily," said Armand with a slight smile toward his sister. Unlike Gianni and Daria, Lord and Lady Devenue could not touch each other in public. They had to feign separation until the formal marriage ceremonies could take place, even though they had exchanged their vows.

Dimitri turned to Gianni. "I know it is not what you prefer, knight, but I hope that the villagers and the people of this valley will all come and listen to Father Piero, as they might have once flocked to hear the disciples. Our priest is a good man, but he is confined by the ways of the Church. I believe the Gifted are here to change the course of history. And I aim to do my part in aiding that cause. So they will come, hungry for the food you can provide, and I doubt it will be longer than an hour before they arrive."

He reached down and helped Anette to her feet. "With the count's permission, I have asked Father Piero to baptize as many as will accept the gift, right here at the river."

Daria could not hide her gasp. The count, the countess, Lord Devenue, and Father Piero all looked in her direction. "You shall bring down the wrath of the Church upon us. Why tempt them so? You all know as well as I that if it is discovered that you have been married without the cardinal present, there shall be repercussions. And a mass baptism . . . Why? Why taunt them?"

Piero raised his hands in a placating manner. "It all will be well, Daria. I agree with Lord Devenue. If this is the time and place, if his healing speaks to Christ's people and they desire to make a public proclamation of their faith, I shall not hesitate to answer their call. Every day without Christ is a day lost. These people need the Holy Spirit in their lives. Who are we to keep them from him?"

Daria sat back, stunned at his decisive tone. Clearly he thought it the right thing to do. "You are drawing a battle line, Father. The Church will come after us on multiple counts."

The small priest smiled at her. "You must know that our battle is already upon us, daughter. The letter speaks of it . . . our map points us to Avignon. We go nowhere and do nothing that God does not see. He is with us. Is it not best to have as many possible with us? There is safety in numbers. Numbers persuade even the most powerful."

"They will declare us Cathars," Gianni put in simply, still sitting on the rock.

"They are more likely to declare us heretics," Piero returned evenly. "But truth will be our defense. Think on it," he said, looking at each one in the group. "When the Apostle Paul spoke of the armor of faith—the breastplate of righteousness, the shield of faith, the belt of truth—only one reference was to a true weapon. And what was that weapon?"

"The Word, the sword of the Spirit," Daria said in little more than a whisper.

Piero stared at her for a long moment, a nod bobbing his head. "What was your defense against evil when Amidei imprisoned you?"

"The Word."

"Yes. The Word will be what we need most in the battle. The Word is what will force our accusers to face their own iniquity and failures. The Word will be our Defender and our Light and help us strike against the dark." He reached down and pulled Daria's precious family Bible from the folds of the leather satchel. He raised it so they all could see. "The Word became flesh. Jesus was the Word. We will force them to see him again, before them. To remember his words. To recall what he said, and what he did not. Our Church has become an institution of ritual rather than an institution built on the truth of Christ. This is what we have been called together to do. We need not the third portion of the letter to know this. The spiritual gifts that Paul mentioned in Corinthians were there to show that the Holy One was present in our lives. We are together to be the Body of Christ, his witness to the world. Our gifts . . . they are present only so that we might call attention to the One we adore, the One we worship. It can never be about us. Never, ever. It is always about Him. Always and forever."

He paused and looked at each one of the Gifted, from Daria to each of the knights, to Gaspare and little Tessa. "Who is most in need of this Word of truth?"

"The Church," Gaspare said.

"Yes, yes. Our precious Church. We need the Church, people to guide and correct us in our walk. To rout out true heresy. But the Church needs to return to the Truth and the Light and the simple Gospel promises that Jesus preached. The Church needs to turn inward first and rout out the sin and greed and pride that is leading some of the powers that be, deep within, astray."

Daria sighed heavily. Ever since they knew they were to go to Avignon, she had known their battle would come to the Church's door, at least on some level. But could it be true, that they were called together to correct the path of the most powerful entity in the world? Not since Roman times had one power had such reach, such wealth. How could their small group take on such a task? How could God ask them to effectively change the world?

Gianni squeezed her hand and she met his gaze. In his green eyes, she saw reassurance and peace. Faith. Even in the face of this, this idea that they might have to challenge the Church he once loyally served. He nodded toward Lord Devenue, reminding her of what they had witnessed, not three days past.

Dimitri rose, conferred with Anette and Armand, then walked to the priest and knelt before him. His lady did the same, and the count followed suit, kneeling beside his brother-in-law. "We swear we shall do everything in our power to aid you and yours," Armand said simply. "We shall command forces to protect you, gather friends to come to your aid in the papal courts, provide you safe passage. Most of all, learn from you and pray for you. We recognize what you speak as God's own truth and will die defending you and yours. This is the very call upon on our lives, greater than any we have ever known before."

Piero smiled down upon them. "Dear nobles, my daughter and sons. My sister and brothers, what you have discovered is the call of Christ upon your hearts. Know that regardless of what transpires with us, nothing is more important than this moment. We accept your offer of friendship and protection, but I ask you to always remember, whether we live or die, always remember this day and God's call upon your lives. This is all that matters, truly. That you might accept the Christ as your own Lord and Savior. That you serve him, ultimately, and only him. That you might know love in full. This is what buys you the keys to doors of heaven—simply embracing Christ as your Lord. Loving and serving Christ, learning what that means, shall bring you fulfillment and joy beyond anything else. What say you? Shall you do that?"

He looked each in the eye until each said, "I shall."

He reached out and touched their heads, then made the sign of the cross and lifted his face to the bright skies of the valley, raising his hands wide beside him. He knelt down beside the nobles. "Pray with me, brothers and sisters. Father God on high, Lord of truth and light, Protector, Redeemer, we thank you for the miracle of this day. For Lord Devenue's healing. For our friends, whom you have brought to us to aid us. You have begun a good work within us. Complete it, Lord, complete it."

Daria moved to her knees and Gianni did the same, each raising their faces and hands to the skies. The steady *thrum* within Daria grew until she felt she was fairly resonating sound, light. They could feel the Holy Spirit enveloping them here, surrounding them. One by one, the others in their group did the same as Father Piero continued to pray. It was as it was when Vito and Ugo had become baptized. It was as it was in the dungeon of Amidei's dark isle. It was as it was when Lord Devenue was healed. As if angels surrounded them, moved about them. They were not alone. They were never alone! Despite what might come before them, they were surrounded by the mightiest of warriors! Daria smiled, full, full to overflowing with the purest joy.

"Use us, your children here, for your good purposes. Drive fear from our hearts and replace it with courage and might. Let us never look away from evil, but drive it from our paths. Let us not tolerate it within our own hearts. Let us be constantly confessing our own failures, learning to be less our own and more your own. Let us teach love and peace and joy to your people. Let us remind other lost souls that you alone are the Way. Let every word from our lips be as if from your own, Jesus. Use us, Lord." His voice cracked with emotion. "Use us. Our lives are meaningless without you. With you, we have all. Enter us, fill us, move us, teach us, protect us, guide us. We are yours, Father. Amen."

"Amen and amen," said Armand, in a softer tone than Daria had ever heard from the count.

"Amen and amen and amen," said the others.

"Come, preach and minister to the people at my side," Piero said, rising with some effort on stiff knees, then offering a hand to Daria. He looked her deeply in the eye, seeing the now familiar desire there, the call to move and heal another. He raised an eyebrow and smiled, then looked about, realizing that the people had already begun to gather, close to a hundred already watching them with wide eyes. He raised a hand in warm greeting and leaned toward Daria to say, "You are schooled in the language of Provençal. We shall read the Scriptures and they shall hear it for the first time, as those in Italia did. Anette will sing. We shall heal and baptize . . . and many new sisters and brothers will know the Word as their own for the very first time."

Anette took Dimitri's hand and rose to stand beside him. Daria went to Anette's side and Armand went to Dimitri's. Father Piero raised two fingers and made the sign of the cross before them. "We begin in the name of the Father, and of the Son, and of the Holy Spirit . . ."

ﻌﻌﻌ

VINCENZO, watching the group from his hiding place above them, recoiled at the sign of the cross. But Ciro was beside him, bolstering him. He was thankful for his presence, one he did not normally welcome. But without Amidei here, Vincenzo felt somehow weaker, less sure of himself.

"Has the spy arrived?" he asked, his eyes never leaving the group below him.

"Moments ago," said the hulking knight.

Vincenzo was torn, half filled with revulsion, half pulled by something about them, in them. Daria and Gianni held hands. Fury at their public display of affection nearly cast him down the side of the mountain, sword in hand. How dare the knight touch her! She belonged to them! To them!

"What news has he?" Vincenzo forced himself to ask.

"The Duchess and de Capezzanas, the countess and Lord Devenue—both couples were married last night by the priest at the Devenue mansion."

"It cannot be," Vincenzo said, staring at Ciro. "That is political madness. If word reaches Avignon, they shall enter the papal palace with the lions already pacing and hungry."

Ciro shrugged. " 'Tis the truth of it. Both couples consummated their vows last night. The countess and Lord Devenue plan to keep their matrimony a secret and wed in a cathedral sometime soon. The de Capezzanas feel no need to do anything further."

"Such knowledge shall serve us at some point," said Vincenzo. Abramo's training came to him, then. The call of the master was to find every person's secrets, desires, weaknesses, and exploit them all. When they did so, their enemy faltered even as their own power grew.

"The villagers will join them there," Ciro said. "They have sent them to gather others and come and worship here, right before us. We should attack now, divide them, kill as many as we can."

"Nay," Vincenzo said. "We shall wait. Wait for them to feel the dulling effects of victory, glory. They shall not anticipate us then. Look, look even to the girl now. She does not know we are here. She is entranced by the worship ceremony, as she will be as they preach to the simpletons. The others believe us gone, probably having heard word of Abramo leaving the area. If some of their group depart, the count will send some of his men with them to protect them. When the Gifted are separated from the nobles of Les Baux . . . Then, then, is when you shall attack."

He slid a hand onto Ciro's shoulder and gazed down below them. "The day shall ultimately be ours. But patience will be our ultimate weapon. Summon the archers and all the men you can garner. Take up the positions we discussed. And wait for my archer to let her first arrow fly."

CHAPTER ELEVEN

THEY rode hard from Avignon, twelve knights de Vaticana by their side. Word had reached Cardinal Boeri that Abramo Amidei had entered Avignon and sought an audience with the pope. Now his cause was twofold: to bring the Gifted to the pope, and to bring Amidei down. He knew Lord Amidei's reach was vast, that his tentacles already interlaced with the men within Avignon and beyond. But he had to expose the Sorcerer. Collect evidence and testimony against him. If he could do both—bring the Gifted into line and into service for the Church, and bring down Amidei—his brothers could do nothing but crown him with the papal crown at the next conclave. And then he would bring the papacy back to her true home in Roma.

He winced with each impact of his steed's step. His hips ached as his horse galloped beneath him. He was accustomed to a more leisurely pace, or a wagon, but there was no time. If he was to keep Hasani as an ally, he had to placate the man's need to rejoin his comrades immediately. When they paused to water the horses by the Rhône and eat a bit of bread and cheese, he went to his horse and unlashed the bundle at the saddle. He nodded to two knights, and the men went to unlock the manacles around Hasani's wrists. Hasani looked at the cardinal, still chewing his bread, as the men released the irons. He rubbed his wrists, raw and tired from the metal, still staring at Boeri, measuring him, considering him. Cardinal Boeri tried to give him a small smile of friendship. *You can trust me,* he wanted to say. *Trust me. I am on your side, ultimately. I want much of what you want.*

He neared the man and handed him the bundle. Hasani took it and then slowly unwrapped his long, curved sword and sheath. "You shall need that, ahead," Cardinal Boeri said. "If the arrows are flying, the Duchess will need another defender."

Hasani nodded once, in a gesture of appreciation, still wary, but becoming more open. Boeri could feel the door widen slightly.

⚓ ⚓ ⚓

WORD of Lord Devenue's healing spread quickly, as he knew it would, and the people came in waves, growing in number from ten to twenty to fifty to more than a hundred. Piero drew children to him, tender in his care and his wording. "Blessed are the children," Daria translated into Provençal, "for they shall see the kingdom of the Lord."

Together, they preached the gospel, calling for people to commit to Christ as their Savior or recommit their lives, to embrace faith as a calling, not so complicated that one had to learn Latin to understand, but requiring a simple step of faith, belief, to come truly as little children.

" 'Let the little children come to me,' " Daria translated, moving toward a young blind boy and kneeling before him. " '. . . and do not hinder them, for the kingdom of God belongs to such as these. I tell you the truth, anyone who will not receive the kingdom of God like a little child will never enter it.' " It was this child that God called Daria to heal.

This was the one.

She searched his face, unable to keep herself from touching his shoulders, tears springing to her eyes. Did he know? Did he know what was about to take place?

"Leave him," said one of the villagers. "He is a child of sin with no father to claim him. He bears the mark of their sin in his blindness."

Tessa moved in front of him as if she meant to defend him, a child of Il Campo de Siena defending another orphaned child.

"Nay," Daria said, drawing the boy closer with one arm and placing her second arm around Tessa. She smiled at the people around her. "This child has remained blind so that you would know the power of God is real. He does have a Father to claim him—our Father in heaven. And our Father wants us to do his work here in the world. Jesus said, 'As long as it is day, we must do the work of him who sent me. Night is coming, when no one can work. While I am in the world, I am the light of the world.' "

She rose and led the child to the river, bent low, and scooped up some fine, silty mud. Daria packed it atop his eyes, and Gaspare, Piero, and Gianni came near to pray with her over him, asking for healing. "Amen and amen," Daria said as they finished.

Daria took the boy by both shoulders. "Child of God, your Lord has delivered you. Your sight is but a sign of that deliverance."

"But, m'lady," the boy said. "I cannot see."

"Of course you cannot," she whispered with a smile. "There is mud all over them. Bend low here, at the river, and wash. When you are done, behold your Father's light. Believe. *Believe.* Your God has healed you."

The slight child opened his eyes and where once an opaque, white film seemed to cover them, there were dark green irises and pure black pupils. He stared at her, utterly still for a moment. Then his pupils narrowed and he gasped. He fell back, crying, touching his face over and over as if he were in a dream and trying to wake, then touching her. "M'lady," he whispered. "M'lady," he said louder, finding his voice. "M'lady! M'lady!"

Daria laughed, tears streaming down her face. "Tell us, child. Tell us."

"I can see! I can see! You are even lovelier than your voice!" He turned to his mother, weeping beside him. "Oh Mama, Mama! I can see! I can see you!"

A woman screamed beside his mother. Two men scrambled away, intent on sharing the news. Gaspare moved forward. "Wait!" he commanded.

The two men paused and looked back to the fisherman.

"Go and tell of this miracle," he said, stumbling over a language he had barely picked up from other fishermen in Venezia. "Tell the people that your God is alive and well in the land. That Jesus longs to come and abide with us all. That he is your Savior and your guide. Tell them that we are but humble servants. Do you understand me? We are but humble servants of the Christ Jesus!"

The two men nodded, fear etched in their faces as if he might do them bodily harm.

"It is of the utmost importance that word of the miracle—the healings of this child and Lord Devenue—carry exactly as I have said," Gaspare said to the crowd at large. "Please, do not embellish. I beg of you, my friends. If we are to carry on our ministry, if we are to heal others and do our work on the Lord's behalf, you must carry forth these stories as I have laid out. Tell your friends that it is God moving, not us. We are but servants. We are only here to serve the Christ. Understood?"

The crowd nodded as one, sober in their promises.

"Thank you," Piero broke in. "It is wise to be cautious. We already have enemies. Please help us from gaining others. Now, I believe there must be some among you who wish to be baptized. Come now and say the words of promise and accept your ultimate healing and union with your God of grace."

More than twenty men, women, and children moved down the banks of the river to where they stood. The first was the boy, who came without hesitation, rushing into the water to receive the gift of all gifts. One by one, the faithful followed and were baptized, immersed as sinners in the cool waters and brought upward cleansed and filled with the Holy Spirit.

Daria, Piero, Gaspare, and Gianni were all waist deep, holding one after another, embracing them as brothers and sisters as they emerged. The people ashore clapped after each baptism, seemingly aware that something larger than anything they had experienced was transpiring. Toward the end, all were wearying. Vito and Basilio went to Daria's side, seeing her knees buckle, and helped her out of the frigid waters. They felt weak but full, as if after the longest, hardest, but best of days, ready to fall into bed and enjoy the deepest slumber of all. Already, Dimitri and Anette and eight of the men had departed, too tired to continue and in dire need of rest.

Piero, a bit wan, looked up and gazed about the group. Wearily he made it to shore and spoke in love to the crowd. "We must depart, my friends. We are tired and must rest so we are prepared for what is ahead."

"We want to come with you!" shouted a woman, mournful.

"Nay. We cannot feed or care for all of you. Please, go and serve our God. Be his light to the world. Share his word with your loved ones, anyone who will listen. There may come a time that he calls you as he is calling us now. Pay attention to how he speaks, here," he said, patting his chest, "deep within. Listen. Pray. Follow. This is the call upon your lives now. You are children of the Light. Live your lives as such. Tell of the miracles you have experienced here, always giving glory to our God, and not to us."

⚓ ⚓ ⚓

THEY were two miles away from the Pont du Gard with the sun setting in the west when Hasani kicked his mare into a full gallop. The man leaned down, as if to urge the horse faster. His body was too big for the small country horse, but the mare was strong and determined, moving forward with surprising speed.

The knights about him looked up in surprise, and then back to the cardinal.

"Go, eight of you," Cardinal Boeri said, aware that he could not keep up that pace nor keep Hasani from his people any longer. That left him four knights, adequate guard for an aging man of the cloth from another land. Mayhap the men would get to the Gifted in time to keep what he feared was about to transpire from occurring.

👁 👁 👁

THE Gifted were moving back across the Pont du Gard, absently admiring the golden streams of sunset cascading through the arches and the silhouette shadow cast upon the far hill, when the archers came into view. There were four on either side of the second tier of the bridge, directly above them, blocking an exit from either side. Like the bridge's shadow, they were little more than dark forms against the fading light of winter's day. But the Gifted knew them well. It was these same women and more who had attacked them in the grove, and again in the streets of Siena, and again off of Abramo's dark isle.

But this time, there were not two with uncommon skill and deadly aim. There were eight.

"Tess, under the arch, quickly," Daria said, pushing the girl to the side, still staring upward, as if to offer herself over the child. Gianni, several paces before her, turned. "Take cover, Daria!" he shouted.

As one, the archers let the arrows fly, a pale blue sky seeming to propel them onward. The Gifted, the remaining Les Baux knights, and the few villagers who still clung to their path all scattered, taking cover behind the ancient bulwarks of the Pont du Gard.

Daria moved toward a pillar, saw it was too crowded and turned, too late, toward the other side. She looked up, even as she ran, seeming to smell the arrow before it came, as if the scent of poison were upon the wind.

She could not outrun it. It was too fast. She was too late.

Her eyes met Basilio's, already barreling toward her.

She shook her head. Nay. It could not be. But it was as if she had Hasani's foresight. She knew what was to come.

Basilio turned and leaped, bringing his brawny chest as wide as possible in shielding her, bringing her down beneath his dead weight.

And the arrow entered, making a sickening, sucking sound as it did so.

Basilio grunted, instinctively rolling into it, as if to give the shaft more room, to take away the pain slicing his belly. He rolled off Daria and toward the edge of the bridge, blind in his pain. Five other knights, all Armand's, were down as well.

"Basilio!" Daria screamed. She moved toward him, but Gianni reached her then, pulling her back beneath the protective arch. More arrows rained down about them, two more striking Basilio in the side. In his agony he inched even closer to the bridge's edge.

Rune shouted and wrenched himself free of the two knights who held him back, running to Basilio's aid. Three arrows immediately pierced his back.

"Nay!" Daria screamed, wincing as if they had pierced between her shoulder blades instead. "Nay!"

Rune staggered at the impact, then turned and aimed his longbow, letting one arrow fly and then another and then another until he sank to his knees in exhaustion, beside Basilio. Two of the female archers fell to the river, but the others were moving closer. Daria could see by the angle of the arrows that they were driving the knights backward, to their deaths. Rune took another arrow in the shoulder; Basilio, another to his arm. The archers steadily moved in closer to the rest of them, huddled beneath the arches of the ancient bridge below.

Basilio opened his eyes and whispered something toward Daria.

"Come, come to us!" Gianni shouted to his men. "You must move over here." They were only ten feet away, but it might have been a Roman mile. Tessa was weeping, hysterical in her fear. She yanked away from Daria as if she meant to go and pull the men to safety.

Rune staggered to his knees after a fifth arrow pierced his chest. His lips parted and his eyes closed in breathless agony, and then he looked over to Basilio, defeat etched in every line of his face.

Basilio returned his look and whispered the same words, eyes wide, already fading.

Rune tried to grab his friend, help him, but took another arrow to the shoulder, almost sending him backward, over the edge himself. Rune looked to Daria, to Gianni, to Piero. Daria sank to her knees, weeping with Tessa, wanting to look away from her friends, but finding it impossible. Her fingers moved to her shoulder, expecting a hot, seeping wound there. But there was nothing. What was Rune saying? He was desperately trying to say something!

"*Post tenebras, lux.* Believe . . . you helped me . . ."

Basilio fell to his side.

Gianni knelt down then, hand to his shoulder, feeling Rune's piercings as his own. "Please, my friends. I have no shield. It is but a few feet. Please. Come to us. We will help you. But we cannot come to you."

More arrows rained down. They were getting closer. Soon, the Gifted would have no choice but to stand and take on their aggressors. And surely it was not merely the six archers who attacked them.

A shout went up from the end of the bridge. A cry of rage came from the man in front, a hulking black man with a shield over his head and a long, curving sword in the same hand that held his horse's reins. "Ha-Hasani?" Daria asked, rising in wonder. Hope surged within her. Could it be?

Eight other knights charged behind him, similarly armed. Armand's knights, given the distraction, immediately moved out in pairs, one shielding, one letting fly an arrow. Arrows passed back and forth in the air.

Two struck Basilio and Rune, a final wave of impact, sending each backward. They hovered on the edge—Basilio on his side and rolling away, Rune slipping over the edge, catching himself, hauling himself up but for a moment—each seeming to wordlessly say good-bye.

Daria screamed. The sound seemed to hang in the air.

And then they were both gone at once.

Daria wrenched forward, out of Gianni's arms, crawling toward the bridge's edge as fighting went on all about her. Horses clattered to hurried stops. Men shouted. Swords clanged. More arrows cascaded about them. Dimly she knew that their attackers now began to recede back into the shadows whence they came.

But all Daria could see was the backs of her two knights, her dear friends, her brothers, as they floated to the surface of the Gardon, facedown, side by side down a pale blue river lined with white cliffs.

She moved as if to jump after them, weeping hysterically as the phantom pain of the arrow piercings receded, telling her the men were dead.

A man hauled her backward, up into his arms. But it was not Gianni, who she could see had moved off down the bridge to defend Tessa and Piero from a knight with a fearsome sword. It was Hasani, holding her close, willing his strength into her, protecting her, shielding her as he always had.

Together they watched the bodies float out of sight, their tears dropping to the waters far below.

Gaspare arrived beside them, and she knew he was searching for the Lord's call as well.

"Do you think we can save them? Can we bring them back? Gaspare? Gaspare!"

The wide, strong fisherman winced at the impact of her keening cry and slowly shook his head, sorrow etched into every line of his face.

He had to be wrong! Daria searched her heart, yearning for the same glimmer that told her their God would save Piero. Could they find the men, haul their bodies from the river, heal them? Would God grant them such favor?

But there was no whisper in her heart, no shimmering hope. Basilio and Rune were gone. Lost to them. Rune's last words echoed through her head.

Post tenebras, lux. After the darkness . . . light?

ๆ ๆ ๆ

THE following eve, in the safety of Lord Devenue's mansion, she sat back in a chair, watching the fire. Basilio's and Rune's bodies had been laid out in the next room, so still. She knew she would need to force herself to stand beside them, to trace their faces and remember smiles and grimaces. They were good men, brothers in arms. How could God allow this blow at this time? The Gifted needed them! Needed them! They had been through so much . . . Even Piero had not the wisdom to comfort her. He seemed to be at a loss himself, grieving the men.

Tessa was on the edge of the room, pacing, still angry with herself for not sensing the enemy's presence before they attacked. Over and over she worked the story of the prior day, trying to figure out what had happened, why she had so little warning. There were no words to help her; Daria had not the strength to try.

Hasani hovered near, and she reached out to take his hand, patting it as she studied the flames before her, so thankful for his quiet strength, her oldest friend, beside her once again. So thankful that he had been restored to them as suddenly as Basilio and Rune were wrenched away. When Gianni entered, Hasani sank back into the shadows, giving her husband his rightful place, but still near.

"Daria," he said, laying a tender hand on her shoulder. "Cardinal Boeri would like to meet you. Are you strong enough for the task?"

She glanced from Gianni to Hasani. "It was he who rescued Hasani from the Turkish slavers?"

"The doge's men did, as I understand it. Fortunately for us, the slavers elected to try to leave the lagoon without paying the required taxes, probably because they lacked the proper documentation on Hasani. Cardinal Boeri had befriended the doge and persuaded him to release Hasani into his care, confident that he could find us and restore him to us."

Daria looked to Hasani, and he nodded in confirmation.

"Daria, he has been to Avignon and came to us only because Hasani insisted. He knows of Amidei, and I believe he is already well aware that you are the healer of Siena, the healer of the lepers outside Venezia. I would not be surprised if he knew that we were behind the excavations of the churches, or that there is a glass map. He's always enjoyed the occasional mystery to unravel. It is in our best interests to confide in him, tell him of our story. He may be our best asset when we reach the papal courts of Avignon."

She glanced again to Hasani. The man was slower to respond this time, but after several long seconds of thought, he, too, nodded. "And Piero?" she asked. "What does our priest have to say on the matter?"

Father Piero arrived, as if he knew they might be talking of him.

"He concurs," Gianni said.

"You agree? That Cardinal Boeri may be an asset to us? That we should share our secrets with him?"

"I doubt we have many that he does not already know, Daria. And yes, as Count Armand suggested, we shall need allies familiar with the papal court, all we can find, in order to avoid the flames of heretics."

Daria stared into the flames of the hearth a bit longer and then turned to Tessa. "Come here, my sweet," she beckoned.

The girl walked to her, head hanging low, shoulders curved in defeat. "Tess, it was not your fault. We all feel the loss of Basilio and Rune. They were dear to us all. But we are in a battle and must keep our eyes on where God is leading us. We must move forward and honor their memory by keeping to the task at hand. It is what they would have wanted, right?"

Tessa shrugged her shoulders. Daria pulled her into her arms and gave her a long embrace. Daria shared a look over the child's shoulder at Piero. She moved Tessa to stand beside her. "Please, child, we need to know more about your gift. The archers moved very rapidly last night; they were upon us faster than any of us ever expected. You seemed hesitant to enter the bridge. Were you not?"

Tessa nodded her head. "I should have said something!" she said, raising her face. Twin tracks of tears ran down her face. "But it had all been so grand . . . your wedding, the worship, the baptisms, the healings! It felt so wrong to speak up, to shout out a warning when I felt unsure about it. It was only once we were on the bridge, only a few horse lengths along, that I knew for certain they were coming." Her voice cracked in a sob. "But then it was too late."

"Shh, shh," Daria said, trying not to cry again herself. "It is all right. You are but a girl. A girl with an unfair task upon such slender, small shoulders. It is all right, Tess. Basilio and Rune would have understood."

They held each other for a few more minutes. When Tessa quieted, Daria dried her tears with a handkerchief. "Please, Tess. Tell us what happens when you sense good or evil in another."

She sat in silence for a bit, watching the fire, considering. "It is simple when a man is good, such as Father Piero, or Hasani, or Gianni. It is also simple when a man is bad, such as Lord Amidei or . . . Baron del Buco." She hesitated before naming Vincenzo, aware that mentioning his loss still brought Daria pain.

"What happens when Amidei or Vincenzo draws near?" Father Piero asked. Gaspare and Vito entered behind him, joining their circle.

"I become weak, sick to my stomach. It is cold; a deep chill enters my very bones."

Daria nodded. Was it her imagination, or did she feel a bit of the same when either man drew near? She looked to Piero and Gianni, and both men were nodding as well. Vito, Hasani, and Gaspare concurred.

"And when there is a good man?"

"Utter peace. Security. A warmth within me that allows me to breathe freely."

"Yesterday," Piero cut in, "when Basilio and Rune were struck, did any of you feel a touch of their piercing?"

Slowly, reluctantly, each in the circle nodded.

"Did the same happen when I was pierced off the isle as we made our escape?"

Daria thought back to that night, how even in the dark of the storm, they could see the arrows hurtling through the air, piercing their small priest as he rose to protect Gianni, as Basilio had protected her on the bridge. The memory pained her, and then she remembered the feel of it. As if the arrows had pierced her. She remembered all of them falling back, hands clutching chests, as if they had each felt the arrow strike their priest.

"We all felt it. Every one, Father," Vito said.

"And again yesterday," Gianni said grimly. "It is not good, this progression. It weakens us. We feel not only our own wounds, but those of our brothers and sisters within the Gifted. It is a disadvantage in the fight."

"God would not allow us to suffer it if it was not to our gain," Piero said. "We are the Body, personified. Together, we are working for God's own good. It makes sense that we might bear one another's burdens as well as triumphs. But we must be cautious because of it. Tessa was feeling the glory of the day and it made her a bit less sensitive to darkness lurking near. I might be so caught up in Daria's healing or Gaspare's miraculous acts that I might forget the way of wisdom."

"And yet, together, we are accomplishing ever greater things," Daria said. "With Gaspare and you others praying with me, we have seen angels about us! Seen Lord Devenue healed! A blind boy granted sight! Surely the Lord is still with us, even in this bitter hour."

"*Post tenebras, lux.* After the darkness, light." Piero said.

"What did you say?" Daria asked sharply.

"After the darkness, light."

"Did you say that to Basilio? Or Rune? Sometime before yesterday?"

Piero considered it, pursing his lips. "Nay. I do not remember doing so."

"He said those very same words to me, just before he . . . died," Daria said. "Rune repeated them."

The group was silent.

"He knew . . . knew we would suffer over their loss, but that their time was over," Daria said. "He knew that we would need to remember the light ahead, the promise, even in the midst of the darkness. Just as I had to tell myself during my time as Amidei's prisoner."

"It is what must characterize us, from here on out," Piero said firmly. "In spite of how things may appear, in spite of persecution or loss or failure, we must always believe that our God can see us through. That ultimately he will rule, supreme. We are but his servants, to go where he sends us."

"To Avignon now?" Gianni asked.

"Not yet. We are wounded, mourning. We shall return to Les Baux, see to our farewell to our comrades and regain our strength before we enter the city."

"And what of meeting with Cardinal Boeri?"

"If not for Cardinal Boeri and his men," Piero said, "we might all be laid out in the next room. Amidei left, knowing it would be a ruse we were likely to want to believe. And he seized the opportunity to try to take us down, or at least thin us out. His plan came perilously close to succeeding." He looked about at them all. "We shall meet this cardinal. But if any of you—most of all you, Tess—sense any hesitation over bringing anyone into our inner circle, you must speak. Understood?"

The girl nodded soberly, and they all agreed.

"What of our prophet? When might we come across him?" Vito asked.

"Or her," Daria put in.

"We may already know him . . . or her," Piero said. "Hasani was with us for some time before we knew of his gift. Or we may have yet to run across him. The Lord will bring our prophet to us when it is the right time."

"Let us hope that he carries a sword as well as the Word," Vito said. "We are short on knights, without our brothers."

"Remember, always remember," Piero said, "that our ultimate weapon is the Word. God will take care of us if we always fall back to using it to parry against attacks. Now, Gianni, let us meet your old friend, Cardinal Boeri. It is high time we all offer him our thanks for delivering our friend Hasani, and us, upon the Pont du Gard."

Chapter Twelve

Basilio Montinelli and Rune of Germany were dressed in Les Baux finery and, according to Les Baux tradition, set upon huge funerary pyres on the cliffs beside the castle, overlooking Les Fontaine Valley. Daria had borrowed a fine white gown from Anette, and together they walked the parapets and guard walks of the castle. Daria lifted her face to the cold winter winds, feeling the welcoming sting of it in her grief.

Anette took her arm and seemed to hold her up. "How do you fare, my friend?"

Daria shook her head, pushing back the quick tears that sprang to her eyes. She tried to smile at Anette. "What I wouldn't give to relive this week again! I'd urge my new husband to gather the men and take us home to Italia."

Anette gave her a rueful smile and pulled her forward along the walkway. "How many times did your men come to your aid?"

"Many. Many, many," Daria said, willing herself to take one step and then another. "Rune barely made it out of my mansion in Siena, with three arrows in his chest. We were under attack. Just like . . ." Her breath left her chest as if she herself had been impaled.

"Two days ago," Anette whispered. "How did he recover then? Did you heal him?"

Daria shook her head. "They were poisoned arrows. Even in touching one point as I pulled it from him, I was sliced and poisoned. Rune, Tessa, and I nearly died in Siena before the others prayed over us and we were healed. Have you ever been to Siena?"

Anette shook her head.

"Tessa was a child of the *campo* before she came to us. It was she who led us to safety out of the city. And Basilio . . . he has been wounded more than once to protect or free us."

Anette shook her head. "You have already suffered much. God must have great plans for you, my friend."

"But why not spare my men now? Why bring them so far to allow them to die here? On the edge of . . ." She paused. The edge of what? Completing their mission? Discovering some answers? None of the words sounded right in her mind. Did that mean it would never be done? The Christian call never came to an end. There were always more to reach, people who had not heard the Word. But would they never be able to rest? Resume some semblance of a normal life again? And if they did, where would that be? She longed to take Gianni home to Siena, but there was no home left to her there; both mansions had been burned to the ground by Vincenzo and his men.

"No one understands all the ways of our Lord, I least of all. At times, only the months fading away gives us the perspective we seek. If Dimitri had been healed long ago and not now, would I have loved him as much? Would I have glimpsed God in my midst, known his presence as real? Would we have been as likely to be your aides among the nobility?" She shrugged and gave Daria a slight smile. "I would like to think so . . . but if I am honest, I would say no to all those questions. So while there are painful things we must endure, I believe with all my heart, Daria, that God can use them for his good purposes if we allow him."

"After the darkness, light," Daria mused.

"*Oui*." She gave Daria a curious look. "You have seen the inscription, then, above our chapel door?"

"*Post tenebras, lux?*"

"*Oui*."

Daria gave her a small smile. "Nay. I have not. But apparently my men had."

They arrived on the cliff face, and the winter wind took their very breath. Anette moved to Lord Devenue's side, also dressed in royal white finery, and Daria to Gianni. She clung to his elbow, feeling the muscle of his bicep as if it might lend her strength. His hand at the small of her back was a welcome, warm presence. Could it be that they had exchanged vows only three days prior? In many ways, Daria felt they had shared the bonds of marriage for months. But now it was real, a stance of love and hope . . . just as the bodies of her men took position as death and despair. She felt pulled apart inside by the extremes of joy and sorrow warring within her heart.

The others had already assembled, even those they had left behind to heal—Ambrogio, Ugo, and the boys. Many of the Les Baux villagers attended behind a ring of nobles that Daria did not recognize. She shared a look with Piero and Count Armand. Already, the nobles of Les Baux worked on their behalf to tie other powers to the Gifted.

Numbly, reluctantly, Daria listened to Father Piero go through the funerary rites and prayers. She let the words in Latin and Provençal wash through her, absorbing her. So tenuous, was this life. Only one heartbeat, one lungful of air away from death, the afterlife. But she wanted to live. To live and grow old with Gianni! To see her friends to safety and old age themselves.

What madness was this holy calling upon their lives? And yet, without it, where would she be? Making do with a solitary life at home, with her beloved Sciorias, but no man. Finding respect as co-consul of the guild, but not wholeness. Not the healing she had found in Christ. Not love, not love like this, even in the face of such sorrow. Not *life*. It was as if she could feel God sustaining them, holding them up, telling them to keep their eyes on him alone. All this would pass away.

"Dust to dust, ashes to ashes. We live in this world," he said, looking at each of them. "Embrace this world, as if it is everything. But it is simply a span of time, after all, one leg of our journey. The greater journey is ahead, in the afterlife. And because of the blood of Christ, we have entry to it. Saved, delivered, set free, as our friend Hasani has recently experienced. As our friends, our brothers, Basilio and Rune, have experienced as well. They now walk in the palace of the King of kings. Their trials are over, their sorrow erased. They are in glory. Something we can look forward to as well. Be at peace over them, friends. They are."

He turned and resumed the rites in Latin, prayed, and then nodded to the knights carrying torches that flowed and flickered broad orange flames in the fading light of day. They laid the torches to the dry tinder beneath the knights' pyres, and instantly the fire grew and spread, arching in the wind, forcing the group to back away. Within an instant, the bodies, with hands gripped around their swords, were consumed, only a vague outline of human form amid the flames that grew white-hot with heat.

Slowly, silently, the mourners turned toward the castle, leaving six knights to tend to the bodies of their brothers. They all attended the funeral feast, forcing themselves to eat and speak with others. One by one, Armand and Anette and Dimitri introduced them to the nobles in attendance . . . the Lord and Lady Bonapart of Tarascon, the Duke and Duchess Richardieu of Villeneuve-des-Avignon, the Lord and Lady Blanchette of Uzes, the Count and Countess Duvin of Nimes. They had been summoned here for the official wedding of Countess Rieu des Baux to Lord Devenue, set to take place the following day. Conspicuously absent was Cardinal Saucille; Anette, ignoring convention, had asked Cardinal Boeri to perform the ceremony.

Ambrogio, Daria's old friend who had unwittingly been drawn into the intrigue and adventure of the Gifted, was speaking animatedly with another she believed she knew, from Siena. Where, how had they met? Gianni, noting her interest, steered her toward them.

The man, seeing her, bowed low in her direction. "Duchess d'Angelo," he said, taking her hand and kissing it. "It is an honor to see you again."

She remembered him now. Another artist, of course, but with a large, sloping nose and ears that stuck out. "Simone Martini," she responded, "you have grown up since I saw you last, and your fame precedes you. You are the pride of Siena, with your work complete in Assisi." Martini had indeed captured the attention of many, with his depiction of the life of Saint Martin in the Lower Church of St. Francis.

"You are overly kind, m'lady," he said.

"Nay. I speak the truth. You and Ambrogio—together you shall change how the world sees our God. It is a great responsibility."

"One I do not take lightly, Duchess."

"I should hope not," she said. "Please, may I introduce you to my new husband, Gianni de Capezzana?"

Simone, dressed in finery that bore witness to his new wealth, studied Gianni with new interest. The two shook hands. "I imagine you know that it has long been debated who might win the lady's heart."

"For good reason," Gianni returned, sliding a smile toward Daria. "I thank our God each day that I chanced upon her."

"Who chanced upon whom?" Daria said with a grin.

"I thank God each day that we chanced upon each other," Gianni amended. "But I thank God every hour that she agreed to take me as husband."

"Well spoken," Simone said. "You must meet my friend, a poet. He enjoys fine words. He is here, somewhere."

"We shall look forward to it," Gianni said.

"What brings you to Provence?" Daria asked. Father Piero joined their small group, along with Cardinal Boeri. Obviously the artists had already spoken with them, for they merely stepped aside to gain them room.

"Cardinal Stefani," Simone said. *The Cardinal of Siena*, Daria thought. Rarely at home, the man preferred to abide with the pope, enjoying the palace and its accompanying pleasures, leaving the work of the Church to good men like Bishop Benedicto and the priests of Siena. She glanced at Boeri. How different was he? Were they of the same cloth? According to Gianni, his cardinal remained at home, saw to the needs of his people—and protected them from the dangers. Daria looked about the room, caught Tessa's eye, and subtly invited her to them.

"Cardinal Stefani's a patron of the arts," Ambrogio said. "He brought Simone in to help paint new frescoes within the palace. Simone has asked if I might wish to come back with him to Avignon to assist."

"Assist?" Simone said. "I shall give you an entire room of your own to paint. The cardinal shall be delighted."

"As he should be," Daria said. "Two of Siena's finest painters in one place!" She caught Ambrogio's eye. Ambrogio understood her silent warning. To paint within the papal palace was as dangerous as a rabbit hopping about a snare.

"But there is more you need know of us, Simone, before I take you up on your kind offer," Ambrogio said.

"Oh? And what is that?"

"I believe the de Capezzanas and Father Piero plan to share more with you all in short order." Every noble and person of influence in this room had been invited by Armand to be brought into the Gifted's fold. It was understood that this night, the Gifted would share their story and hopefully gain friendships that would sustain them even as they ventured into Avignon.

"Most intriguing. I shall look forward to it."

Daria struggled to engage with the task at hand, continually drawn back into memories of Basilio and Rune, not wanting to plunge forward. And when she did dare to look ahead, visions of the dangers that might lie in wait for them terrified her.

Cardinal Boeri turned and greeted a thick-necked, middle-aged man warmly. Count Armand joined them, shaking the man's hand as well and turned to introduce him to the group. Tessa took Daria's hand and stood before her, smiling politely at the lords and ladies who complimented her on her dress, as if it were the only thing on the girl's mind. Only Daria could feel how her hand grew taut or relaxed around the others. But mostly the girl was at ease, warm, among them all. It comforted Daria to know it.

"May I introduce you all to my friend, a fine poet and noted critic of the papacy, Francesco Petrarch."

Daria almost gasped. To meet a poet, and one as fine as Petrarch! How many of his poems had she mulled over, digested as if they were fine foods? How much had the poet shaped her mind? He had always been a critic of sorts, his poetry distributed and read for years now, but she had never read anything explicitly taking the papal court to task.

Avignon

ABRAMO Amidei was not stupid enough to demand an audience with the pope himself. From long experience, he knew that it was best to manage the Holy Father the way it was best to manage any king or count or doge— through his underlings. *Own the men who answer to the man in power, and you eventually own the man in power.* So it was that he entered Avignon and headed directly toward Cardinal Josue Bordeau's mansion.

He gasped for air as he and his men moved deeper into the winding streets of the city. The town was crowded with people, but there was no sewer system in place. Animal carcasses and garbage lined the street. Only a papal edict kept the citizens of the city from throwing their excrement and urine to the streets. Every day, each household was expected to haul its chamber pots to dump them outside the city. Ditches were dug into the center of the cobblestone streets in an attempt to facilitate some drainage.

Abramo shook out a handkerchief and held it over his nose, thankful that the city had recently seen its share of winter rains. Never would he enter these city gates in the heat of summer. Still, he drew a perverse sense of pleasure from the horror. This was a city that was ripe for disease, damp like peat. Here he could sow seeds of the dark down deep, and they would take root and grow. A clean city was more difficult to woo, infiltrate. A dirty city was always looking for a new leader, new hope, new vision. He could fulfill that role.

His men led the way up one street and down another until they reached the highest part of town, near the Rocher des Doms, the ancient cliff that rose above the Rhône river. He closed his eyes and could almost hear the ancient songs of those who had known the dark and worshipped upon the rock, the screams of the innocents and the enemy as they were killed by Moors and Romans as the region was conquered and taken, again and again.

Abramo smiled. It was here that the Templar knights had once had their headquarters—and it was here that the master had seen their foundation begin to crumble, watched their very own protectors and supporters bring them down. He let out a laugh. How fitting that the Gifted would come here. Here his master had known sweet victory more than once. Here they would know bitter defeat.

One of Abramo's men bent to talk to a merchant and obtained directions to Cardinal Bordeau's palace. The cardinal was one of six key men who helped guide the pope. While Clement V and John XXII had handed out red cardinal hats as if they were candy, Cornelius II had been more restrained, choosing to rely upon men he had known for years as a cardinal himself. Two years into his papacy, he had built a new papal palace, but had named only twelve new cardinals. Most in his court were trusted members, personal friends. Only a few were placed as political necessities. This made him a more difficult target. But not impossible.

They arrived at Cardinal Bordeau's palace, and his men dismounted and knocked at the door. Once it was clear that the cardinal was at home, Abramo dismounted and waited with his men, pulling off one glove and then another as he entered the courtyard. His horse was led off to the stables. Only three of his men and one of his archers remained at his side.

Cardinal Bordeau de Orange, a dark, handsome man who would have made a good womanizer but instead had a taste for young things of all shapes and sizes, emerged from the dining hall, his napkin still in hand. His eyes widened a bit at the sight of Abramo's eye patch and the long, ugly scar that extended beyond it. He managed to cover his surprise, however, reaching for Abramo's arm and then pulling him into an embrace.

Les Baux

THE poet bowed deeply, turning to greet each in the circle of nobles. Father Piero studied each of them, their reactions. Some Petrarch clearly knew; a few were new to him. "It was not my desire to become a critic of the court," Petrarch said. "But if a body deserves criticism and I do not speak, it is as if I experience strangulation. Words are my medium, my lifeblood. To not speak would be akin to a stoppage of my heart."

"And what is it you see?" Cardinal Boeri asked.

"May I speak plainly, Cardinal? You yourself were just in Avignon, were you not?"

"I was. And yes, you may."

Petrarch studied the man, dressed in the most subtle of cardinal robes, and then turned back to the group. "Our pope, a Cistercian monk by training, has done many fine things. He has squelched some outward sins and abuses by his court, and even among the priests who abused their power farther out in the papal realm. Many, many wrongs were righted in his first two years as pope. I applauded his efforts. But in the last year, Pope Cornelius has been swayed. He has tripled the taxes, and his churches demand more and more of the poor, while his coffers grow thick with wealth. He has just completed a new palace, and while I understand the need for a regal place to house the heir of Peter, that place is already established in Roma, not Avignon."

"Well said," said Cardinal Boeri. And he seemed genuinely supportive, Piero noted. It might be that the cardinal would be their greatest support in Avignon. What mighty work was this? God bringing a powerful cardinal to their aid?

"And," Petrarch went on, daring to hold up a finger to Boeri, "while I support a regal palace painted in finery such as our friends Simone and Ambrogio might paint, I loathe the obscene amounts of food, the women who are little more than papal courtesans, and the sin that is ignored even within Cornelius's own walls."

Boeri nodded. Several of the nobles shifted uneasily. The pope's power was far-reaching. Many undoubtedly had been entertained at the tables that Petrarch now took to task. But they remained. They did not speak against him.

Count Armand caught his eye. Now was the time for Piero to speak. Now was the time for the Holy Spirit to claim these sons and daughters. Now was the time for the Gifted to move forward in their quest to spread their message of hope. Now was the time for them to regain some of the strength they had lost when Basilio and Rune fell from the bridge.

"My new friends," Piero said. "Frances raises valid concerns." All eyes turned to him. "Count Armand Les Baux has graciously called you here, not only to help us say farewell to our brothers, Basilio and Rune, not only to discuss the threat of the invaders who brought our comrades down, nor only to solidify ties. The count considers each of you trustworthy friends, and therefore, we do too. He has brought you here so that we might share more of our mission with you."

The nobles stared at him, a funny-looking little man, a common priest who nonetheless demanded their full attention. Piero knew they were un-used to such command, were undoubtedly confused by it.

"I was but a young man when I first learned that God had a greater call upon my life than my simple vocation." He went to a table and pulled the ancient leather scroll from inside the satchel. "What I am about to tell you is a tale of mystery and intrigue, but moreover, a story of hope. I am here to tell you that you are a part of something magnificent and holy. Something that God intends to use to change the world, and every believer within. We are on the precipice of change, of a new era."

He looked about the room, meeting every eye. "And you are each a part of it. Every one. I will tell you a story of us, God's Gifted. But you must first hear this—there is not a one in this room who is not gifted by God. We are all a part of the body, Christ's hands and feet to the world. The question is, are we hands and feet that move, that act? Or are we merely limbs that sleep, as if numb?"

Avignon

ABRAMO ate at Cardinal Bordeau's table, enjoying an excellent roasted game hen; *fougasse,* a flat olive bread; and a *tourte des blettes,* a pie made of chard, raisins, and pine kernels. The cardinal waved to a steward, and the man jumped to pour more wine into Amidei's goblet. He knew that his men and the two women who had traveled with them were being fed and catered to in the servants' quarters. Here, his troop could abide as long as they needed. His relationship with the cardinal ran deep and long.

"So, when shall you tell me what happened to your eye?" the cardinal said, sitting back to sip from his own full goblet.

Abramo sighed. "A she-cat. Caught me unawares."

The cardinal threw back his head and laughed easily. "I always warned you that your taste for women would be your downfall."

Abramo leaned forward, elbows on the table, goblet cupped between his two hands. "No more than your own hunger might lead you to trials, my friend."

The cardinal shrugged and then raised his goblet in toast. "We all have our vices to confess." He eyed Abramo. "So who was she? A woman who dares to disfigure you is a woman who may just intrigue me enough to sway my own interest."

Abramo laughed but hesitated. How much to tell him? All of it? Or just enough to bring him into the game? And no one, *no one,* would have Daria d'Angelo before he had her . . . just before he watched her die. Yes, that would be the end of her. Serving him in death, if not life. Knowing him, his power over her, his master's supremacy, before she knew darkness in the full.

His eyes moved back to the cardinal. Nay, his old friend would never truly stray to women. Abramo knew his tastes. "Have you heard of Lady Daria d'Angelo?"

The cardinal sat back. "Yes. They call her the Duchess . . . of Siena?"

"Once of Siena. Lately, traveling with a troop who call themselves the Gifted, who have been preaching, teaching, healing, and more from Siena northward. Even now, they travel here, to Avignon."

Josue took a long, slow sip of his wine. "She is the healer? The one from Siena? From Venezia? The one we've heard so much about?"

"So the pope knows of her?"

"Indeed. There is little like it that so holds his interest. He will enjoy the fact that she comes here, to him. He was considering sending his knights to fetch her and hers."

"No need. They will be here within a fortnight."

"Tell me more. Is your she-cat the leader?"

"Somewhat. There is the healer, Daria d'Angelo. Also a knight, once a captain of the guards de Vaticana de Roma, named Gianni de Capezzana. But it is really a priest, one they found outside Roma, a Father Piero, who guides them." He took a sudden, deep draught from his goblet. If only his master had known of the priest earlier, before the Gifted had gathered, then Abramo could have seen to his demise while still in the hills outside Roma. He had been right there, right there . . .

"So you are here to capture the woman? Is it retribution you seek?"

"In part," Abramo allowed. "But it is in our mutual interests to see the Gifted put down. Now."

"Killed? Or imprisoned? Or merely chastened back into their proper roles?"

"One way or another, they each must die. If they are allowed to live, they will continue to do damage to my causes. And they will undermine your own office and that of the pope. You can be certain that they shall address any vice they see. They dare greatly. And they preach, m'lord Cardinal, in the common tongue. They baptize and commune anywhere they find themselves."

It was the cardinal's turn to sit forward. "You have failed to bring them down, curb their path. And so you look to the holy office of the pope to do your work for you? Do you not find that a bit ironic, Abramo?"

Abramo shrugged and leveled a gaze at Josue. "It matters not to me how it is accomplished. But it must be accomplished, one way or another. And immediately."

"There has been a man in the court of late who I believe you know," Josue said. "Cardinal Boeri de Roma."

Abramo felt himself grow cold at such news. This was a man who knew him as a sorcerer. Who once worked with de Capezzana. He had been with the doge in Venezia. Had the cardinal told tales of his work in Roma? In Toscana? In Venezia?

Josue watched him with animated eyes, then slowly picked up his goblet for a sip. "Calm yourself. He spoke not of a noble practicing the dark arts, but of a curious group called the Gifted."

Les Baux

As soon as Daria heard the word *healing* leave Piero's lips, her eyes had been drawn to Lady Blanchette, across the room from her. This was a woman who had suffered, who knew abdominal pain even now. The woman, pale and sallow, slowly looked about the room and met Daria's eye. It was as it so often was for Daria . . . the Lord drew her attention to those he intended to heal, only at the time when it was right.

But there was a second yet in the room. A man, leaning in to hear Piero's words. Duke Richardieu of Villeneuve-des-Avignon. Now she remembered him speaking too loudly through the evening, as if he were thirty years older, rather than the young man he was, no more aged than Count Armand. It was as if she could see into his inner ears, to the place where scar tissue grew atop scar tissue and blocked his hearing. God intended to clear the passages, to give him his hearing back.

She sent the boys off to light more candles about the room. Piero wanted no mistake made here, now. He would want these nobles to bespeak of the miracles about to take place to others, with awe, but no claims of magic. Daria caught Gaspare's eye, and he gave her a smile of understanding, nodding. So he felt it too. Mayhap he would add his own gift to the evening, make it a night none would soon forget. Daria's thoughts went to her lost knights, Rune and Basilio, of her longing still to reach out and heal them, bring them back from the funeral pyres that had taken them away forever, out of their own realm and into God's. Although surrounded by people, with her new husband nearby, Daria felt the loss of their presence acutely.

Piero finished his preaching, reaching for Daria's Bible and reading Paul's words in Provençal. " 'Do you not know that in a race all runners run, but only one gets the prize?' Many are your prizes, great is your wealth, my noble friends. But I speak of the *prize*."

He grinned at them all, excitement building in his eyes. "We speak not of a perishable wreath, placed around your shoulders for a day, but an eternal crown—one that will truly make you a noble among the saints of heaven. Paul said, 'Run in such a way as to *get* the prize. Everyone who competes in the games goes into strict training. They do it to get a crown that will not last; but *we* do it to get a crown that will last *forever.*' "

Many of the nobles smiled in wonder and surprise at this funny little priest who demanded their attention with his words that seemed to grow and expand within their chests. Tessa squeezed her hand, but Daria could already feel it, the Holy drawing near. She smiled back at the little girl, who was grinning, eyes shining. The hairs on the back of her neck stood up, not from fear, but from anticipation and joy.

She caught Dimitri's eye and gave him a nod. Now was the time.

Lord Devenue stepped forward and lifted his hands out to the crowd as if in invitation. "All of you have asked how it is that I might have been so miraculously healed. Most of you saw me more than two years past, and could attest to the fact that I was nigh unto death. Rest assured that my plight became even more dire, my countenance no less than that of a monster. I had almost given in to death, wished for death every day, every hour, until the Gifted, these friends before you now, came to me. With them, they brought the Lord's own healing." He gestured toward Anette, and she came to his side. "The Count and Countess des Baux were present. They can attest to the fact that God entered my mansion; stole into the dark, dusty, forgotten halls; and reclaimed me."

Anette nodded. "Just as he has here, now."

Armand nodded as well. "These are the Gifted, God's own on his mission. And we all, every one in this room, are called to protect and aid them. To serve God by serving his servants. To learn from them what it means to run this race for God's own glory, not our own. It is why we are here. It is the greatest call upon our lives."

"God knew we would be here, on this day, with this before us," Armand said. He rose and walked over to the tapestry on the wall and drew it to one side. "Long have our families been crusaders, fighting for what is right."

Claude Richardieu jumped from his chair and strode over to the ancient fresco. "It is the fox, our family herald."

"And our heraldic lion," Lord Blanchette said. His eyes flicked from Armand to Claude to Piero, still not entirely convinced. He shrugged his shoulders a bit. "We have known for some time that the Blanchettes have long been friends with Les Baux."

"But what of this? Daria's heraldic peacock? And Amidei's dragon?" Armand rushed to Lord Blanchette, face flushed, with the speed of someone bent on striking another. But he did not, only knelt on one knee, one hand gesticulating wildly. "This is no coincidence, m'lord. This is the Lord, speaking to us, calling to us. He knew the Gifted would need us, here, now. He knew it." Armand waved back at the fresco. "That is but one reason we should believe."

Daria walked across the room and took Lady Blanchette's hand and drew her forward, to the center of their circle. Piero bowed his head and began praying, hands lifted to the ceiling, alternately in Provençal and then Italian and then Latin, and on a deeper level, with invitation and then Scripture. He went to his knees as he prayed, and each of the Gifted followed suit, forming a circle. The nobles about them, still standing, shifted uneasily, unsure of what to do. Some knelt out of deference to the nobles of Les Baux. Others reserved judgment, remaining where they were.

But Daria would lead them. She looked to Lady Blanchette and saw the yellow in her eyes and that of her skin, as if her body were poisoning itself. They stood together, Lady Blanchette's hands in hers, amid the praying, kneeling Gifted and the others. "Lady Blanchette," Daria said. "How long has your liver been ailing?"

The woman's mouth dropped open. "For three years, now." She tore her tearful eyes from Daria's and glanced about the nobles. "Did someone here tell you of my ailment?"

Daria smiled. "Yes, m'lady. Your Lord and your God."

Lord Blanchette slowly sank to his knees as if they had collapsed beneath him.

"M'lady, your God, the Lord of heaven and earth, intends to heal you, now. Do you believe?"

The noblewoman stared at Daria. "I have been to doctor after doctor. They said I shall die. That it is a cancer."

Daria gave her another small smile. The woman wanted to believe, but was afraid to hope. "You must give in to hope, my friend. I know you have been fearful for some time. That you have hoped for a cure, a miracle, but have been disappointed. It is damaging, such experience. Well I know what the heart can endure . . . or cannot. But I beg you, friend. Believe once more. Believe not in me, not in magic, but that the healing presence of the great Physician is now in the room. Believe that the God who healed Lord Devenue can now heal you as well. Do you believe?"

Lady Blanchette stared at her for a long moment. The tiniest glimmer of hope stole into her gray eyes. Slowly she sank to her knees, still holding Daria's hands. "Lead me, holy woman. Heal me."

Daria knelt as well. "I am holy only inasmuch that God chooses to dwell within me, as he chooses to dwell within you, too. This is of your Lord and your God, not of me. I am but his instrument."

She urged the lady to lie down upon her back and waved Gaspare and Piero nearer. She found Lord Blanchette and invited him closer too. "I must ask your permission, m'lady, for us each to place a hand upon you."

The lady nodded, fear and wonder in her eyes. Piero was at her head, anointing her with an oil and praying in a whisper. Gianni reached to take a hand. Lord Blanchette held the other. Gaspare laid a hand on the lady's belly. Tessa leaned in to touch the lady's shoulder. Daria placed one hand on her liver and lifted the other to the ceiling.

The others in the room seemed to hold their collective breath. It was utterly silent.

"Father God," Daria prayed, closing her eyes, feeling the Holy Spirit cover every inch of her, sending a shiver down her back. "Thank you for drawing near. We praise you for being present, here. Now. You have called for this lady to know healing. Cover the cancer that invades her belly now. Hold it in your hand, Lord. Take it from her. Squeeze it into oblivion. Fill her belly with healing balm. We ask this of you now. Our King, our Savior. Please, heal this daughter. Let her know you are here, now, Father."

A surge went through them all, like the force of a mighty wind, at once upon them and then gone, as it had been with Lord Devenue. Lady Blanchette cried out.

The nobles gasped. One woman gave a little shriek of fear. Then they waited.

After a moment, Lady Blanchette began to laugh. First a breathless chortle, then a longer laugh. Gianni helped pick Daria up from the floor, and Daria smiled at Gaspare and Piero, then at Lady Blanchette. The noblewoman gave in to another free, deep belly laugh.

Her husband went to her and studied her face and then began smiling as well. But Daria and Gaspare were already moving toward Duke Richardieu, who was on his knees and looking at them as if he knew what was to come. He accepted Daria placing her hands on each of his ears, Gaspare's hands on each of his shoulders from behind.

Everyone was now on their knees.

Everyone felt his presence.

"Do you believe in the Lord God on High, my brother? Do you believe he cares about you and knows your plight?" Daria asked, intuitively knowing that this man had always believed, known God in an uncommon way, waited upon him in trust and faith. She could see it in his eyes. They were as clear, as knowing and open as his ears were blocked.

"With everything in me," he said.

"Then be healed," Gaspare said.

"Yes," Daria said, "Today, now in the name of Jesus Christ, your scars shall fade away and you . . . shall . . . be . . . healed."

Daria stumbled backward into Gianni's waiting arms. But she was entirely focused upon Duke Richardieu.

Eyes wide, he slowly looked over to his wife. "Say something to me in a whisper," he said, his tone no longer too loud.

She whispered something to him, eyes full of wonder and tears.

And then he laughed, laughed until tears crested his lids and tracked down his face, glittering in the glowing, flickering candlelight. He turned to Daria and said, "I can hear. I can hear everything. The Richardieus, m'lady, are in your service."

Chapter Thirteen

Abramo walked down the candlelit hallway to his quarters, confident that he had Cardinal Bordeau firmly in hand. He had agreed to bring his closest comrades among the cardinals to meet with Amidei on the morrow.

Abramo met two of his men walking in the opposite direction and paused to confer with them, handing each a bag of silver. They were to bring back the choicest flesh they could find to appease the cardinal's carnal appetites. He paused in his own quarters only long enough to take a long, hooded cape from a chest and pull it about his shoulders. It was raining again outside. He could hear the steady drumbeat of the raindrops atop the ceramic tiles of the roof.

Abramo swept down the stairs, shaking his head when two men tried to accompany him as guards, and again when a beguiling woman, one of his archers, matched his steps. "No, *cherie*," he said, turning to kiss her. He nipped at her lip, drawing blood, and she came after him more urgently. They stood in the hall, kissing hungrily, until he took her firmly by the arms and set her aside. "I shall be back in a few hours. Be waiting for me in my quarters."

"As you wish," said the woman, turning at once.

Amidei tore his eyes from her and continued down the stairs, wishing he had not left her sister behind to aid Vincenzo in his attack. How had they fared? Had they managed to divide the Gifted? To lay any of them low? Why had the man not sent a messenger with word of their progress?

He was in the stables, waiting for the boy to bring his saddled horse, when a messenger at last arrived, worn and wet from a long, hard ride. He moved toward the man, recognizing his cape. "You come with word from Baron del Buco?"

"Indeed, m'lord," the man panted. He dismounted and fished a letter from his side satchel. He grinned as he handed it to him. "M'lord, permit me to tell you the best of it."

"Be about it, then," Abramo groused. There was little light to read a letter anyway. He would read it later. "How does the baron fare?"

"Very well, m'lord."

"And?"

"And your orders were carried out," the messenger said lowly. "We were able to take down two of the Duchess's knights."

"Killed them?"

"They are dead."

"Well done," Abramo said, clapping him on the shoulder as if he were del Buco himself.

"We would have taken more had not the cardinal come to their aid," the man said.

"Cardinal?" Abramo asked, feeling the pain of his empty eye socket when he narrowed his eyes with a frown. "Which cardinal?"

"A Boeri. De Vaticana de Roma."

Abramo rocked back on his heels. This was poor news. He had been here and told the pope of the Gifted. Now he went to their aid?

"He had with him the slave, the man captured in Venezia."

Abramo's consternation and confusion grew. "The slave? Daria d'Angelo's Hasani? How is that possible? I sent him off with Turkish slavers." He paced back and forth, his mind racing.

"Mayhap they were intercepted."

"Mayhap." The doge's men, most likely. Abramo stifled a growing need in his belly to growl out his frustration. Hasani was a direct threat, with his gift of visions. He should have killed him, before Daria's eyes, flayed the flesh from his bones until none was left.

What had Hasani seen ahead that he himself could not see? Would he keep the Gifted from falling into his trap, here in Avignon?

He stuffed Vincenzo's letter into a pocket of his cape and mounted his stallion. He must get to the woods outside Avignon, deep inside the cave, and find communion with his master. His master would know what to do, give him guidance and direction, as he always did. And once he had his orders, he would return to the palace to ease his fury in the woman who awaited him even now.

Les Baux

"THEY will lay waste to you and yours," said a grim Duke Richardieu. Healed, whole, he was their patron, fully in their service, but he grew more and more agitated when he knew it was their aim to go to Avignon to address the pope himself. "Why not continue your ministry in secret? Why not continue to travel and heal and preach and minister to those about the country? Why must you march through the gates of a city that is destined to bring you down?"

"Because we can do the greatest good if we can persuade the pope to think differently, to see that God is alive and well and calling to us, his people, to worship him as king, instead of the Church, his earthly vessel."

"You do not believe the Holy Father thinks his God is alive and well?"

"Alive and well," Piero said, pacing, his small hands clenched together behind his back. "But I fear he sees God as his instrument in the heavens, rather than himself as God's instrument on earth. We are but poor vessels, able to do only what God deems best. But the papacy . . . it is an office fraught with difficulty."

"Cornelius is widely known as a wise and prudent man. His Cistercian roots serve him well."

"Indeed. But already he has built a new palace where the old would no longer apparently do."

"Ignoring the vast buildings at his disposal already, in Roma," Cardinal Boeri put in.

"In his stead," Piero continued, "any man might be swayed by the power, the prestige. You must know the perils yourself, my lord. A simple man knows his place. With a surfeit of money, success . . . one begins to think himself a rival of God."

" 'A rival of God,' " Petrarch remarked, chin in hand. "Mind if I borrow that, Father?"

Gianni watched as Daria leaned farther into the corner of her chair and raised a tired hand to her brow. The healings had sapped her energy. He caught her eye and gently nodded toward the door with a smile, urging her to take her leave.

He looked about the room. "Gentlemen, ladies," Gianni said, "mayhap we might continue this conversation come daybreak. The night is deep and much has transpired. Let us take our rest and return to our discussions with sharper wit and mind come morn."

"Well said," Piero agreed. He rose, and one by one, the Gifted and the nobles filtered out of the room. Only Gianni, Piero, and Hasani, standing as if a sentry in the corner, remained.

"All in all, an inspiring day," Piero said to Gianni, reaching up to pat the large knight on the shoulder. They turned toward the door and looked back to see if Hasani was following. "It will be—"

Piero broke off and fully turned to study Hasani, trembling and wide-eyed in the corner. The man stared into the distance, as if watching a troubling scene play out before him. His breathing was shallow and fast.

The small priest pulled Gianni to a halt, not wishing their movement to disturb the seer's vision. Patiently they waited for Hasani's vision to come to an end. Never before had they witnessed their friend in the midst of one.

When it ended, Hasani slumped against the wall.

Gianni took a step toward him, but the tall man was already righting himself. He glanced at Piero and Gianni and then looked away, as if embarrassed at having been caught. How long had it gone on? Could he control it at all?

"You must draw what you have seen," Piero said.

But Hasani was already on the move. They trailed him upstairs, to the count's private hall, to the desk, parchment, and ink that Gianni knew Armand had given Hasani permission to use at any time.

"Is it all right, man?" Gianni asked. "To watch you work?"

Hasani ignored him, already pulling the stopper out of the ink.

"I would take that as approval," Piero said with a dry smile.

He was clumsy at first, eager to get the drawing down, as if fearful he might forget what he had seen. They soon saw that there were three drawings, and Hasani did a rough outline of one, moved to the next, then the next.

Gianni eyed Piero. They could not yet make anything out of any of the drawings.

Hasani moved the other two drawings to a side table in order to dry without smearing, and set upon the first with amazing skill and speed. In short order, Gianni could make out Abramo, with his eye patch, walking with two cardinals, men Gianni did not know. "Mayhap Boeri can identify them," he whispered to Piero.

"We must warn these men of the evil in their midst," Piero said.

"Mayhap they are already one with him. We must tread carefully."

Piero groaned. Even after all they had seen, discovered, witnessed, it pained him to see Christian brothers potentially deceived and in league with the enemy.

In minutes, the second drawing was taking more shape: a giant of a man, hovering with the hilt of a sword in both hands, ready to pierce another on the ground with full force. As Hasani added facial features, he paused and glanced briefly at Gianni. Sweat dripped down his black temples and down his neck.

The giant was Ciro, the knight who had taken Hasani captive in Venezia, stolen the papers he carried that declared him a freed man. The one who had haunted them in Siena, nearly taken them down on Amidei's dark isle. The leader on the pier, who had ordered the archers to send their arrows flying toward Gianni, piercing Piero instead. A man close to both Amidei and del Buco. The same man who had threatened Daria again and again.

"Still alive, it seems," Gianni growled, kicking out his chin, urging Hasani to move on, do what he must.

Hasani dipped his quill in the ink, glanced at Gianni again, and completed his drawing.

The man on the ground was Gianni, wounded, his own sword several paces away. Gianni stared at the illustration for several minutes, unmoving.

So this was how it would end for him? Dead by Ciro's sword?

He laughed hollowly. "Do I not even deserve Amidei's own blade? Vincenzo's? Will the Lord not honor me in death with an equal opponent?"

"Cease," said Piero. "Do not continue that train of thought. You do not know what will happen before this moment"—he paused to tap the drawing—"nor after it."

"Look at it, Father," Gianni said bitterly, waving at the parchment in agitation. "You, a holy man, may not recognize a death blow, but I do." He pounded his chest. He wanted to live . . . live to get through this with Daria and the others and see them all to a time of peace. He wanted to return to Italia with Daria, to know a life with her that did not include constant danger. He wanted . . .

He turned away, hiding the sudden tears in his eyes. Rune and Basilio's deaths were too recent, the threat too real. Hasani had seen them struck down as well, before it happened . . .

"My son, Hasani also saw me 'die' at the hands of our enemy. Remember Ambrogio's description of me upon the cell wall? As it was seen, it occurred. I was struck by those arrows, but the Lord, in his great mercy"—Piero paused to cross himself—"saw fit to restore me to you all. Mayhap you will find a way as well. Mayhap God has shown this to you so that you shall be ready to avoid Ciro's death blow."

Hasani grunted, gaining their attention as he sketched, fast and furiously, a driven man. He completed two more figures in the drawing, beyond Ciro and Gianni, near a tree. The tiny muscles in his cheeks and the veins along his neck bulged as he worked, adding detail. Drops of sweat fell from his brow to the drawing, smearing it a bit.

But they all could clearly make out the two figures.

It was Abramo, with one hand around Daria's slender throat.

The men all paused for several long moments. "And so our battle will continue with Amidei as well as with the Church," Piero muttered.

Gianni swallowed hard, trying to get past the disappointment. He could endeavor to defend Daria all he wished, but all their lives were in God's hands. Was this their end? Daria strangled by Abramo? Himself eviscerated by Ciro?

Piero reached up and pulled down on Gianni's shoulder. "God has not seen us all this way to watch us die. I tell you, this is not the end."

Gianni ignored him, unable to tear his eyes from Abramo's gloved hand upon Daria's throat, her eyes, wide in terror . . . when they had saved her from the isle, she had borne bruises upon her neck, made by that same hand . . .

"Gianni de Capezzana!"

He glanced at the priest. "I tell you," the short man repeated, inserting himself between the drawing and the knight, pushing him a step backward, "*this is not the end* of the story. It shall serve us as a warning. Nothing more. Do you not see? We have an advantage. God has shown us how dire this moment will be. Who is missing in this picture? Who?"

He moved away so Gianni could once again look upon the drawing. He noticed more details. Rocks and cypress trees more common to Italia than this dry and arid land they abided in now. But the priest was right.

There was no sign of . . . "Vito. Ugo. Hasani. You. Gaspare . . . any of the others."

"So any of us might yet come to your aid." The priest tapped the drawing with a stubby finger.

"Unless we are alone, separated somehow."

"Which we shall not let happen." He took the bigger man by the shoulders, attempted to shake him. "Faith, man. God is asking you to dig deep again, into the depths of his courage, valor, promise. *Hope*. Battle against this darkness," he said, waving backward at the illustration. "But prepare for what is to come. We must see this warning as a gift, always a gift."

Gianni lifted a hand and rubbed his eyes wearily. Daybreak was only a few short hours away. Daria most likely already slumbered upon their bed . . .

"Shall we show this to Daria, too, then?"

Both men looked at him with alarm, shaking their heads.

"She would be furious if she were to find it and know we kept it from her," Gianni said.

"She would be nearly incapacitated once she saw it," Piero said firmly. "You know how she fears being taken by Amidei again. We have enough work to do in simply preparing her to see him, in the flesh, in Avignon. He is there, as Hasani has seen, working his magic among the lesser cardinals." Piero glanced back at Hasani and nodded in relief. "Nay. You see Hasani is in agreement. He knows when it is right to share his drawings and when it is not."

Hasani was hovering over the third illustration, waiting. At last they realized that he waited for them to depart.

Neither man spoke as they left the room and then parted company in the hall, both lost in thought.

If Hasani did not want them to see the third, just what would it depict?

Gianni gently opened the door to the luxurious quarters Count Armand had assigned them. A fire had burned down to coals, no longer giving off much heat. As expected, Daria was deep in slumber, lying on her side. Gianni raised his candle, letting the flickering flame wash his wife's curve and contour. Her hair lay in curling waves across the pillow behind her, having escaped her sleeping cap. Her breathing was soft and steady, peaceful. He undressed and slipped hurriedly from the cold of the room under the feather-filled blanket, just behind Daria.

Carefully, he moved to mirror the bend of her legs, so that she was cupped, enfolded by his body. He moved a tendril of hair aside and slowly, gently kissed her neck, the very neck he had to protect, somehow, some way.

She stirred, moving sensuously before him, and then awakened with a gasp, springing away from him.

"Daria?" he asked in concern.

She was at the edge of the bed, facing him with eyes wild in fear.

"Daria, 'tis me. Your husband."

She panted and frowned, as if trying to force his words to filter through her foggy mind and settle her frightened heart. Slowly she stood up straight and pushed back the hair from her face, leaving a hand on her head. "Forgive me, Gianni," she whispered, turning partially away, lost in thought.

" 'Tis I who should apologize," he said, rising and coming around the bed to her. He opened his arms, waited for her to enter them, then held her close, letting his fingers massage her scalp. "Your mind went to him, yes? Our enemy?"

She nodded.

Gianni sighed and still held her. "He manhandled you. Abused you. But attempted tenderness as well? Seduction?"

She paused, and then nodded again. It was a wonder they had been able to consummate their marriage at all, if images of such abuse were in his wife's head.

"Daria, my love. We must speak plainly, in order that you might be free of it. Did Amidei force himself upon you?"

He held his breath, then let it out slowly as she shook her head.

He took her face between his hands, waited for her big, olive eyes to meet his. "Did he try?"

"Nay," she said softly, taking his hands into her own. "He always said I must choose to be his servant in such a manner. It seemed important that I chose it willingly. That he would be more my conqueror, somehow. But he . . . he came to me . . . mayhap it was magic . . ."

Seeing she was paling, Gianni led her to the edge of the bed and knelt before her, tucking her hair behind her ears and then taking her hands again, waiting.

"In Venezia, in the Morassi mansion. Somehow, when I was changing for the dance . . . the contessa slumbered. I was changing, looking at my image in the mirror. And I thought it was you, Gianni." Her eyes searched his, desperately asking him to believe her. "It was about then that I knew I was falling in love with you. And I was aghast at my own wanton nature, but I welcomed your touch. For you were in the room with me—I thought you had sought me out. I was staring in the mirror and you were behind me, touching me, kissing me on the neck . . ."

Gianni furrowed his brow in confusion and shook his head. "In the mansion? I was seeking you, but—"

"It was him," she interrupted bitterly. "Abramo. Some magic trick, making me believe it was you at first. But it was his hands. His lips upon my neck." She shook her head, shivered. "I know not how he accomplished it. When I looked back to the mirror, I saw his face, not yours. I screamed, and then he was gone."

"The Sorcerer," Gianni said simply. "We know he was about. Undoubtedly it was he who caused the fire. And I've experienced his black magic as well. The way he seems to be present . . . as he appeared to you in Dimitri's mansion."

"He was outside," she said, staring at the candle, her eyes still lost in dark memory. Never had they spoken of that night, that night when she was lost to Gianni in Venezia. "I awakened in the water, the Canalazzo. The Morassis' mansion was afire—"

"Yes. I was looking for you, mad with worry," he said, tenderly touching her face, anguished by the memories of his failure to protect her.

"And he pulled me from the water and closed his hand upon my neck, until I could no longer breathe."

Gianni swallowed hard.

"I clawed at his hand, but he knew right where to press. My vision swam . . . all I remember is the great flames of the house becoming like waving streams across the sky. And then I was gone. I awakened a prisoner upon his isle. Bound. Alone. So cold . . ."

She looked back to him, noted his own anguish, and pulled him closer, so that their heads were together. "Forgive me, husband. Forgive me for dredging up such dark visions of our past."

"Visions of our past, but not so distant. Amidei remains near, seemingly intent on killing us if he cannot capture us."

"Yes," she agreed soberly. "The abuse was meant as a means to sway me, beat me into submission, into doing as Abramo wanted. Denying him, then wounding him, there was the line in the sand. I do not doubt that if he gets the opportunity again, he shall try and kill us all."

Gianni avoided looking into her eyes, fearful she would see the note of foreknowledge within his own—afraid she would force the truth from him about what Hasani had forseen—frustrated that they could not flee this place, go east, west, anywhere there might be safety. Why them? Why now? Why must they be the ones to carry out such a mission? And yet, now that they knew what they did, the import of their task, how could they do anything but everything possible to succeed?

"Daria, I know not where this will lead us. If you and I shall ever share any semblance of a normal marital life. You know that I will do whatever possible to protect and guide you?" he asked.

"Yes," she said in response, tears slipping down her cheeks.

"You know that I will forfeit my own life to protect your own?"

She nodded.

"But Daria, my sweet and lovely wife. We are here, together now, by the grace of God. By some miracle, you have bowed low to welcome me as your adoring husband. And I am thankful," he said, kissing her hands, bathing them with his tears, "so utterly thankful that our God has graced us with this reprieve, this joy in the midst of the sorrow."

Daria leaned forward and kissed his forehead, his cheeks, the bridge of his nose. "Gianni, faithful and true. No woman could ask for more from her husband. We shall trust our fate to the Lord. We are seen and watched over by his own angels. I shall strive not to forget it."

"Even now our enemy plays upon our fears. Our memories of the dark, hoping we will forget the light." He shook his head in dismay, frustration. "I am weak, Daria. I, supposedly gifted in faith, *faithless*."

"Nay, Gianni. Speak not such untruths. Your faith is ever present and serves us well. You are merely still mortal." She waited until he met her eyes and smiled. "Come, husband. I bid you come, now, to our bed. I want you and only you in my head when I feel kisses upon my neck. Come and make over my memory. Heal the healer."

CHAPTER FOURTEEN

Avignon

To one he appealed through sin and deviancy, to another he appealed through rules and righteousness. It mattered not how they came, Abramo decided, as long as they came to him.

Before arriving in the city of the pope, he had counted upon the support of three cardinals, already in debt to him in one way or another, all with a history of licentiousness that he could feed. In the week since his arrival, he had met with three more, two of which were more swayed by his rhetoric of restoring the Church to glory, of pulling in the faithful through the ascetic tones of rigorous rules and guidelines. Of controlling with severe punishment. To these three he went in a simple robe, his wealth evident only in a heavy emerald ring he wore upon his left middle finger.

The last two, Cardinal Corelli of Pisa and Cardinal Gabriel Morano of Madrid, were exceedingly close to Pope Cornelius. Morano was his closest advisor, famous for swaying him to issuing several widely discussed edicts, one that protected the Jews in their quarter of Avignon from daybreak to sunset—praised throughout the land in spite of how many cities treated their Jewish population; another that increased taxation throughout the papal realm in order to gain the funds needed to complete his new palace, and the last to put in place an indulgence—paid to the Church, of course—that would supposedly speed a loved one's passage through purgatory and on to heaven in half the normal time. The indulgence was unique in that it paired both financial compensation and a pilgrimage to an established holy site at least a month's travel away, which the good cardinal saw as aiding the pilgrim's faith as much as the dead loved one.

Nonsense and foolishness, Abramo thought. But if that was what the cardinal favored, he would help inspire more of it. Hard-nosed and given to ascetic punishment of the flesh, Abramo knew exactly how he would draw Morano in, first as confessor and guide, making him think he was forming Amidei's mind and spirit, while all the time, Abramo would wind his fingers around the roots of the man's heart, until the time of consequence came, and he could pull those roots as a puppeteer pulled his doll's strings.

Ah yes, Gabriel Morano was a difficult and challenging conquest. But the master had shown him exactly what to do, how to win him, own him. And if he won Morano, Corelli would undoubtedly follow. Then, with these six powerful cardinals in hand, they would be prepared for the Gifted to enter Avignon, and would take them apart by using their own precious Church. Stefani? Boeri? They would not be able to stand against them.

Cardinal Morano entered the sitting room at last, and Abramo rose and bowed in deference, leaning forward to kiss the man's ruby ring. He was dressed in the common red hat with wide brim and tassels that his contemporaries wore, but Abramo noticed there was no white ermine liner to his red cape, only simple, white silk. He was a handsome man, not much older than himself.

"Your Eminence, God be praised that you would see me," he said humbly, staring at the floor for a long moment, as if gathering his words. He did not look up nor rise. "I am a noble in need of a confessor and you, being a cleric of the highest standing, came to my mind as the perfect man for the task. Will you hear my confession?"

"I am well aware of you, my son, although I do not believe we have yet met in person. You are always welcome here. And I thank you for your generous donation to my own Santa Maria, last time you came through my beloved Madrid." He spoke in an elegant, cultured tone, laced with a heavy Spanish accent.

"Each and every time I pass through, you may count on me to donate the same amount, as a sign of my faith and thankfulness."

He did not look up, but he could feel the delicious waves of greed warring with the cardinal's desire for the holy.

"Your generosity takes my very breath," said the cardinal. "The people of Santa Maria shall be most grateful, as will her priests."

And their cardinal, Abramo thought.

"Now, come, sit with me and tell me what plagues your mind." He gestured to a seat beside him.

Abramo sat down and paused, as if mustering up the courage to confess. "I have sinned, your Eminence. I have sinned widely against our Lord and our God." He bit out the words, willed devotion into the nouns that only stirred hate within him.

"Tell me of your sins and be rid of it, my son."

"I have slept with many women, outside the marital bed."

"I see. How many women?"

Abramo closed his eyes. "It is nearly beyond my count, your Eminence."

The cardinal paused, studying Abramo's face. "Countless? Surely not—"

Abramo did his best to force misery and sorrow into his features. "Forgive me for troubling you with such sin, my lord Cardinal. I wish I could tell you a different story. But I speak the truth."

"I see." Gabriel paused, obviously wishing he could make absolution over this generous benefactor and church patron before him, but pulled by the enemy to do his sacred duty, to see the confession fully through. "What shall keep you from taking another abed?"

"I know not. 'Tis where I hope you shall aid me," Abramo said. He rose and paced, as if highly agitated. "I am weak, so weak . . . if only there were a way you could be with me, every day, every hour, keeping me from falling." He moved to Cardinal Morano and knelt before him again. "Here, now, I feel strong." *Stronger than you know, Cardinal.* "You give me strength." *And you shall give me more.*

"A wife. You are handsome, even with your injury, my son, a danger to all good Christian women who have a weakness for carnal wanderings. Yes, you are in need of a good Christian woman to keep your mind on those things holy and appease your appetite. Through a union with her, you could take your ease and raise another generation of faithful sons and daughters of the Church."

"Yes, yes," Abramo agreed, as if he had never thought of it before. "It is wise counsel. Mayhap it is best I settle. Find a good woman." He thought of Daria, of how delicious it would be if, somehow, she yet became his bride. But he fooled himself. She was lost to him. Destined for death and nothing else. "I travel widely and am rarely at home," he said, letting a whine settle into his tone. "What am I to do before I find a wife? Or when I must leave her to attend to my business?"

The cardinal studied him with the dark, long-lashed eyes of his Spanish ancestors. There were crinkles at the corners, as if he laughed often. But he was unsmiling and serious now, making him foreboding and strong in stature. If Abramo could turn this one to his own aim, Gabriel would have his own pick of the women of the dark . . . how the master would revel in Abramo's accomplishments!

"There are ways to remind the flesh that it is but flesh, and that the Spirit is ever stronger," the cardinal began.

"Indeed?" Abramo asked innocently, knowing full well where this would lead. His master had been right, so right.

The cardinal rang a bell, and a servant appeared immediately. "Fetch a spiked belt and a spiked chain, please."

The male servant bowed and disappeared, and the cardinal again met Abramo's eyes. "I, too, suffer from a draw toward the sins of the flesh," he said. "I find it helpful to wear the belt of remembrance, forcing me to think of our Lord's suffering, on days when I am weak or facing temptation."

The servant appeared again and handed his master the leather belt, studded with tiny spikes, and a long chain, with quartets of spikes along its length. The cardinal lifted the belt. "Wrap this around your thigh. The spikes will pierce your flesh and not let you move without reminding you of their presence. Some wear it until their skin heals and fuses to the belt, so that it is always with them, one with them, counting it a blessing that any errant movement causes their flesh to rip and weep like our Christ's own tears."

Abramo took the belt and gazed upon it. Such delicious agony. Pain. The very thought of it aroused him, made him hunger.

"The flagellant's whip," the cardinal said. "On days that even the belt is not enough, turn to this after fervent prayer and confession. Take it firmly in hand and let it fly over your shoulder, and again, around your rib cage." He gestured, empty-handed now that he'd passed it to Abramo, showing him how to flick his wrist at the end. "As you do so, remember the wounds your Savior took to save you from your sins."

"Oh, I shall remember," Abramo said, bowing to cover his smile, nodding as if humbly accepting the direction. Could it really be as simple as this? If it was this easy to wheedle one's way into the mind of the pope's advisor, why not take the Holy Father himself? He remained where he was, swallowing his smile.

"You hesitate, my son. Do you wish for me to see you through this first exercise of pain? I shall hear your every confession and see you through the process. It is the first step toward freedom, absolution. I promise, you have never experienced such a feeling of cleansing until you have experienced this. You shall be restored. *Restored*."

Abramo raised his face to the cardinal, hoping the tears of glory in his eyes now appeared as holy sorrow to the man. "Show me, my lord Cardinal. Forgive my sin and show me the way to dominating the flesh rather than succumbing to its wiles. Help me locate a suitable wife. I place my life in your hands."

Les Baux

GIANNI awakened to find himself alone abed. He rose and rubbed his face, not remembering when he had slept as long and as deeply as this. By the bells, he knew that his comrades had long since broken their fast, and the castle was already hard at work.

He poured water into a basin and then splashed his face, neck, chest, and arms, toweled off, shivering in the chill of the room. He considered, briefly, lighting a fire in the hearth, but gave it up for the greater need to find his wife and see what the day had in store. Had the others already gathered, met and planned without him?

Dressed, he opened the door to find Vito lounging against the far wall, a sly grin on his face. "Marriage has made my captain slovenly," he said, pushing off from the wall. "Might I ask you to accompany me to the knights' quarters for a round of sparring, or will you wish to follow the Duchess?"

Gianni scowled at his friend and pushed out his chest as he patted it with a fist. "Gianni de Capezzana follows no woman about like a sick pup."

"Except the former Duchess d'Angelo," Vito said.

"Except her," Gianni said without missing a beat. The two smiled at each other. "How fare the others?"

"Well enough," Vito said with a shrug, his smile fading. "They feel Basilio and Rune's absence."

As do we all, thought Gianni. How he wished Basilio would round the corner, his big nose going before him, his tall German friend ducking beneath the low ceilings of the palace corridors to follow behind. He kept thinking that at any moment he would see them appear. It had been a long time since he had lost fellow knights, close to his heart. Not since the grove outside Roma, where Abramo's archers had felled brothers of the soul . . . every man Gianni had counted upon in his last years as a knight de Vaticana de Roma.

He swallowed hard against the bitter bile that filled his throat and mouth, fought to concentrate on the words Father Piero had trained him to think upon. God's justice, in his time. Grace. Mercy. Mission.

He followed behind Vito as the passageway narrowed, down two staircases and past the cold and drafty dovecote hall, where small caves had been dug out of the bedrock for two hundred birds that served as both messenger and meal. The entire castle had been dug out of a giant limestone cliff face, making one entire flank impenetrable, her towers atop the rock formed by the hand of God. They passed women and men carrying buckets of water, wood for fires, baskets of fresh food for the kitchens from the storehouses. Briefly they walked outside, now below and moving beyond the castle to the stables and training area for Les Baux knights, through yet another tunnel and down another set of stairs.

"The count has agreed to house and keep our people until we send for them. Roberto, Nico, and Agata will remain behind. And much to Daria's disappointment, her bird, Bormeo."

"I hope the people of Les Baux do not consider a white falcon the supreme luxury for feasting," Gianni said.

"Do not let the Duchess hear such a jest!"

Gianni laughed. He highly doubted the bird would actually remain in Les Baux. Daria seldom went anywhere without him anymore. "Ambrogio took his leave?"

"He is undoubtedly already at work within the new papal palace. He will serve us well, with an inner knowledge of the *palais* and her pope."

"Indeed," Gianni said. "I had hoped to have the opportunity to speak to him before he left."

"Father Piero did. They arranged to meet when we arrive in Avignon. We shall send a message to him."

"Good," Gianni said. Had he lost command while he slumbered with his new wife?

"The count insists we take twelve of his men when we go. I have located the strongest—both in flesh and in faith," Vito said.

"Well done. I bid you thanks for taking up the task. I have been distracted of late—"

"Say no more, Captain," Vito said, smiling over his shoulder. "I understand. You are the envy of more than one kingdom, taking Lady Daria as your bride. I believe our own Count Armand would have been first in line, had she dismissed your begging."

Gianni laughed and shook his head. " 'Tis not only my new wife that distracts me. Speaking of my wife, where has she gone?"

"Left you aslumber, did she?" Vito said, throwing another wry grin over his shoulder as at last the passageway widened and they could walk abreast. "She's on a ride with the countess, and well guarded."

"You sent out scouts to make sure our enemy is not about?"

"As well as Ugo, Gaspare, Dimitri, and Hasani as armed companions," Vito said. "They'll stay near the castle."

Gianni shoved down his fears, only possible because he knew Hasani rode beside Daria. Only he, among them, knew the vision and the full threat of Daria's inevitable capture. He must trust the safety of his bride to his Lord at times, as much as it chafed, and concentrate on other matters. "I take it you wish to introduce me to the men who shall accompany us into Avignon."

"Indeed. They are fine men, all."

"Do you not think we shall gain unwanted attention, arriving in the city with such a grand retinue?"

"I think we can hardly risk any less of a security force," Vito said, deadly serious now. "Our arrival will come as no surprise to the pope. And as we have seen, the enemy has gained strength, either in number or by those he has hired. We faced a good number of professional mercenaries atop the Pont du Gard. Had not Cardinal Boeri arrived with his knights de Vaticana . . ."

Gianni nodded. Vito did not need to say more. They might have all been in the river, every last one.

"We are to meet the priest, the count, and Hasani in the chapel after our noon meal. They have uncovered yet another clue for us there."

"Indeed?" Gianni asked, raising his eyebrows. And then he was startled that he was unsettled by such information. Had not the Lord brought them signs and wonders all along their path? He smiled at Vito. "Have you arranged the rest of my day as well?"

"Nay, m'lord," Vito said with a grin. "As much as I enjoy the role of steward on occasion, I remain your knight more than your *secretario*."

"Good," Gianni said, clapping the man on the shoulder. "Well satisfied am I, that you and your brother still serve our Lord and our cause. Thank you for your faithfulness, Vito."

Vito blushed at the neck and briefly bowed his head. "We would wish to be nowhere else, m'lord."

Gianni offered his arm and the two gripped to the elbow, eyeing each other. Gianni studied Vito, a man he had come to love and trust as a brother. Would he lose this man as well to the fight? Had Hasani envisioned his death as well?

And could he say the same words that Vito had uttered? That he wished to be nowhere else? Had he not wished for another time, another place, just last night?

CHAPTER FIFTEEN

CARDINAL Boeri, Gaspare, and Daria accompanied Gianni when he went to the chapel. He had taken his noon meal with the knights and approved of Vito's recommendations. Between Boeri's men and these men on loan from Count Armand, they would create quite the stir upon arrival in Avignon. But it was wise counsel, on both a safety and a stature front, he believed. With Amidei about, they might suffer an attack at any moment. And arriving with so many knights-at-arms would force the pope to address them as the nobles they were, regardless of their lack of lands or formal position. They had earned the high regard of many, thanks to the nobles of Les Baux and their friends who still held lands and position. And those new friends would join them soon in the center of Christendom, to help them with their cause. What all would transpire between now and then? Gianni mused. He frowned. Just where might they encounter Amidei and those of the dark? A sense of urgency set his heart tripping into a fast beat. What if they could not counteract the damage Amidei was already undoubtedly inflicting? They must not tarry much longer . . . they must be on their way to see through this holy mission, vague as it might be.

They moved through the narrow passageways to the castle's chapel, near the count's quarters. The front of the chapel was fairly new, with a giant rose window of colored glass, set high in the entry apse. Gianni loved to see the light come through at the end of the day as the sun set in the west and sent golden light streaming through, casting it upon the altar as if in benediction.

They had worshipped here together, observed the Hours with Father

Piero, prayed before the altar. As was custom in private chapels, the sanctuary was small and narrow, capable of holding no more than thirty people. The tombs of four lords of old had been placed in cruciform fashion, beneath purple marble slabs, the Latin words noting their names and dates of life. Gianni frowned, seeing Piero, Hasani, and the count at the front, with the altar moved to one side. What had transpired?

Hasani saw they had arrived, and excitedly gestured them forward. They formed a circle. On the floor was a curious indentation in the limestone, as if a slab had been cut out, at an angle.

Count Armand looked to Gianni and Daria. "Your priest told me of your glass map, and I asked to see it."

Gianni raised a brow. "You have more of it?"

"Mayhap. Or something related." He moved out of the circle and gestured upward to the domed ceilings above. "Castle Les Baux was conquered and destroyed two hundred years ago. It took my ancestors twenty years to gain permission to rebuild, and another fifteen to do so. When they did, they commissioned an architect from Paris to design this chapel, presumably atop the old footings."

"It is beautiful," Daria said, obviously aware that the count pointed out the architecture for some deeper reason. They all studied formidable oak beams, hand-painted frescoes of stars in the domes that were to denote the heavenly realms. And newer arches and ribs that met in the Frankish Gothic style.

"Indeed. However, the old servants used to tell my sister and me stories, tales of the older, original chapel that was once hewn deeper and lower into the cliff. And Father, before he died, mentioned the chapel."

Gianni's hair stood out on the back of his neck. Another hidden chamber?

"When the castle was razed, our family assumed that our sacred relic, a piece of our Lord Jesus' manger, brought back from Palestine by Balthazar, had been stolen. The invaders took everything, allowing my people to take nothing but the clothes upon their backs. But curiously, the holy relic has never reemerged. It is a relic worthy of a grand basilica. So one would assume that it would have emerged ages ago as the pride of some city within Christendom."

"Even as a stolen article?" Gaspare asked.

"Was not the body of Santo Marco stolen from Alexandria and brought to Venezia?" Piero returned.

"But it has not emerged," Cardinal Boeri said, stepping forward. "You believe it remains here? Beneath your altar?"

"We shall see," Count Armand said, waggling his eyebrows. "Beneath our altar has always been a most curious indentation, one that was original to the first chapel, and remains here today." He moved aside so they might all clearly see it. The indentation was set at a forty-five-degree slope. "Some thought it might be natural to the rock, but see here? It bears a stone mason's mark." He looked up at them. "When I saw your glass map, I recognized the similar form."

Count Armand gestured to Hasani, who bent to open the chest that held the glass pieces. Together the men pulled it out, piece by piece, and set it within the indentation.

It was a perfect match, except for one piece at the bottom center. Cardinal Boeri gasped and knelt beside it, crossing himself. "A portion of a vast map formed in antiquity . . ." the cardinal whispered. "Fitting a form hewn centuries later . . ."

"Among my father's things, at the bottom of his trunk," Armand said, "I found this." He unwrapped a bundle in the now-familiar waxed fabric they had found the others in.

The Gifted stood in silence as Armand set it in place. They all waited, as if something would occur now that the map was in its apparent place of destiny.

"Now what?" Vito finally voiced. "Aren't the very rocks supposed to cry out or something, Father?"

Father Piero ignored him and nestled his chin in his hand, studying the map. He paced slowly about the sanctuary, studying each crevice, each ledge, each symbol upon the marble floor tiles that marked the kings' final resting places. He returned to the group, where they all waited, shifting from one foot to the other in expectation. "I have no idea," he said helplessly, arms out in surrender. "Is it merely a sign that we are where we were destined to be? A nod from our Lord?"

The others looked back to him in consternation. Surely there was something more . . . but what? They all set about the chapel, tapping on walls of stone and wood, examining every inch. All except Cardinal Boeri.

"And so the legend is true," the cardinal said in a low tone, moving toward the altar. "An entire map of Christendom in glass . . . I never knew whether to believe it. And when I heard of your attempts to retrieve the pieces in Venezia, I could see God's own plan unfolding." He knelt down and touched the lower center portion in reverence.

"What is that?" Piero asked, kneeling beside the cardinal. He pointed to the center of the piece, where an ivory orb had been inserted into the teal glass.

"I know not," said the cardinal.

"If this is the land mass that forms Italia," Gaspare said, pointing, "this is out at sea."

Again, they all stared at it, thinking that something would happen, now that it was all in place. But nothing transpired. No movement, no sound, no enlightenment.

Gianni glanced at Daria, so beautiful, even in her frustration, especially in the warm streaming light that gained strength as the sun set. The light illuminated russet tones in her dark hair not normally visible, and tiny hairs along her cheek and ear. He reached out to touch her and then paused.

She looked at him with a smile of confusion at his odd hesitation, probably wondering if it was because they were surrounded by others. But he was staring at the rose window nestled beneath the roof and the warm light streaming through, moving slowly forward toward them as the sun set.

"Move, all of you," he grumbled. "Quickly! Stand aside! To the side of the chapel!"

The people all did as he bid, their expressions denoting fear and anger at his demanding tone.

"Look!" he said. "Look to the window!"

They all stared up at the window and down to its stream of light, centered on the rose-colored orb in the middle. It came toward them as a beam from heaven, inching directly toward the glass map, first a Roman foot away, then eating up a finger width at a time.

The hair on the back of Gianni's neck stood on end again. Was that the form of an angel's shoulder in the stream of light? The curve of a head? The bend of an elbow?

Tessa broke through the chapel door, panting as if she had run all the way. Her face was already aglow. "They are here! Here!" she said in a reverent whisper. "Do you see them? *Do you see them?*"

"We see them, child," Daria whispered. "Come, come beside us," she said, lifting a hand to gesture the girl forward.

One by one they all fell to their knees, unable to watch as the light beam fell upon the glass, because they could not tear their eyes from the silhouette of God's holy army within the room. It was as if the angels marched back and forth before them, one moment visible, the next moving out of sight, another replacing the last.

"Look," Tessa said, pointing to the front of the church. "You must look forward."

The others did as she bid. The sun had hit the glass map and cast a reflection on the far wall, evolving as quickly as the sun moved. They were torn between falling flat upon their faces before the altar and staring, unblinking, at the vision at the back of the chapel. On the back wall was a cross and crucifix, of good quality, but like a hundred others in the region. An emaciated Christ figure hung in death, blood streaming from his wrists and crossed ankles, his rib cage sticking out. But as the beam of light streamed over the angled map and illuminated the back wall, a silhouette of a massive Christ seemed to emerge and grow out from the body, strong and sure, arms outstretched but lower, as if in invitation.

Cardinal Boeri crossed himself and went flat to the floor, with the bishop beside him, but the rest remained upright. As the light continued to move, the image changed. The silhouette of Christ remained, but his arms rose higher and higher, until he held them like a master dominating his realm. Behind the figure was a map of the world. Every continent. Every sea.

"They are singing," Tessa whispered in wonder. "Do you hear them? It is so beautiful!"

Gianni listened hard, but could hear only the blood thrumming through his ears. His eyes scanned the map. This was clearly for them. What were they to do? Where were they to go? Surely their Lord did not intend for them to try to reach every nation with their message? The task was too big, too daunting. They were but mortals!

"They grow louder," Tessa whispered again, an edge of fear in her voice.

The rumbling beneath their feet might have been building for some time before they noticed it. Dimly, Gianni heard the screams and shouts of servants and knights outside the chapel. All at once, he became aware of it fully as the ground shook beneath his knees, knocking him down to his arms. He crawled to Daria and covered her with his body, wondering if the ceiling would come down atop them. And then the quake receded.

When he opened his eyes, the light beam was gone, the sun now lower than the cliffs to the west. There were no more angels visible in the room, and to the front of the chapel, no more figure of his Messiah. The front plaster had cracked, massive fissures now visible behind the lonely Christ figure atop his cross.

But then he saw it.

Chapter Sixteen

It was a doorway, or the edge of one anyway.

"When I asked if the rocks would cry out, it was only in jest," Vito whispered over his shoulder.

"Call for a stone mason," Count Armand said, edging near.

"Nay. We must keep this to ourselves," Father Piero said. "Please. Let the servants know that you are all right, so they do not come seeking you. And tell them the chapel is damaged and no one is to enter until you tell them they may."

Count Armand, like an altar boy, obediently set off to do as he bid. Piero reached out and placed a hand on the plaster. It pulled off easily. "Quickly, see if you can help me free it," he directed, eyeing the cardinal. Why did Boeri not seem surprised by this?

The men set to work.

In a short time, they had a narrow entry.

Tessa and Gaspare brought candles near, and Gianni reached for the nearest torches atop the walls, dipping them into the candles' flames and handing one to Father Piero, the other to Hasani. The men disappeared into the narrow crevasse in the wall, warm light inviting the others inward.

Daria gathered her skirt into a bundle so that it would be out of the way and followed them. Directly behind the false back of the chapel was a steep stairwell and then a narrow passageway, which opened up into a shallow but massively tall chapel ceiling.

Vito whistled as he came through, gazing up at towering domes above them, carved out of the limestone. There were three, soaring thirty feet above them, with perfect red Egyptian marble columns. In between were smaller green marble columns, with what he assumed were saints atop them.

"We knew it was here," Count Armand said, looking upward. He took a torch from Hasani and stepped forward. "All this time . . ." His words broke off as the light caught a gold-gilt altar. Beneath it was a golden box, with seraphim on either side.

They all moved nearer, holding their breath as the count knelt and brushed off centuries of dust from the top. Above him was a fresco of the three kings of old, nearing the manger of the Christ.

He handed the torch back to Hasani and tenderly, reverently opened the box, moving aside the lid guarded by images of God's own. He gestured to Hasani to bring the light closer and then cautiously reached in. He took out a piece of an ancient board, rough-hewn and raw, dark with age. "It is here," he whispered. "Our Lord Jesus might have touched this, once."

Slowly they each sank to their knees, overwhelmed.

But the light of the second torch moved behind them, and gradually Daria, Gianni, and Gaspare followed Father Piero's gaze upward. He waited for them. When he had their full attention, he lifted the torch to illuminate the small sculpture atop the first column. It was a soldier, dressed as a Roman of old. But it had Gianni's face. Piero moved to the second, and the others rose from their knees to come closer, no one saying a word. He lifted the torch to the next figure. A patrician woman, with the face of Daria. He stared at her meaningfully, then lowered the torch. On each marble column was the etching of a sixteen-pointed star, and across its center, a peacock feather.

"And so the legends collide," Vito mumbled in awe. "The story of our Lord's manger, and the story of the Gifted."

They moved on, from one figure to the next. A small priest, obviously Piero. A girl child resembling Tessa. A large, broad-shouldered man with Gaspare's eyes and nose and chin. The tall, haunting African face of Hasani. And the last, a gentle, middle-aged woman. "Our prophetess, I assume," Father Piero said, squinting his eyes as if to memorize her looks. "Just as Gaspare's mother's figures represented."

"A woman as prophet? That'll go over well with the boys in Avignon," Vito said.

Daria gave him a playful shove.

"What?" he asked, playing the fool.

Count Armand waited for them to come closer, his face a mask of serious intent. "My ancestors must have built the false chapel centuries before it was dismantled. Somehow, some way, they knew that this chamber had to be hidden away, preserved, with both the relic and the signs that the house of Les Baux and the house of d'Angelo would one day share much." He studied each of them, the torch's flame lighting one side of his face, leaving the other side in deep shadow. "My father had somehow seen this place—there must be another secret entry. He knew you, recognized you. It had to be because he had seen the statues."

A flicker of gold caught Gianni's eye behind the count, but then Armand's words drew his attention again.

"My friends, it was clear from the start that our paths were to intersect. With each day that passes, I know more of our Lord's intent. And his intent for me is this . . . to serve you, with all that I have, all that I can gain. I pledge again to you all my life, my resources, my men. I will do all that I am able to aid you, wherever it might lead. For you serve our one and true God, and your mission is blessed indeed."

Gianni stared at Father Piero, seeing his own question reflected in the priest's eyes. But just where was this mission to end? He stood to take Count Armand's arm, accepting his pledge, but stilled.

The count, confused, paused and then turned to follow his gaze.

Gianni took the torch and raised it higher. "Quickly, Tessa, come here."

The girl moved to him at once, and he handed her the torch, then lifted her to his shoulders. "Raise it high, as high as you can."

The others gathered around them, able to see the gilt lettering reflected in the light of the torch. Around the bottom of each dome were words. In the first the words read, *Deus providet, Deus creat, Deus respicit, Deus ducit.* God provides, God creates, God watches, God leads.

In the second, the words read, *Christus salvat, Christus amat, Christus docet, Christus manet.* Christ saves, Christ loves, Christ teaches, Christ remains.

All were words they might expect to find in a chapel. But what followed was far from usual. *Praediti Dei, communicate dona vestra populis Dei.*

Father Piero moved forward and read aloud what Gianni suddenly had no voice to cover, translating as he did so. "Gifted of God, share your gifts with the people of God."

They all stood in silence for a moment.

Father Piero glanced at Cardinal Boeri, who nodded. The two church-men shared a long, hard gaze.

"Another clue for you, the Gifted," Cardinal Boeri said, still studying the priest. "It is all coming into line now, is it not? With the letter?"

They all stared hard at him, again rendered mute. Only Hasani seemed unsurprised.

"You . . . know of our letter?" Gianni asked. With measured action, he lowered Tessa to the floor. She stared up at him in concern, obviously feeling the sudden tension.

"I know it, my friend. Moreover, I have a missing portion." He looked to Gianni, his expression a mix of confession and intrigue.

Gianni rushed across the room, looking as if he wanted to take the cardinal's robe in his hands and shake him. Bishop di Mino edged closer as if he meant to defend the cardinal from Gianni. "You have a portion of our letter? *Our* letter? You knew? You knew of our prophecy all along? All those years I served under you . . . you *knew*?"

The cardinal shook his head, lifting his hands to placate the large knight. "Nay, Gianni. I always understood you were special, that we were of one heart, with similar goals. But I had no idea, really never considered the possibility that the prophecy might unfold in my time . . . until I knew of the Sorcerer and . . ." He paused, paced, and lifted a hand to his skullcap, looking a bit faint in the face of his furious ex-captain's glare. "My letter contains only pictures of our priest, here, and of a woman who looks curi-ously like the lady atop that column," he said, nodding at the prophetess. "It speaks of pursuing change, change within the Church. It speaks of leading the men back to the road of righteousness. To getting back to the Church that Christ intended. But most worrisome is the prophecy of how the Church will be infiltrated by the devil himself. It was what fueled my work for so many years in Roma, Gianni, the same work that drew you to my side. I did not wish for the evil one to enter the church's walls. I so desired Roma to be pure, a beacon . . ."

"The letter, does it sound Pauline?" Father Piero asked quietly.

"It echoes of Saint Paul, but I believe it is Apollos. I have read other works by him, in the Church archives of Ephesus. He was a learned man, well capable of authorship." He looked about at each of them. "I have al-ways meant to share my letter with you, but I had to be certain . . . utterly certain that you were the Gifted mentioned in the letter. Merely my possession of it places me at risk within the Church, let alone my assertion that it is prophecy worthy of Church canonization."

Daria reached out to place a hand on Gianni's arm. He still looked furious, as if the cardinal had betrayed him. Slowly the knight straightened, and the cardinal ran a nervous hand down the front of his cassock. Gianni turned, gazing back up to the domes of the ancient chapel. "Perhaps . . . 'tis time to fetch the letter and share it with us, Cardinal Boeri."

Avignon

AMBROGIO walked down the massive hallways of the new wing of the palace, following Simone and their benefactor, Cardinal Stefani, rubbing his aching hands as they moved. When Daria had healed him, the bones had been straightened. The feeling had returned to each digit, as had full flexion. But after hours of work upon the frescoes of the pope's dining hall, the massive *tinel,* capable of seating more than three hundred souls, his hands ached, as if echoing complaint of an old, forgotten injury.

Stefani emerged in the *tinel* again, admiring and praising their work in depicting the heavenly realms with an undulating, cloudy blue fresco across the massive, barrel-vaulted ceiling. Bronze stars were already being formed by countless metalsmiths, which would later be inserted among the heavens' clouds.

Ambrogio coughed. Several fires, the remnants of the fresco firing, still spewed smoke into the great hall. His eyes, he knew, were much like Simone's, bloodshot and teary in protest. Their faces and necks were covered in soot. All he wanted was to take a bath, have a bite of bread and several swigs of wine, and lay his head down atop a pillow.

But Stefani insisted upon showing them an inner papal gallery, their next assignment. Pope Cornelius was reportedly very pleased with their work and had asked Simone and his new friend to review the gallery and suggest appropriate frescoes. But still they remained in the Grand Tinel, looking from one end to the other. Cardinal Stefani was suggesting to Simone that more could be made of the lower walls. Mayhap a forest scene? A pilgrimage? The famous wedding feast?

The far door opened again, and Ambrogio watched as two more cardinals entered, followed closely behind by a grand noble dressed in a fur-lined cape. Ambrogio's eyes narrowed as he noticed the way the man pushed back the edge of his winter cape over his shoulder and touched an eye patch.

Abramo Amidei.

Ambrogio ducked and turned. It was imperative that the man not yet know that he was present. He had had so little time to gather information, scant scraps here and there from the scaffolding as churchmen passed below in deep conversation or disagreement, or servants tossed gossip back and forth, impossible to discern truth from lie.

"*Permesso*, my lords," he said lowly, glancing backward to see the cardinals and Abramo edging closer, their eyes thankfully drawn again and again to the ceiling. "I confess I suffer much from the day's smoke. I am in need of food and a bath. Might we see to the papal chambers now and return to this conversation on the morrow?"

Cardinal Stefani gazed at him in consternation and irritation. Ambrogio knew that only his reputation as one of the finest artists available kept the good cardinal from chastising his ill manners, regardless of his physical state. The cardinal forced a smile to his face and raised his hands, gesturing them forward through the door that led to the papal gallery.

Ambrogio was the first one through, and he turned to watch the cardinal and Simone follow, and the men beyond them, now halfway down the massive *tinel* hall.

Abramo Amidei stared straight at him.

⚭ ⚭ ⚭

"My lord Cardinals," Abramo said, still staring at the figures disappearing into the next hall, "who is responsible for this miracle upon the Holy Father's ceiling?"

"Why, it is Simone Martini, of course," said Cardinal Rocher. Abramo had seen that many of his own mansion chambers bore the mark of the accomplished artist's work.

"Ah, I should have known that the pope would invite none but the best to decorate his inner sanctum," Abramo said easily.

"It is Cardinal Stefani who is responsible for it," said Cardinal Saucille, the biggest gossip among the cardinals. "The man will do anything to get into the good graces of Cornelius. He used his political pull in Siena with the Nine to move Martini from his next commission in a cathedral up here, to Avignon." He grinned. "I can only admire his ingenuity, of course, and hope to emulate it myself."

Abramo smiled. "How long will he remain?"

"As long as the pope has walls and he the pigment," laughed the cardinal.

"Who is that that was with him?" pressed Abramo, still puzzling over something that niggled at him. Covered in soot as they were, it was difficult to make out the facial features, but there was something familiar about both of them. He dimly remembered meeting Martini through the years . . . but the other?

"An apprentice? I know not."

"Nay, I had heard they had run across another artist from Siena," said Cardinal Rocher. "They seem to produce fine artists in Toscana as fast as a rabbit spits out babes. What was his name?" He paused and gestured toward a man carrying two pails of ash and embers from the dying fresco fires. "You there, man. Who is Master Martini's new compatriot, the man helping orchestrate these magnificent frescoes?"

The man smiled, revealing missing teeth. "Why it is another master, from Siena. Master Rossellino."

Abramo stilled. "Ambrogio Rossellino?"

The man nodded quickly and then abruptly slowed, seeing Abramo's expression. "*Oui*, that is the one. Now pardon me, m'lords. I must be about my task."

Saucille stared from the workman to Abramo, his small eyes missing nothing.

"That's it!" said Cardinal Rocher. "Rossellino. I believe I will try to get him to do some work in my mansion as well, when his work here is done. Can you imagine the feasts we shall enjoy in this hall? Once the new kitchen tower is complete . . ."

The trio moved forward, and Abramo smiled. So it had begun. The Gifted thought to send a spy forward, a scout to examine the enemy in shadow. It would serve them well.

Let them come, he thought. *Let them know I am here, lying in wait.* His own spies were already in place. He feared nothing. The day belonged to the master.

Here in Avignon, the Gifted would know death and defeat, and Abramo would know revenge and victory.

Let them come. I am ready.

HELL'S KEEP

Avignon

CHAPTER SEVENTEEN

JOSEPHINE Fontaine had spent her life as a blind woman. "It is well that you are blind," her mother said of her, "true enough is your sight. If you had vision atop it, it would be too much for one person to bear." She was the child of a misbegotten union between her mother—a servant in a bishop's mansion—and said bishop; her mother had alternated between blaming the shameful sin of her beginnings for the child's blindness and claiming that Josephine's keen insight was the Lord making things right.

The bishop had been a kindly man, whom Josephine remembered holding her in his lap and singing the Scriptures in Latin, whispering to her the translation into Provençal and talking about what the words meant. The Word unfolded in her young mind, exploding into multiple layers, lodged and continually building like a flood jam in a river.

But her mother and her lover, the bishop, were both long dead. It had been some time since Josephine had been held by anyone, decades since anyone had shared the Word with her. It always flowed out of her, the truth, out upon deaf ears. So frustrating was her cause . . . what good, truth, if no one wished to recognize it as such? Her own life was edging toward the end, she thought, her hips and shoulders aching in the cold stillness of morn.

For years now, Josephine had made a living as a beggar, wondering how it was that the Lord on High had made her first, a woman; second, blind; and third, a prophetess. Prophets were never welcome in their own towns. The people of Avignon held her at arm's length, drawn by her insight, yet repulsed by her forthright honesty. They came to her as a diviner of sorts, but she never made the same money that the fortune-tellers did outside the city gates. The fortuners would tell their clients what they wished to hear. Josephine always told them the truth.

She knew the city by sound and touch. She could walk each block and know exactly where she was. The smell of the fishmonger's market guided her from three blocks distant, as did the tallow and beeswax of the chandler's. She knew the sound of each cardinal's horse, the steep slope of the hill that led to the Palais de le Pape. Beyond it she knew the feel of the wind off the Rhône in any season, the spray of her waters upon her face. Well she understood the sensation of flying when one stood on the edge of the Rocher des Doms, the massive cliff above the old river, beyond the growing, expanding palace. She enjoyed the relatively quiet Université district, rife with professors and students, deep in thoughtful conversation.

And yet she also enjoyed identifying the city's more boisterous characters—such as the shrill voice of the cotton merchant and the twin voice of the spice merchant's wife, women the people said must have been separated at birth, so alike was their tone and their talk.

Josephine moved down the creaking stairs from her third-story room, one hand to the crumbling plaster wall, a basket of woolens at her hip. She spent her days in the vast plaza below the palace, tolerated because of her blind, poor status by the churchmen. Some were kind enough to throw a minor coin in her basket each day. Cardinals Stefani and Morano; Bishops Corin, Barnabe, and Ferdinand. More minor priests and officials.

Although she earned enough for a loaf of bread each day from the coins, and a bit of cheese or meat every other day from her weavings, it was for the people she came. As each passed, Josephine would pray the Scriptures that sang from her heart, those she felt applied most to that person, at that moment, be he beggar or bishop, priest or professor. Here, along Rue de Mons, much of the city progressed each day, entering and exiting through the busiest gate of the city—le Porte du Rhône. Certainly anyone of import. Praying for the people here allowed her to make the biggest impact on the greatest number of people. From here, she had the clearest sense of her sisters and brothers—be they well or ill—and felt the thrumming life of her city.

Yet something was different in these last weeks, within her city's daily song. The cadence was the same, but it was as if another beat had been added, something almost imperceptible, different. And the Scriptures, those words whispered so long ago to her by her father, were no longer content to remain a silent whisper, singing through her mind and occasionally spoken to passersby. Instead, they formed in her mouth until she was desperate to release them—at times like a lump of clay, something she felt compelled to spit out; other times a welcoming kiss, like the finest of olive oils that could emerge as an anointing. She never knew what was to come until a person moved before her.

Josephine groaned, feeling the lump begin to form. He had returned. She had hoped he was a visitor passing through, soon gone. But he had passed by five times and now he neared again.

ᖍ ᖍ ᖍ

SHE rose ahead of them, trembling as if enraged. Abramo knew her immediately as *other*, as threat. She looked toward them with eyes opaque in blindness and yet it felt uncannily as if she stared straight into his soul. Why now? He groaned inwardly. He traveled with Cardinal DuPree and Bishop Corin, en route to another cardinal's mansion to dine.

Cardinal DuPree, seeing her distress, pulled his horse up short. "Be at peace, woman. The night is drawing near. Should you not gather your basket and head toward home?"

"Well I should, Eminence," she said, with a slow nod. "But you travel with someone who is a danger to you."

The cardinal laughed. "Not Bishop Corin? He's as harmless as a dove!" He cast a teasing glance at the bishop, but his eyes hesitated over Abramo.

"Nay, Eminence," said the woman, her face still pointed toward Abramo. "I have a word for the third man who travels with you."

"Lord Amidei?" Again, the cardinal chuckled. "Then by all means, tell him what you must. I shall enjoy listening."

"Cardinal DuPree, should we not be on our way?" Abramo asked, barely concealing his agitation. "Might we not be late?"

"Nay. We have plenty of time. Cardinal Rocher's household hardly runs on any sort of schedule, due to his slovenly spirit. Go ahead, good woman. Tell Lord Amidei what you must. If it's worthy, I shall give you a gold florin this day instead of a silver gros."

She paused, then poised her face toward Cardinal DuPree. "Forgive me, Eminence, but God himself has given me this word for your companion, now . . . *'Propter quod abiicientes omnem immunditiam* . . . Therefore, get rid of all moral filth and the evil that is so prevalent and humbly accept the word planted in you, which can save you.' "

The cardinal, dumbfounded by the beggar's fluent use of Latin, pulled slightly on the reins. His gelding moved a step backward.

Amidei scoffed in irritation. "Surely you shall not let a beggar speak to us with such insolence—"

She turned to the cardinal and bishop. " 'Has not God chosen those who are poor in the eyes of the world to be rich in faith and to inherit the kingdom he promised those who love him? But you have insulted the poor.' "

"If the poor have no manners then—" Amidei began.

" 'Is it not the rich who are exploiting you?' " the woman cut in. " 'Are they not the ones who are dragging you to court? Are they not the ones who are slandering the noble name of him to whom you belong?' "

♋ ♋ ♋

JOSEPHINE knew she had slipped from Latin into her native Provençal at some point, but she could not stop herself. Never had the words come so fast and furious. It was as if they welled within her, surged and spewed, unaided. At one point, the Lord's words were for the cardinal, the next, for the bishop, the following, for the newcomer. All were for her, for anyone who would listen. Holy words of wisdom, from the pen of James, if she remembered that right. But she had to stop . . . she would be imprisoned . . . right after she said what was next . . . " 'If you really keep the royal law found in Scripture, "Love your neighbor as yourself," you are doing right. But if you show favoritism, you sin and are convicted by the law as lawbreakers. For whoever keeps the whole law and yet stumbles at just one point is guilty of breaking all of it. For he who said, "Do not commit adultery" ' "—she paused and faced the newcomer—" 'also said, "Do not murder." ' " Josephine swallowed hard, knowing by the intensity of these words that the newcomer was both adulterer and murderer.

The newcomer, Amidei, sighed heavily. "Shall we be on our way now, Cardinal? Surely we need not subject ourselves to the wild rantings of a madwoman . . . I'm to meet Baron del Buco. I really must not tarry."

"What is your rush, m'lord?" asked the cardinal. "Are you not the least bit curious? Here is a woman, aged and poor, who seems to know the Scriptures both in Latin and what they mean in Provençal."

"A trick," Amidei said. "Meant to garner larger coins for her basket in the company of holy men. She should be jailed for attempting to take advantage of your tender hearts."

Danger! Danger! her mind screamed. But she could not stop herself. She sank to her knees, clasping her hands before her. " 'Speak and act as those who are going to be judged by the law that gives freedom, because judgment without mercy will be shown to anyone who has not been merciful. Mercy triumphs over judgment!' Mercy, m'lord Cardinal. I beg you. Mercy. Mercy."

She had heard of people imprisoned within the dark dungeon of the Palais de le Pape, those who suffered the Court of the Rota. She had smelled the burning flesh of those heretics burned at the stake, right here in the plaza. What was she doing? What madness was this, this path her Lord forced her to take? *Mercy, mercy, mercy. Protect me, Lord God on High!* She sank to the ground, her nose to the cobblestones. Would they order her dragged from this spot? Place her in stocks? She prayed that they would simply leave, that her task was complete.

The cardinal cleared his throat. "Good woman, were you once a noble? How have you come to know the Scriptures?"

"My father taught them to me," she said in misery, her face still pressed to the ground.

"What is that? I cannot make out your words. Come now, fear no longer. I am curious more than angry. Rise."

"M'lord Cardinal—" Amidei began.

Apparently the cardinal urged him to hush with a gesture or look, for the newcomer fell silent. She could feel the waves of danger from the man, the hatred that pulled more words from her . . . As he had asked, Josephine rose, feeling the full misery of what undoubtedly would now transpire.

"Come now, you face a father of the Church, not an executioner," the cardinal said. She could hear him dismount and step closer to her.

"*Oui*, Eminence."

"Was your father a scholar? One who favored James?"

"He favored much of the New Testament."

"I see. And he taught you both Latin and the Holy Scriptures? A worthy cause. But are you aware that it is not permissible to speak the Word in the common tongue? If we allowed such madness, the villeins would distort what is holy and none would remain pure."

"I am aware, Eminence," she said. "But does not the Word say, 'Do not merely listen to the word and so deceive yourselves. Do what it says.' "

"Quite," returned the cardinal. "I must—"

" 'Anyone who listens to the word,' " she rushed on, " 'but does not do what it says is like a man who looks at his face in the mirror and after looking at himself, goes away and immediately forgets what he looks like. But the man who looks intently into the perfect law that gives freedom, and continues to do this, not forgetting what he has heard, but doing it—he will be blessed in what he does.' "

"Your father was a professor specializing in James, I take it," the cardinal said.

"He was a student of many biblical books," she returned. More words were rising in her throat, begging to be let out. She bit on her tongue until she tasted the copper essences of blood, forcing them back, clamping her lips shut. She could not say anything more. She could not!

"I see that you feel the full force of your contrition, and grant you absolution." She could feel the breath of air about her face as he made the sign of the cross in front of her. "See that you sin no longer."

He turned, and she could hear the creak of the leather as he mounted his horse again. She shook her head in frustration and angst. There would be no halting the words. "I shall do my best to sin no longer, but if it is sin to speak the Word of God, then so be it. Be aware that you ride with sin, m'lord. The snares are wide and vast ahead of you, already surround you—"

"Cardinal!" Amidei barked, knowing she was about to lay into him again. "You cannot allow such madness!"

"Woman!" the cardinal shouted. "You shall cease!"

" 'If you harbor bitter envy and selfish ambition in your hearts, do not boast about it or deny the truth. Such "wisdom" does not come down from heaven, but is earthly, unspiritual, of the devil.' " She spit those last words toward Amidei. " 'For where you have envy and selfish ambition, there you find disorder and every evil practice.' " She leaned backward, aching as the words left her mouth, as if they had battered her while she pushed them down and left her bruised.

"We shall speak of this further on the morrow," said the cardinal lowly. And with a snap of his fingers, Josephine was grabbed by two knights, her basket left behind, her feet barely touching the cobblestones en route to the dungeons beneath the Palais de le Pape.

ቀ ቀ ቀ

LATER that night, Abramo Amidei and Baron Vincenzo del Buco rode back to the cardinal's residence, alone but for Ciro and another knight. Vincenzo seemed at odds, weak. It was good that he had arrived. Here, Amidei would refortify him. "I learned from the messenger that you were successful with our quest," Abramo said.

"Indeed. We killed the short, dark-haired knight, and his companion, the tall German."

"Very good," Abramo said with a nod. "They were formidable knights, a significant force together. De Capezzana was wise in choosing them. Fierce must his loss be, greater our gain."

"We had hoped to take more of them, but Cardinal Boeri arrived with his knights de Vaticana. We were driven off."

Abramo shrugged and pulled his cape a bit closer. "You did what you could. You did well."

"You are not dismayed at such word of Cardinal Boeri? His aid to the Gifted?"

Abramo smiled. "If all the cardinals fell to us, it would hardly be fair, would it? And the messenger told me of Boeri, and how he reunited Hasani with the Gifted." He sighed. "That is what dismays me."

"Agreed. He aids them with foreknowledge. How are we to battle that?"

Abramo looked to his friend. "Wit and strength, as always. The Gifted think themselves smart and prepared as they make way for Avignon. But they really have little idea what is ahead of them."

"Yet they gain strength. And Daria . . . I have it on good word that she and de Capezzana wed, shortly before we departed."

Amidei raised his chin, taking that information in like an unwelcome rain settling on his shoulders. So this was the root cause of Vincenzo's downtrodden demeanor. He had always had a tender heart toward the woman, the woman whom Amidei once had wanted for himself. And that she had spurned both Vincenzo and Amidei made him want to reach out and strangle her now . . .

He sighed. "It will be well. We shall use their union against them. Love shall make them weak."

Vincenzo coughed. "Why not leave them behind, Abramo? Pursue our own course? This is a vast land. . . ."

Abramo pulled on the reins, and his horse pulled up short. Vincenzo's mare moved forward several steps and then pulled around to face him. Ciro and the other knight moved off several paces in either direction and then waited, respectfully keeping watch as their lords spoke.

"Lord Amidei, forgive me. I am weary . . ."

Abramo swallowed back the bile that rose in his throat. "You are in need of succor, strength, my friend. I understand. You have been on the front of our battle for some time. And I have been away. . . ." He sighed. "You have forgotten that we must draw the line here, now, and drive our enemy backward. I met the last of them today, the last of the prophesied Gifted."

"Here? In Avignon? Who is he?"

Abramo smiled and laughed without breath. "*He* is a blind woman, a beggar at the entrance of the Palais de le Pape. Honestly, I do not believe our enemy has any sense when it comes to choosing the people he wishes to lead others. Look at them! Other than the duchess and de Capezzana, who do they have? A homely priest, an African ghost, a child of Il Campo, an old fisherman, and now a blind beggar woman . . . Hardly the sort of group who might attract others."

"And yet they do. The Count and Countess Les Baux have invited many powerful friends to their castle in the last week. I fear they may lend support to the Gifted."

Abramo listened to his words, staring into his eyes as if he were in another place. He suddenly sat straighter in his saddle and snapped his fingers, waving Ciro over.

Ciro moved closer.

"Did you get a good look at the woman we spoke to earlier this evening, the one who addressed us and was taken away to the *palais*?"

"Yes, m'lord."

"I want you to wait for her to emerge. The cardinal will have no stomach for detaining a blind old woman for more than a night or two. When she is released, you are to follow her into a dark corner of the city, kill her, and send her body to the bottom of the Rhône. Do you understand me?"

"It shall be done, m'lord." The big knight set off at once.

Abramo returned his attention to Vincenzo. "So they gain in strength . . . and are finding support. We have cut them to the quick with their loss of those two knights. And we will keep them from their prophetess, who they believe will aid them."

"If they find her."

"If we do not vanquish them here, Baron del Buco, they shall haunt us forever. Our tasks cannot coexist in peace. This is war. They must be killed, every last one. And we shall use their own Church to take most of them down. If the Church fails us, we shall see the task through. Do you comprehend this? The import of this task?"

Vincenzo stared at him dolefully, unspeaking.

"Do you understand?" Abramo shouted.

His voice reverberated through the city streets. A window popped open above their heads, but when its owner saw the lords below, it immediately shut again.

At last, a nod from Vincenzo.

It was good he was here, with him. He had weakened without aid in Provence. Here, in Avignon, he and the master could bring him back in line.

"Good, good, my friend." He moved his gelding forward, and Vincenzo moved beside him again. "As I said, I know the road has been long, that this has cost you much. But remember what you have learned, how vast your fortunes have become. There is a cave just outside Avignon. It is deep and long. I have met with the master there, counseled with him. In three nights, with the full moon, our faithful shall gather. After that, we shall be fully prepared for the Gifted to arrive . . . and to watch them fall."

CHAPTER EIGHTEEN

Les Baux

VITO awakened with a start, drawing his dagger and leaping to his feet as soon as he knew someone lingered beside his bed.

A small gasp made him blink, trying to break through the fog of deep slumber and early-morning light. "Tess? What are you doing here?" he whispered.

Seven other men slept on, some snoring. One, in the corner, would waken the entire castle if he didn't turn over. Tessa was wringing her hands, pacing back and forth. Suddenly Hasani arrived as well, his eyes wide, sweat running down his face even in the cold of a winter's morn. Ugo, aware now that they were not alone, sat up on his cot, staring over at them in concern. He immediately reached for an overcoat and joined them.

Vito frowned, pulled on a shirt, and led all three outside the knights' hall. "All right, out with it, both of you. What has transpired? Why have you come to us?"

"I know not," Tessa said in a high-pitched voice, still wringing her hands. "I only have a terrible sense of foreboding. I was so eager to set off for Avignon on the morrow. I was certain we were to meet another of our Gifted. There are good people ahead of us, Vito, not just bad. We shall not be alone. Surely we shall not be alone . . ." She paced back and forth. "Mayhap it is only that I know that Lord Amidei and Baron del Buco will be there as well . . ."

Hasani grunted and shook his head. He gestured to them and led them down the hall, to where the torch still burned. There, he knelt and pulled a scroll from his robe, spreading it flat on the floor before them.

It was an older woman, once pretty. And she was clearly the same woman depicted in the Les Baux chapel statue and Gaspare's tiny figurine. But her expression was a mask of terror. She reached out to the wall, as if it steadied her. Her head was bent, as if she were listening, seeking.

Tessa's hand went to her mouth and Vito put his arm around her, comforting her.

Behind the woman was Ciro, a sword drawn, closing in.

Beyond Ciro stood Abramo Amidei, cape flowing, barely discernible from the deep shadow.

Gaspare arrived, his hair disheveled. He knelt down, looked at Hasani's drawing, and looked up at each of them. "Our prophetess. She is in Avignon, and Amidei knows she is there. We must get to her now if we are to save her."

"I'll go and fetch the others," Ugo said, setting off for the other side of the castle, where Gianni, Daria, and Father Piero lodged.

Avignon

JOSEPHINE huddled in a corner, shivering in the predawn light. Blind since birth, she could make out bright light and deep shadow, but little else. The other women in her cell had descended upon her as soon as the guards had gone away, taking her overdress and woolen stockings from her, leaving her bruised and wearing nothing but a thin chemise for the long, hard night.

It was not the first time that others had preyed upon her weakness of sight. Long ago, she had learned that it was easier to give the thieves what they wished. Capitalizing upon her blindness, they thought themselves strong, and Josephine a victim who could not later identify them. But eight out of nine times, she had been able to find her attackers again, haunting them with truth until they confessed. In the light of day, Josephine felt less vulnerable, and the thieves more open to conviction and repentance.

The words formed in her head and heart. She waited for the women to stir, rise from their sleep, knowing they were apt to feel as cramped and sore as she herself felt, even though she was likely twice their age.

She heard the scratch of movement that could not belong to a rat, and then a low moan and yawn as another stretched. Josephine rose and walked three steps forward to the center of the floor, and then knelt down. She positioned her face to hopefully bespeak kindness and love.

"My daughters, good morning," she said softly. "Good morning, good morning. This is the day that the Lord has made. Let us be glad in it."

One of the young women laughed without humor. "We are not your daughters. And we see no joy in this day. Go back to your corner, old woman."

"I shall go, but first I must say what I must," Josephine said. "One, I know that both of you were deeply loved, mayhap are still deeply loved, by a mother or grandmother. You knew what it was to be touched. To be held. To be taken care of. These women fed you. Washed you, mended your clothes. They bespoke love, and in them, you caught a glimpse of what life was supposed to be like, even though you are far from that life now."

Neither of the young women said a word or moved.

"Those women looked at your faces, deep into your eyes, and they knew you as a prize, a gift from God. They thanked him for you. They prayed for you, for your future, that you would find hope, and peace, and love. They wanted more for you than they had themselves, did they not?"

Again, neither young woman moved.

"I understand you are imprisoned. I know not your transgression, nor how long you must remain here. But I am here to tell you, as a messenger of the God your mothers and grandmothers knew, that this is not the end of your life. This is but the beginning. In Christ, we can begin again, at any time. We simply must confess our sins and endeavor to try better this time. To act and speak in ways our mothers and grandmothers would be proud of. To act and speak in ways our Lord would be proud of."

"Who are you?" dared one at last. "A nun?"

"Nay. I am but a blind beggar woman."

"Why are you here?"

"For speaking words to a cardinal he did not wish to hear."

The two young women giggled over that and then were silent.

"Do your mothers still live?"

"Hers does. Mine wishes she didn't. If she cared for me once, she cares not any longer."

Josephine listened, absorbing the full weight of the girl's words. Judging from her thin, girlish voice, she could not be older than thirteen or fourteen. "Our loved ones will always fail us. Even the most true. Only God is perfect, unfailing. Only he can be ever-present for us." She rose and waved about the room, smiling. "He is here, now. There is nowhere we can go where he does not go with us."

The second girl guffawed. "God is in prison?"

"In prison. On the Rocher des Doms. In the *palais*. In the corner pub. He is everywhere. All-seeing. All-knowing. Ever-loving." She took a step closer to the young women, reaching for the words. " 'For God so loved the world that he gave his only begotten Son.' Jesus came for us, died for us. He left his Holy Spirit here, with us, so that we would never feel alone. He is our Counselor, our Friend, our Guide. Our Comforter. Trust in the Holy One, daughters, and he shall lead us out and onto a better road. I promise it."

A cough at the cell door made Josephine turn. By the intonation alone, she knew who it was. Cardinal DuPree. By the sound of boots upon the stones, she knew he was accompanied by two guards. "I see that a night in the cell has not changed your ways," the cardinal said dryly.

"Nay," returned Josephine, letting her hands fall to her sides. "Cardinal DuPree, although it may be a rule of man not to utter the Word in the common tongue, it is not what Jesus Christ himself did. Did he not speak to his followers, his disciples, the crowds, in Aramaic? Did he not wish for them to understand exactly what he was saying?"

"Jesus Christ left the keys to the Church in Peter's hands. Those who were blessed enough to be in the Lord's presence were uncommon, hand chosen and worthy."

"Indeed they were. But never can I imagine that our Lord Jesus would have hoped that the keys he placed in Peter's hands would become this." She raised her arms and looked above her. "What must he think, right now? Seeing a daughter imprisoned beneath the palace for saying nothing but Scripture to his cardinal?"

Josephine could feel his anger, prayed for the right words to reach him. "Your Eminence," she said, going to her knees. "I beg your forgiveness for any insolence you have felt from me. But I do not regret using holy words given to me from on high. Can you not believe that God can use a blind woman as surely as he might a small shepherd boy or fisherman? Are we not all his creations, with a song that is bursting from our breast?"

The cardinal stepped closer. "I absolve you of your sins," he said. "I do not wish to keep you here any longer, woman. But I will detain you for the day, to fast and pray. Before you leave, I ask only that you consider one thing—might our Lord Jesus be calling you into his service? Might you be able to sing your song as a blessed sister of the Church? Trained and blessed, you could move forth and minister to others in your world, and know when to speak, and when to be silent. Will you agree to pray over that question?"

Josephine stilled. People in the streets playfully called her "Sister Jo," but never had a man of power within the Church suggested she truly study and take the vows. Nuns were typically women from families that had a dowry to give, but no husband to take. "I—I have no money to give," she said.

"If you decide to take the vows, I shall cover the gift myself," the cardinal said. "Pray over it. If you decide to move forward, come to me upon your release at dusk. If you do not, go in peace and sin no more."

He turned then, striding off in long steps. Josephine walked to the bars and leaned her head against the rough, cold texture. Was this her answer? She knew she was called to something bigger, something more. It had been steadily growing in her heart over the last few months, an awareness that something was soon on the horizon that was bigger than she. Had the Lord been calling her toward the Church, to take her vows and serve? But how could she serve a Church she felt called to question? How could she fall into line with priests and bishops and cardinals she felt were more pharisee than disciple?

The two young women were beside her then. One took her hand and laid her stockings in it. The other gently helped her into her woolen overdress. "Forgive us, sister. Forgive us for taking your things."

Josephine could feel the change in their tone. They feared her now. Feared what she could do to them as a woman of the Church. "Thank you, daughters, for helping me. I was confused for a moment by the cardinal's offer. But I do not seek your fear. I seek your respect. Come, let us sit and talk. I have much to tell you before we part."

Les Baux

"I think we should remain together," Daria said for the third time. She grabbed Hasani's horse's bridle and looked up at him and Vito. "If you will give us but another hour, we can all be on our way."

"Begging your pardon, Duchess, but we can travel faster without you," Vito said. "Let us go. Ugo, Gaspare, Hasani, and I. We can ride hard and fast through the day and get to Avignon before nightfall."

Daria sighed in frustration and looked to Gianni as he approached.

"Will you tell them? Avignon is a city of thousand upon thousands. They cannot ride in and get right to our prophetess."

Gianni moved past her to Vito's saddle, reaching low to snug up a leather strap and tuck the end away. "The count says there's but one place in the city that has stones of that size to the walls, and that's by the Palais de le Pape. They know where they're going. God will show them the way to our prophetess."

He looked up to Vito. "Count Armand is sending Lucien and Matthieu with you. They are fine fighting men. We will follow, arriving on the morrow about noon. Meet us at the bridge." He reached up and offered his hand. Vito clasped it above his wrist and looked him in the eye. "On the morrow at the bridge at noon. We shall see you there, Captain."

"You shall need me," Tessa said, appearing beside Daria, already in her overcoat and a pack over her shoulder. "I can assist you in finding her."

Vito reached down and took the child by the arm, swinging her behind him, onto the saddle. She wrapped her arms around him. "She's right," he said to Daria with a shrug. "We need her. If she doesn't sense the prophetess, we know she'll sense Ciro and Amidei."

"Absolutely not!" Daria cried. "This is madness!"

"Nay, Daria," Gianni said grimly, "this is battle. We send forth some of our strongest, in an effort to gain an advantage over the enemy and save one of our own. Will you keep them from it?"

Daria stared up at him, then glanced at Hasani, Gaspare, Vito, Ugo, and the two knights who rode up behind them. Father Piero appeared. She'd already tried to get him to agree with her, but he did not. She licked her lips, looked away, and then back to them all. "Go with God, my friends. We shall pray over you, every step of the way." She took a step toward Vito and tapped him hard on the leg. "And you, you never take your eyes off Tess, you understand? Let her come to harm, and I shall beat you myself."

Vito pretended to shiver. "My, Duchess, you are fearsome!" He smiled and patted Tessa's small arms, still clinging around his waist. His face softened. "Fear not. I shall give up my life before I allow her out of my sight."

"That does not make me feel better," Daria said with a sigh.

" 'Tis all I can give you, m'lady. Trust us. God has asked us to go. We must follow where he leads."

"On the morrow at the bridge," Vito said to Gianni. "After the darkness . . ."

"Light!" shouted the others in farewell. But the six horses were already galloping away, Count Armand's knights carrying a flag bearing his coat of arms in front like an angel of protection.

Avignon

AMIDEI had sent a messenger to retrieve Ciro from his post and give him a day of rest, having discovered that the woman would be released that evening or taken into the labyrinth of the Church's keep. He fervently hoped she declined Cardinal DuPree's clever offer of sponsorship into a nunnery and emerged on the streets. He toyed with the idea of having Ciro squire her away, making use of her at the ceremony in two nights' time, but then decided against it, knowing it was best to destroy this one before she aided the Gifted in any way.

"Sorry, my dear, you simply must perish," he whispered with a smile, staring out the wavy glass of the bishop's windows. The thought of watching Ciro take her life made his heart pound with pleasure. Yes, he would go and watch his man take this one. He would aid him in hunting her down, make her know the greatest fear of her life, before her throat was cut. Yes, yes, yes. Would the Gifted feel it, too, when she died? Would they know they had suffered a blow? Or would he deliver her body to their doorstep when they finally dared to enter this city to face their enemies?

He would leave it to the master. The master would appear to them in two days, at the ceremony. There they could present her body to him and ask what to do with it. He would know. He always knew how best to manipulate men. Abramo shivered. How blessed was he to be the chosen one! The man who was destined to control his own empire. He already owned controlling interests in businesses from Paris to Sicily, and many of the men in between. In a decade or so, he would launch his political campaign to own them outright.

He flung off his overcoat, pulled the long jerkin from his torso, and walked to the mirror. The glass was dim and flecked with black, but he could see his naked form. He was still in his prime, muscled and broad in shoulder, his jaw strong and full of color, even in the dead of winter. Abramo fingered the patch, remembering Daria, her hair flying about her as the storm wind blew through the window. He remembered her whirling, chest heaving, wiping her mouth with the back of her hand. Her fingers, clinging to a bloody piece of glass, the glass that had claimed his eye.

His hand went to the studded belt, given to him by the cardinal, took the strap, and with a quick move, pulled it another notch tighter. He closed his good eye against the pain, fighting for breath. But in the pain was pleasure, pleasure that equaled what he had experienced upon his master's altar. He opened his eye and watched as blood streamed down his muscled thigh and down his knee, mingling with the hair and running onward like tiny rivers. And then he laughed.

He would make each of the Gifted know pain and fear before they knew the release of death. No easy passing would it be for them, nay. They would know his power, know the full extent of his wrath. He would take Gianni— nay, the girl—and he would make Daria watch as he cut her eyes from their sockets. Yes, he sighed. Yes. That would be the retribution he sought. One at a time, he would kill them, leaving Daria last, so that she would know the full force of her poor decision to deceive him, maim him, deny him.

He laughed again hollowly, running his fingers over the belt. "I shall find you again, Daria," he whispered, tapping the mirror as if it were her visage before him and no longer his own. "I shall take you and lay you upon my master's altar and punish you for your wrongdoing. Your loved ones will all be slain. You shall be alone. And I will watch the hope die in your eyes even as the blood drains from your body. It will be a new era. The Gifted, vanquished. And the world, ours. *Ours.*"

He pulled on his long shirt and his overcoat again, returning to the window, eyeing the setting sun casting a pale yellow hue upon the Palais de le Pape. "You think you can come here and change the world," he said with a scoff. "It has already been purchased."

Abramo swung the heavy woolen cape around his shoulders and strode to the door. "Fetch Ciro," he said to the guard in the hall. "Tell him it is time."

ಶ ಶ ಶ

THE six men and the girl arrived in Avignon, having ridden hard for hours. Hasani eyed the setting sun as they gained entrance through the gates and looked in consternation toward Vito, Ugo, and Gaspare, then Tessa. They had come in through the Porte de l'Oulle gate, near the Palais de le Pape, but were still several streets below it. They could see the mammoth structure, the biggest Vito had seen in many a land—and still under construction from the look of it—rising above the buildings along the Rue Rempart du Rhône.

It boasted silver-stoned tower after tower, with crenellations and guards atop it as if it were the keep of a warring king instead of Saint Peter's distant kin.

Vito lowered Tessa to the ground near a public well and then dismounted, leading her to the well for a drink. The child drank as if she had just emerged from a desert.

Vito took the dipper from her, handing it to the woman who tended the well, pulling buckets from the deep in exchange for a small coin. He tossed her a larger coin, pointing to the six horses that already waited at the trough with expectant looks in their eyes.

Gaspare handed out bread and dried meat to the men, taking in sustenance for the battle ahead while giving Vito room to encourage the girl. He stepped forward and handed a hunk of bread and several slices of jerky to Vito, who pulled off a smaller chunk for Tessa.

She stuffed a bite in her mouth.

"Tess, we need direction. Where shall we start?"

The girl continued to chew, then closed her eyes and lifted one hand out, as if she were touching something animate. Slowly she turned in a half circle, from one wall of the city at her left to the other wall at her right. Several times she paused and moved on.

When she retraced her steps in an agonizingly slow fashion, as if she were atop a wheel and the rope were being winched back in, Vito had to turn away. They had no time for this! The sun was soon down!

∞ ∞ ∞

"The cardinal would have your decision now," said the guard from the cell door, turning a key in the squeaky lock and opening the gate.

"I shall be on my way," said Josephine.

"You do not wish to enter the nunnery?" he asked. She could hear the surprise in his voice. Would it not be the answer for any beggar she knew? To have a roof, clothing, food, purpose for her life, all magically provided for her? But she had her purpose. And if she entered the nunnery, she knew it would not last. They would not stomach her talk for long before calling her to face the Lord's Commissioner. She almost welcomed the idea, relished the challenge. In him she would find a worthy mind, and with God on her side, she just might get him to see her way of thinking. But she would face him in God's time, and this was clearly not her path.

"Be at peace, daughters," she said to the girls. "I shall pray for you each and every day until your release."

"And we for you, Josephine."

"Remember what we talked about this day. You end this day changed, free. His."

"We shall remember," said the other.

"Come along," grumbled the guard. "I want to get home to my stew before it grows as cold as the streets." He took her arm and pulled her down the passageway, past prison cells that Josephine could feel open like gaping, cold caves. "Stairs," he said, half a second before she would've tripped. They turned left at the top and then right, then went up another staircase before Josephine could smell the city. As foul as it was, it was divine compared to the pit of the dank dungeons below.

The guard dropped her arm, bent, and put another key in a lock. A massive wooden door opened, and Josephine was free. She turned to say something to the guard, the Lord having given her a word for him, but the door slammed in her face. She heard the lock jam back into place and smiled. "That stew must be quite good."

She turned back around, trying to detect where they had released her. She cocked her head and listened, hearing the gentle sounds of the river and the more jarring sound of the sailors and fishermen, crossing even the muffling, massive city wall. The far side of the *palais*, she decided, but a few steps from Rue Banasterie. It made sense. It was here they saw to the riffraff of the city, fed the poor, ushered prisoners in and out. The front plaza was reserved for honored guests and statesmen, with beggars merely tolerated on the outskirts.

Josephine lifted her face. The sun had set and darkness was fast descending. Best to get home straight away and find food on the morrow.

ॐ ॐ ॐ

"THERE," Tessa said, staring straight ahead over her arm, pointing to the palace.

"The *palais*? Please tell me you don't believe she is in there," Vito said, looking up.

"Not in it. Beyond it. I can feel her, Vito," she said, a sudden grin of joy upon her face. "She's but a few streets away! Let us be about it!"

"All right, all right, keep your stockings on," he said. She was running to Hasani's horse and turned back to wait for him. But then her face stilled and her smile faded.

Vito turned and he groaned inwardly. Knights of Avignon approached, a patrol retinue, four men strong. They would want to know what the knights of Les Baux were doing here. And it wasn't likely that they would allow them to charge off to find a woman whom they could not yet even name.

"Give me the words, Lord," he whispered.

"Vito!" Tessa cried, her face white. "He is there too! *He* is nearing her!"

"Excellent," Vito mused sarcastically. He looked up to the skies. "A mite of assistance possible, Lord?"

Two of the knights of the city dismounted, their faces awash in consternation at the girl's alarming tone.

Hasani, Gaspare, and Ugo swung up and into their saddles.

"Halt!" said the captain of the patrol. "You shall remain here a moment longer."

"We are on an urgent errand of Count Armand Rieu des Baux," said Lucien, carrying the count's banner. "Do not detain us if you care to keep your position."

"Let me see your papers," said the captain. He stood his ground, but the knight's words unnerved him.

"We have reason to believe that a friend of the count's is in grave danger," Lucien said. "She is an older woman, a beggar to your eyes. But she is much more than that. We must get to her, and get to her now. It is vital."

The knight of Les Baux handed the captain his papers, knowing there was an even chance he could read. But that bore the sixteen-point star of Les Baux, anyone could make that out. "The man speaks the truth," Vito shouted. "Let us be about our task."

"Be at peace," said the captain, handing the papers back to the knight. "Tell me the woman's name and we shall aid you in finding her."

"She is about sixty years of age, with a basket about this wide, full of cloth. A weaver? A seamstress? She resides in this district."

"And her name?"

"*Vito*," Tessa whispered. She was as white as a sheet, trembling now. Panting, her eyes wide. Twin tracks of tears ran down her face, dirty still from the dust of the road. "They're moving *away* . . ." Hasani reached down and hauled her up in front of him. He looked to Vito, ready to ride without permission if necessary.

"What ails the girl?" asked the captain, his eyes narrowing. "Is she ill? If she is ill, we must place her immediately in quarantine! And does your African have papers? I must see those as well."

ぐ ぐ ぐ

CIRO and Amidei tracked the woman as she walked down one street and then the next, moving toward the Université district on the east side of the city. She moved slowly but methodically, as if counting her steps. Surely that was how she maneuvered through the twisting avenues, he thought. Counting.

"Give me a little room to toy with her," Amidei whispered to Ciro.

"As you wish, m'lord."

Abramo moved forward, chanting a spell of confusion as he stared hard at the woman in front of him. "Eighteen, twenty-five, ninety-one, thirty-six," he said silently, willing the words into her mind. The woman stopped, put a hand to her head, and then slowly turned in a circle, sniffing the air. He inhaled with her and barely stifled a cough at the stench. Here, the streets narrowed. There was barely a path down the center, where rotten meat or refuse or excrement did not lie.

Somehow the woman managed to avoid it all with each footfall. Was she truly blind? Having found some olfactory landmark, she turned and headed down another street. As darkness crawled through the city, its citizens disappeared within their own doors. Abramo, Ciro, and the woman were three of only eight within sight.

Again he neared her, this time passing by her. "Forty-five, twenty-one, eighty-four, eighty-eight, eighteen, eight."

The woman stopped, dead in her tracks, behind him. "Who are you? Who is there?" She turned in a slow circle. "By the words within me, you are of the dark. Lost . . ." She grasped her chest, as if able to hold her beating heart. "So lost . . ."

He continued on, not looking back. She was strong, this one. It was good they were removing her now, before she joined the others. With one glance at his towering figure, two men left their perch where they had been sharing a pipe, slamming the door behind them.

Abramo turned and with a nod, gestured to Ciro to send the others from the street. He immediately turned, grabbed a man and a woman, and shoved them around the nearest corner. The street was suddenly silent but for the old woman, with Abramo and Ciro blocking any escape.

❦ ❦ ❦

"Hasani," Tessa whispered through her tears, her gasping. "There is no more time. We must go to her, *now*. She has not long. They close in as we speak. I sense her . . . and our enemy. Amidei is not alone."

Hasani did not hesitate. He turned his gelding in a tight circle and they were off, with Ugo and Gaspare right behind them. Vito jammed a fist into the jaw of the patrol captain, sending him sprawling, and spooked the next knight's mare so that he reared, sending him off the back. Both were knocked out cold.

The third knight on horseback drew his sword, but Matthieu was already upon him, jumping from his horse to the next. Both went to the cobblestones, turning over and over, each landing punches. The Les Baux knight rose, victorious, but bled from his lip.

Vito tackled the fourth knight on foot, regretting that a third punch was necessary to put him down. He did not want to kill any of them. They simply had to be away. He looked up and saw that Hasani, Tessa, Ugo, and Gaspare were already out of sight. Men and women around the well stared at them as if they were monsters. Slowly they backed away, fear lining their faces.

Vito sighed and ran toward his horse. "Daria is going to flay me alive," he muttered, jumping into the stirrup and immediately urging the horse into a gallop in one fluid motion. The Les Baux knights were directly behind him. They rode hard, leaning down behind their horses' necks, praying they would not slip on the slick cobblestones.

❦ ❦ ❦

"Tell me, old woman," Abramo said, nearing her. The night was falling fast, deliciously fast, and it was cold with the wind off the water. "Do you feel the chill?"

"I know you," she said, turning a half step behind him as he circled her like a cat playing with a mouse. "The man with the cardinal. We have no quarrel."

"I beg to differ," he said with a smile, smelling her fear-filled lie. "Our quarrel is vast. But alas, I cannot even tarry to begin our conversation. I must silence your tongue now, this night."

"Why? Why me?"

"You know why it is I hunt you," he said, stopping at last. "You are one of them. My enemy." He glanced up. There was a hint of rain upon the wind, and fast-building clouds. A storm?

"Now I know why it is that I have these words for you . . . 'The Lord rebuke you, Satan!' "

She stepped forward as he fell back from her words. " 'I saw Satan fall like lightning from heaven. I have given you authority to trample on snakes and scorpions and to overcome all the power of the enemy.' " She paused and looked upward. "Nothing shall harm me."

He turned away, running into the wall as if thrown, and then slowly faced her, hate racing through his body, his fingertips itching to grab her throat, to rip it apart before she uttered but one more word . . . he would show her harm! She would *know* harm!

"God's remnant shall be pulled from exile to carry out his mission. If I am a part of that mission, so be it. If I am not, if you succeed in killing me this night, I shall die praying for those who will. You, newcomer, *shall not be victorious*."

He rose, eager to watch her die. He took a step forward, but the sound of a sword striking another drew his attention down the narrow street.

Hasani passed Ciro, who now battled the one named Ugo, and was heading straight for Abramo, his curved blade high in the air.

The Gifted had arrived. Why had his master not warned him?

Abramo turned, saw the old woman stumbling away, already eight paces ahead, moving faster than he expected her age or blindness would allow. He must reach her, kill her, then disappear. He leaned down and, using the toe-hold of a cobblestone, set off after the woman, his left hand on the powder that would help him disappear, his right on the blade of his dagger.

He pulled the dagger from beneath the fold of his overcoat, lifted it over his right shoulder, taking aim, when a lightning bolt came down from the sky, blowing him backward down a tiny alleyway. He paused a moment on the ground, momentarily stunned, dimly hearing the scream of Hasani's horse, the sound of a girl's cry.

Abramo shook his head and rose, trying to see after the blinding flash of light. Ciro was still out there, fighting Ugo. There were only two men, the knight and the slave, and the girl was here! They had to take them, lay hold of the child and kill the woman.

He rose. It was time.

CHAPTER NINETEEN

HASANI leaped back to his feet, turning only briefly to make sure that Tessa moved. She was crying, but she was moving, rising from the cobblestones. The lightning had startled his horse, sending them both to the ground. He reached for his great, curved sword from the stones and advanced upon the alleyway, now deep with shadow, where he was sure Abramo Amidei had disappeared.

The old woman had paused down the street, hunched over as if defending herself, ten paces away. He grunted to Tessa, pointing toward the woman with his chin. The girl set off down the street, still crying in fear. "He is in there, Hasani," she whispered through her tears, edging past, keeping Hasani between her and the alley. "He is in there! He yet lives!"

Hasani knew it already. He could feel the chill of the alley, in a way that went beyond a normal city's stone cold feel. The dark was here. He let his eyes slide to the right, where Ciro battled with Ugo and where Gaspare still was on his knees, his arms stretched out to heaven in prayer. It was he who had asked for the lightning bolt, and their God had answered.

It was here he might find retribution, might find the moment to end his enemy's life. Hasani would make Abramo Amidei think about each stripe his whip had laid into Hasani's back, every punishing blow that Daria and Ambrogio and Nico had taken, before he killed him and turned toward Ciro . . .

Abramo was upon him, stronger than he expected, pushing him back, nearly taking him down. Hasani grimaced, chastising himself. He had been distracted by thoughts of revenge rather than the task at hand. He narrowly blocked a blow of Abramo's sword, stopping it just short of his neck, and then pushed away, just before the Sorcerer's dagger thrust would have pierced his belly.

Abramo advanced, his eyes piercing Hasani. "I should have killed you on the isle." He circled him. "I should have watched as Ciro flayed every last bit of your skin from your back." He smiled. "Yes, Hasani. Hate me. Hate me. It shall feed you. Feed you."

Was there a deeper shadow behind Abramo? It was suddenly so cold . . . as if snow were on the wind!

Hasani raised his sword and sliced downward and then circled and brought it down again in the other direction. Both times, Abramo narrowly avoided the blade.

"Was it you who foresaw this night? Do you fancy yourself an avenging angel, come to save an old woman?"

Hasani thrust forward, bending low on his forward knee. His sword hit something beneath Abramo's clothes, something that made the Sorcerer wince but kept it from driving inward. He whirled and wrapped his cape around Hasani's sword, sending it with a flick down the road toward the woman and child. He advanced on Hasani, his sword poised to strike, speaking as he stepped toward him. "Did you really think that you, a slave, could amount to anything? Did you think you could save the woman? I shall kill you, kill the woman, and take my time with the child. I like her fear. And then, then I shall move on to the others."

Hasani thought about his drawings. Why he and Vito and Ugo and Gaspare were not in that scene with Ciro and Abramo and Daria and Gianni.

Is this where it ended? Here? When they had just arrived in Avignon?

He gripped a dagger at his belt, behind him, slowly easing it from its perch and into his fist. He only needed to wait for the right moment . . .

The sound of horse hooves upon the cobblestones grew louder in their ears. From the shadows came three men on horseback, one bearing the flag of Les Baux. The flag fell to the ground as the knights all drew their swords, roaring their disapproval in a move designed to invoke terror in their enemies. One paused beside Ciro and Ugo to help take the hulking knight down, but the other two tore down the street toward Hasani and Abramo, with Vito in the lead.

"So you live to die another day," Amidei whispered to Hasani.

And with that, he stood straight, lowered his sword, and disappeared within a small exploding cloud of white.

Hasani threw his dagger, but it bounced off the far building's wall and fell to the ground. He looked to his left and saw that the woman and Tessa were well, Tessa lifting his heavy sword from the ground with everything she had in her, then dropping it as she saw Vito coming hard. She grabbed the woman's arm and pulled her to the side, narrowly keeping her from being stomped beneath Vito's horse's hooves. Lucien of Les Baux was right behind him.

Vito pulled the horse to a stop and circled around. "Where is he?"

"He disappeared! And yet he is still near! " Tessa cried. "I can feel him, here. Oh, he is on the move! He is running away!"

"Ciro is gone as well!" cried Ugo from up the street, throwing up his hand and sword in dismay and frustration.

Hasani took his sword from Tessa, then lifted her up toward Vito. He immediately turned, as if guarding them from the night. But the street was utterly still. No doubt city dwellers hovered behind their shutters, not daring to open them, but still watching their every move through the cracks.

Vito deposited Tessa safely behind him. "I beg you, lady," he said to the old woman, "take the knight's hand that is reaching toward you. We are here to bring you aid, not harm."

Tentatively, the old woman reached upward. In a quick move, Lucien had her settled behind him. "Who is this nobleman? Why does he menace us?" the woman asked.

"An enemy of old," Vito said. "He knew you as one of ours, and therefore wished to kill you before we reached you."

She paused. "And who are you?"

"We, m'lady, are your new family. Your protectors and friends, here to aid you in fulfilling your call. On the morrow, you shall know all."

∞ ∞ ∞

"Why did you not take me with you?" Vincenzo asked lowly.

"I thought it best to leave you to your rest," Abramo said. He moved forward and paused, bending over at the waist and gasping in pain.

"M'lord, you are hurt," Vincenzo said.

"Nay." He held out a hand, keeping Vincenzo from taking another step. "That foul man of Daria's merely managed to inflict a wound upon me." He patted the belt beneath his leggings and tentatively took the overcoat off. A bloodstain seeped across his thigh.

"M'lord!"

"Nay, nay, it is all right." Abramo sighed and rinsed a cloth in a basin of water. "The Gifted have nothing to do with this. It is a gift from Cardinal Morano, a bit of corporal mortification, my means of ensnaring him."

"We must take it off you."

"Nay. It remains where it is. To be truthful . . . I find the pain pleasurable. It has been some time since I have felt this alive."

Vincenzo sat down on the edge of a chair in the corner of the room. "And it is your means to garner the cardinal's good graces?"

"Yes. We have the five others. This cardinal demands the utmost in piety. I confessed to him that I have lain with many women and could not control my carnal urges."

"And he offered the belt as absolution."

"Indeed. In addition, a flagellant's whip. If one's mind is on the pain, if every move inflicts more, then it is rather difficult to consider being close to another."

He turned to show him his back, crisscrossed with wounds. It reminded Vincenzo of Daria, and of Hasani, of how flayed their backs had been in the prison cells of Abramo's castle. They made Abramo's wounds appear as mere scratches, but he did not doubt his master had suffered under the whip.

"And so the cardinal will see your stripes and remain confident in your piety, regardless of what the Gifted claim."

"Indeed. By my own stripes, I am healed." Abramo reached for a fresh, clean jerkin and eased it over his broad shoulders. "And the good man has also agreed to find me a wife."

"A wife?" Vincenzo asked. "You do not prefer to choose among your own faithful?"

"Nay," Abramo said. "It will be good this way. The Church can choose my wife, the one who will carry my bloodline and be blessed. Should my new wife one day wish to join us in our ceremonies, so much the better. Yet she'll have to understand that in the dark, of the dark, I am shared by more than one woman . . . I am the lord of all."

"Your people must have access," Vincenzo said dryly.

"And I to them." He pulled on his surcoat and stared into the mirror. "It is a suitable arrangement. My hope is that the good cardinal chooses one of his own kin for me. That will tie him more firmly to my side."

Vincenzo shook his head. "You venture very close to the line, Abramo."

Abramo smiled. "It is daring, yes. But I always flourish where I dare. Now come. You must accompany me to the cardinal's home. He will welcome you, along with me, for dinner. I shall report to him about my progress with the belt, and we will be fully prepared to meet the Gifted on the morrow . . . or when they dare to near. They are coming in waves, and we must be prepared for each one. The men and girl were not the first to arrive."

"Who else is here?"

"Ambrogio Rossellino. He is at work in the *palais*."

Vincenzo paused, obviously surprised.

"Our enemies are not foolish. They will use every asset they have. Hasani knew what would transpire with the old woman," Abramo said bitterly, gruffly pulling on his gloves. "They were surely an advance party—by the look of them, they'd ridden hard all day."

"So we can expect the priest, the de Capezzanas, and others later."

"They will not tarry. We have seen how they favor staying together. They shall arrive this night or on the morrow at the latest."

"And you believe we are ready?"

"Oh, yes. Here, the Gifted shall meet their end. We shall haunt their every move, make their nights a misery. Use the Church to destroy them. And if the Church fails us, we shall do it ourselves." He whirled out of the house and strode toward the stables.

Vincenzo paused. He was too old for this. His mind, his body cried out for rest, for a place by the fire. This constant battle . . . and Abramo's most fervent desire to kill every last one of the Gifted wearied him. He did not feel sorrow or fear, but neither did he feel joy or pleasure. He felt dead. On leaden feet, he moved after his master, thinking back to the last time he had felt alive, felt pleasure. When had he last known love?

Daria, before she had seen that he was now owned by Amidei and the master. Before that, Tatiana. For a while, in Siena, when Abramo was first mentoring him, he had experienced power and pleasure like none before. But it was fleeting. Every attempt to surpass those weeks was met with defeat, frustration. His wealth, his power had certainly grown; never had his bank accounts been so fat, the business potential so grand. But every day, every hour felt like nothing more than more hours spent, acting as he was expected to act. What he had thought was to be his route toward glory, strength, failed him.

"How do you fare?" Abramo asked, staring at him in consternation. He had paused beside the stable door, watching Vincenzo move across the courtyard, lost in thought.

"I am fine, m'lord."

Abramo clasped his shoulder and looked deep into his eyes. "You are in need of our ceremony. It will give you strength. We will sup from the cup and eat our fill of our devoted. Wait until you see this new cave. It is vast and magical, with golden stalactites clinging to the roof. Perfect for the mysteries of our ceremonies. It is the master's plan that we draw more than ever before . . . even now, our people speak of our secret meeting. They will come from afar. And we shall be renewed, you and I, ready for the battle at hand. Do not be troubled, brother, all will be well."

Vincenzo forced a small smile to his face and nodded. Satisfied, Abramo turned. But all Vincenzo could concentrate on was the swirling, dark eddies of his master's cape.

Chapter Twenty

AMBROGIO walked behind Cardinal Stefani, watching as his swirling crimson robe curved and flowed with each step, wondering how he might catch that on either canvas or wall. His work had new depth and vitality now, mayhap because he had experienced more of light and dark firsthand. Simone was openly admiring, seeming to hold little competition in his heart, only wanting to learn. Their days moved swiftly, and for hours at a time, Ambrogio lost himself in his work. He was thankful for the respite, for a taste of the world he had known before, a world he was glad to return to. Here he had stature, reputation, purpose. Following Daria and Piero and Gianni, he had known holy cause, but also pain and agony like he had never before suffered.

He glanced behind them, down the hall, thinking that Abramo Amidei would magically appear merely because the memory had slipped through his mind, setting his heart to pounding. But he was not in sight. In fact, Ambrogio had not seen him since that day in the Grand Tinel.

Cardinal Stefani waited at the doorway of the chapel, a question on his face as he looked back toward Ambrogio, who had slipped behind.

They had left the rest of the Grand Tinel to the work of apprentices, and checked on them daily. But their attention now turned toward one of the pope's private chapels, a lesser oratory than the Grand Chapel, but a lovely abode to be dedicated to the two Saint Johns—the north and east walls to depict Saint John the Baptist, forerunner of the Messiah; the south and west walls to depict Saint John the Evangelist, apostle and messenger to the world. He and Simone had spent all night on charcoal sketches, swirling, rough outlines of figures and placement, the beginnings of an architectural rendering to present to the cardinal, and after him, Pope Cornelius himself.

Simone's Saint John the Evangelist was fleshier, depicted like a man lauded and honored in every city he traveled through. Ambrogio's Saint John the Baptist was leaner, stronger, somewhat like Vito—a man who could survive under harsh conditions. Ambrogio wished he could bring Daria, Gianni, Father Piero, and Vito in to come and model for them when the Gifted arrived. It would gain them a sense of familiarity for the vast *palais*, a toehold before the battle was upon them.

If Cardinal Stefani approved of his direction, of course. It always came down to this—the wooing of the one in charge. Every chapel, every basilica, every noble hall he had ever painted required this step. The only difference was that Cardinal Stefani was a true patron of the arts, humble and accepting and encouraging. Never before had Ambrogio met a man such as he. It made him want to paint in these hallowed halls until the end of his days.

The cardinal allowed Ambrogio to enter and followed quickly on his heels. He was excited to see what the two artists were to present.

Three easels were set up in preparation. Simone moved to light five torches on the raw walls, illuminating every corner of the room. The sketches had been done on a series of light wood panels, canvases on which they would make their presentation. Ambrogio began first.

"Here on the easels, you can see a sampling of the pigments and dyes we have chosen for the frescoes. There will be spots of bright colors, but we are mostly seeking a harmony of colors. Since the figures will be predominantly pictured in natural settings, this will be simply accomplished."

"Good," the cardinal said, already moving on to the next easel.

"We plan to paint the Baptist to the north and east walls, over here," Simone said, waving his arms up to their left, "and the Evangelist over here," he said, moving to the right.

The cardinal bent low to look at each easel, one depicting in miniature the scenes that Ambrogio would take lead on—the Baptist, from birth to beheading—then the scenes Simone would take lead on—the Evangelist, from vocation to Jesus' recommendation of him to the Virgin.

When he straightened, they moved to replace the overview sketches with more detailed rough sketches of each panel, each scene.

"Their faces," Cardinal Stefani said, standing back, chin in hand. "Their eyes . . . is it not a bit too . . . close? Too intimate? Should they not all be a bit more passive? As if they were above it all? I know that Pope Cornelius prefers—"

"Passive?" Ambrogio said in frustration. "How could they be passive?" He moved to the scene of the women with the babe, John. "Elizabeth had felt this child move, leap, when his cousin drew near! She is beyond her prime, and yet pregnant . . . and Mary, she had the *future of the world within her womb*. How could they be passive?"

"Ambrogio . . ." Simone said in warning.

Cardinal Stefani held up his hands. "Be at peace. I am only saying that these were people God used for a grand and glorious purpose . . . would that not set them apart?"

Ambrogio sighed. Mayhap this churchman was no different from any other. "Set apart? You mean when Salome asked for the Baptist's head? Or when the executioners sliced it from his neck, presented it on a plate?" Cardinal Stefani blanched, but Ambrogio continued on. "Do you believe that those people, Cardinal, were set apart? Nay, they were foul, common, sinful. *Us*. We need to show them as such."

He riffled through the drawings and brought up the picture of Jesus upon the cross, the two Marys at his feet, John to his left. He stared at it for a long moment, as if he were being transported through time and place to stand with them. It grieved him, every time, to paint scenes of his Lord's death. He turned to show the cardinal, holding it in front of his chest. "My lord Cardinal, surely we cannot do one more depiction of this darkest of days, without feeling what these people must have felt. Trust me, please. Trust us. If we can show emotion, show the passion for a portion of what it truly was, it will move all who enter."

Cardinal Stefani stared hard at him for a moment, angered by his insolence but softening in the face of his obvious devotion. He bit his lower lip and then dropped his hand from his chin, turning to go. He paused at the doorway. "I shall bring the Holy Father by on the morrow after breaking our fast. You shall present your ideas to him. But Simone must do it. He is aware of how we must speak in the Holy Father's presence. You," he said, pointing a finger of warning at Ambrogio, "must remain silent. Agreed?"

Simone was nodding. Ambrogio hesitated a moment and then gave his assent.

"One more thing. Who is your model for the executioner?"

Ambrogio turned in confusion to the panel on the floor, to a knight who was striking the old man's neck with a massive sword. There was no detail, but it was undeniable who he had been thinking of when he sketched it. Thankfully the cardinal had not noticed the others. "Oh, no one in particular, my lord Cardinal," he said smoothly. "Why? Does he appear familiar?"

"Indeed," said the man, lowering his brow in consternation, unable to place him. "Well, no matter. See you on the morrow. Good work, gentlemen."

He disappeared into the dark hallway, and Simone came close to clap Ambrogio on the back. "I think we convinced him. It will go a long way in convincing the pope." His eyes slid to the executioner's panel. "Who is your model? Come. You can tell me."

Ambrogio smiled and raised an eyebrow. "You will see his face clearly when the fresco dries."

Simone shook his head. "Now, Brogi, if you get us in trouble—"

"It will be well," Ambrogio said, turning to stare at the panel. "The man who will serve as my model will never give this chapel more than a passing glance. Let us just say that he is less than devout."

The men moved about the chapel, dousing the torches and setting them back in their iron holders. Simone promised a shortcut and they moved out into the hallway, through a vestry lined with ancient manuscripts and royal robes. Ambrogio paused, staring at the hundreds of volumes that lined the shelves, many of which would undoubtedly boast lovely illuminations. If only he had time to look through them . . . but Simone was already entering another hallway. Ambrogio sighed and followed him down a narrow staircase.

CHAPTER TWENTY-ONE

THEY had arrived after nightfall, a magnificent retinue of fine knights and horseflesh, the red and white peacock crest of Daria's family on one flank, the white sixteen-pointed star on a bed of red of Armand's family on the other.

In the end, even Agata and Roberto and Nico insisted they come along. Daria rode across a beautiful brown gelding, with Bormeo on one arm. Beside her was Count Armand, and behind them the Lord and Lady Devenue.

Although the city gates were closed for the night, the nobles had little trouble entering. In fact, the guards, seeing the flag of Les Baux, opened them wide, and they never paused.

Armand had sent word ahead to the Duke and Duchess Richardieu at their estate in Villeneuve-des-Avignon about their impending arrival. The new city across the Rhône was where many nobles chose to live, outside the stench of Avignon proper. Daria and Gianni had disagreed with Armand's plan for a grand entrance, wishing to slip quietly around the city, but Armand had won them over.

"We enter battle. We must never signal anything but utmost strength and stature. I always enter Villeneuve through Avignon, announcing my presence. We shall not hide now. Besides, the entire city will know of our arrival by morn anyway. Why not use it?"

He set off, and they followed him, their countly herald, seemingly appointed by God himself. And so they marched through the city streets, largely silent at this late hour. But here and there people opened their windows to gaze upon the processional, wondering if they be but politician or pilgrim.

In some ways, the Richardieu mansion in Villeneuve-des-Avignon was immensely more comfortable than the Les Baux castle hewn from the stony cliff. The rooms were larger and more luxurious. There was a constant fresh breeze off the water, a welcome, cooling air, not the deep chill that pervaded the castle. The meeting places were larger, more welcoming. And if the Gifted thought they had been waited on hand and foot in Les Baux, it would be nothing compared to this noble mansion in the city.

Gianni widened his eyes toward Daria, telling her he was reluctantly surprised by the wealth shown here. But in his eyes, she detected admiration and appreciation as well as surprise. They emerged in the central hall, a massive room alight in the wash of a hundred candles, with a staircase that curved upward on two sides, like the welcoming arms of a maiden.

It was there that the Duke and Duchess Richardieu found them, sweeping down that same staircase to cry out their greetings and share embraces. By the time they were done, each and every one of the Gifted felt welcomed, at home.

The duchess turned to the chief steward, standing ready at her side. "Laurent, have your people see Lord Rieu, Lord and Lady Devenue, Sir Gianni, and Lady Daria to the north rooms. Give them the larger suites. Ensconce the priest, Father Piero, beside them, and the others in rooms that extend from there."

"Yes, m'lady," said the steward, bobbing in a quick bow. Six men emerged and took their bags and satchels from them, and the steward led the way.

"I shall see you all in the morning, at first light," said Armand from the hallway as they parted. "Let us take our rest and we shall make our plans come daybreak."

Daria and Gianni nodded their good night and followed a maid to the right. "You have traveled a good distance this day, m'lady," the maid said to Daria.

"A good distance, yes," Daria agreed. She laid a hand on her stomach, trying to hide her grimace.

"Are you hungry?" asked the maid. "I can fetch you some soup, bread, and wine immediately."

Daria eyed Gianni, seeing him turn with a look of displeasure. She had little on her mind other than disrobing and falling into a deep sleep, but her husband was probably hungry. "Please, mademoiselle. That would be most welcome."

"Right away, m'lady. I shan't be more than a bit." She bobbed in another curtsey, and Gianni shut the doors behind her. Daria was already crossing the wide, marble floors to double doors, visible in the light of the candle left behind by the maid. She opened the doors inward and gasped.

Gianni was behind her, taking her bag from her shoulder, tossing it across a bench at the foot of their bed, and then returning to encircle her from behind at the rail. Beneath them, the Rhône wound in a cascading ribbon, silver in the almost-full moonlight. It was surrounded by old cotton-woods, thick at both trunk and branch, winter dormant, standing as quiet, regal sentinels on guard.

Her cheek was cold to the north wind, the *mistral* as the locals called it, but Daria could not tear herself away. Across the river, beyond the bridge of Bénezet, a bridge that had weathered centuries of storm and floodwater, was the imposing Palais de le Pape. Her towers climbed into the half-lit sky, and Daria could even make out the small shapes of guards atop her walkways.

"It has been a very long time since a place had such a firm sense of home, for me," Daria said, leaning her head to the side as her husband edged in.

"But we barely know the Richardieus."

"Mayhap it is that we took part in Claude's healing . . ."

"It is good to see him, is it not? Or rather, *hear* him, not shouting at everyone."

"Thrilling! Yes, I think that is part of this sensation within me . . . but Gianni, *home*. Think of it. I long to return to Toscana, to see people I know and love. To have you there with me."

Gianni hesitated for a long moment, wrapping his arms more tightly about her. "What if . . . what if we are on this road, constantly moving about, forever?"

"Forever?" She frowned and turned to face him, studying him in the dim light.

Gianni raised his head and stared out toward the bridge, the river, for several breaths. "Daria, this is not a stretch in the road for us. It is *the* road. God has placed us upon it. We will walk it as long as he continues to allow us to place one foot in front of the other."

Daria listened to his words, heard them as the slow wisdom of faith, but cast them aside. "I do not wish for a lifetime of this. I wish for quiet. Solitude. Time with you beside a slow, sparking fire in the hearth. To sup with friends. To worship." She turned, looking up into his eyes, reaching up to run her fingertips over his hard chiseled jawline, to his ear. "Oh, husband. I long for peace."

He did not smile, just nodded softly. "Peace is here. With you. In the eye of the storm." And then he bent down to kiss her. "At least we travel this road together."

"Together," she whispered, stepping up on her toes to kiss him again.

"Daria," he said, turning her gently back toward the river, pointing out six horses approaching.

"Tessa!" she cried, rushing past him and down the stairs.

Gianni smiled, leaning his arms down on the railing, watching as Vito, Ugo, Gaspare, the two knights of Les Baux, a girl, and an old woman crossed a small bridge over a creek and entered the Richardieu mansion's gates.

But his smile faded as he saw Tessa turn in the saddle behind Vito, search the woods, and jump off, despite the knight's barked warning.

Gianni searched the woods beside the river, those that extended upward, to the cliffs and on toward Montpellier. What danger did she sense? Whom did she fear? Was Amidei already near?

ʘ ʘ ʘ

"STEADY," Abramo said lowly to Ciro and Vincenzo. They could plainly see the knights arrive upon the road below, and across the narrow valley, Sir de Capezzana and his new bride, Daria, on the small portico. "We will have our opportunity with them in time," Abramo said easily. "They shall be invited to Prince Maximilien's ball, given in honor of the pope. If that doesn't force their hand, we shall. Given their inability to hold their tongues, they shall soon find themselves in the Court of Apostolic Causes, before the Lord's Commissioner. We hold, gentlemen. Hold. And allow their Church, their precious Church, to be their own undoing. We shall merely aid them upon their way. Taunt them. Tease them forward, before they know they've entered a trap."

He laughed, and his laughter echoed across the stippled waters of the Rhône.

They watched as the girl child, Tessa, jumped off the horse from behind Vito and stared up the hillside, as if she could see them. Her arms were at her side, her chin lifted, staring as if she could see in the dark.

"It's unnerving, how she does that," Vincenzo said in a whisper, shifting in his saddle. "Do you believe she can actually see us?"

"Senses us. Not actually sees," he said, staring down the hillside, un-moving, as if memorizing every inch of the girl. She stood there, her silhou-ette visible in the moonlight. The knight joined her, looking upward, hand on the hilt of his sword. "She feels us, knows we are here. It is most unfor-tunate she is in the Gifted's company. Imagine, a small child being such an obstacle for us. But a child shall not be invited to the ball, so they shall not have their fierce little guard to warn them of our presence."

"You are certain that the Richardieus and their guests shall be invited to the ball?" Vincenzo asked.

"My friend," Abramo said, turning his horse and setting off toward the bridge of Bénezet, "the invitation is already inside the Richardieu mansion. Les Baux dare not decline. They need Prince Maximilien on their side, and if Armand refuses, it shall be an outright slap in the face of both prince and pope. Nay, Richardieu's household, and all honored guests within, will be equally obligated. We shall see your old friends, your beloved 'niece' Daria, in two nights' time. Isn't it interesting," he said, pausing, still looking forward with his horse, "that it is the very same night as our ceremony?" He turned in the saddle and eyed Vincenzo, although his face was in deep shadow. "The tide is about to turn again, my friends. It is turning while we yet ride back into Avignon. It is almost as if the mighty Rhône might shift directions as we ride across it."

ᘓ ᘓ ᘓ

Nico and Roberto, having heard the riders approach, tore down the stair-way, past Daria, and out the front door of the grand house. Daria watched as Roberto trailed behind and felt a pang of guilt. Months ago, in Siena, she had promised to see to his well-being, his healing. His awkward gait had become more pronounced in the last months, even as he grew taller. Now probably nine years of age, he was in a growth spurt, which had made his deformity more apparent.

As a younger child, Roberto had had a serious break in the leg; because he was as a beggar child of Il Campo, it had been poorly set, if it had been set at all. The result was that his lower leg and foot were at an odd angle. Pain was evident in him from hip to ankle, and for the hundredth time, Daria wondered how he had made the trip from Siena to Venezia all on his own—intent on warning the Gifted of Vincenzo del Buco's treachery and the crimes he had wrought against her household. It was obvious that God had a purpose in placing him among them. Roberto had aided their escape from Amidei's dark isle, helped them collect the letter and the glass pieces of the map. "Do you wish for me to heal him, Lord God?" she whispered, rushing down the stairs and finally exiting the manor. She pulled her cape close at the neck.

There was no answering tug to her heart, the becalming, warming feeling when she knew she was to do as the Lord bid. She groaned inwardly, watching the children greet one another. She would need to consult a surgeon physician, someone to assist her with rebreaking the bones to try to repair the deformity. It would mean months of recuperation. Risk of infection. Learning to walk again.

"When, Lord?" she whispered, opening her arms and smiling at Tessa as the girl ran to her. When would they have that kind of time? Rest? Calm? They faced the biggest battle ahead of them, one that very well might demand sacrifice—of cause, of purpose, mayhap their very lives. What would happen to the children if this quest ended upon the Inquisitor's stake?

And dear, loyal Roberto, so patient, so deserving. Why could it not be him that the Lord chose to heal? Her thoughts went back to Vincenzo's beautiful wife, Tatiana. Of others, deserving, true to the faith, that God did not choose to heal. It confounded and frustrated her, but as always, she gave in to the trust in her Maker, the One who could see far beyond in time to his own goals and purposes. She would not doubt him. She would not. But it did not mean she would not still give in to irritation over his timing.

She hugged Tessa, holding her close, so thankful to be reunited again, and reached out to lay an appreciative hand upon Vito's arm for bringing her back safely. Father Piero appeared at her side, ready to greet the others, and behind them, Gianni.

Vito bowed with a grin and then turned so she could see an old woman behind him. "M'lady, Captain, Father, may I introduce you to one of our own? We have found the last of the prophesied Gifted, and narrowly succeeded in saving her from Lord Amidei. Josephine Fontaine, meet Lady Daria de Capezzana, Captain Gianni de Capezzana, and Father Piero."

The older woman reached out a shaking hand to touch Daria's cheek, pausing before her for a moment, then turned to Father Piero, who took both of her hands in his with a smile. After a moment, she turned to Gianni, and reached up to rest her age-spotted hand on his shoulder, high above her. She nodded, tears running down her face. "Do you know? Do you know how long it is that I have waited for you all?"

Her trembling suddenly was so intense that she looked about to fall. Gaspare neared, holding her arm, then wrapping an arm around her as he gestured inward. He turned to Daria. "Let us get to know one another by the warmth of the fire, shall we, m'lady?"

"Of course. Josephine, are you ill?"

"No, m'lady. 'Tis difficult to describe. More weak with relief."

"Please. Come inside. Nico, please go and see if the maids in the kitchen can bring us some tea and bread." The boy set off as she bid.

Gaspare led Josephine into the manor, and Daria and Gianni shared a knowing look behind the couple's back. Was it merely age that brought them together? Father Piero, hands clasped behind his back, turned to lift an eyebrow at Daria and Gianni, obviously seeing the same thing.

There had been a similar tie between Agata and Gaspare at first, but they were plainly nothing more than dear friends, drawing together over the commonality of age. Gaspare led Josephine toward the hearth, set her upon a bench, and gently took her ragged shawl from her shoulders and wrapped a new, soft woolen blanket around her. The woman shivered, but Daria could see that it was not from fear. Deep wrinkles lined her forehead, as if she had fretted for decades, but her opaque, blind blue eyes had an unnerving sense of sight about them.

Daria forced a smile, even though the blue eyes reminded her of Rune. *And so you bring us another warrior with eyes of blue,* she said to her God. Josephine accepted the cup of tea from the maid, took a sip, and seemed to sense the two knights of Les Baux and the others approach.

She spoke in Provençal, and Daria quietly translated her words for the children. "How is it that you know me? How is it that you knew that I was in danger?"

"We have sought you for some time," Father Piero returned in Provençal. "And there were many clues that you were both female and older." He glanced at Count Armand, remembering the statue. The face upon that pillar was uncannily similar to the prophetess before them now. Count Armand's mouth was slightly agape.

"Clues? Such as?"

Gaspare returned from his room and held out a wooden box, one his mother had given him as a child, with the peacock carved into the top. "Hold this in your hands."

Josephine set aside her cup of tea and took the box in both hands. Her fingers, with ragged, dirty nails, traced the carving in the top of the lid. "A bird?"

"A peacock. Our lady's family crest, visible in many clues left for us by saints that have gone before us," Piero returned steadily. "By God himself."

Josephine nodded and then slowly opened the lid. One at a time, she fingered each figurine, recognizing each shape before handing them to Gaspare. The figurines had been playthings for Gaspare, given to him fifty years before. An old fisherman, a small priest with long head, a tall African warrior with curved sword, a young girl, a lady, a knight. The Gifted.

One more figure remained within the box, but Josephine was weeping, her small shoulders shaking. Gaspare knelt beside her with head bowed, lending her comfort without touch, silently encouraging her to do what she must.

With a shaking hand, she pulled the final figure from the box: an old woman. Tears slipped down her cheeks, and her face was alight in wonder. "How is it that you know this is not coincidence?"

Father Piero let out a scoffing sound. "Come now, woman. I can hear that you do not believe that is so."

"And as Piero said, it is but one of many, many clues that our God has given us," Daria said, kneeling beside Gaspare. "You are a part of us. It is why Amidei wished to kill you and your God spared you."

Josephine nodded, tears still slipping down her weathered cheeks. "Vito and Gaspare told me all about you, the Gifted. I am your prophetess. I know it as surely as I do my own fingers, that I belong with you. Do you know how long I have looked for you? All my life, my head has been filled with the Word, the truth. But all along, I've waited for this feeling."

"And what is that?" Daria asked.

"Home. Family. Belonging." Her last word cracked in her throat, and a sound of such heartbreak and loneliness escaped that it made all of them take a collective breath of sorrow.

"Well I know of your plight," Gaspare said, taking the lady's hand. "I, too, was alone, wondering why God would give me a gift that set me apart, left me without kin or connection. But those days are over. Here, among us, you have come home. We are your new family."

Daria smiled and laughed a little, wiping away her own tears. "There is much more to tell you, Josephine. We shall spend the day together on the morrow, all of us, so that you shall know our story to date, and we shall know yours. You must know why we're here."

Josephine nodded gravely, her smile fading. "You are called to the Palais de le Pape, just as I am."

"Indeed," Father Piero said. "We know not where our journey will end, or if we shall escape with our lives, only that we are to do this and no other. It shall have bearing on the course of the Church, indeed, upon all of humanity."

"Not to lend any pressure," Vito put in. He grinned at them all. " 'Tis a grand adventure, if nothing more."

Josephine smiled as Gaspare translated the knight's words. "Oh, 'tis much more." She gazed around the room at them all. "You believe that this is where it all ends. I can feel it within you. But my friends, my new family, this is where it shall all begin."

Chapter Twenty-two

"They have arrived, Your Holiness," said Cardinal Bordeau to the pope, bowing low in front of his chair and leaning forward to kiss his ring. Morning light streamed through leaded glass windows at their right, in the private papal apartments.

"Oh?" said Cornelius absently, settling back into his thronelike chair, a bit tired after morning mass. "And who might that be?"

"Those Cardinal Boeri spoke of. Those I have warned you about," said Cardinal Bordeau. The pope flicked his fingers toward him, and the cardinal stood and took a seat. "Those who believe their coming is foretold. They believe they are in possession of a lost letter of Saint Paul, or at the very least, Apollos, a letter that bespeaks of power within the people. Do you remember my speaking of this matter?"

"We do."

"They arrived in the company of the Count Rieu des Baux, and have already collected quite the following among the Provençal nobility."

"And how have they accomplished such a feat?"

"Apparently," the cardinal said, sitting forward, eyes aglitter, "there is some truth to their prophecy. Word has it that the lady does indeed hold the power to heal; the priest, the gift of wisdom; the knight, the gift of faith. There is even one among them who can produce miraculous acts, and a child who can discern light from dark. What's more, there is one of our own city now among them . . . an old, blind woman who claims to be a prophetess."

"It is bound to be nothing more than magic," the pope said, scowling.

"Such spiritual powers have not been seen since the days of the apostles. And never would our Lord God deign to gift feeble women as such. It is preposterous. And dangerous."

"Agreed," said the cardinal.

The pope settled his chin in his hand, thinking. "Did Cardinal Boeri intercept them? Is he with them?"

"He is."

"They must know that this is not a safe place for them. Why not hide out among the people as the Cathars did? Why present themselves to us as sheep to the slaughter?"

Cardinal Bordeau gave him a rueful smile. "I believe they hope to persuade you to support them."

Pope Cornelius laughed, his brow lifting. "Such audacity!"

"Not if one believes oneself holy and called," said the cardinal.

The pope sat back in his chair, studying him. "They will end up in the Court of Apostolic Causes. Their judgment shall be final, might cost them their very lives."

"You must tread carefully, Holiness," said the cardinal, rising and pacing toward the window. "There is word of a miraculous healing for Lord Devenue. He has just entered Avignon."

"Dimitri Devenue?" the pope said, mouth agape.

"Indeed," nodded the cardinal. "Again, this is not all rumor. Their claims are not without merit. Lord Devenue was grotesque in the end, merely waiting in self exile, praying to die, these last two years."

"Hideous was his deformity."

"And now 'tis entirely gone. His head is as any other man's. He is thin, but handsome as ever. And he has wed the Countess Rieu des Baux."

"They wed?" said the pope, a bit surprised. "We do not recall receiving an invitation. Not that we would have attended, but 'tis customary . . ."

"Indeed. It was rather sudden. Cardinal Boeri presided in Les Baux, much to the consternation of Cardinal Saucille."

"Hmm. The good cardinal de Vaticana de Roma came to us, certain that he could guide this group, bring them into line. He believes they might be an asset to us, not heretics on the prowl."

"That would be ideal," Cardinal Bordeau allowed, rising to pace, chin in hand. "Ideal. But from what I know of them, there would be much work for the cardinal to do. This group does not seem like those who wish to conform. There is a rumor that the countess and Lord Devenue married without sanction or blessing—that Cardinal Boeri conducted rites already spoken by their common priest."

The pope's eyes widened with displeasure.

"And we've seen before what religious fervor can do for heretics . . . and how the masses gravitate toward them."

"Much has transpired of late, it seems, at Les Baux. Yes, much has transpired. How is it that you know such intimacies?"

The cardinal smiled. "It is my aim never to fail you, Holy Father. My network of people loyal to the papacy has grown quite vast. Well beyond Provence."

"Hmm. As evidenced by the handsome sum that goes to pay for it."

"Well worth it, to be prepared, no? Lord and Lady Devenue entered the city last night, and are now at the Richardieu manor on the river with her brother—and this intriguing group we have spoken of. Word has also reached us that the doge intends to arrive on the morrow, along with Conte and Contessa Morassi de Venezia."

"For Prince Maximilien's menagerie ball?" the pope asked. "That is a long way to travel for the festivities."

"There are others. The Bonaparts of Tarascon, the Blanchettes of Uzes, the Duvins of Nimes."

"And all of these nobles have ties to this group?"

"Indeed."

The pope rested the back of his head against his high, carved chair and stared upward. His light brown eyes flitted across the ceiling, searching the massive wooden beams as if they could give him guidance. "It is unsettling," he mused. "They have amassed enough power that we cannot quietly deal with them."

"Exactly their intention, Holiness."

"And so we are forced to catch them in some outright act of heresy that no noble would dare defend."

"Indeed."

Pope Cornelius steepled his fingers and sat in silence a moment longer. "They shall be at the menagerie ball?"

"Yes, Your Holiness."

"Be certain that we are seated near one another, will you?"

"Consider it done, Your Holiness."

The man turned to go, and Cornelius waved away his secretary and guard, eager to be alone. Seeing the pope's face, the last guard turned and closed the double doors behind him. Cornelius stared at the wooden doors, remembering copies of a forbidden letter . . . hidden deep within his own library. Could it all possibly be true? Prophecy unfolding before him? He grimaced. This would become quite a mess before it was over. He could feel it in his bones. Wearily he rose, went to the window, and lowered to his knees to pray.

ಈ ಈ ಈ

"ABSOLUTELY not," Gianni said, pacing in front of Count Armand. "We shall not attend a masked ball. We shall not be able to know who is friend and who is foe!"

"We really have no choice," Armand said. "I have already sent my men to Marseilles to retrieve two suitable animals for the pope's new menagerie. You must sit immediately, along with the others, and be fitted for new clothing. What you wear is hardly suitable for a ball."

"We shall not attend," Gianni said.

Armand rose and leaned closer to him, pointing a finger. "You shall."

"Nay," Gianni said, leaning a little closer.

Piero, roused by the raised voices, entered the room and edged between the men. "What are we not attending?" he asked quietly.

Gianni held Armand's gaze a moment longer, seething, and then turned away with a sigh. He ran his hand through his hair and then pointed toward Armand. "The count wants us all to attend Prince Maximilien's menagerie ball. For the pope."

Piero studied Armand, who was plainly having difficulty holding his tongue, and then looked to Gianni. "Is it not what we are here for? To reach the pope with the good news? To help enlighten him? Bring him into the new era of the Church?"

Gianni laughed without mirth. "And this is the way, Father? We engage him at a dance? To say nothing of the danger of such a show. Think of it! We enter, all in mask and finery. Who else do you think shall attend?"

"Abramo Amidei," Piero said evenly.

"And his minions. They will seize every opportunity to get to us."

"But we shall be surrounded by nobles," Piero said.

Gianni paused. "You are not considering attending . . ."

"At some point we must engage the pope, Gianni. Why not come bearing gifts?" Piero looked over his shoulder at Count Armand, who was visibly relaxing with the priest's support. "It will be an affront to the pope if all honored guests within the Richardieu manor do not attend the festivities. Count Armand is right—we cannot do anything but attend. So we may as well make the most of it."

"Do you not remember what transpired the last time we attended a public dance?" Gianni asked, visibly paling. "Do you not *remember*?"

ob ob ob

DARIA fingered the elegant invitation and carefully lettered font of the words, and stared over the small portico that looked out at the Rhône. She remembered the ball to which her husband referred in his fury last night—when she and Hasani were abducted and the Morassi mansion burned above the curving Grand Canal. She stared out at the river of Provence, high and sparkling in the winter sun, remembering the Venetian waters.

The seamstress took her hips in hand and forced her to straighten. It was her second fitting for her gown. Daria frowned down at her. No servant had dared to touch her so.

The seamstress caught her look of disapproval but ignored it, concentrating at the task at hand. Word had come down that all ladies were to wear the finest dress possible, with a bit of wild animal skin worked into the creation somewhere. Men were to do the same with their coats. Every seamstress in the city had been working deep into the night for weeks.

"It is as if we prepare for some vast drama," Daria said. "Is the pope so bored with the work of the kingdom that he must turn to the exotic?"

Josephine stood beside her, her hands constantly running over the elegant fabric of her gown, still slightly aghast that she wore such finery at all. " 'Tis not the pope, but those who influence him. Deep within him beats the heart of a true disciple, a man of God. But he is led astray, more and more, by the wealth and deceit of others."

"It is encouraging that you believe he remains true, deep within. If I had whatever I wished at my fingertips, and the devil whispered in my ear, it would be difficult to defend myself." Her thoughts went to Abramo, his whisperings. She closed her eyes, remembering how near she had come to falling, failing her Lord and giving in to the dark lord.

"The dark one is insidious," said Josephine. "He uses any edge he can to get between us and our Savior. Sometimes, even truth."

"Indeed." Daria glanced at her. Could this one, too, read her thoughts? She had often wondered if Piero had the gift.

"You have come close to the dark," Josephine said quietly, still staring blindly ahead of her. She picked up pauses in speech as Daria relied on expression to read what people chose *not* to say.

"Yes. The same man who sought to kill you in the streets was the same that hunted me. I was his prisoner for some time."

"Until the Lord found a way to free you."

Daria nodded, already tired of the conversation. She did not wish to remember those days. It made her fear what was ahead. Seeing Amidei again. Gianni had already warned her that they were likely to encounter him at the ball the next night. She laid a hand on her stomach, suddenly queasy.

"You are ill, m'lady?" asked the seamstress, looking up at her in alarm.

Daria tried to take a deep breath, then ran for the deck and vomited over the side. She returned, thinking back to how long it had been since she had had an appetite, how the very thought of food made her feel ill. Since they had set their course for Avignon, she thought, or soon thereafter. It was most likely the grief, the trauma of the last few months, the concern over what was ahead. Even in the midst of the joy of her union with Gianni.

"I do hope you did not muss your dress," said the seamstress.

"I did not," Daria said in irritation. "And I am well, thank you for your concern."

The seamstress gave her a rueful smile and resumed her pinning of the hem when Daria again stood upon the small platform.

"You are well," Josephine said with a small smile. "How long have you been our brave captain's bride?"

"Little more than a week now," Daria said.

"And already carrying his child. Blessed are you."

Daria whipped her head around and stared at the woman. "Carrying . . . nay. That is not possible."

"Oh? Then it is normal for you to feel so ill?"

"It is the upheaval, the difficulties we have faced. I mourn two of our knights. They were killed by Amidei."

"Oh," Josephine said. But her opaque blue eyes rested on Daria, waiting.

Daria turned away from her, feeling the older woman's piercing gaze as suddenly too intimate. As if she were not blind, but rather could see in an extraordinary fashion. Slowly she lifted her eyes to the mirror before her. Her mind raced, thinking back to the last time her menses had passed, more than five weeks now. The stomach upset, the ache in her breasts when the seamstress pulled the bodice tight . . . And then she ran again, this time making it only as far as the chamber pot.

She sat down on the edge of the bed and turned to look upon Josephine. " 'Tis not possible. You see, I am . . . I am barren." Her words emerged in little more than a whisper.

Josephine's eyebrows shot up and she gave her a small smile. "Not any longer, m'lady."

It was too soon after their wedding night. Too soon to be sensing the first signs of pregnancy. Wasn't it? Daria lifted a hand to her brow and stared at the wall, at delicate paintings of flowers and vines that filled false architectural panels. Was it even possible? Might God have blessed her at last with a child? And how could she forfeit her life if it meant forfeiting a babe as well?

She turned back to Josephine and eyed the seamstress, who had turned to Josephine's hem in her absence, ignoring them as if this were naught but idle talk. "It is imperative you not tell anyone of this. Yet."

Josephine remained facing forward. "I cannot tell a lie, m'lady. It is not in me."

"I am not asking you to lie. I am asking you not to share word of this . . . possibility."

"Until?"

Daria stared back at the wall. Until she knew for sure? Until this was over? Hadn't she just searched for a time to see to Roberto's surgery and recovery and come up empty-handed? When would be the right time to tell Gianni? The others?

She shook her head and sighed. Nay. They would all become impossible if they knew the truth. Gianni was nearly impossible now, when it came to her protection. If he knew she carried his child . . . if the others knew . . . God had not brought them this far for a babe to get in the way of his plans. She owed it to them all to see it through. When they were on the other side of the battle, safe, she would tell them.

Her hand went to her belly and she shook her head again in wonder, looking up to the ceiling, thinking of how long she and Marco had waited, wanted a baby. An heir. It would have made their handfast a betrothal. The vows would have been exchanged. She would be at home in Siena, married to one of the Nine, enjoying life as she once knew it with the Sciorias and Hasani, spending half her year in the bustling city she loved, and half in the rolling green hills that she loved even more. Ambrogio would just be completing his task for the Nine, in the Palazzo Publico on Il Campo, and Vincenzo . . .

The thought of her lost dreams did not bring her the hollow ache of old, the grief that had once sent her to the convent where she met Piero. All of that was gone. In its place was this new life. If she had been granted that most fervent of wishes, if God had smiled upon her prayers for a babe, she might never have known what it was to heal in the Father's name. She might never have met Piero or Gianni or Tessa or Roberto or Gaspare or any of her knights. She might never have known the vast power of the Holy and his war for his own, against those of the dark. She might not have seen life for all it was—this portion, here on earth, a mere itch on the vast horizon.

She smiled. How good it was to know she was where she was supposed to be. With Gianni, Piero, and the others. And on the track God wished her to take. Her homes had been burned behind her. Many of the people she had loved had been taken or killed. Vincenzo was lost to her. But here, now, she knew love again, and a pervading sense of peace.

Daria finally turned to Josephine. "Until it is right."

Josephine paused. "You know you are asking a prophetess to keep her tongue. That is nigh unto impossible."

"Please, Josephine. It is important."

"I shall do my best, m'lady," she said with a nod. "It is all I can promise."

Chapter Twenty-three

"You are certain?" Abramo said to the young woman at his side.

"Heard it from her own lips, a day past. She believes she carries a babe," said the young seamstress. "But she swore the old woman to secrecy."

Abramo laughed and turned, picking the young woman up in his arms and twirling her around. "Great shall be your reward," he said, smiling up into her eyes. He set her down on the ground and kissed her until he felt her ease beneath him, bending to follow every curve of his body.

"You are certain that the knight does not know? Nor the priest?"

"The lady forswore the old woman to silence."

"Excellent. Most excellent."

"What is that?" Vincenzo asked, entering the stables in his own finery.

"Our Daria de Capezzana. I have received the most intriguing information."

"And that is?" The baron came closer and pulled on his gloves. He was all in a fine brown silk, other than a hem of leopard spots, just as Abramo was all in black, with a hem of zebra at the edge of his overcoat.

"She apparently is with child."

Vincenzo stilled. "That is not possible. She is barren."

Abramo pursed his lips. "Apparently not any longer. Mayhap when she was healed in my prison cell, the enemy cleared the way for a babe as well. It is his way—to promote life. But he is foolish, here. I shall use her pregnancy to my own advantage. It weakens Daria, and therefore, weakens them all."

He stepped into a stirrup and mounted his horse, then gestured back at two servants to bring the caged creatures they were bringing to the ball, set atop a broad wagon, pulled by two oxen. The horses had been too skittish with their cargo to be of any use, constantly threatening to bolt. The cage came into view, and inside, a pair of magnificent Bengal tigers paced back and forth.

Another servant handed him a mask covered in zebra skin, and then handed Vincenzo his mask of leopard skin. "Come, baron, let us be off," Abramo said in irritation.

Vincenzo stared up at him. "What is it that you intend to do with the babe? Daria's child?"

Abramo stared back at him, puzzled by his sudden hesitation. Could he still care for the woman? After all this time? After she had denied them? Taken Abramo's eye? "I know not. We shall consult the master this night at our ceremony. No doubt he shall have the best plan. Tonight, we shall but taunt them, play with them, remind them of their enemy's strength."

Vincenzo still looked a bit ashen, but he mounted up and was soon beside Abramo. They joined Ciro and three other knights outside, as well as his two finest archers, dressed in seductive dresses that made Abramo anxious to be done with the ball and on to their ceremony. Yes, tonight would be the finest of all. The battle was at hand. And soon, the Gifted would be vanquished.

♋ ♋ ♋

DARIA released Bormeo to the sky and strode up to Hasani, who had stood outside the gazelles' cage ever since they had arrived an hour past. He was dressed for the ball in a long, elegant coat of black, but had only agreed to deer skin at its edge. The sacrifice of animals for such human foolishness plainly grieved him. Daria shifted uneasily, hesitating, since at the neckline of her own cream-colored silk bodice was a delicate white fur—that of an arctic hare, said the seamstress. In her hair, elaborately tied and pinned behind her head by Tessa, was a matching white fur half-moon cap from which descended an ivory net, which held her heavy hair as if in a hammock. While Contessa Morassi would have positively gleamed over her appearance, Hasani held no such notions of keeping up with fashions.

Hasani, sensing her presence, turned and glanced at her in brotherly fashion from head to toe, then turned back to the gazelles. He looked magnificent in his own new white shirt and black silk overcoat, like that of an

African noble. Still, his curved sword, in its old and worn fringed sheath, was at his side, just beneath the new coat.

She ventured near and stared at the gazelles, trembling and huddling together on the far side of the cage. "What is it, Hasani?"

His dark eyes slid to meet hers and then miserably turned back to the animals.

"Do you remember . . . do you remember animals such as these from your childhood?"

He paused, and then nodded.

"And it brings you pain? To see them caged?"

He thought about that for a moment, then shrugged.

Daria lifted her hands and rested them on a crossbar of the cage. "It is almost as if we are building Noah his own menagerie. The children beg to come with us so that they might see them all."

He eyed her and made a sound that meant, *Why not?*

"We shall face Amidei and Vincenzo there, as well as the pope. We need not endanger the children as well."

" 'E-ahh," he said. He wanted to bring Tessa at least.

"Because you think we need her?"

He nodded, staring back at the gazelles.

"Nay, we shall keep the children safe as long as possible. They are all in dire need of rest." She turned to go, but Hasani reached out and grabbed her arm. She looked back to him.

He was staring into her eyes and slowly let them slip to her belly, then back to her eyes. He knew. He had seen it.

Daria swallowed hard. "You must keep it to yourself, Hasani. For now."

He gave her a long, searching look, and then nodded once.

She turned to go and then glanced back at him. "Have you seen . . . do you know . . ." She lifted a hand to her brow, suddenly sweaty even in the winter chill. "Will I hold this babe in my arms?"

He paused and then shook his head. He was not saying no. He was saying, *I know not.*

Daria turned away, pained that he had not seen if she would live to hold this child. For it had taken only her a few hours to fully know the truth of it and want this baby with everything she had inside her. She was pregnant, having conceived in the first night or two of her marriage. She shook her head at the wonder of it. "I hope your plan is wise," she whispered to God, as she returned to the manor.

Tessa came bursting out of the house, Nico and Roberto right behind her. Bormeo screeched, high overhead, as he circled. Tessa smiled, looking at Daria, now in her gown, which matched the dress. "Oh, m'lady, can we not go with you?"

"Nay, Tess," Daria said for the tenth time, reaching out to pinch her chin, then patting each of the boys on the shoulder. "You three are to stay here with Agata and five of the Les Baux knights. You are to remain indoors, with the doors locked. Understood?"

"Understood," they all said sorrowfully.

"Can we not simply ride along?" Roberto tried. "We could remain in the servants' quarters."

"Nay. It will be no place for children."

"We have been in many a place not meant for children," he said.

Daria laughed. "Yes. Unfortunately that is well true. But I shall do my best to keep that from happening on a frequent basis. Because of our task at hand, you three are thrust into more than your share of circumstances that demand an adult's shoulders to bear the weight. I am so proud of all three of you—what you have managed to navigate. What a gift you are to all of us! But nay, I shall keep you safe and out of harm's way for as long as possible."

"You mean you shall be in danger this night?" Tessa asked, her eyes narrowing. She had had been fingering Daria's gown, running her fingers over the arctic hare hem.

"We shall see our enemy this night," Daria said levelly, "but he dare not move against us. Not in the midst of so many of our friends."

Tessa shivered. "I do not wish to see Amidei or Vincenzo anytime soon."

"I'm afraid you shall see them again sooner than you wish. Take your ease this night, my sweet. The servants can show you how to play the Mameluke cards."

"Truly?" Nico asked, eyes widening. He had always loved games, playing for hours with his granduncle in Siena. Count Armand had introduced them to the oversized cards that came from the East, and they had spent an evening playing in Les Baux. Ever since, the children had been begging to learn.

"Truly."

The boys took off running to the house, pushing each other, tackling the other, falling, laughing, and then running again. Daria laughed at them and then looked back to Tessa, who was circling her, looking in consternation at her dress.

"What is it, Tess? Do you not like it?"

"It is beautiful, m'lady." She circled her again and paused, reaching out to touch it, then pulling her hand back as if scorched.

"Tess?"

"It is a magnificent gown," she said. "But one of the dark has touched it."

Daria frowned at her, but just then the men emerged, all heading toward the stables, with servants who carried their trunks for an overnight stay near the castle. It was time to depart. Right after them came the countess, who searched about for her. Two Les Baux knights came out the front door, looking for their third charge.

"Never thee mind, Tessa," Daria said, "go, go to the house now. We shall see you on the morrow."

"Our prayers go with you," Tessa said, holding her hand for a moment longer, then trailing away.

Daria smoothed her gown down, feeling bile rise in her throat. Just who of the dark had touched this cloth? She pulled on the leather gauntlet, raised her arm to the sky, and called for Bormeo to return.

⚛ ⚛ ⚛

THEY journeyed for several hours, along the river, until the castle came into sight. Prince Maximilien was the reigning monarch of a kingdom that stretched from the edge of Villeneuve-des-Avignon to nearly Valence. His castle boasted four turrets with a crenellated, manned walkway between and stood on a high cliff above the Rhône. Flags with long, streaming colors waved against a robin's-egg-blue sky, making their gold and red seem all the more dramatic.

Directly across the wide Rhône was a larger castle, dominating the hillside. It was there that the king of France hovered, as if a bird of prey about to pounce. It was only Prince Maximilien's presence, and Queen Jeanne of Naples, who owned Avignon, and the pope directly behind them, that seemed to keep the Frankish king from taking the rest of this territory. He rested for now, as he had for some time, in an uneasy truce with Prince Maximilien, each seemingly content to remain on his own bank of the Rhône. But this night, even the king was expected to attend the festivities.

As they neared, the Gifted could see hundreds upon hundreds of servants, horses, and mules hovering around royal tent after royal tent. It was an uncommon gathering of nobles from near and far, with so many in attendance that neither the prince's nor the king of France's castles could hold them all. Each large tent bore a royal flag or family herald. Odd animal sounds filled the air. Gianni pulled up his horse beside her. "An elephant. Somewhere down there, they have an elephant." They could hear it trumpeting, almost like an angry sheep bleating his complaint.

As they entered the camp, every person masked as instructed, they spotted bear and an ostrich and every sort of hoofed animal possible. Leopards growled and restlessly paced their cages. Daria looked up at Bormeo, who seemed unfazed by any of them until they came upon twenty tiny, impossibly yellow birds that inhabited one cage. Bormeo moved, digging his claws into her gloved arm in agitation.

"Easy," she said, "you shall get dinner soon enough. None of the pope's rare birds for you."

They passed through the muddy avenue between the tents, smelling food on the many campfires. Elegant ladies and finely dressed gentlemen in masks entered and exited the tents, made of a durable cloth that would repel most of the rain, should it fall.

"It as if we are in the camp of Bedouin kings," Piero said, edging his horse beside her.

" 'Tis a wonder. I wish now that the children were with us to see it."

"Nay. It was a wise decision to leave them behind. No telling what mischief they might have entered here. We have enough potential trouble without them in the mix."

Two Les Baux knights rode up to them, bearing the flag of Balthazar. A group had set out at daybreak to prepare their tents and provision them for their arrival. They led them into the meandering tent village to a group of eight tents at the edge, each in a crimson red with white flags atop their points, perched on a hillside.

Count Armand grinned at Daria. "I thought you might approve of the colors." Then he smiled at Gianni. "And I thought you might approve of a position of strength."

In front of four of the tents was the d'Angelo peacock, staked into the ground and waving in the breeze, and in front of four of the others was the Les Baux sixteen-pointed star. They looked beautiful all together.

"It was a wise choice," Gianni said approvingly. It was always better to be high, above your enemy, than down below them.

"Will not all the heraldic flags tell everyone our identity?" Daria asked idly. "Why wear the masks?"

"The men already search the grounds for Amidei and his dragon," Gianni said. "We shall use it to our advantage."

"It is a farce," the count said, dismounting. "But it does lend an air of gaiety to the festivities, does it not? Everyone looks so mysterious and intriguing." The count reached up to help Daria down. "Your wife is a vision," he said to Gianni, still smiling down at Daria. "Every eye in the room shall be upon her."

"That does not make me feel better," Gianni said, coming near, leading his horse by the reins. "And I beg your pardon, m'lord, but I must insist you stop staring at my wife like that, or I shall be forced to strike you."

"As well you should," said the rakish noble. He reluctantly turned from Daria and clapped Gianni on the shoulder. "Never fear, brother. Your love affair is a grand thing, a story I shall tell for many years in the halls of Les Baux. I could never get in the way of such a tale, still unfolding right before my very eyes. But you cannot stop me from being jealous."

"I shall have Father Piero come and pray for you."

Count Armand laughed. "He can try. But the other lovelies about these tents will probably do me one better."

"You mind your behavior, brother," Anette said, drawing near. "Set your mind upon honorable things and do our friends a service."

"Oh, I shall," he pledged, raising an eyebrow. He looked again to Gianni, suddenly serious. Then to Daria. "I jest. Play. But you must know you already have many friends among these tents. All the nobles you met at Les Baux will be in attendance this night."

"It is not they that concern me," Gianni said.

"They shall not ambush us here," Armand said, spitting out the words in distaste for their enemies' cowardice. "We are prepared. Let them come." He leaned closer to the de Capezzanas and put a fist to his chest. "Me and mine," he pledged again, "shall die fighting for you and yours."

He turned and Daria stared after him. Would this cause take his life, too? Just how many lives would be spent upon their holy endeavors?

"Daria?" Gianni asked, looking down at her. He slid a hand down to her lower back and his other lifted her chin. "Are you well?"

She forced a smile. "As well as can be expected, husband."

ᘒ ᘒ ᘒ

THERE was a mass of blessing inside the castle as the sun set, over which the pope presided, but only the highest nobles could attend. There simply was not room for the rest, so the remainder stood in the stone hallways and were instructed to remain in silence, heads bowed, all still in masks, from the time it began until the time it ended.

Daria, standing on the stair near the front entrance, watched as the pope and twelve cardinals, twenty bishops, and other papal court higher-ups processed through the castle and into the chapel, the only ones not in animalia costume. Armand, Anette, and Dimitri were in the chapel, and she had glimpsed the Conte and Contessa Morassi, as well as other nobility she had met. But she remained outside with the rest of the Gifted, her knights and the mass of others, as she well preferred.

She had not sensed Amidei's or Vincenzo's presence, and while she startled at the sight of numerous men who resembled them in stature, she was sure she had not yet laid eyes on them. It helped her breathe easier. Mayhap they had not yet arrived. Better yet, mayhap they were not coming at all.

Knowing she was to keep her eyes to the ground did not make it easier. The staircase was calling her, constantly guiding her upward. Again and again she pulled her head downward, until she realized that it was her God who urged her upward. Who was up there?

A young woman. Daria searched her mind, but could not determine her ailment. But there was a woman above them whom God was crying out for her to come and heal. She itched to move immediately, but forced herself to stay in place. She tapped her foot, until Gianni quietly took her hand, silently urging her to stop. He met her glance and frowned when he saw what was in her eyes. By now, he knew exactly what she was thinking.

Was it really necessary for them to remain here? In silent vigil for a mass they could not hear or take part in? She moved an inch, and Gianni's hand tightened around hers. "A few more minutes," he urged in a whisper.

She closed her eyes and prayed for the strength to remain still. When she opened her eyes, she heard the blessed chorus of men singing a hymn and thanked her Lord it was over. The pope and cardinals and bishops processed out of the chapel and on to the gardens outside, which overlooked the river, and where the feast and festivities would take place. Everyone else went after them, except for the Gifted, who looked to Daria in concern as she stayed rooted to her spot, like a rock in a river of people.

They were alone in the hall at last.

"There is a young woman upstairs I am to heal," Daria whispered. She straightened and smiled at two male servants who came down the stairs, waiting for them to pass.

"Ugo and Hasani," Gianni said, "you two remain here, on guard. We shall send down word as to where we end up." They turned to go, and at the next landing, paused.

"She is higher still," Daria said, her eyes going to the next sweeping staircase.

"Vito and Josephine," Gianni said, "You shall remain here."

"I always get to rest with the prettiest girls," Vito said, smiling at Josephine.

"Remember," she said, thrusting a finger in his direction, "I know the truth of your words. You offend me."

"This is not good. A woman who can judge the truth of a man's words. No one told me I'd have to endure such suffering."

Gianni rolled his eyes and told Vito to run down the stairwell and tell the others they were heading to the third floor, then he turned and ushered Piero and Daria upward, Gaspare hard on their heels. He said in a low voice, "If we are asked, we will say we are lost."

"It is good that we left the truth teller behind us," Piero quipped.

Daria moved into the third level, heading toward one wing, then abruptly stopped and went the other way.

"This has to be the family quarters," Gianni said, his face awash in concern. If they were discovered here . . .

Daria continued down the hall, lit by several torches, and then paused at one door. Inside, she could hear creaking upon the boards, as if someone paced. Tentatively, she knocked upon the door.

The crying stopped. "Who is there?"

"It is a friend. We have come to help you." She looked at Father Piero, who was frowning and rubbing his chest, where he had once been wounded. Gaspare glowered behind him.

"Go away. I am in no need of assistance." The creaking resumed as the woman continued her pacing.

"Ready?" she whispered to Gianni, not pausing for an answer. Inward she went, Piero and Gianni right on her heels.

The woman was slight, mayhap sixteen years of age. Her hair was long and stringy, unkempt. Her gown was simple but of the highest quality. A noble? In such a state on a feast day?

"What ails you, m'lady?" Daria asked.

"Who are you? How do you know I am unwell?" Her eyes were wide, and even in the bright torchlight they were strangely dilated, making them look almost entirely black.

"We are friends," Daria said smoothly. She stepped forward easily, as if invited. But the room was oddly cold, much colder than the rest of the castle. She looked to the windows, but the shutters were lodged in place. Daria frowned and glanced back to Piero, who still rubbed his chest as if to massage away the pain there. His wounds . . . from Amidei's arrows. This cold . . . so like that of the dark isle.

"You have been touched by the dark," she said to the girl, trying to cover the alarm in her voice, only halfway succeeding. Gaspare was edging near, from the other side. She could see from his face that he had understood what lodged here from the start.

The girl recoiled. "I know not of what you speak. My father says I am unwell. Unfit for the festival. But I have been visited by a healer. I feel better than I have in months."

Daria took another step closer. "Your healer. Who was he?"

"A woman. From the north."

She took another step, advancing upon her. Piero and Gianni were behind her now, understanding at last what was before them. "What is your name?"

"Ariana."

"Ariana. What did the healer do to ease your pain?"

The girl's eyes went wide with wonder, and an eerie smile spread across her face. "I had been in such pain. Terrible stomach trouble. I had lost so much weight . . . could not eat. And then I heard of this healer, a woman. She reminds me a bit of you . . . Forgive me. What is your name?"

"I am Lady Daria de Capezzana. I, too, am a healer. Tell me, I am always looking to learn more about my craft. What did this woman do to heal you?"

"She spoke in a different language, like that of the Ottomans, I believe. She was magnificent, m'lady. You would have been enraptured, being that you yourself are a healer. Undoubtedly you could learn much from this one."

"Undoubtedly. What did she do?"

Ariana paced. "I don't remember it well. It is almost as if it were a dream. She snapped her fingers and covered my belly with a blessed fabric from the east, and whispered a beautiful prayer. Almost instantly, I was better. And it was she who sent me to the master, to continue my healing." She turned away, rubbing her hair in agitation. "But my father has cut me off from the master. He will no longer let me out of his sight, and refuses to come and see what the ceremonies are about. If he would only come, he would see . . ."

"Does your father not see you are healed?" Daria asked quietly.

Ariana's smile was gone, her eyes again wary. "My stomach is not right again. It is always better when I go to the ceremonies, take part in the mysteries. But my father says I am not myself. That I am somehow changed." She shook her head and splayed her fingers in agitation. "He does not know what to do with me now that I have seen God."

Daria, Gianni, Gaspare, and Piero stilled. "What does that mean, that you have seen God?" Piero asked.

The girl scoffed at him. "What would you know of her, priest? You are but a babe, lost in the woods!" She leaned close to him, her words coming with spittle in her haste. "God is a woman. A beautiful, white-winged woman who comes to us in the forest, in the deep of night. She leads me forth, to the cave. There have I understood what it means to *live*, to have *power* over myself, over another."

"Long have you lived in this castle," Daria said, edging between the priest and the girl as Piero wiped his face and rubbed his chest, his face ashen.

"All my life. Though they keep me chained here more as a prisoner than a princess," she groused.

Piero neared again. The girl's eyes followed his movement on his chest, seemed to linger there hungrily, as if she could see his scars. She licked her lips, as if she could taste the blood that was once upon it. Piero forced himself to pull his hand away and sighed. "This girl has been touched by the hand of our enemy. He has taken a crack in the door and made it a wide passageway into her heart."

The girl laughed. "What do you know of my heart?"

It was Piero's turn to laugh. "Too much, child." He stepped forward, reaching for her.

"Do not touch me," she sneered, backing away. "You are unclean. You are *enemy*."

Piero ignored her and grabbed her arm. "Lord Jesus Christ, we ask you to enter this house, this room, and lay claim back upon this child, Ariana."

The girl writhed and bent to bite the priest, but Gianni grabbed her and pulled her head back just before she clamped down on his forearm. Gaspare laid hold of her from the other side. Daria ran to close the door, then rushed back to them.

"Father God on High," Gaspare said, placing a hand on the girl's head, "we ask that you silence the evil spirit that has laid claim to this daughter's heart. Keep him silent now, as we work to do as you have bid, in the name of Jesus Christ."

The girl writhed in Gianni's and Gaspare's arms, but she was rendered mute, as clearly as if they had gagged her. Outside, they could hear music and the swell of crowds.

Daria hoped that they would have time to heal this one before they were discovered.

გიგიგი

THE master caught Abramo's eye as he moved through the crowd waiting to present their gifts to the pope. It was a long and crowded train of people, interspersed as they were by the caged animals, a thrilling string of ladies behind masks, and men as well. All people to be drawn forth, enticed toward the deep night's ceremony. Abramo watched the master move in and out among them, whispering in their ears, unseen, and the results behind— leering, whispering, hidden touches, laughter.

Men with casks of wine upon their backs already wove their way among the people, pouring liberally, and behind them, maids carried trays laden with cheeses and fruit. The feast would be hours ahead, but Prince Maximilien knew well how to care for his guests.

The master stilled among the people and caught Abramo's eye again. He looked up the palace wall to the third floor, where Abramo knew the prince's young daughter resided. She had visited them and their ceremonies. She already belonged to them. Abramo smiled in victory, but the master did not return his grin.

Something was wrong. The Gifted. That was why they had not yet seen them. They were with Ariana.

Nay. They could not have her. She belonged to him. He needed her. Needed her ensconced here in the castle, ready to serve him.

He turned and pushed his way through the throngs, slowly making his way back to the castle, with Vincenzo and Ciro right behind him.

The master was there, suddenly, right before he entered the castle. "Use the servants' stairwell," he said in a hiss. "They guard the main stairwell."

"Of course, master," Abramo said, bowing his head in shame for not having foreseen such obvious facts. His master was good to him, ever patient, ever guiding.

"Just who are you referring to as a master?" said a regal young lady before him. Dressed in a delicate rose silk and peacock feathers, she was anything but male. And she appeared to be momentarily without escort.

Abramo smiled, realizing he had spoken aloud to his lord, invisible to the masses. He bowed and grinned down at the young woman, with a long neck and pleasing cleavage that peeked from behind a screen of peacock feathers. Her neck and the feathers reminded him of Daria, undoubtedly above them in the castle now.

He gave the young woman a rakish grin and stroked one of the peacock feathers slowly, seductively, until his fingers brushed the very edge of her skin. Her eyes widened in surprise at his audacity, but her lips parted in pleasure. "Fine feathers, m'lady," he said.

She shivered and looked about, suddenly aware they were not alone. "Who are you, m'lord?" She peered around his shoulder, at the hulking Ciro and the more lean, graying Vincenzo.

"Ah, our identities are to remain a secret as long as possible, are they not? Is that not the charm of such a masked ball?"

"I know not," she giggled. "I have never attended one before."

"Nor have I," he said secretively, leaning closer to her. She smelled of roses, fresh and innocent. Just as he liked them. Only oranges and cloves would be better . . .

"I shall find you this night, during the dances," he promised.

Impulsively, she pulled one of the five feathers from her bodice waist-band and rubbed it across his cheek, handing it to him. "See that you do, m'lord."

He smiled and turned away. A girl playing with womanhood. He would show her what it meant to be a woman . . .

"So we shall hunt more than one peacock this night, m'lord," Ciro said, edging closer.

Abramo laughed and ran the smooth edge of the peacock eye feather again past his cheek. "And so we shall . . ."

⚭ ⚭ ⚭

ARMAND Rieu des Baux had noticed the Gifted's absence after the service. They had arranged to reconvene after the mass, with Daria and Gianni and the rest coming to join them in line to greet the pope and pass along their animals. He had been looking for them as night descended and the river val-ley grew colder, as had his sister and her husband.

"Armand," Anette said, taking his arm. She pointed with her chin in the direction of the castle.

Abramo Amidei. His knights had identified him, Baron del Buco, and those who belonged with them, carefully describing what they wore in cos-tume. He was talking to a young woman, it appeared, and now he was mov-ing off toward the servants' area of the castle.

Lucien finally returned and leaned in to whisper his report. "M'lord, the Gifted are inside. Lady Daria and the others are above. She has been called to heal a young woman on the third floor."

Armand looked to Amidei and the others, disappearing inside the kitch-ens, with men and women rushing in and out, madly at work to prepare and serve one course of food after another for the hundreds in attendance. Then he looked up to the windows, shuttered and shut high above them. "Captain de Capezzana left guards on the stairwell?"

"He did. That is where I found them."

"But he forgot the servants' stairwell," he said. "Go to the others. Tell them their people have been discovered on the third floor, or soon will be. You and you," he said to two others, "come with me."

"Armand," Anette said, her hand again on his arm in concern.

"It shall be well, sister. Remain here with your husband, and pray for us."

Armand set off, trying not to show his agitation as he and two knights made their way at an agonizingly slow pace through the crowded court-yard and to the kitchens. A cheer went up as seven massive bonfires were set ablaze at once. The fires bathed the massive courtyard in firelight and warmth.

ᚴ ᚴ ᚴ

GASPARE wrapped his meaty arms around the girl's shoulders and pinned her arms against her sides, as if he were embracing her. His head was bowed in fervent prayer, repeating again and again, "In the name of the Lord Jesus Christ, we command you to release this girl and be away from this house."

Gianni had moved to her legs, clasping them in his arms, keeping her from writhing.

Daria hesitated. "Does she not need to ask to be healed?"

"She asked to be healed, just of the wrong healer," Piero grumbled. He leaned closer to Ariana. "Daughter, you were claimed in baptism by the God on high, but you have relinquished authority to the enemy. We are here to free you and bring you true healing. Long will be your sorrow if you do not allow it."

Ariana grimaced and then looked as if she laughed, but no sound came out. She laughed and laughed, but her eyes were wide, giving her a maniacal appearance. Piero leaned in to pray over her, and Ariana spit in his face. The priest barely paused to wipe his face this time, already lost in his prayer of hope.

Daria knelt beside her and took the girl's hand in hers. Ariana dug her fingernails into the back of her hand, but Daria ignored it, wanting her to know she was here to stay until she was freed. God had called them to heal this child. And they would remain until the task was done.

ᚴ ᚴ ᚴ

THEY climbed the curving stone stairwell of the turret, one turn, then two, then three, up and up. Amidei paused and smiled. "Do you smell that?" He closed his eyes and inhaled deeply, catching their scent above the smells of roasted meats and baked goods in the kitchens below them.

"Oranges and cloves," Vincenzo said tiredly.

Amidei eyed him warily. What was troubling his brother? He deeply needed time in the caves. Tonight would restore him . . . and if they could find victory here against their enemy before they returned to Avignon, how sweet might that be?

"Oranges and cloves," he repeated, with a nod and a grin. He rushed up the final flight of stairs that clung to the turret wall, and paused at the door that led to the third floor. He inhaled again and closed his eyes, remembering Daria, so close to him, so nearly his own. It was a pity, really, that she had to die.

But she had decided wrongly. It would please him to watch her suffer greatly, watch them all suffer greatly, before he watched the light of life disappear. Daria especially would pay. Yes, in their deaths, he would become stronger. The master had promised that.

"Lord Amidei," Vincenzo whispered.

Abramo glanced back at him.

"I thought we were to leave them to the pope. That he would bring them down."

Abramo smiled. "Mayhap an earlier opportunity has arisen. We must go where our master has led. And he points us here, now."

ᚙ ᚙ ᚙ

HASANI frowned at the knight of Les Baux rushing headlong toward them, clattering through the halls on heavy boots. Before he could even speak, Hasani knew the warning in his mouth, understood that they did not guard all entrances to where Daria and Gianni and Gaspare and Piero were lodged. *The servants' staircase.*

He turned and ran, Ugo hard on his heels, not asking where they were going, understanding the unspoken warning. Josephine and Vito, aroused by their fast and heavy footsteps, were already looking over the edge, watching them come.

Vito turned and ran, two stairs at a time, drawing his sword as Ugo and Hasani had. All three passed the old woman. Vito paused at the top and looked to Matthieu, the knight of Les Baux. "Guard the woman with your life, man. Your very life."

"Upon my word," said the man. He reached for Josephine and tucked her carefully behind him.

❧ ❧ ❧

AMIDEI opened the stairwell door and swore under his breath at the sight of Vito, Ugo, and Hasani arriving halfway down the hall, swords drawn. He turned back inside the stairwell, seething with frustration.

"Lord Amidei!" cried a voice from below. "There you are!"

Abramo frowned and looked downward. Two curves of the stairwell revealed Count Rieu des Baux and two of his knights. Abramo could feel Ciro and Vincenzo tense beside him. "Do not draw your swords," he hissed. He feigned a smile, just as his foe below him had done. They had clearly been identified, and the enemies knew their precious Gifted were in danger. "Count des Baux! It has been some time since our paths have crossed!"

"Indeed. I hear tell that you were near my castle and never came to my door. What is an old friend to do with such worrisome information as that? I have sought you out now, to make sure all is well between us. And here I find you, sneaking about as if you had a lover to attend to! Come, come and share a cup of wine with an old friend while we wait to be received by the pope."

Abramo settled his lips in a steady smile, thinking through his options.

"He is here! Lord Amidei!" Count Armand cried, to someone in the kitchen, as if he had heard someone inquire. A maid? Another noble? One of Prince Maximilien's councilmen? It mattered not. He was exposing him, telling others that Lord Abramo Amidei was on the servants' staircase. No noble took the servants' staircase unless he had intentions he meant to keep in shadow.

This was a man who must be removed. If he would dare to take Amidei on here, in such a public fashion, he would not fear taking him on again in private. He lent the Gifted too much power . . . his backing meant too much for them . . . Amidei turned and edged past Ciro and Vincenzo on the narrow staircase. "This castle is so large," he called down, "I confess I got a bit turned about."

Armand smiled and lifted his arms wide, shaking his head as if he entirely believed him. "Well I know it. It puts my own humble castle to shame. I might fit two of mine in this one wing!"

"If you had the king of France across your valley," Amidei said meaningfully, nearing the count, "you might refortify your castle." He reached out and clasped the younger man's, elbow to elbow in the manner of knights.

"If it were the king of France, well I might," said the count, staring into his eyes. "Instead, I only have thieves and robbers, hiding in the caves of Dante's *Inferno*. Hell's Keep."

"Hell's Keep. Sounds fearsome."

"Nay," said the count with a dismissive smile, releasing him, but still looking into his eyes with an ease that only true power yielded. "When one rules with the blessing of God himself, there is nothing to fear in one's enemies."

Amidei raised his eyebrows. "Pride goeth before destruction, Count."

"Not pride, Amidei. Divine understanding."

Abramo stared into his eyes, thinking of different ways to dispose of this nuisance before him. "So it is out beyond you? The line to see our favored guest? If so . . . lead the way. You promised me a cup of wine."

"Indeed," said the count, gesturing past him. "Please. I shall follow you out."

☙ ☙ ☙

Vito, Ugo, and Hasani rushed down the hall, paused at the scene unfolding at the far end of the countess's room, then eased forward, seeking the servants' staircase.

Quietly Vito edged open the door and leaned in, catching the end of the count's conversation with Amidei. He grinned and silently saluted the count, shaking his head at how God intervened on behalf of the Gifted. What wonder was this? A count of Provence, so firmly entrenched on their side?

He turned and whispered to Hasani and Ugo, "It is well. The count must have caught him here, before he made it in. He cuckolded him into returning to the festivities below."

Ugo smiled and lifted a brow. Hasani only looked relieved. All three turned and headed back. Vito and Ugo positioned themselves, one at the countess's door, one at the top of the staircase with Josephine and Matthieu. Hasani moved inward, joining the others.

☙ ☙ ☙

Father Piero knew when Hasani joined him. He could feel his presence and his ease as the tall man knelt down beside him and placed his long, black fingers atop his own, praying for this child of God.

Daria was growing tired. "Father in Heaven, you asked us to heal this child. We ask that you take over her heart, that you drive out the demon that has imprisoned her. Free her, Lord Jesus. Free her."

Hasani reached out to rest a hand on Daria's shoulders, feeling her frustration and concern. Silently, he was encouraging her to give in to the prayer, to block out the enemy outside. To trust in the Holy.

"Lord Jesus, you are our King. We invite you in, into this room within a castle that is nothing compared to your kingdom. Come and reign here, now. Lay claim to this child of yours. Wrestle her away from your enemy. Drive him away from this room, now and forever." She leaned down, weeping at last over Ariana. "We know you have the power to do this, Lord Jesus. The enemy has a firm hold upon her, but you have a greater hold. For you are the power . . . and the glory . . . forever and ever. Amen."

Daria sat back, eyes alight as Ariana laughed, the first sound they had heard from her since Gaspare had prayed she would be silenced. And it was not the laugh of a maniacal, possessed woman, but the free, light giggle of a young woman in bloom.

CHAPTER TWENTY-FOUR

ARIANA allowed Daria to choose a dress for her, brush out her hair, and pin it up. She settled a delicate gold band around her head, befitting a princess.

"I have no mask for you," Daria said sorrowfully.

"It matters not," the girl said. "My papa will wish to see me without my mask at last."

Daria smiled back at her in the mirror and squeezed her shoulders. "How glad am I that we were here, now."

"No more than I," said the princess. She covered Daria's hand with her own. "You, m'lady, shall have my undying gratitude."

"Not us, princess. Always remember that it is God who has freed you, and he is the guard who shall keep the enemy from your gates. But you must be very wary of inviting our enemy inside again."

"I shall remember. Now let us go to my father."

Daria sighed and looked to Gianni and Hasani and Piero. They were ready as well. Together, the group headed down the stairs, with Matthieu, Vito, and Ugo before them, hands on the hilts of their swords, and Hasani and Gianni coming behind the women.

⚜ ⚜ ⚜

"How long," Amidei said, eyeing the count after they had left the pope's side, "do you think you can keep them safe from me?"

Count Armand pursed his lips and tapped them. "Hmm, I do not know. Mayhap forever?" He grinned audaciously at Amidei.

It had been some time since an enemy had taunted him so. Abramo could not remember the last. The count intrigued him, like none other since Daria. If he could bring this one down, how great would be the master's victory? An insider, a supposed ally, that Abramo could use to reach others within the Gifted . . .

"What if I promised you wealth beyond all you could imagine?" Abramo asked. Vincenzo eased in from the other side, while Ciro watched the beginnings of the dance take form among the massive bonfires.

"Nay," the count dismissed. "What more could I want?"

"The next kingdom? And the next? All of France?"

Count Armand scoffed. "You are promising me all of France? Does the king know it is for sale? Mayhap we should go over to him now. He's right over there. Shall we go and ask about the highest bid?"

Abramo ignored his taunts. "You and I both know that kingdoms are not truly won and lost in a battlefield of swords. It is the mind," he said, tapping his temple, "and the money that control most kingdoms."

"I confess I love women more than money," the count said. "And I am quite content with my own kingdom."

"A count who never seeks to take the next will soon lose his own."

"I do not fear invasion. Many are my friends and few are my enemies." The smile faded from his face. He tired, too, of their games.

Abramo stepped in front of him and turned, chin in hand. "Is it women you truly desire, Armand? Come with me tonight, to my ceremony, and you shall experience mysteries unparalleled with anything you have ever dreamed of. You shall feel like a god. And all the world, your servant. There are no rules in my realm. No one shall deny you."

The count hesitated.

"Ah yes, I can see it in your eyes. You are intrigued by a place without rules. Constrained, a life of a count must be. Courtly conduct and all of that. Come and see what it is to experience life without any demands at all, only gifts to be unwrapped."

Armand swallowed hard and then stood up straight, nearly as tall as Abramo. "Lord Amidei, our time has come to an end. I must see to my honored guests." He leaned closer, taking Abramo's shirt in his fist. "See that you stay in Hell's Keep and away from me and mine," he said fiercely. Then he forced a smile, released his shirt, smoothed it out, patted him firmly twice on the chest, and walked away.

"Pity, that," Abramo said with a sigh to Vincenzo.

"What, m'lord?"

"That he should have to die with the rest of them. Come, Vincenzo," he said with an easy smile, "let us see if our peacocks have emerged for the dance. We shall collect them." He nodded to the moon. "It is soon time."

ↂ ↂ ↂ

THEY entered the vast courtyard that bordered the cliff, overlooking the river, far below them and sparkling in the moonlight. Torches and bonfires were ablaze all over, lending both light and warmth, and while Prince Maximilien, the king of France, and the pope still received the remains of the line of people, the party was well underway. The men with casks continued to circle around, taking up new casks when their own were empty, serving one and all who were present. Maids now served skewers of roast pork and chicken and duck, interlaced with onions and potatoes. Others served delicate breads, laden with pats of butter.

To the side remained two knights of Les Baux, guarding the Gifted's own gift to the pope, the two gazelles, and obviously awaiting their arrival. Gianni waved them forward, and the two jumped from their posts to do as he had bid.

"The Count and Countess des Baux?" Gianni whispered.

"Come and gone," said one of their knights.

"With Amidei?"

"Indeed," said the other, eyes wide still, in surprise at the sight. He relaxed when he saw no surprise on Gianni's face.

They moved closer, watching as the pope, king, and prince received the group ahead of them, clearly bored and tired by now, after receiving more than three hundred guests before them.

Two priests took the people's invitations, authenticated them, and then looked for their names upon the list in hand, a vast scroll, before letting them move forward to the dais where the guests of honor sat. Two other armed guards stood on either side of them, axes on long handles ready across their chest. Six others stood in a line behind them—two from Maximilien's guard, two from the kingdom across the river, and two from the pope's own *Honneur Gard*.

Daria searched over her shoulder nervously, as if worrying that Amidei might be closing in from behind even as they faced a new potential enemy before them. Only Cardinal Boeri's presence on the dais made her capable of breath. But all at once, the princess was moving forward, edging past the guards and priests, going to her father in a full curtsey, reaching out her hands to him.

With one look into her eyes, the prince was on his feet, mouth agape. His wife stood up beside him, emerging from the shadows. "Ariana?" she asked. She hurried to the girl, took her face in one hand, staring at her as if to ascertain it was truly her daughter, even as the prince took the girl's hands and bid her rise.

"Ariana, my daughter? You are free?" he asked.

The girl smiled back at him and nodded. "I am healed, Papa. I am returned to you," she said meaningfully.

He leaned back in wonder, looking her over as if she were to be relearned as kin. How long had the evil one had his hold upon her? Piero mused.

But his eyes turned to the pope, who had awakened from his party doze. Cardinal Boeri was whispering in his ear, and the man was studying each of them, one after the other, as the cardinal continued to talk.

Piero's knees shook. He could not help himself. Here he was, before the Holy Father, the Bishop of Greater Rome, the man who held the keys of Peter. From him, the entire Church flowed; he was like the spring that produced a river that led to a sea that covered the earth.

Piero frowned. He had not anticipated this, this thrill, this awe, in meeting the pope. He had been called to the Church, served the Church, for many, many years. Nearly all of his life. Who was he to question what God had put into place and what he had not? Was he not but a lowly priest from the outer reaches of Roma?

He focused on Ariana, the young beauty before him, and remembered what she had been like but an hour before. He glanced over his shoulder, as Daria had before him, looking for Amidei. The devil would use any edge, any wedge he could find, to worry a crack into a chasm into a valley between him and his Lord. It was his way. Piero knew that. He shook his head and whispered a prayer of covering for himself and the Gifted. Because standing here, before the pope, the Holy Father—the man from whom all Christendom received guidance—sent his knees to quaking again.

ⴆ ⴆ ⴆ

GIANNI looked back to Piero in confusion, looking for him to lead here, but Ariana's reunion with her parents, their obvious surprise and joy at her appearance, their questioning glances to the adults behind her . . . all had set things off in the wrong direction, as if a boulder had broken loose and headed toward the valley floor unhindered.

"How is it, Ariana?" asked Prince Maximilien. "How is it that you are well again?"

"These people came to me," she said, reaching back to Gianni and Daria with girlish delight. "They freed me, Papa. Healed me."

"You no longer suffer from stomach trouble?" asked her mother delicately, sliding a glance toward the pope, who now stood beside her husband, obviously anxious to avoid further detail.

"No troubles at all," gleamed the young princess.

"So this is Sir de Capezzana and his bride, the former Lady d'Angelo," the pope said, taking another step toward them.

Daria, Piero, and Gianni immediately knelt. "Yes, Your Holiness," said Gianni, again waiting for Piero to speak, and then stepping in when he did not. What ailed their priest?

The pope leaned forward, allowing them each to kiss his ring. "You may rise and remove your masks for a moment," he said.

"We brought you two gazelles for your menagerie, Holiness," Daria said, doing as he did.

"Thank you, daughter. They shall be well looked after and bring light to our new gardens and menagerie." He reached forward and lifted her chin, and nodded once. Did he hesitate, as if he recognized her? "You are as beautiful as you are fabled to be, Duchess. Are you truly a healer as well?"

Daria's eyes flitted to meet his, glanced at Boeri and then back to the ground.

Gianni's muscles tensed at another man's hands upon his wife, old holy man or not. But he remained where he was. Clearly the pope knew more of them than they expected. What all had Boeri told him? His heart raced. He had promised to shield them, introduce them in a prudent manner that would not elicit a response of might . . .

"You may look upon us, daughter. There is nothing to fear here, with us. Tell us of your story. We expect it shall be the most intriguing thing we hear this night. But first introduce us to those who travel alongside you."

Two cardinals edged nearer, on either side of Boeri, and Piero rubbed his chest, still puzzlingly silent.

Daria raised her chin and slowly, elegantly rose from her deep curtsey. "Holy Father, may I present one of your own, Father Piero, my chaplain."

"Ah yes, Father Piero," said the pope, leaning down to place his hand on the man's head in silent blessing. When the priest did not look up, he moved on.

"We travel with my friend and freed man, Hasani, Gaspare de Venezia, Vito and Ugo Donati de Siena, Josephine Fontaine de Avignon, and others."

"We see," said the pope. "Quite a varied group. You are a collector of people as well as a healer, Lady Daria?"

Daria hesitated, eyeing Piero, still with head bowed.

"She healed me, Your Holiness," said the young princess, coming beside them, clearly attempting to ease the tension in the air and aid them. "This very night."

"Oh? And what ailed you?" asked the man, eyeing her. "Stomach trouble?"

Ariana hesitated and then nodded. "I have not felt this well in some time, Holy Father. These people freed me. Healed me. I swear my life upon it as truth."

The pope raised an eyebrow. "No swearing, please, daughter, in our presence." He looked to the king and Prince Maximilien. "May we take these honored guests away from you? I have sat so long, I need to stretch my legs. And you must be eager to join the others in the festivities."

All three nobles nodded their heads reluctantly, clearly wishing to take part in that conversation, and the pope laced a hand through Gianni's arm and another through Daria's. "Come along, little brother," he said to Piero. The priest obediently rose and followed. It made Gianni want to turn and shake him. Despite years with Cardinal Boeri, he was ill prepared for this, time with the pope himself. "You, too, mother of Avignon, and fisherman de Venezia, and freed man of Siena. Where is the girl child? We must speak with you all."

"She is safe at home," Gianni said, holding his breath. "She did not come with us." What did this mean, that he knew of each of them?

"No matter," said the pope, waving his hands in dismissal. "You may relate our words to her."

They walked through the vast garden, led by two of the guards of the *palais* in Avignon, and followed by the two cardinals. Evidently Cardinal Boeri had been instructed to remain behind. He had met Gianni's glance with a helpless look.

The pope moved slowly but consistently forward. The festival had reached a new height, with laughter and singing and dancing engaging almost everyone present. He paused at last, at the edge of the cliff. The castle across the river was alight with torches on every level, sending glittering, reflected streams across to them as if lifelines. The full moon cast its own wave of light across the water.

"We stand at a precipice, my new friends," the pope said, looking dolefully downward, into the dark abyss before the river washed the rocks below. "You must see that you walk a path that is like that we see here, perilously close to taking you down."

Piero looked up, and his eyes glittered in the moonlight. He rubbed his chest and eyed the men in red behind them. Gianni followed his gaze to Cardinals Bordeau and Corelli. Had these two been touched by Amidei and his minions, as the young countess had? What were the weaknesses? Where were the wormholes that had made way into their hearts, giving them entrance to evil?

"We are here," Piero said, finally finding his voice, "because we can be no other place. God himself leads us. We merely follow."

"Worthy words, little brother," said the pope. "But pray, tell us that the stories we have heard are not true. That you have not deigned to use your gifts outside of Church sanction? You have not purported to truly heal?"

"We have healed, at God's own bequest," said the priest, "under his advisement and leadership."

The pope raised his chin and studied Piero. "Then pray, tell us the truth of this as well. It is but rumor that you have baptized, upon a river bank."

Piero swallowed hard, but his gaze did not waver. He clearly was not telling him anything Cornelius did not well know already. "Upon the river bank and elsewhere, just as John and the others did before us."

A long moment of silence followed. "And what of communion?"

"We have communed in many places, many a time."

The pope eyed Gianni and Daria. "And the sacrament of marriage?"

"Again, in the full view of our God on high."

Cornelius sighed and paced back and forth. He began to speak, paused, and then resumed his pacing, his chin again in hand. "We must speak of this further," he said at last. "We shall spend time in prayer and fasting, and you shall come to our palace very soon. There we shall wrestle through what is to become of your eternal fate."

When it was clear that Piero would say nothing, Gianni said, "Begging pardon, Your Holiness. But we are the Gifted, prophesied to come together centuries ago. And we firmly believe that while you are in a holy stead, no one but God himself shall decide our eternal fate. We shall come to you as you have asked, but we shall brook no argument that anyone rivals the God on High. It is our enemy's best argument, and we fervently hope that you shall not use it as well. Now, may we have your leave to depart?"

Cornelius stared at him coldly. "Do not make us your enemy, former knight of the Church."

Piero roused again. "We do not wish to do so, Holiness. Never have we wished it. But if your dearest friend suddenly is in the wrong, what can one do? One must argue for truth and light, and pray that that friend sees the way. Must one not?"

Cornelius studied him, and smiled a little. "We believe we shall have many spirited discussions before we turn you over to the Court of Apostolic Causes. It shall be our goal to turn you back to the truth that you mention now, little brother. Because if we cannot, you shall face the Lord's Commissioner. And that rarely ends well."

CHAPTER TWENTY-FIVE

THE dance, which took place on the other side of the castle, atop the rocky cliffs, was something that none in attendance would soon forget. As Daria and Gianni moved into the crowd, seeking their comrades, with Piero right behind them, Gianni continued to feel as if he were walking through a dreamscape, what with the masked men and women all about. Some had gone well beyond the feathered, furry, or skinned masks that most held to their eyes. A few had entire hollow heads of a zebra, or the long, skinny neck of a giraffe. One fellow had a massive elephant head, and a second followed him around as the elephant's tail.

Such foolishness and expense. Gianni grabbed three goblets from a passing maid and handed two to Daria and Piero. It was a fine, smooth wine, unwatered. Mayhap from the pope's own vineyards, world renowned for their quality, although the grapes grew from dry, rocky soil that no one could imagine would produce anything, let alone a fine wine. They called it a miracle of God.

He watched the people about him, some already stumbling in drunkenness. He knew Amidei and Vincenzo and Ciro were somewhere near. These people were weak, defenses down, victims in the making for the likes of their enemy. How long until they drew them to a dark cave? Would they be a party to another child sacrifice, as Gianni had witnessed outside Roma? His hands itched to unsheathe his sword, hunt Amidei down, and end it here, now.

Daria knew well what he feared. Her hand tightened on his arm. "Gianni, the moon." She looked over her shoulder at the priest, who gazed upward with them.

A full moon. It was then that he knew that this party was just the beginning for Amidei and Vincenzo. On a full moon, their master called them to their foulest acts. Their attention had been so focused upon the pope and other royals that they had neglected to pay attention to the waxing moon . . .

Gianni turned to Daria and took her hands in his. "Daria, promise me. Promise me that you shall do everything in your power to remain right by my side this night. We must not let anyone separate us. Anyone."

She frowned at his intensity, but squeezed his hands. "Right beside you, husband."

"We must gather the others and make our way back to the tents," he said to them both. "We shall be safe there, together. But we must find the others." He dropped one of Daria's hands and pulled her behind him, searching for their comrades.

But as soon as they neared the raucous crowds, men and women pulled at them, inviting them in to the dance. Groups of musicians wandered, all matching the rhythm, through one tune and then another, and there were multiple circles of people lining up to dance, bowing to partners, turning. Never had they seen such a feat. The nearest thing to it was at the Morassis' mansion in Venezia, but that had been no more than a hundred people. More than three hundred were dancing here.

Gianni frowned, seeing men and women kissing passionately, out in the open. It was unseemly behavior, but no one looked upon them with surprise, all intent on their own pleasures. "We must get . . ."

A man, singing with another, fell backward into him, and all three went down. The big man fell so hard against him that Gianni fell flat on his back, hitting his head upon the hard limestone of the cliffs. He gazed at the moon, but it swam in the sky, shifting and then streaming as if now a comet. Piero's face appeared above him. "Gianni?"

"Da—Daria . . ." he said, reaching up.

Piero looked away and then left him.

꧁ ꧁ ꧁

Two women in leopard dresses grabbed Daria's hands right as the men collapsed into Gianni, taking him down. "Come! Come and dance with us!"

Daria frowned, looking over her shoulder. "I cannot. Please. Let me go."

They dragged her down the hill, and Daria fought to find a toehold to resist them. They were laughing and smiling, beautiful girls, but something was wrong. Daria could feel it within her.

Men took her hands from the women and pulled her into a loose ring of people, dancing in time with the music. The women were gone.

"Pardon me, I must excuse myself," she said to each of her dance partners, and turned to move up the hillside again, to where she had left Gianni. She had promised—

"Duchess," Abramo Amidei said, bowing low before her.

Daria's hand went to her throat.

It could not be. Not again.

She turned to run, but he caught her wrist and whipped her back around to him. Vincenzo was now at his side, but Abramo commanded all her attention. His mask gone, she could plainly see the eye patch and long scar where she had maimed him.

"Would you care to see it, healer? Might you be able to bring back the eye you stole from me?" he asked, pulling her close.

"My Lord does not heal his enemy," she said, struggling to get away from him. "I prayed that infection might spread through your entire body and take your very life."

Abramo laughed at that. "Not very holy thoughts from one of God's own."

"Yes, well, we all have our sins, do we not? You, unfortunately, have too many to name."

"You left us, Duchess, after promising to do your duty in my ceremony."

Daria laughed bitterly. "I had a change of heart."

"Ahh. I think I might have to cut the heart from your chest and eat of it. You see, now we have no choice but to hunt down and kill each of the Gifted. If we cannot turn you, bring you down, you must die." He lifted a hand and pulled a coil of her hair to his nose and smelled of it. "A pity, that. But Daria, what of your child? Do you not wish to live so that he might live as well?"

Daria froze. He could not know of her pregnancy. It was not possible . . .

Abramo suddenly froze as well, instantly mute. A second later, he released her, hands in the air. Count Armand walked around him, sword following his neck as he circled him. Daria looked up and beyond him to see Gianni, hand to the back of his head, Piero beneath his other arm, holding him up. Vincenzo and Ciro were each detained by Lucien and Matthieu of Les Baux.

The count pulled Daria back behind him, sword still pointed to Abramo's throat.

"That is twice, Count des Baux, that you have gotten between me and my quarry."

"You shall not have these people, Lord Amidei. I will do everything in my power to keep them safe from you and yours."

Abramo lifted a lazy, relaxed eye to study the count, as if there were no sword hovering near his Adam's apple. "And how shall you keep them safe from your own?" he shot back.

"My own?"

"The pope. The other nobles. Oh, I am well aware you have assembled a multitude of supporters. But it shall not be enough when the Gifted reach the Court of Apostolic Causes. No one can save them from the Inquisitor." He laughed, slowly at first, then a great belly laugh. He reached up to wipe a tear from the corner of his eye. "It is poetic, really. Beautiful." He glanced at Daria, then up the hill at Gianni, who was slowly making his way to them. "They cannot do anything but move forward with their 'prophesied cause,' driven forward by their God. But that cause will cost them their very lives."

Eight of Maximilien's men rode up on horses, swords drawn. "Gentlemen, what goes on here?" shouted the captain.

"A friendly misunderstanding," Abramo yelled, staring into Armand's eyes.

Neither of them wanted the battle to become a full-blown war here. Now.

Armand gestured to his men to lower their swords, eyes still on Lord Amidei.

Abramo leaned close and eyed Daria over his shoulder, then whispered to Armand, "Get between me and the woman again, and you shall die."

Armand stepped forward and took hold of Amidei's shirt. "Get near her again and it shall be you who forfeits his life. Or mayhap I shall take your other eye, leaving you unable to ogle the innocents." Then he stood back, forced a smile, and patted Abramo on the chest.

Amidei looked upon him with such hate that Daria barely held back her shiver. The dark lord had grown in power since their time on the isle. She could feel the magnetic pull of him, at once repulsive and undeniably attractive.

He closed his eye, as if he could feel it, too.

Gianni was there, then, and without pause he pulled back and punched Abramo with everything in him.

Amidei spun sideways and fell to the ground. Vincenzo and Ciro drew their swords, and the knights of Les Baux stood beside them.

Maximilien's knights shouted out a warning, unsheathing their swords.

∞ ∞ ∞

Dimly, Gianni could hear women screaming. He could feel people rushing about him, behind him, away from them. But all he could see was Abramo Amidei, crouched as he was, on his feet again, circling him. Neither man drew a sword.

He knew it was not part of the plan. But he could not contain his anger any longer, his desire to kill this demon and send him back to hell.

Gianni raised his chin, but he was still dizzy from hitting his head upon the rock. The Sorcerer whispered in his right ear. "Gianni, I shall have your woman."

Gianni whipped to the right, but he was not there.

He whispered in his left, "I shall make you watch as I take her life."

Gianni pulled a dagger from his belt and spun around, trying to keep up with the Sorcerer as he circled and circled and circled . . .

He could hear Daria call out to him, crying.

But she was dim, in the background. Abramo's words were echoing, resounding in his ears. "I shall kill every last one of the Gifted, and take you and Daria last. You shall not win this round, knight of the Church. I will bring you down, and the Church with it. Imagine little Tessa . . ."

"Nay!" Gianni cried, striking out at the phantom.

His knife struck into the man's gut. Gianni smiled when he heard his gasp of breath, and drove the knife deeper, wanting Abramo to die . . . die . . . die . . .

"Gianni!" Daria screamed, weeping, tugging on his arm. "*Gianni!*"

He looked to his quarry, wanting to see him take his last breaths.

But it was Count Armand, mouth wide open in pain, blue eyes open in surprise, as he fell to his knees before him.

Count Armand with Gianni's dagger in his belly.

"Nay," Gianni whispered. " 'Tis not possible . . . Nay!" he shouted, helping Armand to the ground, pulling his bloody dagger from him as he did so. He looked about, only to see Maximilien's knights moving in upon them.

Amidei was no longer in sight.

Chapter Twenty-six

Gianni was dragged off from them, weeping, screaming, reaching for Daria, for Armand. "Forgive me! I thought he was Amidei! It was a trick, the Sorcerer's trick! Oh, God in heaven! Please! Please!"

Daria was torn, wanting to see to her husband, but Piero drew her attention down to Armand, who was gasping for breath. Daria began to weep in earnest, because there was no urge, no call within her to end this nightmare, to heal her friend. She fought for breath, as if she could feel the wound deep within her own belly. It was a nightmare. Surely this was not real. *O God, please, let this not be real. Not so soon after Basilio and Rune.* She could not take it. *O God, please!*

"Armand," she whispered, her tears falling to his face. She took his hand and held it to her chest, using her other to pull away the blood-soaked cloth and see the wound beneath. She closed her eyes, fighting for breath. It was a death wound, surely having sliced kidney or liver. Gianni had driven it hard, so hard, into their friend, believing him to be Abramo . . .

Armand tried to smile, but it only made him appear ghoulish. Blood was seeping from the edges of his mouth, and his teeth were red. Anette broke through the crowd then, along with her husband. "Armand? Armand!" She went to him, lifting his head into her lap, looking down to his belly and then to Piero and Daria, panic lacing every action and expression.

"What has happened?"

"A terrible accident, Countess," Daria began.

"Sister," Armand gasped, taking her hand. "It was Gianni."

"Gianni?" Anette gasped, looking madly about.

"Sister," Armand said, trying to will calm into her. "It was Amidei's trickery. You must not . . . you must not allow Gianni . . . you mustn't let . . . tell him . . . I understand. Do not let them . . . punish him. It was done in error . . . in error . . ."

Armand looked to Daria. Piero was uttering last rites. It was cold, so cold there upon the rock, under a wide full moon high above them. "It is well, Daria. I know . . . you would do—" He paused to gasp against the pain, and then forced another smile. "You would heal me . . . if you could." His breath was coming fast now, a constant pant. "Do what . . . you came to do." His eyes widened. "Do not let this dissuade . . . you from God's call. Oh! 'Tis beautiful! Oh, if you could only . . . What I see . . . Sister, friend, what I *see* . . ."

His face and eyes froze in that expression of utter joy and pleasure. Daria and Piero both felt a wave of warmth wash over them and into Armand. She looked up quickly, hoping it was God's healing, bringing Armand back to them, but it was not.

It was Count Armand's final healing, his coming home. Angels were again present around them; they could feel them, glimpsed them in the moonlight. But then they were gone.

Anette rocked back and forth, cradling her lifeless brother's body to her, and let out a keening wail of such pure pain and grief that Daria could do nothing but join her.

❦ ❦ ❦

AMIDEI watched the scene from the second story of the castle, alongside Ciro and Vincenzo. He laughed, hollowly. "The count is out of the way, killed by the hand of the very people he swore to protect. It shall cost them some of their support among the nobles. Gianni shall be hanged for his crime, leaving the others more vulnerable than ever." He reached out to clasp each one on the shoulder, and stilled as the women wailed in grief. The music had long ago died, the people drawn en masse by the commotion. A gasp washed through the crowd as word passed that the Count des Baux was dead, murdered at the hand of a friend.

"How did you manage it?" Vincenzo asked, leaning against the railing, staring down at the people. "How did you make Gianni think you were still there?"

"A simple trick of the mind," Abramo said. "When people are impassioned—by love, by fear, by anger—they are the most vulnerable to it. Come, friends. Master shall be so pleased by our success this night that he shall undoubtedly reward us greatly. Let us gather the people and depart."

TOWER GUARD

Avignon

Chapter Twenty-seven

Lord Devenue and Anette des Baux escorted the Gifted back to the Richardieu manor in Villeneuve-des-Avignon, barely able to meet their eyes. Daria grieved, grieved as she had not since her own parents died. Armand's passing, Gianni's imprisonment, the wedge that death had placed between them and the house of Les Baux—brought up unspent tears over Basilio and Rune, as well as tears of fear over their collective future, her baby's future.

She had wanted to see Anette home, to accompany her and grieve with her as Armand was burned upon his funeral pyre, as Basilio, Rune, and the count had been burned in the past month. She had wanted to hear Anette sing as the flames reached the sky and she sent her prayers up to God with both villager and priest and family member. But Anette had gently, firmly told her to stay where she was.

"I shall return to you all, Daria," she said, holding her hands in the receiving courtyard of the manor. "But I must take some time. To pray through this, accept it, before I have the strength to fight alongside you once again."

Daria nodded, unable to speak around the lump in her throat.

"Daria," she said, waiting for her friend's eyes to meet hers. "I know that Gianni was tricked. I shall see him released. I have two lawyers working on it as we speak."

Upon Anette's pleading, the prince had released Gianni to the pope's *Honneur Gard*, to be detained in Avignon until it was decided what was to be done with him.

" 'Tis a royal mess."

"Indeed. But Armand did not want his death to cause you or yours harm. He made that abundantly clear before he . . ." She squeezed Daria's hands, trying to maintain control and not give in to more tears. " 'Twas a cruel blow Amidei dealt us. I need a bit of time. I simply cannot think of anything but . . . I need to see Armand home." She looked over to the wagon, her blue eyes huge in a wan face. "We shall not be away longer than a week, a fortnight at the longest. We shall return to you with my strength back. Together, we shall return to battle Amidei and any other who endangers what God would have you do. Armand pledged our lives to your cause, as did my husband. I have not forgotten that, Daria. Nothing has changed."

"Well I know your grief, Anette. Gianni and I would do anything we could to change what happened. Our enemy is wily, but Gianni . . . Amidei spotted a weakness within my husband and exploited it. He turned Gianni's rage into his own revenge. If only—"

"Armand would not stand for us spending time on *if-only*s, Daria. He and I knew, from the day we stepped into the old chapel, that we were a part of something grand, something of God. We were honored that God brought you to us. I am still sure of that, still honored, despite the cost. But the cost . . . This terrible cost. I was ill prepared . . ." Her blue eyes, so like Armand's, drifted right, wide and glossy with tears.

Daria smiled and the tears ran down her face again, her heart heavy with grief, but she clung to the hope within her friend's words. "Sing of his honor, Anette, his valor, his life. As his body burns, sing for me. I shall pray for you and remember you, weep with you, as you say your final farewells."

"Thank you," Anette whispered. Then she turned and accepted Dimitri's open arms.

He took her to a wagon and passed her up to a waiting knight. The young lord took a crate of pigeons from the back of the wagon. "If you have immediate need of us, send one of these home to Les Baux."

Daria nodded and took it from him, not trusting herself to speak without breaking down again.

Dimitri climbed into the wagon. "We shall return, Daria," he said lowly, repeating his wife's pledge. The wagon driver flicked the reins and the company moved off, but Dimitri held Daria's gaze. "You are not abandoned. Look for us within a fortnight."

"We shall," Daria said, raising a hand to the sky in farewell.

The wagons moved toward the bridge, one carrying the body of the count of Les Baux, under the flag of a sixteen-pointed star. The Blanchettes, the Duvins, and even the Richardieus followed behind, casting Daria sorrowful looks. They would see Anette and Dimitri through the funeral and then return with them.

She knew Piero was behind her without turning.

"We must rally, Daria," he said as the wagons and men turned along the bend in the road. "Find the strength for another battle."

"I am weary," she said, lifting a hand to her head. "So weary. I believed we were free of Amidei and Vincenzo, their master, for a time. I made myself hope. For love. For life." Her hand went to her belly and she stroked it, as if she could hold the tiny babe in her womb. Amidei knew of her pregnancy. Would he take her child? Would that be his final blow?

Vito and Ugo neared, Hasani right behind him. Gaspare and Josephine rounded a corner, and the children, playing by the water, stood to watch the procession of wagons rumble by, and ran back to the group assembling.

"They stare down upon us, not knowing whether to protect or kill us," Daria said, looking up to Lucien and Matthieu, and four other knights of Les Baux, left behind to guard them.

"Hush," Piero said, eyeing the knights. "You know as well as I that they grieve their count."

"A count who would now still live, if we had not accepted his hospitality," Daria said.

Piero moved into her line of vision. "A count who demanded we come; a count who sent his knights out to collect us. A count who spoke to his father once more because we entered his realm. A count who saw his sister rediscover love, because we came. A count who knew faith, wild and free, of a God who transcends time, *because he knew us.*" He placed his small hands on her upper arms. "Daria, it will be well. It will be. But you *must* believe. You must hope. You must stand firm!"

The small priest walked before them all. " '*Qui autem confirmat nos vobiscum in Christum, et qui unxit nos Deus,*' " he said. He turned to Daria. "Translate it for them, Daria."

She paused, searching the ground, thinking of running.

Away from them. Away from all of it. The pain, the fear . . .

"Daria de Capezzana," Piero ground out. "Translate it. '*Qui autem confirmat nos vobiscum in Christum . . .*' "

" 'Now it is God who makes both us and you stand firm in Christ,' " she said in a whisper.

"Louder, please."

She raised her face, furious at the impudent little man. " 'Now it is God who makes both us and you stand firm in Christ!' " she shouted.

The others stood mute, wide-eyed, watching their priest and lady.

"Good," Piero said, giving her a thin-lipped smile. "Let us go on. *'Et qui signavit nos, et dedit pignus Spiritus in cordibus nostris.'* "

Daria turned away and sighed. " 'He anointed us, set his seal of ownership on us, and put his Spirit in our hearts as a deposit, guaranteeing what is to come.' "

"A deposit," Piero emphasized. "Now, from Ephesians. Translate, please . . . *'in quo et vos, cum audissetis verbum veritatis, Evangelium salutis vestrae, in quo et credentes signanti estis Spiritu promissionis Sancto . . . laudem gloriae ipsius . . .'* "

He paused and watched her. She looked at him angrily, stubbornly holding to her grief, not yet ready to embrace hope, light. How dare he slap her with Scripture, use it as a weapon . . .

"Daria . . . *'in quo et vos . . .'* "

" 'And you also were included in Christ when you heard the word of truth, the gospel of your salvation. Having believed, you were marked in him with a seal, the promised Holy Spirit, who is a deposit guaranteeing our inheritance until the redemption of those who are God's own possession— to the praise of his glory.' "

"Again, the deposit, with the hope in the future . . ."

Daria sighed and sat down upon a boulder. The words were easing her anger in spite of her stubborn hold, easing away the blackness in her soul and filling her with light.

Piero looked at them all. "Satan's greatest advantage is if we act like the unholy, if we act as we *feel*. He wants us to believe ourselves defiled, unclean, unworthy of entering the King's court. He wants us to serve ourselves, our own ambitions, our own concerns, our own whims and emotions, rather than answer our Lord God's call." He paced in front of them. "But we are sealed by Christ, and within us abides *the Holy Spirit.*

"My friends," he said. "Painful though this blow may be, we must believe that our God will ever be victorious. We must cling to the truth, always and forever. We must praise him through the sorrow, through the pain, through imprisonment, through loss. Through it all, he must reign victorious in our hearts and minds, or our enemy shall win again. Do you want that?"

"Nay," whispered Tessa, looking up at her priest. The others shook their heads. Even Daria.

Piero drew near her again and laid a hand on her shoulder. "Take joy, daughter, in our King, for even when all seems dark, he is present, ready to hold us. And the day is soon at hand, when he shall rule again. *'Et subvertam solium regnorum et conteram fortitudinem regni gentium et subvertam quadrigam et ascensorem eius et descendent . . . fratris sui . . .'*"

" 'I will overrun royal thrones,' " Daria whispered in translation, staring at the river, " 'and shatter the power of foreign kingdoms. I will overthrow chariots and their drivers; horses and their riders will fall, each by the sword . . . of his . . . brother.' "

She glanced up at Piero, faltering over the words, tearing up again, but he continued on, steadily staring back at her, willing her to find the strength to continue, to begin again, always, always beginning again. " 'On that day, declares the Lord Almighty, "I will take you, my servant . . . and I will make you like my signet ring, *for I have chosen you*," declares the Lord of Armies.' "

I have chosen you. Daria rose and looked to the river. On and on the river ran, through time and space, making its way onward as men and women were born and others died along its banks. Ever present, ever constant.

And across it rode a most welcome sight, a vision from her past, her present, and now her future. Ambrogio Rossellino.

"You people certainly do not know the first thing about keeping to the shadows, now do you," he said, dismounting and coming to Daria, embracing her, lifting her tenderly in his arms, then moving on to greet the others. He turned back to Daria, his arms around Tessa's shoulders, who grinned.

"I have seen your husband," he said. "He is well. Unhappy as the pope's new animals in their cages. But well enough." He eyed the priest, Hasani, the others. "Word has it the countess shall not press charges, that she believes her brother's stabbing was an accident. But the pope shall use Gianni's imprisonment to press his hand. Prepare thyselves, friends. Your greatest battle is soon upon you."

Chapter Twenty-eight

Cardinal Boeri came to him on his fourth day of imprisonment.

Gianni glanced up at him and then back to his fingers. "You betrayed us," he said. He sat in the corner of a barren stone cell.

The cardinal gestured to the guard to unlock the cell door and let him inside. The guard locked them in together, and with another gesture from the cardinal, left them to speak. No others were held in this group of cells, everyone else freed and pardoned in honor of Maximilien's generosity. Gianni had been alone the entire time, giving him plenty of opportunity to rehash the fateful night, his failures, and where the blame might ultimately reside.

Cardinal Boeri leaned against the wall. "I did not betray you. I would have come sooner, but I was only now granted access. They have fed you? Given you water?"

Gianni sighed and rose, brushing off his pant legs. "You told the pope all our secrets."

"Not all."

"You told him of our identities, gave him cause to hold me, take me, after . . ."

"I had not foreseen that occurrence," Boeri said sorrowfully. "What happened, man?"

"Trickery," Gianni said, going through it for the thousandth time in his mind. "Amidei was there. I was furious. He had Daria, *Daria* again. I couldn't let . . . I wanted to . . ." He paced back and forth. "He is the Sorcerer, Cardinal."

"I know."

"He turned my fury, my desire for revenge into—"

"Confusion."

"Yes," Gianni said, feeling the pain again in that moment of realization that something had gone desperately, terribly wrong. "I thought I stabbed Amidei. I thrust my dagger in, and I swear, it was our common enemy's face before me . . . and then it was Armand."

His legs buckled beneath him and he bumped heavily into the wall, sinking then, face in his hands.

Cardinal Boeri let him weep for a moment, then leaned over and patted his shoulder. "Our enemy is crafty. Well he knows how to make his way into the human heart. Now get hold of yourself, Sir Gianni, and rise. Rise. We cannot make war upon the enemy if we are not on our feet. Or at the very least, upon our knees in prayer."

His tone awakened something within Gianni, something he had not felt since leaving his father's fields outside Siena and going to the holy city to discover his future as a squire of a knight de Vaticana de Roma. He pushed upward on weak legs and faced his former employer, wiping his face of tears.

Cardinal Boeri reached up and took his cheek in hand. "Do not feel your sorrow as shame, my son," he said. "You have lost a friend, a friend by your own hand. But turn your sorrow into righteous determination to see this thing through, to honor Count Armand's life, given in the midst of a noble cause." He dropped his hand and paced before him, then paused and looked back to him. "I have my own confessions to make."

Gianni studied him, waiting. Could he bear another blow? More deceit?

The cardinal sighed heavily, as if trying to draw strength to say what he must. "I confess I set out to use you and yours, Gianni. I wished to control you, the Gifted. To make you make the pope see he must return the papacy to the Vaticana de Roma."

"Your dream," Gianni whispered.

"Indeed. Forgive me, friend. But there is more. I had thought that if I were to have you all firmly in hand, if you owed me a debt, if I could control you, I could use you for more than that. I had terrible dreams, Gianni, terrible ambitions. I wished to use you to become pope myself."

Gianni watched his face, saw his own misery and guilt reflected in his cardinal's eyes. The cardinal set to pacing. Gianni waited for him to continue.

"My time with you, back here in Avignon, and at Maximilien's masquerade. Afterward, I saw . . ."

His eyes were drawn to the window, and his face blanched at the memory. "I glimpsed . . ."

Gianni sighed. "Did you attend Lord Amidei's ceremony?"

Cardinal Boeri started and turned. "Ceremony? Nay. But Gianni, there is something foul among my fellow cardinals. Amidei had made his way among them. He owns a few of them. I glimpsed unspeakable things. Terrible things. They tried to bring me in, persuade me to join them. They promised gifts that you cannot imagine. Of the flesh, of power . . ."

Well he could imagine. Daria had faced such temptation. But it was he who had succumbed to Amidei's trickery.

"Their draw was powerful, so powerful . . . Gianni, they believe themselves gods. Amidei had done that—made them see themselves as gods. They cloak their goals in language of the holy, but this group of men are on a most unholy course."

He crossed the few feet between them, his face awash in concern and anger. "But naming their sin as such served only to convict me as well. I understood at last that my call was not to bring the papacy home, nor for me to be pope—that is only my own ambition. My call is to support you and yours to battle against the one who has been our enemy all along—the dark lord. That is why I was given the letter, why you came to be the captain of my guard. God knew it all along, that we would join together to fight his foe. If we can defeat him, it will be a victory for all within the Church, from the least to the greatest."

Gianni nodded at him, well understanding weakness, failure, accepting his apology.

"Forgive me, friend. I have not been a father of the Church. I have ministered only to my selfish ambition."

"You are forgiven," Gianni said, clasping the cardinal, elbow to elbow. "Now hear my own confession and let us plan as absolved and free men."

cho cho cho

"WORD has it," Ambrogio said, sitting down at the Richardieus' table with the others, "that the countess has demanded Gianni's release. Her lawyers have refused to leave the *palais* until it is done, claiming the pope had no jurisdiction when he took Gianni from Maximilien's home."

"Go on," Piero said.

"And since the countess refuses to press charges, supporting Gianni's claim that it was accidental, they are having difficulty finding the means to keep him imprisoned.

"So I would expect him to be released within a day or two," he said. "But you all shall be brought before the pope again, soon. Are you prepared for that?"

Piero looked troubled. He paced, chin in hand, thinking. "The countess has departed just this morning, taking her brother's body home to Les Baux to see to his funeral. We do not know how long she shall be gone."

"A week or two, she promised no longer than a fortnight," Daria said.

"But without her," Piero said, "what will become of our noble compatriots? We had thought we would venture into battle with them at our side."

"We must be prepared to venture forth," said Josephine, "without anyone beside us other than our Lord and Savior. If he has brought us this far, for this purpose, we can do nothing but carry onward. He shall see us through."

"There is something very dark indeed among the halls of the *palais*," Ambrogio said. "I have heard whisperings of foul happenings. The cardinals, they are unraveling; it is as if they are boats that have slipped their moorings and been cast upon the river."

Piero stared at him. "Amidei."

Ambrogio nodded. "I have seen him among them."

"Not all of them."

"Nay. He has not had time. But six of the most powerful are most firmly at his mercy. There is a wild look in their eyes. They barely make it through their duties before they slip away from the *palais*."

"Is the pope aware of what is unfolding within his palace?"

"Nay. Not entirely. He is absorbed in the expansion work, the building of the new wing, the duties of seeing to all of Christendom." He looked at them all. "Do you know that the *palais* receives more than three hundred missives a day? From as far away as the Orient? That more than five hundred people are employed by the *palais* on a daily basis? That four thousand directly report to the Holy Father?" He shook his head. "I have never seen a king so busy. He can hardly be blamed for not recognizing what is unfolding beneath his very nose."

Piero studied him. "You have had opportunity to spend time with him, Ambrogio? See him talk with others, counsel others?"

Ambrogio nodded. "From afar. Be encouraged. I believe him to be a good man. Distracted, at the moment, by his countless duties and the constant building within the *palais*. He has made some misguided decisions over indulgences to raise funds."

Piero let out a breathless laugh. "Indeed. Selling papers to get people into heaven, *bah*." He sobered. "But deep within him . . . Brogi, do you think Amidei has reached him as well?"

"Nay," Ambrogio said firmly. "But there are two cardinals who seem closest to him: Cardinals Morano and Corelli." Ambrogio looked at the children and motioned for them to depart. "Just for a bit," he said with a sorrowful smile. "This is not for young minds and hearts." Reluctantly all three rose from the table and left the room as instructed. A knight shut the door firmly behind them.

"It pains me to tell you this. It may only be rumor, but it makes sense with the way Amidei works. Amidei has been seeking out Cardinal Morano—by all accounts, an exceedingly faithful man—for spiritual counsel. Amidei confessed a terrible appetite for women," he said, eyeing Daria. She looked away to the window. "He confessed to bedding many. To desiring more. To experimentation . . . The cardinal absolved him of his sin, gave him a spiked belt to wear and a whip to use upon himself when the desires grew too great."

"If only he would flay himself to death," Vito said.

Piero lifted a hand to silence him, but the knight only bespoke what they all were feeling.

"For weeks this has been apparently unfolding. The cardinal has gone on to find a suitable bride for Amidei, thinking that if he eases his need with a Church-sanctioned wife, his carnal days are over."

Vito laughed aloud.

"Amidei has accepted his recommendation—"

"We cannot allow that marriage to occur," Daria interrupted, standing.

"And Morano is so pleased at Amidei's progress, he has reportedly begun to confess his own sins to Amidei."

"What?" Piero asked, flushing red at the neck.

"Such is the way our enemy works," Gaspare said.

"They spend a great deal of time together. Amidei and Vincenzo have resided in the cardinal's mansion for a week now. An eavesdropping maid, my source, told me the cardinal confessed carnal sins committed long ago, before he took his vows. But he said the desires remain."

"Such is the way *flesh* works," Piero said. "Only God can fill our minds with the holy. But we must ask it of him."

Ambrogio paused.

"There is more," Piero said flatly.

"Five nights past, after the masquerade, Amidei and the others had one of their ceremonies. It was widely attended. By maid and cardinal alike."

Daria closed her eyes, leaning her head against the cool plaster wall like a cold cloth against a fever. Not wanting to know what he was about to say, yet aware she must hear it.

"My young friend, the maid, was horrified, properly rushing back for confession and a declaration never to enter any room that Lord Amidei is in again. She has left the cardinal's employ."

"Take care, friend," Piero warned. "Fill our minds only with the barest of facts."

Ambrogio grimaced. "Well I know of what you speak. Wide is Amidei's reach, and spreading," he said to all of them. "He must, must be stopped. If he infiltrates every cardinal's mind, every cardinal's heart, it will not be long until he controls the pope himself. All of Christendom is in danger."

"It was so bad?" Daria asked, daring to look at her old friend.

"No eyes have seen the depravity of that ceremony. And what is worse, Amidei turned it in their heads. In their eyes, in their memories, they believe it a holy venture, an enlightening ceremony where they saw at last how things ought to be. God must have had his angels around that girl."

Daria's eyes met Piero's, then Gaspare's and Hasani's, even Josephine's blank eyes that so strangely seemed as if she could see.

It was time to get to the *palais*. Even before the pope demanded their presence, they must demand his.

"I must confess something else," Ambrogio said.

"Speak," Piero said, tensing.

But Ambrogio smiled. "The Chapel of Saint John was fully prepared for frescoes. It merely needed the right artist to lay pigment upon the plaster. While you were away, Simone and I, working long into the night, completed them."

Daria let out a curious laugh through her nostrils, seeing the mischief in his eyes. "So you wish to confess that your weariness produced . . . unworthy results?"

"Nay, the results are grand, as usual," he said, raising an eyebrow. "But the executioner who took John the Baptist's head? The face of Satan, hovering in the corner at Golgotha? The face of Judas, at our Lord's table? All three bear a striking resemblance to men we know."

Daria let out a breathy laugh of disbelief. "You did not."

"I did," Ambrogio said, nodding. "It shall not be long until one of the cardinals ushers our friend into the new chapel for a look."

Vito clapped him on the back and began laughing, and they all joined in, laughing so hard they cried.

ഷ ഷ ഷ

It took everything in him to bear the entrance into the chapel, to pretend admiration for Simone Martini's work. But he dearly wanted to make his way into Cardinal Stefani's mind and life as he had so easily with the others. This one was difficult, resistant to him.

And while Stefani oversaw all the pope's endeavors to make the *palais* something of world renown, he was also the keeper to the keys of the cells far beneath the *palais* floor. If he could befriend the cardinal, he might gain access to the prison and kill Gianni before the man was released.

Vincenzo trailed behind, obediently admiring the new frescoes that had been added in the past week, the vast array of bronze stars set into the vast, barrel-vaulted ceiling of the Grand Tinel, the first of the pope's private compartments—done by apprentices of Martini—and then up to the Chapel of Saint John.

"It was just completed yesterday," Stefani said, opening the doors and ushering them inward. "You are of the first honored guests to lay eyes upon it." He looked up. "Is it not magnificent?"

"Magnificent," muttered Amidei, feeling physically ill. What kind of prayers had already been uttered here? He had not felt such presence since he had been beaten back by the Gifted and their God on the isle, and before that in Il Campo de Siena . . .

His eyes stilled on the scene of Golgotha, relishing the Lord Jesus upon the cross, running across his dying body as if it gave him sustenance. But as his gaze traveled over the faces of the mourning, glorious in their defeat, he stopped on the ghouls and the face of Satan, painted in blue in the corner. His face. Abramo Amidei's.

His head whipped to Simone Martini's, the artist now visibly shaken as he looked from Amidei to the face of Satan. "It is not I who painted that, m'lord," he whispered. He swallowed hard.

"Lord Amidei," Vincenzo whispered, nodding up to another panel above them, this scene depicting the beheading of Saint John the Baptist. The executioner, with axe in hand, was again clearly Abramo. "You are not alone," Vincenzo whispered, nodding to the upper right panel, a scene of the Last Supper. Judas, with Vincenzo's face.

Abramo Amidei seethed, searching his mind. He whipped his head back to Simone, ignoring Stefani, who stood, mouth agape, seeing what they had already discovered. It would take only hours for word of this to spread throughout the *palais*, for all to come and see it with their own eyes. What traction would be lost if the cardinals saw this?

"Who assisted you in this chapel?" he asked, striding over to the small man, already knowing the answer.

"Ambrogio Rossellino," said the artist, trembling before him. "I swear, m'lord, I had no idea it was your visage. No idea—"

"I want it destroyed," he said to the cardinal, over Simone's shoulder. "Now. Destroy it this instant and repaint it. Close off these doors and allow no entrance."

"Nay, m'lord," Cardinal Stefani said, looking at him as if he were half mad. "I can understand your embarrassment at the apparent likeness—"

"I want it destroyed!" he screamed.

Two knights came running, swords drawn at the uncustomary shouting so near the sacred chambers. Behind them were a bishop and Cardinal Saucille. All rushed in.

Amidei turned and walked out and down the stairs. He had to get to the men who could see his task done. Immediately. He paused in the Grand Tinel, feeling Vincenzo pause beside him, closed his eyes, and pinched his temples with middle finger and thumb.

"Lord Amidei," said a small voice.

He opened his eyes to see the pope, Cardinal Corelli, two bishops, and four secretaries trailing behind him.

Amidei went to his knee, reaching forward to kiss the pope's proffered ring, feeling the bile of hatred rise in his throat even as he forced a proper expression to his face.

"We take it you have seen our new chapel, Lord Amidei," said the man, not giving him permission to rise. Vincenzo still was kneeling, just behind Abramo, but was ignored.

"I have, Holiness," Abramo said evenly.

The pope smiled, staring down at him without blinking. "The artists took some creative license with their interpretations. By and large, we are well pleased."

Could he have missed the resemblance? Might it all be in Abramo's imagination?

"We all would do well to pay attention that Satan still lingers at the foot of the cross," the pope said.

Abramo could feel his smile fall. This man missed nothing. "The enemy is always about, Holiness," he ground out.

"Always," said the pope, still staring down at him. "Vast is our holy realm, Lord Amidei, but do not underestimate our power to closely watch those things that are of the greatest importance." He brushed past him, leaving him on his knees.

Abramo frowned and met Vincenzo's gaze over his shoulder.

"I understand you wished to pay a visit to Sir Gianni de Capezzana," the pope said from behind him.

Shoving down his anger, Abramo shifted around to face him, still on his knees. The man toyed with him. "An old friend from Toscana. I thought I might bring him a word of encouragement."

"Hmm. We highly doubt that. But you needn't seek him out. Upon Countess des Baux's urging, we thought it appropriate to release him an hour past. He shall return with the rest of the fabled Gifted in three days' time, in a private audience with me." He strode forward. "Lord Amidei?"

"Yes, Holiness?" Abramo ground out.

"See that no harm comes to Sir de Capezzana nor any of the others between now and our private audience. If anything dire does transpire, you shall be the first we come to. Deep is the division between you and them. We have seen it. Do not cross the divide. Is that understood?"

"Most clearly," he said.

The pope sat back on his heels and studied him. A small smile grew at the corners of his mouth; he undoubtedly was seeing Abramo's face as Satan's own. When he got hold of Ambrogio . . .

"We shall assign six knights to follow your every step, Lord Armidei. Do not be surprised to see them behind you," said the pope.

He turned to go, leaving Abramo sputtering in rage. Just what exactly was transpiring here? When had the tide turned? When had the Rhône again shifted direction?

CHAPTER TWENTY-NINE

DARIA ran across the narrow footbridge to meet him, and Gianni swept her into his arms, holding her close, tenderly, whispering over and over, "Oh Daria, I am so sorry. So sorry."

At last she pulled away and looked up into his green eyes. "You did as any one of us might have," she said. "Armand understood you had been tricked. He could see it all. And Anette . . ."

"Anette?"

"She grieves. But she knows the truth of it, too, Gianni. She will return to us."

Gianni looked up into the winter-dormant tree branches. "She left, then."

"To say her farewells to Armand. See him home."

He sighed heavily and wrapped an arm around her shoulders as they began to walk back to the river manor. "I would have liked to do the same."

"I know. We all feel it. Father Piero has proposed a remembrance ceremony of sorts. We shall honor Count Armand's memory here, even though we shall not be at his funeral pyre."

"They will burn his sword with him?" Gianni asked.

"In the manner of all the valiant," she said. Her eyes went to the ground, but in her head, she could only see Basilio and Rune and Armand's father, all clutching their swords in hand as the fires were lit beneath them. The flames rising to the sky, heat so great they had to back away . . .

"So much death, in this life," Gianni said.

"So much life, among the death," Daria returned. She had to tell him of the baby. It could not wait any longer. She turned to face him, but a shout went out from behind her. They turned together, to see Vito, with Tessa across his back. The two cried out in joy and rushed to them, embracing Gianni. Their shouts roused the rest of the household, and soon all were about Gianni.

Daria backed away and watched as they enfolded him as a long-lost brother. Even Lucien and Matthieu came near, tentatively reaching out an arm for Gianni to grasp, silently giving him their blessing, their forgiveness. Piero had spent some time with them of late, explaining Amidei's great power over the mind, the flesh, the heart. He had explained enough of Daria and Gianni's history with the Sorcerer that they might see things from Gianni's perspective, understand how things might have gone so desperately wrong.

She could see from the tender look upon Gianni's face that their embrace and welcome meant the most to her husband. As they reached out, touched him, held him within their gaze, he found some of the absolution he sought. Daria knew that only when he was forgiven by Anette would this journey be complete.

"Come, husband," she said, taking his hand and leading him into the manor. "You must bathe and eat and tell us what you have learned while in the pope's close care."

Gianni smiled. "Close care? If that is his close care, then I would hate to be in his prison."

"We wouldn't want that," she said with a grin. "Go upstairs. I will bring water for a hot bath," she said.

"Only if you join me in it," he whispered.

She shoved him away and yet smiled at him. "Mayhap in the second bath," she said. "You smell of pig slop and lesser things."

He gave her a shrug and turned and headed up the stair, his weariness plainly evident in every step he took. He bore the effects of five nights in a prison cell, the grief of the loss of a friend, but she could detect no abuse. "Thank you, Lord Jesus," she whispered, filling a huge kettle to set atop the cook's fire.

Gianni was asleep, facedown across their bed, when she and the maids came up, buckets of water in hand. They poured it into the massive master washtub, filling it halfway with the steaming water, then returned to the kitchen to fetch five more, letting the captain nap.

Daria looked outside and then down at her snoring husband, aware that it was but three in the afternoon. If he slept for the night now, he might awaken partway through the night and prowl the manor, awakening them all. Nay, it was best to rouse him now with a bath, help him remember life, hope, love. Then he could tell them what he had learned in the *palais* and retire for the night.

She smiled and locked the door, then went to the bed and slowly undressed. She stared at her husband and rubbed her belly, aching with the need to tell him. But she wanted him alert, his attention solely on her, not so distracted, not so terribly weary. Daria leaned forward and gave him delicate kisses atop his temple and ear, wrinkling her nose at the rank smell of him. He roused and opened one eye at her.

Immediately he rolled to his side and held his head in one hand, gazing upon her. "What mischief are you up to, wife?"

"Mischief?" she asked, a puzzled expression upon her face. "No mischief. Just a bath as you requested." She turned and slipped into the sudsy, hot water, then looked back to see his grin. "Come, husband," she said, reaching out a wet, bubble-covered arm. The soap reminded her of home, with its scent of juniper berry and anise . . .

ᘒ ᘒ ᘒ

"THE cardinal came to me and confessed a greater ambition in his heart," said Gianni, sitting with the others around the great dining room table after they had supped.

"Which ambitions?" asked Father Piero, fingering his knife, stabbing a rind of pork fat and stuffing it in his mouth.

Gianni remembered the priest's strange hesitation with the pope, shoved it from his mind, and continued. "He confessed that he had hoped to use an alliance with the Gifted as a means to bring home the papacy to Roma. And moreover, he confessed his own desire to be crowned pope."

They all stared at him, absorbing the information.

"He has come to see the error of such desires," he said, looking each in the eye. "The Lord has made it apparent to him that his task is not to ascend to greatness, but rather to assist us in our monumental task. He now sees it as the rationale for my coming to him and serving alongside him in the hunt for the Sorcerer and others of the dark, for how he came to be the keeper of a portion of our letter. And moreover, why he is a cardinal. He has been kept separate, untainted by the work of Amidei here in Avignon, and yet he still has a favored voice within the pope's ear. He has warned the Holy Father of what is transpiring among the cardinals, of Amidei's widening web."

Piero studied him. "Are you certain that he is now a trustworthy ally?"

"Upon my life," Gianni returned.

ඊ ඊ ඊ

THE Gifted rose just before daybreak, building a massive fire and holding a vigil of silence for Count Armand Rieu des Baux, just as they knew their friends did at the same time on the limestone cliffs beside the castle. The fire lit easily, for the men had stacked wood dried last autumn high, and laid the kindling well.

Piero spoke in a hushed whisper. "Good is the Lord, for he brings us friends along this difficult path, friends we shall see yet again, in our Lord's own kingdom, a kingdom without end." He took the torch from Vito and passed it to Gianni, who threw it across the kindled pile. It immediately caught and spread, moving about the pile at a steady pace until all was aflame.

The fire's light drove away the last bit of darkness, even as the sun rose over the eastern horizon. "The enemy considers death his own victory, when he might extinguish the Lord's light among the world," Piero said, walking between the Gifted and the flames. "But God knows that death is but the beginning. In the hereafter, we are relinquished . . . to peace, to hope, to nothing but freedom and worship of our Lord God on High."

They stared back at him, eyes drawn to the flames and back to their priest again. "Armand is lost to us, but not to the Father. Large is his reward in heaven, as it shall be for us. We shall not fear death," he said, looking each in the face, waiting until each acknowledged him. "We shall not fear death. *We shall not fear death!*

"The devil presumes it is his greatest weapon. We can take this weapon from his hands. If we believe, brothers and sisters, truly believe, that our very lives are in God's hands alone, then no one, no one can ever instill fear in our hearts again. This life is temporary, fleeting. The eternal is ahead, a life in the Garden, as it was meant to be. How many of our friends have pledged and given their very lives to our own cause? Lucan, Aldo, Beata in

Siena; Basilio and Rune on the bridge." He stopped before Gianni, observing his abject misery. He reached out a hand and laid it on his shoulder. "And now Armand.

"Mayhap they saw it more clearly than we ourselves have. No matter how we try, how we fight," he said, again pacing before them, forcing each to look into his eyes, "we cannot cling to a life that is not our own. We must relinquish our rights to the Father, and trust that he will see us to *his* end, come pain or glory. Do you believe this as truth?"

They nodded, understanding the import of his words, why he lent such intensity and vigor. Well each could imagine the wrap of rope around chest and waist and hands and legs to a stake. Well each could imagine the Inquisitor's nod, the flames alight at their feet. They had no choice. No choice but to lay their very lives in the Father's hands just as their friends had done before them. It was their only hope.

How many had died for this cause? Daria wondered. In protection of the letter, or portions of the letter? What had become of the prophets who had painted their portraits among the borders? Of those who had painted their faces among frescoes, of those who had woven images of peacock and dragon into holy tapestries, of those who had sculpted them into figures that had lain dormant, deep beneath the recesses of Les Baux? How many had lived and died, all a part of the Father's long plan?

All at once, the import of their task, the slow arrival of their Master's making, made her knees weak. She fell to the ground beside her husband, weeping with him, half in grief, half in overwhelmed awe at the task before them, the long coming of this time. She watched and worshipped her Lord and Savior as his sun, birthed from his Father's hands, arose in the east. Dimly, she felt her brothers and sisters coming to their knees as well. Her life, her child's life, her husband's life, were not her own to hold.

She must relinquish them to the King. Daria opened her hands before her, in front of flames that singed the tips. "Take us all," she whispered, "we are nothing if we are not yours, my King."

Gently, Father Piero knelt beside her and lifted her up and embraced her, seeing that she had taken in what he was trying to impart. "Come, daughter. Let us share the Truth with the others."

She rose and followed behind him, translating his words from the Latin as he read the Scriptures. At some point, she became aware of the four knights of the Palais de le Pape sitting atop their horses, mouths agape, watching them. But she ignored them, taking their presence in as part of the Lord's grand plan. Their task was greater still . . . instilling courage among the Gifted, come what may. Every word bolstered her own heart, lifted her own chin. She had little doubt that it would do the same for the rest.

" 'The cords of death entangled me,' " Daria translated in little more than a whisper, barely discernible above the crackling of the fire behind them. She cleared her throat. " 'The anguish of the grave came upon me. I was overcome by trouble and sorrow.' "

Piero continued in Latin.

" 'Then I called upon the name of the Lord; O Lord! Save me!' " she continued on, translating now for the Gifted, in the language of Toscana, and again in Provençal, wanting the knights to hear. " 'The Lord is gracious and righteous; our God is full of compassion. The Lord protects the simple-hearted; when I was in great need, he saved me. Be at rest once more, O my soul, for the Lord has been good to you. For you, O Lord, have delivered my soul from death, my eyes from death, my feet from stumbling, that I may walk before the Lord in the land of the living.' "

She shared a look with Piero and continued on. " 'I believed, therefore I said, "I am greatly afflicted." And in my dismay, I said, "All men are liars." How can I repay the Lord for all his goodness to me? I will lift up the cup of salvation and call on the name of the Lord.' "

Daria turned toward the papal knights and strode toward them, still translating the priest's words as she walked. " 'I will fulfill my vows to the Lord in the presence of all his people. Precious in the sight of the Lord is the death of his saints. O Lord, truly I am your servant; I am your servant,' " she said, pausing as she realized her husband was beside her.

" 'The son of your maidservant,' " Gianni said, looking down at her as they walked toward the knights together, taking her hand.

"The *daughter* of your maidservant," Daria whispered.

Piero's Latin words came to them in a shout, encouraging them onward.

" 'You have freed me from my chains,' " said Gianni.

" 'I will sacrifice a thank offering to you and call on the name of the Lord. I will fulfill my vows to the Lord in the presence of all the people,' " Daria said, reaching up to take the scroll from a young, stunned knight's hands.

Piero continued in Latin from behind them.

" 'In the courts of the house of the Lord—in your midst, O Jerusalem. Praise the Lord,' " ended Gianni. He gathered his wife in the safe nestle of his arm and turned her away from the knights, men who would soon ride hard back to the *palais* to report all they had witnessed.

But for now, it was only them. The Gifted. Safe within the Father's own hands.

CHAPTER THIRTY

"How shall we approach it?" Gianni asked as they rode toward the palace two days later, having supped and feasted the previous night as if it might be their last opportunity. They rode across the bridge of Bénezet and the palace rose, high and still and strong in the early-morning light.

"Forthrightly," said Josephine. "Truth is truth. Begin at the beginning. Leave nothing out. Force the Holy Father to face God's own story, woven among his people. What he does with it is out of our hands."

"Well spoken, sister," Piero said. "It shall be as she says. We shall begin at the beginning, telling the pope all of it."

"That shall take the better part of the day!" Daria exclaimed.

"So be it," said Piero. "He has called us into audience. We have prayed that he would be shown the light, that darkness shall not prevail. We shall entrust the rest to our God."

They rode on across the bridge, breathing deeply of what they all thought might be their last free breaths of the air above the Rhône. All were in attendance, from little Nico to aged Agata, from Ambrogio to Piero, although only a portion were summoned to the papal court by name. But they had pledged to live and die together, and come what may, they would endeavor to remain together.

Abramo Amidei and Vincenzo awaited them at the far end of the bridge, atop their own mounts, smiling in victory as they passed. The Gifted looked to the knights beyond them, assigned as Cardinal Boeri had shared, to watch and make certain Amidei did not harm a one of them. With that promise in each of their minds, they resolutely did not look upon Amidei with more than a passing glance, which plainly infuriated him.

"Sir de Capezzana, your grief must weigh heavily upon you," Amidei said, edging near the knight. "Great is your woe, losing the count."

Gianni ignored him.

"Your friends shall have to watch themselves. None of them wish to be stabbed by you and die like Armand," he added in a whisper.

Gianni clamped his teeth shut. He would not respond. He would not give this devil entrance to his heart again.

Giving up on the knight as they neared the papal *garde* at the end of the bridge, Abramo wheeled around and rode up beside Ambrogio, some distance back from Daria and Piero and Gianni.

"Remain here," hissed Gianni, circling his mare back to face the Sorcerer and protect Ambrogio, as Vito and Ugo did. Two knights of the *palais* followed.

"You think you can dare me so and not live to feel the pain of my wrath?" spat out Abramo, edging his horse into Ambrogio's. "I should have killed you when I had the chance."

"Yes," Ambrogio said, staring levelly back into his eyes. "You should have."

A *palais* knight edged between them and stared hard at Abramo. "Lord Amidei," he barked. "You shall give these people passage without harm."

"As you wish," said Abramo, still staring at Ambrogio with hate. Slowly he backed his horse up, allowing them to pass.

Gianni and Vito looked back at him, guarding Ambrogio's back as they moved away. Ugo rode beside him.

"My, those paintings must be quite fine," said Vito.

"Quite," said Ambrogio, raising an eyebrow at him and grinning.

"I would pay a king's ransom for a look," said Ugo.

"I might be able to arrange a quick viewing," promised Ambrogio.

"Take care, gentlemen," Gianni warned, "We must watch where we tread."

Ambrogio nodded and turned again in the saddle. They had reached the *palais.*

Together, they paused, taking in the soaring towers, fifty meters above them; the square Campane tower to their left, hovering over the church of Notre-Dame-des-Doms; the Familiars' Wing with its high arches; the Angel

Tower directly above them; and the elegant and imposing Chapeaux Gate, immediately to their right.

Piero blew out his cheeks, watching ten and more knights stare down upon them at the Chapeaux entrance. "After the darkness . . ." he muttered, already heading inward.

"Light," the remainder said, following behind.

ᴕ ᴕ ᴕ

It was soon after they arrived that the Gifted learned the pope was ill and would not see anyone that day. They were shown to simple but comfortable apartments in the Familiars' Wing and told to stay within the palace grounds while Pope Cornelius recovered.

"Is the Holy Father in need of care?" Daria asked, that first night.

The secretary gave her a small smile and raised one brow. "I think not," he said. "The Holy Father is already under the care of his own trusted physicians." And with that he departed, leaving Daria to smile over at her husband.

"I think the holy secretary does not trust me."

"Shocking," he said, enfolding her in his arms. "Good of the old fellow, in any case, to give us our own room."

"Nicer than the papal dungeon?" she asked.

"Infinitely," he said, kissing her on the crown and holding her close.

She thought again of telling him—telling him that he was to be a father. That they had been blessed with a child. "Gianni, there—"

A knock at the door made them both turn.

He held up a finger to her and walked over to the door. "Who is it?"

"Us," said Tessa's voice.

Gianni smiled and opened the door, looking out at the group in the hall.

"We are going to see the pope's own Grand Tinel, and the chapel, where Brogi emblazoned Amidei's and Vincenzo's faces on every evil face possible," Tessa said, eyes alight.

"Ahh," said Gianni. "I must put a stop to that, beloved." He gestured them all inward and closed the door behind them. "It may appear that we are the honored guests of the pope, given freedom over his *palais*. But it is not as it appears. If we are discovered in places where we ought not to be, it will not go well for us."

Tessa, Nico, Roberto, Vito, Ugo, Hasani, and Ambrogio all took in his words with sober faces, nodding. "We understand your warning, Captain," Tessa said. "We shall return to our apartments and see you in the morningtide."

"Good night," Gianni said, opening the door and then closing it behind them, gratified by their ready acceptance.

"You do not really believe they shall stay put," Daria said, wrapping her arms around him, kissing him in the center of his back.

He turned and looked down at her, running his fingertips down the edge of her face in a light touch that sent shivers down her spine. "Nay. But their lives, like our own, are in God's own hands. And as much as I'd like to see Ambrogio's work, I'd rather lay my eyes on God's own work, right here, in the shape and form of my wife."

᪣ ᪣ ᪣

"THE captain is right," Ambrogio said in a whisper, again in the dark hall just outside the de Capezzanas' room. Piero had drawn near, curious to see what they were up to.

"And we shall return to our apartments," Vito said, "just as we promised."

"But not until we have laid eyes upon Ambrogio's masterpieces," said Gaspare, joining them with Josephine.

The group smiled at one another, but Ambrogio paused. "You cannot see it anyway, Josephine. Why not stay behind?"

"Because," she retorted, "if it is a hall that strikes a blow to my enemy, I wish to say a prayer within it."

"Mutiny," said Vito, raising a brow. He gestured forward with a flourish. "Lead the way, Brogi."

"Stay close," said the man, already heading down a hall. "Stay close to me."

The group set out, scurrying down the Familiars' Wing and through the quiet of Cornelius's vast chapel, smelling of old incense and pooling, cooling beeswax candles—now extinguished for the night until Lauds—on through the kitchens, dormant for several more hours before the bakers began their daily task. Ambrogio paused at the entrance of the Consistory Wing, waiting for two priests to pass by, then led the way onward. In another moment, they passed through two doors and headed upward to the second floor. They emerged on the next, hushed and remarkably quiet for a group of ten souls.

Ambrogio reached for the lone torch alight on this floor and waved them forward. He set the three others inside the chapel alight, and a warm glow spread through each curve and dome. "Daria always said I liked to show off my work," he said unapologetically.

"As well you should," Gaspare said. " 'Tis magnificent, brother."

"Simone did half of them," Ambrogio said. "See if you can guess which half."

Hasani moved forward, looking at each inch of each fresco with the hungry eyes of another artist, eager to see how a hand was drawn to not appear like a paddle, how eyes depicted emotion. He backed up and looked at all of them, then pointed to each of the panels Ambrogio had done.

"Indeed," Ambrogio said, pretending to applaud for the man. "How could you tell which were mine? Other than our enemies' depiction?" Abramo's and Vincenzo's portraits were not in the five other panels Ambrogio had painted.

Hasani gestured toward his face, waving two fingers about his own black oval, then drawing two fingers across each eye, as if drawing a mask.

"Well done," Ambrogio said. "Simone prefers to keep his figures distant, as if uninvolved in what is transpiring. He calls it 'divine distance.' I prefer to engage my subjects wholly." He considered the black man, tapping his lips in thought. "Would you care to try your hand at a fresco at some point, Hasani?"

Hasani glanced at him and gave him the barest of smiles, the hint of intrigue, surprise, and pleasure visible there.

"Consider it done. Somewhere, sometime, we shall not be otherwise engaged, and you and I shall create a magnificent chapel, a chapel that will sing across the ages." His eyes left the man and looked to the others, most of whom still stared upward or directly ahead of them, putting biblical scenes in context in their mind's eye. But his eye soon rested on Tessa, who stood at the far side of the room, her hands against the wall.

He moved toward her. "Tessa?"

She looked up at him, eyes wide in her small face. "He is on the other side? His room? Is the pope down here?"

Ambrogio pulled his head to one side. "There are three rooms between us, but yes." Gaspare, Josephine, and Piero drew near them. "You can sense his presence there?"

Tessa looked at all of them. "His and more. We must pray for him. There is much good within him, but the dark . . . they hover, looking for a way inward. *We must pray.*"

And together, they all knelt at the far wall, hands atop one of Simone's frescoes, as if they were instead laying hands on the Father of all Christendom.

Chapter Thirty-one

THE pope's steward entered the papal apartments and opened one shutter to allow in light, but not send it directly over the Holy Father. The pope roused and turned, his breathing seeming easier now, not quite so congested. But when he pulled himself to a sitting position, the cough was as lusty and wet as it had been the day before. The poor man coughed until the steward thought he might bruise a rib, choking on his own mucus.

At last clear for the moment, the pope sank back upon the pillows and closed his eyes. "Mayhap we should summon the healer in the Familiars' Wing," he said.

"That would rankle the cardinals," said the steward with a grin. He handed the pope an Eastern *siwak* stick, used to clean teeth, and two glass goblets, one that held cold, spring water, the other serving as a spittoon.

The steward stood aside as the pope finished his teeth, took the goblets from him, and then followed behind as he moved to the next private chamber to move his bowels. That task completed, they returned to the papal chambers to give the Holy Father a sponge bath, performed quickly in the cool, morning air that even a hearty fire in the hearth had not fought off. The pope slipped on new undergarments and then the royal robes.

They could hear the bleat of a goat, the wild cry of a jaguar, and more in the gardens down below the papal chambers. "Mayhap the menagerie was a poor idea," said the pope wearily. "Come summer, with the windows open, the noise will be intolerable."

"We shall find new land for the menagerie," said the steward. "Mayhap up above, toward the Rocher des Doms? That would be a fine place to wander the menagerie. You could extend the gardens."

The pope sat down on the edge of the bed, suddenly a bit dizzy.

"Your Holiness?" asked the steward in alarm. "Are you still not able to endure an audience this day?" The chest cold had taken hold more than a week prior, directly after Maximilien's masquerade. It troubled him that the pope still seemed so weak, even after several daily visits from the royal physicians.

The pope lifted a tired hand to his sweaty brow. "We must find it within us to see to some of the business at hand. We can only imagine the stacks of paperwork we must make our way through. Not to mention the people . . ."

"There is quite a line to see you. Much of it can be seen to by your men," he said. "But the Doge de Venezia should arrive today."

"Via the Rhône?"

"How else would the master of mariners arrive?"

The pope gave him a small smile. "You expect him by eventide?"

"At the latest."

"What is his stated purpose for such a visit?"

"Apparently he comes to defend the Gifted."

"Ahh, not to seek restitution with us, the Church. Of course not, the vagabond. It is our troublesome Gifted who draw him, those who wait patiently in the Court of Familiars for me to see to their fate." He rose and went to the window, easing open the second shutter. He stared outward, as if envisioning the doge behind them. "My, have they not managed to collect an impressive following?"

"Indeed. Even de Capezzana's murder of the count is reported not to have damaged his support among the nobility. The countess is due to return any day, after seeing to her brother's funeral."

The pope stared outside for a long while. The steward, accustomed to such silences, waited where he was, allowing the pontiff to think, consider, pray.

"Have you searched the archives for what we asked?" he said, suddenly turning and staring at the steward.

"Yes, Holy Father," he said, with a slight bow. He moved to a table and pulled the stack of papers from the leather satchel. "The chief librarian found three copies, just as Cardinal Boeri described. As you and he both surmised, none were ever canonized by our forefathers. In fact, they appear not to be Pauline at all, but rather one of his followers."

Reluctantly Cornelius reached out to take the stack from the man. "Give us a moment. We shall attend the audience in but an hour. Please siphon off anything that can be seen to by the Lessers, leaving only those issues of utmost importance to us."

"Yes, Holy Father," the man said, bowing even as he drew the twin doors shut behind him.

Cornelius sighed and unclasped the royal cape that threatened to pinch off his breathing and threw it to the bed. Then he took the stack of papers to a desk and sat before them, a hand splayed on each side of the stack, praying for fortification. He had stumbled upon them in the library during his first days as pope, but quickly reshelved them. No pope wished for such controversy. When he opened his eyes, he carefully took the top sheet of parchment, mayhap several centuries old, and laid it in the upper left-hand corner of his desk. He did the same with the following eight sheets, until they lined the entire upper portion of the table.

He lifted two fingers, each bearing massive ruby rings, to the sinuses just above the bridge of his nose, and massaged upward, feeling the pressure release as he did so. But even with just a partial view of the pages, he could see what Cardinal Boeri had described on his own copy of the letter. He would ask for the original pages the Gifted had collected, to see if they were of the same scribe. It would be logical. It could simply be happenstance, coincidence. Mayhap one scribe had impressed another, and what began as merely flattery in copying an art form had become what the "Gifted" interpreted as prophecy.

He had not studied the group for long, but yesterday spent a few minutes on the ramparts above the Familiars' Wing, watching as they moved about the open courtyard far below, talking, praying. They were an odd group, with three older people—the priest, the woman of Avignon, and a fisherman—and three children in their company. The girl had paused in the courtyard while he watched them, and slowly lifted her gaze as if she had sensed him.

Cornelius had stood his ground, backing away from no mere girl, but he fought the desire to do so. Hasani, the lady's private guard, had looked up as well, as silently observant as a sentinel and following the girl's mute attention. And then the lady had moved into the center of the courtyard, lifted her arm, and a falcon—of the purest white, worthy of his royal menagerie—had dived down within the ramparts of the *palais*, lifting his wings at the last moment to flutter down to her proffered glove.

He had seen them at the prince's feast as well, but it had been late, very late, before they were received, the last in line. If Prince Maximilien was to be believed, the Gifted were responsible for delivering his daughter from some great evil. Could it be?

Cornelius picked up a page of the fabled letter and studied the image of the woman in the margin, comparing it to what he remembered of the people he had met. "Daria de Capezzana, the former Duchess d'Angelo," he whispered. Then he picked up another. "Sir Gianni de Capezzana, former knight of the Church." And then a third. "Father Piero, former loyal priest of the Church." He was the most troublesome of all. This group had entrusted their spiritual condition to this little man, and where had he brought them? But it was uncanny, the resemblance. He picked up the second copy of the letter and the third, all admittedly done by different scribes, but all clearly depicting the trio now lodged within the *palais* walls. He sighed heavily and began to read the text again, at once enthralled and dismayed with each word.

಄ ಄ ಄

AMIDEI and Vincenzo made the most of every opportunity to walk the Familiars' Wing, eager to catch the Gifted out-of-doors as they awaited their audience with the pope.

By now, Amidei had access to nearly every hall and room of the grand *palais*. Piero watched as each man entered the courtyard, wary of their adversary. But he had told the Gifted to treat them as if they were not there at all—not to speak to them, engage them in any manner. Gianni had been engaged, and none of them wished to be tricked into any more horrors. "The best defense," Piero had said, "is to turn away. Do *not* allow him access."

"It is difficult when he is in our heads, invading our minds, whispering in our ears," Gianni said, clearly remembering what had transpired on the cliffs.

"Indeed. But not impossible. We must block every avenue he finds. The devil delights in confusion. How do we battle confusion?"

"Concentration."

"Yes," Piero said. "Concentrate on Scriptures. Our Lord was tempted by the evil one. How did he fight back?"

"Scripture," Daria said.

Piero nodded, chin in hand. "The devil said to Jesus, 'If you are the Son of God, tell this stone to become bread.' What did he say in response?" he asked, looking at Daria.

" 'It is written: "Man does not live on bread alone," ' " Josephine said, surprising him.

Piero turned and smiled. "Exactly. Time and again our Savior returns to what is *written*, and that is what we shall do both with Abramo and in our coming arguments with the pope and those who seek to lead him astray. It kept Abramo at bay for Daria on the dark isle. The Word will not fail us now. The Holy Spirit protects us, seals us from him—but if we allow Amidei and his dark master entry, he'll come quickly. Allow him no entry, my friends. No entry."

They were grand words, words of truth, but well Piero knew of how difficult it was to remain focused on Scripture when the dark one came into view. Each time, Tessa set to trembling, running to hide behind Hasani or Vito or Ambrogio, the boys drawing close as if to protect her, one on either side. The adults were more successful in pretending they had not even noticed him, other than Daria, who edged closer to her husband every time.

The beast seemed to feed on her fear, looking as if he meant to truss her up and cook her upon the spit, then gazing out over them all as he pretended to converse with one cardinal or another. His mind play was fierce, and he had grown in power since they had last done battle. They could all attest to the fact that while he seemed entirely engaged in dialogue, he seemed to speak to each of their hearts, playing off their deepest fears, hopes, emotions.

Each time, Piero clung to one phrase, born of Scripture: "I believe solely in the Alpha and the Omega. Who was, and is, and is to come." Vito said he had been reduced to simply repeating the Savior's name, "Jesus, Jesus, Jesus." Collectively it seemed to be working. Abramo and Vincenzo appeared more often each day, intent on drawing them out upon the battlefield. But each time they were constrained by the slow, steady pace of the cardinals they walked alongside, as well as the retinue of guards who trailed them, and the Gifted easily remained on the opposite side of the courtyard.

Tessa looked up at him suddenly, soon after they had arrived that morning, eyes full of alarm. "He approaches. And it is different," she said, her whisper sounding like a screaming alarm in his ears.

"Behind Hasani," he directed the girl, but she was already running.

Gianni stood and moved in front of Daria just as Abramo Amidei and Vincenzo del Buco entered the courtyard, with Ciro directly behind them. There was no cardinal in attendance this day. And no guards. Amidei moved across the grass diagonally, charging toward them.

Gianni, Vito, Ugo, and Hasani all drew their swords as one.

"You shall kill me in the pope's own courtyard?" Abramo asked, smiling at them all as he circled. Daria remained behind Gianni, but then realized she faced Vincenzo. Abramo moved toward Gianni, edging his chest into the tip of his sword, taunting him. "Do it. Do it. I shall die for my master. And you all shall be dead before sunup tomorrow. The cardinals would see to it. The pope would not stand for it . . . murder in his own Court of Familiars of one of the most prominent and beloved men among the cardinals! And your dreams would die."

Gianni trembled, and the veins on his neck stood out as he flushed red.

"Gianni," Piero said, laying a hand of warning on his arm. "Remember, remember the words . . ."

"Nay?" Abramo asked, hands out, daring the knight. "You shall not take down the very man who has touched nearly all of your pretty wife?" He leaned over the sword and eyed Daria, then slid his eyes again to Gianni.

Twin beads of sweat rolled down from the knight's temples, and his breath came in quick pants.

"Come now, Gianni, do you not wish to take me down? Here? I shall only come after you and yours again and again. And someday soon I shall take back what should have been mine in the first place, whether she offers herself to me or not. Right before I *kill* her."

Piero pulled back against Gianni with everything in him, feeling the last vestiges of the knight's control slip.

Ugo grabbed the captain's right arm and held it, slowing the sword as it sliced perilously near Abramo's chest.

But Abramo had already turned and spun, taking advantage of the knight's temporary distraction, and reached out to touch Daria's chin. "Have you told him of your little secret, my darling? Nay?"

Ambrogio sidled between them and pushed Abramo backward.

"Well, and now the artist pretends to be a knight, defending the lady," he said, tapping the smaller man on the chest. "You think your little paintings shall turn them against me?" he asked with a wry grin.

"Nay," Ambrogio said, staring back at him. A small smile grew upon his own. "But you are a most convenient model. When I paint the scene of heaven descending into Earth descending into *hell*, your visage shall surely again be of utmost aid."

Abramo shook his head. "You shall not always be safely ensconced within the pope's own building. And when you emerge, I shall find you and cut off each of your fingers and feed them to the dogs before I hang you from a church rafter beside one of your precious frescoes."

He turned and walked to Josephine, standing beside Gaspare. "What's this? A love affair among the aged of your group? How quaint." He circled them, staring down at each. "A seer who cannot see. A man of miracles with the hands of a fisherman. Tell me, seer, what is before you now?"

She turned away, clinging to Piero's urgent command no longer to speak to him. The priest could see her, closing her eyes, wrestling with words in her mind, either those that Abramo shouted inwardly, or those she wished to release.

"Mute as well as blind, I take it," Abramo said. "You should be with the African instead," he said, gesturing toward Hasani.

"And what of you, fisherman? Why not call down a miracle now? Where is your lightning? One bolt, and I'd be ashes before you, yes?" He peered into the shorter man's eyes, taunting him. "Nay?" He blew out his cheeks. "Your God makes this most difficult for you."

He moved on toward Hasani and Tessa.

﷼ ﷼ ﷼

DARIA could hear Abramo, taunting the others now. Dimly, she realized it was odd, the entire lack of *palais* servants or nobles or churchmen about. No customary guard. How had he arranged it?

But her eyes were on Vincenzo. It had been some time since they had come face-to-face in broad daylight. He hovered in front of her, a mere shadow of his former self. His skin hung in loose folds from his brow and jawline and it was a sickly color, as if his liver failed him. He was strong still, straight and handsome. But it was as if he had aged twenty years.

Her eyes moved to his hand, a dagger within it. Did he intend to kill her? Daria hated him. Hated what he had become, what he had cost her. How could he have given in to Abramo Amidei, so thoroughly, that he allowed this? This constant torment of them all?

He stepped toward her, and instinctively Daria's hand went to her womb, as if she might protect the babe. He paused and glanced down at her hand, then back to her eyes. Was that the smallest glimmer of hope there? How often had they prayed together that she would conceive, that her union would be complete with Marco? His tender look took Daria aback, and she stepped away from him. Just as fast as it had come, the glimmer was gone. He looked down at the dagger in confusion, as if unaware how it had come to be in his hand.

"Vincenzo?" she said, barely opening her hand, making herself reach out to the man who had cost her so much. But once . . . once, he had been so much more. Her father's friend. Her guardian. Her co-consul. Was he merely lost behind the screen of his dark master's making? Had his brain been entwined with the spider's web until it was but one dark mass?

"Baron! Master!" Ciro barked from the far corner of the courtyard, seeming to give them some sort of warning. Did others approach?

Vincenzo raised his eyes slowly to meet hers. And with the barest shake of his head, he turned and strode over to meet Ciro and Abramo. And then they were gone.

♔ ♔ ♔

GIANNI lifted his gloved hand and used the inside of his wrist to wipe the sweat from his brow. He looked over at Piero. "I cannot tolerate much more of that. When are we to be free of him? How?"

Piero looked up at him, over them all. "I know not."

"If it isn't Amidei or del Buco, someone else shall arise to take their place," Josephine said.

"You do know how to impart a comforting word, m'lady," Vito said.

Piero gave him a rueful grin. "Truth is truth."

"So the battle is ever before us," Gianni said, taking a few steps to the left, thinking. "As a knight, I can live with that. But Father, we cannot continue to stand in place. No army can withstand constant attack. We must either abdicate territory or strike back, seize upon what is rightfully ours. A true knight, a good knight, strategically stands, holds, but then he *moves*. Here, in Avignon, I feel as if we've been hovering in one place too long."

Eight bugles rent the air, signaling a royal arrival. "I know that sound," said Vito.

"Venezia," Ugo said with him, eyes raised in alarm. They were still wanted men in the islands of the Rialto, for having ransacked the holy crypt.

They had taken nothing but the piece to their glass map, but the outrage over their daring entrance had had the entire city up in arms.

Piero reached up and patted Gianni on the shoulder. "I believe that is a call for us as well. Soon we shall be on the move again, good knight. Trust our God. He sees us and knows our strength—or lack thereof."

CHAPTER THIRTY-TWO

THE Gifted emerged onto the massive Honneur Courtyard, just inside the Champeaux Gate. Now they could see why the Court of Familiars had been empty—everyone in the *palais* appeared to be here. The Doge of Venezia arrived not only with buglers, but also with banners and elaborate horse dressing, preceded by eight knights, and followed by eighteen more. Four hovered on either flank, on foot, here in the courtyard. Beside him, along with numerous scribes and officials, was Cardinal Boeri and the Conte and Contessa Morassi. The contessa turned, and briefly Daria glimpsed two babies in the arms of a nursemaid behind her.

Daria gasped and started down the steps, but Gianni held her back. Already the papal court officials reached them, welcoming them, ushering them toward the Dignitaries' Wing. It would not be wise to interrupt the process.

"It is good," he whispered in her ear, wrapping an arm around her shoulders while they stood, watching from the shadows. "Surely they are all here to lend us support."

Daria nodded, hoping the Morassis would look up and she could wave, but they had turned in the other direction and walked away, up toward a group of papal officials. To their left stood Amidei, del Buco, and Ciro.

The Gifted held their breath in anticipation, all watching now what was about to unfold. Amidei greeted the doge in a deep bow, but the doge dismissed him, barely looking in his direction. When Daria glanced up at her husband, he was grinning. His eyes moved from the humbled form of Amidei down to her. "Daria, what was Amidei referring to, back there? What secret? Or was it more of his games?"

She glanced at the others, judging distance, wondering if it was at last time to tell her husband, when her eyes rested upon Hasani. "Come," she hissed toward Gianni, already turning in her friend's direction.

They moved the man around the corner, away from prying eyes and into the shadows. Hasani's eyes rolled back into his head, and he allowed them to settle him to the ground. In seconds it was over, and he pushed them away, moving to his feet and then running down the hall, back toward their quarters. They all followed.

Hastily he pulled a piece of parchment out of a shallow drawer and the cork from an inkwell. He dipped and sketched, drawing a man atop a bed, another hovering over him. And in the corner was Abramo Amidei.

" 'Tis the pope," Father Piero breathed out.

Hasani nodded, still drawing. He moved to a new sketch, of a man kneeling beneath a throne, cardinals on either side of him. A conical hat was being lowered to his head.

"A new pope is crowned," Piero whispered.

A knock sounded at the door, and Vito and Ugo went to answer it.

"The pope has cancelled any afternoon audiences, as he remains ill," said the steward, glancing in to see them all curiously crammed in one man's small room. Hasani was entirely blocked from sight. "He shall see to you on the morrow."

Piero turned and pushed through the others to get to the steward, who had already turned to go. "Wait!"

The man turned to stare at him.

"Please," he said, moving into the hallway with him. "Is the Holy Father improving?"

"He had risen today, hoping to attend the audience, but had to return to his bed."

Piero crossed himself and gestured backward, into the room. "Lady Daria, she is well known as a healer."

The steward laughed in his face. "Well we know of your healer. You believe he will send for the very one he must search and potentially try for heretical acts? I think not." He turned to go. He waved a hand over his shoulder. "The royal physicians are already keeping the pope in constant care."

"Wait, brother," Piero tried again, walking after him. "I fear there is dreadful intrigue within the *palais*. Is the pope under careful guard?"

The steward frowned and stepped toward Piero. He lifted a hand toward him. "Do you dare to threaten the Holy Father?"

"Nay, I—"

"Do you have information of intrigue meant to be used against him?"

"Nay, not exactly . . ."

"Then hold your tongue, Father. The *palais* has ears and they needn't any unwarranted false information." He walked away again.

But Piero was not done. "The pope has no enemy in us," he called. "But tell me. He does have enemies, does he not? People who wish to place their own favored cardinal in power? People who would benefit from such an act?"

The steward turned again. "Are you not exactly such people? Would it not benefit a group of heretics to place their own heretical cardinal atop the papal throne?"

Piero sighed, soon nose to nose again with the steward in the hall. "Fine. Consider us all threats, every last one within the *palais* this night. But quadruple the Holy Father's guard. If I were his enemy, if I intended him harm, would I ask you to do that?"

The steward stared back at him. "I shall ask it again. Do you know of something the *Honneur Gard* should know? Shall we go and speak to them now?"

"Call it intuition," Josephine said, moving toward them in the hall. "What is the harm in positioning guards you already have on the premises? What will you feel like on the morrow if something happened to the pope, something you could have prevented? Do you want to endure a lifetime of hellish memories because you did not wish to act on a word of caution? Think on it, man. We may be heretics. But then again, we may *not*. Are you willing to risk the Holy Father's life upon your own judgment?"

The steward stared back at her, then to Piero, considering, and then he turned again and walked away.

"Think he'll do it?" Vito asked, as Piero and Josephine edged back in the room.

"He will. He simply needed to protect his pride and not admit as much to us," Piero said. He walked back to Hasani's desk, where the rest hovered, still staring at the drawings.

A dead pope.

And a new pope crowned, the highly favored Cardinal Morano of Madrid, a man loved by one and all.

Piero let out a breathless laugh and lifted the illustration. "The devil is nothing if not wily and inventive." He glanced at Gianni. "You wished to act? The time is now."

꧁ ꧁ ꧁

It was the Morassis who came to their door an hour later, with a steward who formally invited them to join the doge in his private apartments to sup.

Daria cried out at the sight of them, reaching out to embrace each of them as old family members, then reaching for little Angelo and little Daria, the twins now three months in age and able to smile and coo up at their godmother.

"I cannot believe you ventured after us," Daria said, looking up from her godchildren to the Morassis. They turned and dismissed their servants, closing the door firmly behind them.

"We could do little else," the conte said in little more than a whisper. He looked at Daria. "You look well," he said with a grin, gazing behind her at her husband. He reached out a hand, "I understand congratulations are in order. You certainly know how to pick a bride."

Gianni shook his hand, smiling. "How did you know that we would need you now, here, Conte?"

"Armand sent word of your intent to come here, to the *palais*. Given our pope's firm stance against anything that might even smell of heresy, we thought we should pack up the twins and venture to Provence."

"A bold venture, with two precious children in tow," Gianni said. He hesitated. "About Armand, Conte . . ."

"No need," Martino said, holding up a hand. "We stopped and saw the countess in Les Baux. Anette told us all." He looked upon Gianni with kind eyes that became hard with determination. "Our enemy is common. One who would've burned us all alive in my palazzo in order to accomplish his goals." His eyes flicked to Daria and then back to Gianni. "You are not him. Armand died in battle against our enemy."

"All and the same, I beg your forgiveness," Gianni said.

"You are forgiven, Sir Gianni," Martino said softly.

"We are exceedingly grateful you have come," Daria said, looking at them both with eyes soft with emotion. She glanced down at the twins, now woozy with sleep, and kissed each on the forehead.

"It was for them we came, really," Gracia said. "The pope must know that what you speak is true. Seeing them, hearing our story, may convince him. And the others Anette and Dimitri spoke of . . . Surely, collectively, we can speak the truth to Holy Father and he shall hear us."

"If we get to hold our audience with the *sitting* pope," Gianni said. "Listen, you must lend your shoulders to the cause. Hasani has received another vision. Amidei is again on the move . . ."

The Morassis listened to their story, never interrupting. "You must tell this to the doge, now. He has the power to change things in this *palais*, sound an alarm. The pope, ailing as he may be, has long sought to repair the Church's relationship with Venezia. Mayhap this is all God's doing."

"No doubt it is all within the Lord's sight," Piero said. He had entered the de Capezzana room, invited by Daria, halfway through their story. "But the devil is still on the prowl."

☘ ☘ ☘

"You have passed the test," Abramo said, laying a comforting hand on Cardinal Morano's shoulder. "You observed writhing flesh, comely young bodies, temptation like you have never known, and yet you remained true to your vows."

The cardinal remained where he sat, staring into the fire of his hearth, watching the flames dance. He looked wan, weak, after a week of self-mutilation, beating back the demons that walked through his memory and back again.

Abramo smiled. Still the images were harvested where the master had placed them. And still the cardinal believed himself the victor, capable of keeping them caged in memory. But Abramo could see the spark in his wide eyes, the desire to see it again, experience it again, regardless of the pain that ensued after. The rush of desire, the excruciating pain of mutilation . . . yes, well he knew of the cycle now. He lived it, breathed it, alongside Cardinal Gabriel Morano, future pope.

It was delicious.

"You are to be commended. Few are as worthy as you, Cardinal. I will pay you back for finding me a wife, for leading me out of my own depravity." Never mind that the cardinal had been led away before the culmination of the dark ceremony. Let him believe what he wished. *What is right for him,* the master always led, *shall be right for him.*

Abramo moved to the other side of the chair, watching the cardinal, still staring into the flames. He placed a hand on his arm and closed his eyes, asking his master to show him what so captivated Morano.

The cardinal's lips parted. Drool pooled at the corner. His eyes, wide and limpid, remained on the fire, but his lids opened even wider as if he watched a scene unfold before him.

"Yes," Abramo whispered into his ear. "All of that. You can become pope. You can rule the hearts and minds of all of Christendom. Show them how to live the devout life." He leaned closer. "But if you are to know and protect your flock, you must at some point know the dark. It is an investment in your future, Gabriel. A sacrifice made on behalf of your flock. Did not Jesus bear his own forty days and nights in the desert?"

He moved to his other side, and leaned in again. "You shall venture in, just for a time. To know the full extent of your enemy. To conquer him. Yes, conquer him. You can rule the world of light *and* dark. You are *that* strong. Able to walk in either realm. See how far your faith has brought you? You are to be rewarded. Rewarded. God wishes it to be. It all shall be yours. And I will be here, right by your side, ever grateful for your leadership."

꿏 꿏 꿏

"He has created mayhem in my city," the doge said at last. He had been silent through much of the meal with the Gifted and the Morassis and Cardinal Boeri, as they told the Venetians of what had transpired since they left in the midst of the fearsome storm, barely escaping with their lives.

"He barely pays homage, and he certainly avoids many of the taxes— your own Hasani bearing good witness to that fact."

They all remained silent, waiting for the doge to continue. Every last one of the Gifted and their loved ones were present, sitting about the table in mute fascination.

"He has gathered together the foulest within my city and banded them together, and its effect is kin to common war, though hidden, their work done in the shadows, impossible to rout out. He leaves behind disaster, and I tire of his play." The doge wiped his mouth with the edge of the tablecloth and rose, splaying an arm out in either direction, staring at them all. "I am a man born of the militia, leader of the finest maritime power ever seen by the modern world. From what I have learned, from what I know, the time has come for us to strike. For Venezia. For the Gifted. For God."

"Well I know men of power," Gianni said, sitting beside Cardinal Boeri. To his right was Daria. "You must strike the sea monster at his belly, to bring down the head. What drives this man most?"

"Ambition. Greed. Power," said Boeri.

"Yes. And what feeds those things?" asked the doge.

"Sin, depravity, lawlessness only seem to take him to new levels," Daria said.

"His foul ceremonies with the dark lord," Boeri said.

"His play among the nobility in every city, the foul ceremonies, all of it are but pretty jewels upon his dark crown," said Josephine. "Take away his funds, his wealth, and you strike the belly of the dragon. Now how do we take down a businessman on the level of Abramo Amidei? This is the question we must ask ourselves."

The doge sat down and smiled. "Well you have chosen your prophetess. She speaks the truth." He looked to Morassi. "Together, we still rule enough of Venezia to close him off there, drive out his compatriots."

"Done," Morassi said, with a grave nod.

"I can cut him off at the knees in Roma," Boeri pledged. "He owns several powerful nobles. But we can put them back in their proper places. Providing that we all strike at once."

"Agreed," the doge said.

"And Anette, with the other friends our Gifted have made, could cut him off in Provence," Conte Morassi said.

"They shall support her," Daria said.

"We need Toscana," Gianni said, rising and pacing. "Even if we inflicted wounds there, he would feel it heavily in combination with Provence, Venezia, and Roma." He looked to Daria and Ambrogio. They stared at one another for a long moment, remembering what the d'Angelo name once meant throughout Toscana.

Slowly Daria rose, righteous anger making her appear fierce, and she glanced at Nico, Roberto, and Agata. "The time has come for justice to be served. We shall send a messenger this night, with word to the Nine, from the former Lady d'Angelo, now Lady de Capezzana." Gianni came to her and took her hand, wondering where this might lead.

"I shall tell them that Vincenzo del Buco took the lives of my servants, my knight, kidnapped these three here, ransacked my house for valuables and set it all aflame, all in the aim of controlling me, owning me." She looked to Gianni, asking permission. "I shall send it to Marco. He is one of the Nine now, and highly favored. He has no idea that Vincenzo has fallen so far. That he has used him as well. He shall rally the others to our side."

"Are you certain?" Gianni asked. "That Marco is not more firmly on their side? He was in Venezia . . . his presence helped persuade you to speak to Vincenzo."

Daria stared at him, remembering that fateful night with him. She shook her head. "He was a pawn. Nothing more. Vincenzo used him and sent him home. He was afraid he would learn the truth, and Marco would defend me."

"Are you certain?" Gianni repeated softly. Siena, Vincenzo, Marco . . . ghosts of the past rose up between them. "Are you truly prepared for justice to be meted out?"

"Justice is in God's hands," Josephine put in. "We merely set truth in her proper place."

"Excellent," the doge said, dividing the de Capezzanas' soft glance. "We then shall have Roma, Toscana, Venezia, Provence. With those four firmly in hand, we can lend pressure upon the Visconti, Gonzaga, and Estense families, even upon Firenze, Genoa, and Pisa."

"What of Napoli?" Gianni asked.

"Let him retreat to Napoli," said the doge in dismissal.

"And what if he retreats back to Firenze?" Daria asked. "It was from there he came to Siena."

"Then, dear lady, we shall surround him," the doge pledged. "And take him down there. This battle turns here, now."

They all studied him in silence.

Vito rose and placed his hand in the center of the table.

Everyone else laid their hand atop his, until the doge's hand edged on top.

"After the darkness," whispered Piero.

"Light," said the others lowly, reverently.

"Ambrogio," said Gianni, "can you go to the chapel? Invent some reason for remaining there? It's as close as we can get to guarding the pope as possible, yes?"

"Yes," Ambrogio said, searching his mind for a tangible excuse. "But I am rather sorry when it comes to swordplay."

"No worries," Gianni said, reaching out to lay a hand on Vito and Ugo, pushing them forward. "Meet your new apprentices."

Vito scoffed. "If he's bad with a sword, you should see what I can do with a brush."

CHAPTER THIRTY-THREE

HASANI wistfully gazed after the brothers trailing Ambrogio, but there was nothing for it. In the light of day, the *palais* was like many other houses of power. Black men were relegated to the outer regions or servants' quarters only. It was a wonder they had allowed Hasani to remain with them at all in the Court of Familiars. When they were together, they brought him with them. But sending him off in the direction of the papal chambers . . . nay, Gianni was right in sending the brothers.

Daria turned from her tall, black friend and moved to his desk. She pulled a small piece of paper from the drawer and dipped the quill in the ink, pausing over every other word. It had been more than a year since her handfast to Marco had been dissolved.

20 February, the Year of Our Lord 1340
Avignon

Marco—
I pray that all is well with you in our beloved Siena and Francesca is soon safely delivered of your babe and that he is hale and hearty. Much has transpired in the past year, some of which you know, some you do not.
Upon my life, I beg you to believe the words you must now read, and moreover, I beg you to act as one of the Nine must, with authority and swift decision. I have always trusted your good, sound judgment, even after all that has transpired between us.

Vincenzo del Buco is no longer my guardian and treasured friend.
He is in league with an evil lord, Abramo Amidei. They used you as a
pawn to get to me in Venezia, where they kidnapped me, as they had
Ambrogio Rossellino, Agata and Nico Scioria, and a boy of Il Campo,
Roberto. All four will attest to the fact that it was Vincenzo and his
men who came into my mansion, murdered Beata and Aldo and my
knight Lucan, and burned it all to the ground, taking with it the other
mansions of our calle *that night.*

At the same time, he burned my country manor to the ground, and
under the guise of paying debts incurred by the fire, froze my assets in
banks from Roma to Firenze, cutting me off from any funds that might
see me and mine to freedom.

Well you must know how much it pains me to write this to you.
But it is the truth. I have been freed from Amidei's prisons, narrowly
escaped his utmost attempts to control me, own me, suffering every
torture possible. Still he has continued to haunt our every step, threat-
ening me and mine, murdering other beloved friends.

It is not an overstatement when I say I am in the midst of a holy
war, called as a healer of God. Gianni, my captain, has the gift of faith,
and Piero the gift of wisdom. Our coming has been foretold and much
have I to tell you of the wonders we have seen. We battle one who
wishes for nothing more than to stop our harvest of souls for Christ,
preferring to sow diseased minds in the furrows of his followers, every-
where he travels. Such has it been with his control over our Vincenzo,
and the result is Vincenzo's terrible fall, producing nightmarish acts
neither of us could have imagined.

I beg you to believe me in this, Marco. I need you to act on my
behalf, without pause. Please. In memory of our friendship, our fami-
lies. There is no ill will between us, no vendetta present here. You
must know that I have become Sir Gianni de Capezzana's wife, and
we expect a child of our own come autumn. Life has come full circle,
or shall, if I can free myself of the evil one who seems committed to the
idea that we must die.

Help us, Marco. Persuade the Nine to suspend all of del Buco's
and Amidei's properties and accounts within reach and call them to
testify before you. I shall bring you your witnesses and you can see to

justice from there. Regardless of your decision, send me word through
Countess Anette Devenue des Baux at once.

In the God who lives and breathes,
I wait, ever your friend,
Daria de Capezzana

Gianni came in and leaned against the wall, watching her sign her name.

"You should read it," Daria said.

He moved closer, silent, and leaned over her shoulder to read the missive. She could hear his breath catch when he read over the sentence of the expected child, pausing so long that she turned to make sure he would not pass out. He looked down at her in confusion, almost anger. Did he think it a ruse she used to play upon Marco's emotions?

She reached out to place her hands atop Gianni's own and waited for the truth to reach from her eyes to his mind and heart.

He gasped and came around the chair to kneel before her, taking her hands, then her shoulders, then her knees, then her face in his hands. He shook his head in wonder. "Are you certain?"

She smiled back into his eyes. "Very. I have been trying to tell you for nigh unto a week."

He lifted her up into his arms and cradled her there. "How it possible, Daria? How has my barren wife suddenly become a mother-in-waiting?"

"I know not. All I can believe is that that night in the prison, when I healed you? And was healed as well?"

He nodded, remembering.

"That the way was made. That God healed me in every way possible."

He nodded, so pleased, so happy . . . and then all at once stilled. "Amidei knows. It is the secret he spoke of?"

It was Daria's turn to nod, miserable as he.

"How? How could he know?"

She shook her head. "I have no idea. No one knows but Josephine. She and I were together, the seamstress doing a fitting . . ." She looked up at him, remembering Tessa's reaction to her dress. *One of the dark has touched it.* "The seamstress. He sent a spy into our house."

"Shocking," Gianni said dryly. He cradled her close. "I must tell you that it makes me more convinced than ever that I must protect you. Now there are two of you to watch over."

"I understand, Gianni." She pulled away to look him in the eye. "But just as we must leave justice in God's hands, you must trust our well-being to the Lord as well. Concentration must remain upon our task at hand. Only in seeing it through might we have the chance to resume a normal life with our child."

He stared at her. "I must get the letter to the docks. The doge intends to send all of his own letters on a special ship en route down the Rhône, due to depart within the hour."

Daria turned to fold the letter, place it in an envelope, and seal it with a peacock stamp in red wax. "Go," she said, handing it to her husband.

⚜ ⚜ ⚜

THE pope emerged from his deep slumber, dimly remembering canceling afternoon audience. His breathing was the same, wet and milky, and he fought not to begin coughing, for to begin coughing meant never ceasing.

His physicians arrived, bringing leeches to suck the poisons from his blood, speaking of bodily humors and the odd mix within the Holy Father this night. They laid horehound upon the fire and gave him foul-tasting liquids and he slept again, awaking hours later to again find them in his room, but it was difficult to see in the dim light of eventide. He had missed prayers.

They whispered about him, debating what could be happening deep within his lungs, and possible remedies, including hart's tongue, massive doses of goat's milk, and lungwort wine.

Cornelius kept his eyes shut, watching them through his lashes. His gaze moved to his desk, where the lost letters lay. He felt as though he sat in the corner of the room, watching the scene unfold before him as if actors in a play. The letter lay there, and the images arose from the sheets, almost taking life in front of his eyes. The beautiful healer, Daria de Capezzana. The knight of faith. The priest of wisdom.

He looked to the royal bed, to himself. Pale and in anguish, even in sleep. To the physicians, well schooled but absent of total and complete knowledge. Back to the papers, spread across his desk. It was as if he moved to them, moved over them, greeted them. Well aware was he that his fever soared. But he could not deny the call. He was almost out of time. He was weak, so weak.

Move. His God said to him. *Rise. Speak! Now!*

Cornelius rose, looking through dazed eyes at the startled physicians and his steward behind them. "Fetch the Gifted to attend to us. We are in need of their succor. Let no one attend us but them," he said, falling back upon the pillows.

჻ ჻ ჻

THEY heard them approach, and Ambrogio moved into the hallway to steal a look. The three papal physicians and the surgeon moved past, grumbling, and Vito pulled back, listening. A steward peered out of the papal chambers, telling a sleepy guard to go and seek those in the Familiars' Wing, Sir de Capezzana and his wife, along with their priest.

Vito pushed Ugo out and sent him running ahead of the guard, recognizing the opportunity. Ugo set off, running past the stunned physicians and beyond, down the stairs, in pursuit of Gianni, Piero, and Daria before they were formally summoned. The important part was that they were summoned. That they arrive before they were expected was part of God's plan.

If an attack was imminent, every minute counted.

Vito watched his brother disappear beyond the physicians, and then grimaced as the physicians again moved, to make way for another group, coming forth.

Amidei. And Cardinal Morano.

჻ ჻ ჻

"DRESS and come," Ugo said, throwing open their door without invitation.

He ran on to Piero's door, rapping upon it, then slamming it open as well. "Hurry," he said.

They gathered in the hallway.

"M'lady, captain, Father," Ugo panted, "the pope asks for you."

"For us?" Daria asked.

"For you. The guard shall be here in a moment. We merely overheard the invitation." He looked at all three of them. "I passed Lord Amidei and Cardinal Morano. They seemed to be en route to the papal chambers."

"You all remain here," Piero said calmly. "I beg you to be on your knees in prayer for us, your brother and sister, until we return. More good is done upon your knees, covering us in the Lord's name, than a sword has ever done."

ᘓ ᘓ ᘓ

VITO moved out into the hallway before Lord Amidei, sword drawn. "I am afraid that neither you nor yours shall pass," he said, pulling his sword to his nose and then pointing it toward Amidei.

Abramo looked upon him with a smile, as if he were expected. "Surely you recognize Cardinal Morano. Do you have a death wish, man?"

"Nay," Vito allowed, still staring over his sword, pointed at Abramo's neck. "But neither should you, Sorcerer."

"Get out of the way, before I call for the papal guard."

"Lord of the Night, you shall remain where you are," Ambrogio said, staking his place beside Vito.

The cardinal looked to Abramo in confusion.

ᘓ ᘓ ᘓ

GIANNI, Piero, and Daria set out running, with Ugo right behind them. They walked in hushed steps down the side hall as priests chanted through Vespers, through the kitchens, with maids washing floors clean of bones and cartilage and fat, through the Consistory Wing toward the Chapel Tower.

They met a confused guard, looking back to the man holding Lord Amidei and Cardinal Morano at bay, to them, those he had been sent to fetch.

"Go and bring back six knights of the papal guard with you," whispered Piero, moving past the dumbfounded young man. "There is danger in this house," he said.

With that, the man ran.

The three moved forward, across the hall and around Vito and Ambrogio, who held Lord Amidei and the cardinal from moving any farther inward.

"The pope has invited us to attend him," Gianni said to Amidei. "Not you. Be gone."

"I think we shall remain where we are," returned Amidei.

"Can you maintain your guard?" Gianni asked.

"No problem, Captain," Vito answered. Ugo joined him, drawing his sword.

They moved forward, opening the door into what they supposed was the papal vestry, then on to the papal chambers.

Daria went in first, but she backed up, into Gianni's arms. Piero paused alongside her.

Piero raised an arm and lifted it, as if against a palpable force. He looked to Gianni. "It is as it was with the young princess. The dark has made inroads here. Go. Return with Gaspare, Hasani, Tessa, and Josephine. All must be present to combat this."

"Captain?" asked Vito, hopefully. But his captain ignored him in a desperate run down the hall.

⚜ ⚜ ⚜

"Come," Abramo said to Vito, appealing to him. "This is the Holy Father's own Cardinal Morano, blessed, well known to be of uncommon faith and valor," he said.

Ambrogio edged forward, his own sword drawn. Well Abramo knew that he could slice the artist to chunks before him, but he held back, aware that his control of Cardinal Morano was tenuous, in the balance this night. His master emerged from the shadows behind him.

"Hold, my son," he hissed. "Work at the knight. He is your doorway."

"Vito, you have fought well on behalf of the Gifted," Abramo said. He moved to the right, behind Cardinal Morano, and then back, as if unperturbed by the knight's sword, or the captain's departure for reinforcements. "Vast should be your reward. How long has it been since you and your brother drank of your benefactor's wine, supped at her table, rolled gold florins into your own bank account?"

The other knight, Ugo, edged closer to his brother. Amidei could feel them gaining strength, knew he had to act.

He lunged forward, drawing his sword, but rather than drawing Vito's attack upon himself, he watched as Vito drew his sword to the nape of Cardinal Morano's neck. Abramo immediately stilled.

Vito smiled. "Without him, Lord Amidei, it all falls apart, right?"

It was true. Without Gabriel, he had not the power nor the might to seize the papacy. Gabriel Morano alone was the one who could win it.

He looked into Vito's eyes. Honest. True. Unable to kill an innocent.

"You intend to kill a cardinal of the Church?" he whispered in a taunt, feeling the master, just over his left shoulder. "They shall hang you at dawn."

⚜ ⚜ ⚜

DARIA moved to the pope as if her feet were encased in mud, looking back to Piero with her medicinal chest. But he had paused over the letters, the copies of their own letter, spread across the pope's desk. Three of them, nine pages each in a row. Three additional pages to their own copy. All in a clearly separate hand, an illuminist's hand that had each drawn a depiction of Daria, of Gianni, of Piero. Copies? Nay? Simultaneous or inclusive prophecy. She could see him lift one against the other, side by side, staring back and forth, measuring symmetry, language, curve of line.

Her attention moved to the Holy Father, to the vials by his bedside. She lifted one after another, smelling of each. He was plainly ill with an ailment of the chest. But there was something more, something more . . . beyond the overwhelming sense of evil here. It was similar to when they entered the young princess's room . . . and yet different. Amidei had been here. But what had he accomplished?

Dear God, she prayed, bringing her nose back to the second vial, even as her hand reached for the third. She closed her eyes and inhaled again, taking in the subtle garlic-like odor in a bottle labeled LUNGWORT TONIC.

It was not lungwort, which smelled vaguely of alfalfa. This was arsenic.

An assassin, she said to her Lord. *An assassin within your holy gates, Father. Stop him. Stop him!*

She turned to the pope, barely breathing now, and glanced with fear at the steward. Was he to be trusted? Or were they in the room with a man who tried to kill the pope?

ⱷ ⱷ ⱷ

THE *Honneur Gard* ran into the Consistory Wing, just as Vito swung his sword from the cardinal's neck to Abramo. Abramo parried his strike and then lunged toward the hated Ambrogio, painter of poisonous plots. He had decided to risk the cardinal's life, upon his master's urging.

The guards, seeing swords drawn, roared and unsheathed their own swords, rushing to block the pope's door. Abramo grimly recognized that by position alone, he appeared as the transgressor on attack.

The Gifted scurried in behind the guards, and although they were blocked as he was, they took up position on their knees to one side, with one arm raised to the pope's chamber wall beside them, as if they could draw out the poison already having its way with the weakened man inside, and one arm raised toward Amidei and Morano, as if they could hold them in place by prayer alone.

Their presence infuriated Abramo more than the knights with swords.

"Forgive me, m'lord, m'lord Cardinal," said the pope's steward, who had come out of the chambers at the sound of swords. He tore his eyes from the strange sight of the praying people to Amidei and Morano. "No one else is permitted entrance this night." Abramo abruptly sheathed his sword.

"Surely that does not pertain to us," Abramo said.

"Sorrowfully all," returned the steward.

"Upon whose orders?"

"The Holy Father's," returned the man.

Abramo and his master received the first volley of prayers of the Gifted, taking a staggering step backward, then another. Three papal guards raised their swords toward him, drawn by his odd manner. He grimaced, not having ever sensed such power. They grew more formidable, still. "Come," he managed to say to the cardinal, "We must return . . . on the morrow."

ಈ ಈ ಈ

DARIA went from her medicinal chest to the pope, again and again, hoping to put together some remedy, some answer, held just beyond her experience, her knowledge. But there was no more that could be done. She had purged the Holy Father's stomach. Filled his mouth with herbs that would complete the task. But still the question plagued her. How long since the poisoning had begun? Had their enemy begun his assault a day ago, a week ago, longer? Was the chest cold part of the enemy's attack or merely the opening he needed to usher in death?

She laid the last of her poultice across the pontiff's chest, and laid atop it steaming Egyptian cotton cloths, prized for their thickness, absorbency. But Daria was more interested in their capacity to hold in the heat, store it, diffusing it in spare, even portions. *If I make it through this, Lord,* she found herself praying, *I shall become a purveyor of Egyptian cloths . . .*

She sat beside the pontiff, mayhap sixty years of age, casting back to another scene, another time, in which she watched Piero, struggling for breath after breath . . . .

Breathe, Cornelius, she prayed, wholly conscious that if the pope died this night, his death would be laid squarely at her feet. At the Gifted's feet. *Surely, Father,* she prayed to her God on High, *you did not bring us this far to perish before Amidei, leaving us at the mercy of your own courts . . .*

Daria leaned down and laid her hands upon the pope, the Father of all Christendom, and felt as his chest rose and fell in a death rattle, just as the elder Count des Baux had done weeks before. She eyed the new branch of horehound upon the fire, the poultice drying across the pontiff's chest, and lent her voice to join her brothers and sisters praying alongside her, just outside the papal chambers and those beyond . . .

CHAPTER THIRTY-FOUR

THE pope awakened with a start, as if choking, sitting up so suddenly, hand to his chest, that Daria moved away, startled.

Piero sat up straight at the same time, eyes widening in surprise. He had been half-asleep himself.

He stared hard at Cornelius, watching as Daria and his steward went to him, easing him back among the pillows, then closed his eyes in thanks. *You have spared him, Lord. Now please allow him to spare us . . .*

"Holy Father, drink this," Daria said, bringing a green liquid to his lips.

The pontiff obediently sipped it down, studying her as he did so. "You are," he said between labored breaths, "the very image of the illuminations."

"Or they are the very image of me," she said, smiling back into his light brown eyes.

"They are . . . not Pauline," he said, holding back a cough.

"Does it matter?" she asked. "The text holds with Scripture defined as Pauline. There is nothing blasphemous or heretical about it."

"Nay," he said, eyes watering as he held back another cough. "But what are we to do . . . if more letters appear . . . more people arrive . . . convinced they are . . . part of an ancient prophecy?"

Daria lifted a brow and eased back the sheet, squeezing herbs in a pot by her feet and packing them atop his thin chest. "Are you truly concerned that might happen?"

"Templar Knights, Cathars . . . the Church must be vigilant . . . in watching for dangers to our people."

"Indulgences, priestly vagary, conspiracies among the papal *palais*," Piero said, rising in the corner. "It seems you have enough to keep straight those already within your gates."

"Tread carefully," the pope said, lifting a trembling and weak finger of warning.

He looked back to Daria as she worked. "God nearly called us to his side." His tone had no question, but his eyes asked if it were true.

"Nearly," she said. She looked to his steward, who nodded back at the pontiff, confirming her answer.

So he was a friend? They could use every one.

"What did you give us . . . that our own physicians . . . could not?" He reached out and grabbed her hand, his fingers surprisingly strong.

"Why did you call for us?" she returned, staring back at him.

Slowly he released her hand and glanced toward the desk. "We knew . . . We could feel the slow slide. Losing hold. We were getting worse, not better. And, the letters, the uncanny resemblance to you, the priest, the knight . . . Lord Devenue own recovery . . . the princess . . ."

"God saved you," Daria said, resuming her process of packing the poultice. "I did naught but place yew branches within your hearth, water on to boil and fill the air with steam, and this poultice of sage, fennel, and mint atop your chest," she said, nodding downward. "Your own physicians gave you hart's-tongue tonic, which I would have done as well. But Your Holiness," she said, reaching for the bottle of poison. "Someone was also giving you this, before we arrived."

"What is it?"

"Arsenic, but within a bottle that is labeled lungwort." She held it to his nose. "Smell of it. Do you detect the garlic-like odor? It burns at your innards."

The steward gasped. "Poison? Someone has dared to try to murder the Holy Father?"

"Abramo Amidei," she said, wiping her hands. "Every last one of the Gifted and our company was outside your door last night, praying that God would save you. Guards arrived, narrowly keeping Amidei and Morano from entering. He has had previous access?"

"Amidei is but one of many who has neared us in the last weeks," the pope said softly.

"You know as well as I that he is the dragon, the one prophesied to work against the Gifted, against all who live and breathe to serve God. Look at his coat of arms! Look to your very own copies of our letter!"

"Coincidence," he dismissed with a wave of his hand. "The dragon is . . . a common enough emblem. Amidei has many . . . friends in this court."

"Yes, friends among the most influential of your cardinals," she said. "Great is your intelligence, and wide is your own web in gathering information. You have heard the rumors, of dark ceremonies, of sin masquerading as piety. Cardinal Boeri has told you what Amidei is capable of, and lately he has taken Cardinal Morano under his wing, forming him into the future pontiff. Morano is innocent, I'm quite sure of it, but he has allowed Amidei to use him. Only one thing stood in the way of Amidei's plans coming to fruition. You."

She rose and paced back and forth. Piero urged her on with a silent nod. "He has given funds to many churches, as a means of securing devotion among their churchmen. He owns them, Holy Father," she said, reaching for his hand in her urgency, "in more ways than one. You must wrest them away from his grip before it is too late."

The pontiff stared at her for a moment and shook off her hand. "Leave us now. This conversation is at an end. We shall see you again when we begin our formal audience."

Daria pulled back, confused.

"Grave are your charges, woman . . . against men . . . close to us."

"Yes," she said softly.

"It is only right . . . to allow these men . . . to defend themselves. No more whisperings in dark halls. Open, frank dialogue is what we seek. God will shine in the daylight."

"*Post tenebras, lux,*" she whispered. She gathered up her herbs and cloth and packed them into her chest of medicinals, then looked up to the pope. "Will you not look upon the others outside your door? Give them your blessing, your praise, for calling God to enter these hallowed halls and heal the Holy Father?"

He waved her away, eyes closing in weariness.

She frowned at Piero as he took the medicinal chest from her hands. "How much has Amidei given to his own personal causes to buy him that much devotion?" she whispered. "To allow Judas to hover about?"

Piero raised a brow. "It must be considerable indeed."

⚭ ⚭ ⚭

THE audience was called two days later. The pope appeared, looking considerably better than he had two days ago, and coughed only on occasion. Amidei hovered, entering and exiting the hall at odd times, mayhap a move designed to draw the cardinals' attention to him, remind them of promises made.

For the most part, the Gifted ignored him, focusing on words exchanged between the pontiff, Piero, and Josephine, who arose to be their best defense, turning every question back to Scripture, demanding again and again to show them all where the Word said they were not to be doing as they had been gifted by God to do.

The doge and Conte and Contessa Morassi sat through the entire first day, waiting to be called upon for their testimony. But the pope carefully avoided even looking in their direction, let alone allowing them to say what they had come to say.

And despite the fact they had clearly spared his life—and that the pope had called them to help him out of an apparent, desperate need—he seemed intent upon seeing his sacred duty through. To ascertain, as he put it, "whether you be renegade, heretic, or saint."

"Is it your intention," said the pope now, "to continue to baptize outside Church gates?"

Josephine rose. "Peter said, 'Repent and be baptized, every one of you, in the name of Jesus Christ for the forgiveness of sins. And you will receive the gift of the Holy Spirit. The promise is for you and your children and *for all who are far off—for all whom the Lord our God will call.*' "

"You take that Scripture as justification for your actions?"

"All that we need, Holiness," Piero said soberly, looking from Josephine to the pope. "But God is urging me to speak the Word more than baptize and get into disagreements with you, as Paul did with the Corinthians. 'For Christ did not send me to baptize, but to preach the gospel—not with words of human wisdom, lest the cross of Christ be emptied of its power.' "

"A simple yes or no will do," said the pope dryly. "You presume we do not know our Scriptures, little brother and sister?"

"We beg your forgiveness, Your Holiness. My sole concern is to follow the call that Christ has placed in me, and do so with everything I have in me. This is the core of what we believe: that we are to devote ourselves, like the first believers, to studying the Word, to fellowship, and yes, even breaking bread together. Only within the Word can we find the truth we seek. We do not look to the wisdom or traditions of man, for in man, the Church becomes lost."

The pope rose, waving a bit on his feet, flushing at the neck. "*I* am the Church. You promote heresy, madness among the commoners."

"No, Your Holiness," Piero said, bowing, regretting his words but unable to say anything but this. "We are the Church. We are the Body. Born to live and act in Christ's name, by the power of the Holy Spirit. To do as he bids, wherever, whenever, he bids it. If we were to ignore that call, now *that* would be heretical."

The pope said nothing. Round and round had they gone on these facts, saying them again and again, with every different phrase possible.

"Sleep this night, 'Gifted' of God. But be aware that we must hear far different things from you on the morrow. Our patience wanes. You are on a path toward excommunication and the Court of Apostolic Causes. And you, priest," he said, pointing at Piero, "shall be defrocked."

"It matters not," Piero said steadily, "for God sees me as I am, shall use me wherever I am for the remainder of my days, whether I wear the robes of a priest or wander about in animal skins."

The court erupted.

࿇ ࿇ ࿇

THE next morning, the pope ignored the Gifted and turned to the doge. "You and the Conte and Contessa Morassi must desire to be soon on your way. You wish to say something in public defense of these men and women?" he asked.

"I do," the doge said. He lumbered to his feet.

"Be about it then."

"These men and women came to my city. I can personally attest to the fact that they healed more than fifteen on our isle of lepers, citizens who now work and live among us in the Rialto again. They restored husbands and fathers, sisters and mothers, daughters and sons."

The pope sat back in his chair. "Our court has heard whisperings. These healings have been authenticated?"

"By Cardinal Boeri himself. He was in Venezia when the Gifted came to us."

The pope's eyes flitted over Boeri and back to the doge.

"They healed a madman, long stationed on a corner of the Dusodoro district," he said. "This was a man who screamed through the night, keeping neighbors awake for hours, for years. No one remembers him with sound mind. He now is clean and well and works with the sisters in the Hospital of the Saints."

The pope looked over to Daria. "Your 'madman' must have had some physical ailment. She is a healer. I take no issue with using her gifts as a physician."

"I do not wish to be a physician," Daria said, standing. "I only wish to heal as God bids."

The pope frowned. "What is the difference?"

"The difference is that I go where God, not man, calls me. To those he calls me to heal. I can administer medicines, but only God can heal."

"Did you not come to us, in our chamber, to heal us, when our own physicians could not?"

The court erupted in gasps. Apparently, many had not yet learned of this. Daria studied the pontiff. Was he allowing her an opening? Using his own healing as a means of defense?

"I did, three nights past."

"And the next morning we were remarkably better," he said.

"Because God laid his hand upon you," she said. "I treated you. But God healed you."

"But we had sent for you," he said.

"We were called by God to go to you even before your steward even arrived at our door. We were making our way to the papal chambers—"

The pope laughed. "How did you intend to gain entrance?"

"If we could not gain entrance, we planned to pray for you, as close as we could get to you. And we intended to stop your assassin, even if we had to forfeit our own lives to do so."

A lady screamed and fainted at the mention of an assassin in the house of the pope. Men shouted, and the audience dissolved in private conversation.

"You shall be quiet!" the pope said, rising. He turned to Piero. "How do we know that *you* are not the papal assassin? And if it wasn't you, how did you come to know of this intrigue?"

"Hasani was granted a vision," he said, lifting his hand for the sheets. Hasani rose, handed them to him, and then sat back down.

A steward took them from him and passed them along to the pope. He studied them for a long moment and allowed his eyes to move to where Amidei stood. To his credit, Amidei did not waver under his gaze.

The pope's red-rimmed eyes moved back to Hasani, standing behind Piero. "He is your seer? A slave?"

"Freed man, long a member of the d'Angelo household."

"And how often do his visions hold true?"

"We have yet to see one not come to fruition," Piero said, knowing the pope was seeing Hasani's drawing become reality—the conical hat of the pope being placed on Cardinal Morano's head. "Although at times, the outcome is different than we expect."

The pope rested his elbow on the throne chair and rubbed his temples. "How many of these drawings has he done?"

Piero glanced over his shoulder. Hasani stared downward. "I am uncertain, but I have seen stacks and stacks of them in rooms we have had to leave behind."

"So you have no others here, now?"

"Nay," Piero said, relieved to be able to answer in honesty and not relinquish anything Hasani was not ready to share.

"Are there others in the manor in Villeneuve-des-Avignon?"

Piero's eyes widened, and slowly he turned to Hasani, hoping the man had not left more there, that he had hidden them, somewhere along the way.

Compelled to honesty, the regal, tall man nodded once.

"Go and fetch those drawings from the manor," the pope muttered to a clerk. The man set off at once.

The pope sat in silence for a time, then looked again to Piero. "Your letter speaks of seven in your number. We know Lady de Capezzana is your healer, you a man of wisdom—although we confess we believe that to be a matter of debate—the black man is your seer, one who receives visions. By her tone, Josephine is your prophetess. Sir de Capezzana is your man of faith." His eyes went to the knight, taking in the stance of his shoulders, chin. "Who is your discerner? The one who can determine light from dark?"

"I am," said Tessa, standing on shaking legs. But her arms were at her sides, her hands in fists of defiance.

The pope stared hard at her. After a long moment, he asked, "And your man of miracles?"

Gaspare rose beside Tessa.

ॐ ॐ ॐ

THE pope continued to question the Gifted, the Morassis, and the doge for days, at first seeming to wish to guide them onto a safer path, persuade them to relinquish those things the papacy could not condone—baptism, communion, and other sacraments outside of the Church and not on Church-sanctioned days—and find the means to bless their gifting, utilize it for, as he put it, "the glory of God."

But as the third day edged into the fourth, the pope became visibly wearied and agitated. Daria feared that he had taxed his weakened health, the task too much as he tried to heal. "His color is poor," she whispered to Gianni, but her husband's attention was upon Josephine as she moved forward to once again respond to the pope's questions.

After a time, the pope stared at Josephine with deadened eyes for a long moment, then moved on to look at Piero. Lastly, he looked upon Daria. "It deeply saddens us that it has come to this. However, we see no other recourse. We hereby send you to the Court of Apostolic Causes. We command the court to begin proceedings by defrocking Father Piero. We send any of you"—he paused to look at each of the Gifted and their supporters, including the Conte and Contessa Morassi and the doge—"with the recommendation that anyone who refuses to denounce their previous involvement with these people, recant their intentions to proceed in holy matters when we have specifically asked you to refrain, must be excommunicated."

Piero absorbed his words, closing his eyes at the last. Excommunication—damned to eternal hell, with no method to return. And yet he no longer believed the pope held such power; only his Savior could save or condemn. There was simply no scriptural basis for it. He was more concerned for the people . . . that anyone in papal territory would be sure to avoid them, going as far as to refuse them food, water, lodging, or they would risk excommunication themselves. What would that do to their ministry? Their desire to reach the people with the Good News? But God was not surprised at this; he knew they would face this day. A warm assurance washed over his heart.

He opened his eyes to stare back into Cornelius's. "So be it," he said softly.

ॐ ॐ ॐ

THEY were called before the Court of Apostolic Causes three days later, led by armed guards to the massive hall, with soaring ribs that met in domes, and placed in line behind others condemned to final judgment.

The Great Audience Hall was packed as they at last were called forth. Word had spread that the Gifted were to be questioned, and that the process would begin with the defrocking of a priest. People jostled on the sides, but Daria had a hard time keeping her eyes from Piero. What would this mean to him? Was there not any other way?

He looked back at her, as always making her feel as if he could read her thoughts. He gave her a tender smile and leaned toward her. "I do not fear this, daughter. God can work through all things. You've seen it. After the darkness, light. Right?"

She nodded, quick tears in her eyes.

"Father Piero, chaplain of Sir Gianni and Lady de Capezzana," called a steward, reading from a parchment scroll.

Piero cleared his throat and stepped forward. "I am here."

"Step forward, please," said the man, pointing to a spot right beside him.

Piero moved forward, and the process began, just as he had described to them the night before. At the fore of the massive hall was a round bench at which the judge sat. A barrier separated them from the rest of the hall. Against the east wall was a lovely fresco of Calvary, and on the north wall a massive rendering of the Last Judgment, to remind all under whose judgment they would ultimately sit—Christ's. In the Court of the Rota, named for the wheel-like round bench, up to ten thousand petitions were heard a year. The Lord's Commissioner or chief auditor, a formidable man named Bishop Matteo du Puy, sat beneath a coat of arms and keystone labeled "S.P.Q.R."

Piero eyed Cardinal Boeri, who saw it, too. The initials stood for "The Senate and the People of Rome," a nod toward the papacy's original roots. The cardinal returned his gaze with understanding. No priest ever wanted to be here, in this court, accused of anything.

Atop Piero's simple robe, they placed a cape of gilt ribbons and a white silk. They placed a stole of silver and gold around his neck, with the holy emblems denoting the Alpha and Omega on either tip. Over one arm they placed a censer of gold, its holy fragrance still smoking out the holes. And in his hands they placed a golden box, holding the heavenly host.

Bishop du Puy stared hard at Piero from under bushy, furrowed brows. "My brother, you were once sworn to uphold the causes of Christ, to abide by the authority of the Holy Roman Church, to honor the Rule, to lead life without error and to shelter others. You hold in your hands the treasures of the Church. You wear the most highly esteemed and honorable robes of the Church. Will you forsake us? Or shall you repent and recant?"

Piero looked down and thought for a long moment, holding his slight shoulders straight. Then he looked back to the bishop and said, "Blessed and holy Court, I honor what you do in attempting to keep the sheep within the gates." He eyed Abramo Amidei and turned slightly toward him. "Wolves prowl about and we must be ever vigilant. For we are the shepherds, left to lead and protect the sheep."

"I ask you, Father, to keep your eyes on me," said du Puy, "as you speak to the Court."

Piero turned without pause. "As a fellow shepherd of the flock, I recognize that my ways are unorthodox. That my guidance of my small flock was not along a road I was authorized by the Church to enter. And yet," he said, picking up his chin, "I see no reason for the Church to block a road that our Lord and Savior himself has asked me to walk. If he asks, I shall go. Would this blessed Court ask me to deny a call of Christ? Is it not what brought each of us into the brotherhood of faith? Nay. I maintain there is nothing for me to repent of or recant. To do so would be akin to denying my Savior."

The bishop rose, flushing red at the neck at Piero's impudence. His mouth was set in a grim line. He gave a signal, and they began the process of defrocking Piero as a priest of the Church, beginning a litany in Latin.

Daria's tears crested her lids and slid down her cheeks.

A hand reached for hers. Gianni. And after a moment, another reached for her hand. Tessa. She looked down to the child and over her head and then back again, wanting to make certain that her eyes did not betray her. Anette Devenue des Baux. Her husband, Lord Devenue. And right behind them, the others who had witnessed the healings. They had returned to Avignon as promised.

Daria pulled at Gianni's hand, calling attention to their presence. They were too late to stall Piero's defrocking. But could they aid the Gifted in circumventing endless questioning, torture, excommunication, banishment? Collectively they were the most influential of all of Provence. Armand had chosen well. God had chosen well.

Gianni squeezed her hand in response. *Hope*, said his touch. *Hope*.

Four priests moved forward and took the sacred elements from Piero's hands. They took from him the alb, the stole, the censer, leaving him in his brown robe.

The Court stood and stared at the priest as the final words were uttered, the dissolution nearly complete. "Do you have anything left to say, Piero?" asked du Puy, carefully avoiding any holy title.

Piero smiled at him with kind eyes, and Daria understood his expression. He felt sorrow for the auditor, a desire to show him truth, light, to lead him out of the dark. "Yes," he said. Slowly he undid the rope at his waist and carefully folded it at his feet.

Du Puy frowned, wary now.

Piero reached for the shoulder of his robe.

"Piero . . ."

But Piero continued, lifting the robe from his shoulders and pulling it away from his body, leaving only a flimsy undergown and leggings beneath. People stirred and covered laughter behind hands. But Piero continued, carefully folding the brown Benedictine robe into quarters and setting it down on the stair in front of the bishop, with the rope atop it.

He lifted his hands outward. "M'lord Bishop," he said, staring back into the reddened and furious face of his prosecutor. "I could be naked and my God could still make use of me. The role of priest is a sacred task. I am called to speak to my people wherever I am, to reach them with the truth of Christ, the hope of the Everlasting. Our time on earth is fleeting. The Alpha and Omega is not contained on a gold and silver stole. He is all about us. Dress me in rags, in the clothes of a court jester—leave me in nothing but my undergarments—but you shall never take away the truth."

Piero's voice rose, and he pointed at the ground. "God is here. Right now. He is present. And I, recognized or not, am his servant."

Silence washed over the halls, everyone holding their breath, eyes on Bishop du Puy. His chest heaved, as if he were having difficulty breathing himself in the midst of his fury, but slowly it eased. He sat back down upon his high wooden chair, one hand on the arm of it, the other rubbing his lips as he considered his next move.

At last, he spoke. "You declare yourself as his servant. Do you stand alone?"

"Nay, m'lord Bishop," said Anette. "I stand behind him," she said, stepping forward.

"As do I," said Josephine. Each of the Gifted and their supporters said the same, stepping forward.

"And we do as well," said the doge. The rest of the nobles followed suit. In the passion of the moment, others from the gallery moved forward, including a priest, a steward, and a knight of the *palais*.

The bishop stared down at them, now a collective group of about fifty. He had risen to his feet again as the group grew, obviously wondering when the momentum would taper. "Countess Devenue des Baux," he said, coughing into his hand. "Are you certain that you wish to stand with this heretic?"

"If he is a heretic, then so am I," she said, raising her chin. Gaspare leaned toward her and whispered in her ear. She took her skirts in hand and moved forward, Count Devenue at her side. "M'lord Bishop," she said. "We all know what will come next. You have a holy charge. But you prosecute your own," she pleaded. "Their gifting is something to be celebrated. Honored. Do you not see what they have done for my husband? Will you not give them the opportunity to prove themselves loyal to our God?"

Du Puy frowned.

"Beware of trickery," said Cardinal Zambrotti. Abramo Amidei eased away, as if he had said nothing to him.

"What do you propose, my lady?" asked the bishop.

"I know not," she said with an easy smile, looking back to the Gifted, letting her eyes rest on Gaspare. And it was then that Daria felt it, the urgent need, the desire from within to heal. Her eyes met Piero's, then Gaspare's. Was this the Father's way out? His passage to safety?

"I do," said Daria, stepping forward. "There is one to be healed. Before your very eyes. Would that not prove to you that we are who we say?" Her eyes sifted through the crowd. Who was it? Whom had the Lord picked to heal this very day?

"She has done it before," said Duke Richardieu. "She healed me of my deafness."

"And she healed my cancer," said Lady Blanchette, standing beside him.

"And you have seen me at my near worst," Count Devenue said. "You cannot deny, Bishop du Puy, that at our last meeting, you considered me a dead man upon my feet."

The bishop stared hard at him. Daria could see the truth of it in his eyes. He had counted Dimitri dead, had undoubtedly seen his deformed head, riddled with tumor. And now he stood before the court again, the proud and healed husband of Countess Anette des Baux. He could not be ignored. Something significant, something obvious had occurred. Something that could not be denied.

The bishop's eyes narrowed.

The pope entered, among some fanfare. He appeared better today, but Daria gave him scant attention. She was praying, asking God to identify who would receive healing this day. *A child, Lord?*

Daria searched her heart. Her eyes again ran over the crowd. There were precious few children among them.

"I shall determine who it will be, then," said the bishop. He moved down the stairs and into the crowd before him, to Daria's right.

"He cannot," Daria whispered to Gianni. "It cannot be our determination . . ."

"Trust, wife," he said, squeezing her hand. "God sees us. He knows us and our current crisis. He shall see us through."

"But—"

"Him," the bishop said. "You shall heal him."

The crowd parted, clearing the path between the child he gestured to, then back toward Daria.

Roberto. *Dear Roberto.*

It was not possible. He needed surgery. Months of healing . . .

The bishop stared in cold challenge at Daria. "Well?"

Chapter Thirty-five

I<small>T</small> was then Daria knew the truth of it, felt the familiar pull. She smiled into Roberto's hopeful, wide, patient eyes. "Yes." She nodded, grinning. "It is he that God has chosen."

"I chose him," dismissed the bishop.

"God is a part of everything we do," said Piero as he passed him, heading back to the dais and his chair. The pope took a seat beside him.

"Yes, well you better hope that God is a part of *this*," Vito whispered.

"Our Lord *is* a part of this," Gaspare said, his eyes twinkling with excitement even as Daria moved toward Roberto. He knelt on the floor and raised his hands to the ceiling. "Our Lord on High placed the sun and the moon in place. He is our Creator, and he lives and rules the heavens to this day. No one can stop him," he said, staring hard at Amidei.

Abramo was pacing, Vincenzo now at his side. He looked to Daria, his eyes appearing old and weary, reminding her of the pope . . .

She shifted her gaze to Gaspare. The old fisherman closed his eyes and was praying. Suddenly the windows became dim and then dark. Women screamed. Men rushed outside. Torches were lit. In a moment, one returned. "An eclipse! There is an eclipse of the sun!"

The bishop looked to his counterparts. No eclipse was foreseen. There wasn't another due for months, and it was to be partial, at most.

"The world is in darkness," Josephine said, as Gaspare continued to pray. "Only Jesus is the light."

Daria stepped forward. " 'No one lights a lamp and puts it in a place where it will be hidden, or under a bowl. Instead he puts it on its stand, so that those who come in may see the light.' Roberto, are you ready to let Christ's light shine through you?"

The boy nodded, eyes wide.

"*Post tenebras, lux,*" Vito muttered behind her.

"*Post tenebras, lux,*" Daria repeated. She moved toward Roberto and leaned down. She caressed his cheek. "You have been patient, my friend. God has chosen this day, this moment, to bring you healing. Do you believe?"

He nodded, eyes wide.

"Lie down here, Roberto," she said softly. She looked to Tessa and Nico, right beside the boy, and asked them to stay on either side of him. She spoke clearly, loud enough that their judges could hear.

Piero held his hand out toward the bishop and the pope. "Please, come closer. You are wary of trickery. Bring two of your most trusted men on the Holy Court, and come close. There must be no dispute. What you are about to witness must be corroborated by three or more of you." He looked about the grand hall. "You as well, m'lord Cardinals. Please. Draw near."

He was wise, bringing them close, Daria thought. If enough truly believed what was about to transpire, knew it as truth, they had a fighting chance of making it out of the Court without a death sentence, mayhap even without an excommunication.

Hasani drew closer as well and pulled a parchment from the folds of his robe. He handed it to Bishop du Puy, but Daria began praying then, and his attention was solely upon her. He waved for three torch bearers to come closer.

Daria looked about the boy, now wreathed in the faithful—Hasani, Gaspare, Piero, Tessa, Nico, Agata, Vito, Ugo, Gianni, Josephine. Ambrogio edged near and took to his knees, reaching in a hand to touch Roberto's deformed leg, and smiled his encouragement toward Daria.

Daria rolled up Roberto's leggings to his thighs, leaving his healthy leg exposed as well. She wanted to see what his leg was supposed to look like, the goal before her and her God. She ran her hands over the deformed limb, the bad break, covered over in bone. Ligaments and tendons shortened where they not ought to be. Muscles bunched in knots in others.

She sighed and closed her eyes, making sure she understood all that was ahead.

"Faith," Gianni whispered into her ear, his breath hot. "God can do this. He *shall* do this."

"Faith," she repeated in a whisper.

"Wisdom," Piero added, staring soberly at Roberto's leg. "May you know exactly what to do."

"Wisdom," Daria said.

"Power," Gaspare said. "Know that the Holy One is present. And nothing is beyond his reach."

"God's own power, here among us," she said, a smile growing across her face.

"A word from our Savior," Josephine said. " 'For this people's heart has become callused; they hardly hear with their ears, and they have closed their eyes. Otherwise, they might see with their eyes, hear with their ears, understand with their hearts and turn, and I would heal them.' "

"We turn to you, Lord," Daria prayed. "We understand it is you that holds this mighty power and ask you to heal this child, now."

Hasani grunted and she looked into his eyes. His eyes were at rest, confident. *All will be well. I have seen it.* He smiled at her.

Tessa moved closer and laid a hand on Daria's shoulder. "We are not alone, m'lady," she whispered. "There is evil here, but God's own are moving among us as well."

She looked from the child and into her friend Roberto's eyes. "How long, little man? How long ago was your leg broken?" She spoke more for the bishop's knowledge than her own.

"More than six years past, now, m'lady," he said.

Daria rose slowly and looked to the people beyond their inner circle. "There must not be anyone here who does not believe or wish for God to heal this child. You must believe, hope, and join your prayers with our own, or you must leave." She turned to Lord Amidei and Vincenzo, then back to Bishop du Puy. "Those two men must be ushered out of this hall."

Cardinal Saucille stirred. "That is preposterous . . ."

She turned to the bishop. "This is your test for us, is it not?"

"It is."

"Tessa, are those two men of the light or of the dark?"

Tessa stared where she pointed. "Of the dark, m'lady."

Gaspare said, "Have them go, m'lord Bishop. They must not be present." He looked toward the pope, as if he intended to directly appeal to the Holy Father.

"Take them out," the pope said immediately, throwing a dismissive hand in the air as if to say he just wanted this nonsense done.

Abramo whipped his arm out of the hands of a guard and strode out of the hall, Vincenzo right behind him.

"Tessa, are there any others who must leave?" Daria asked.

The child turned in a slow circle. She pointed out three men, then a woman, and guards took them from the room. She paused over the six cardinals, standing in attendance beyond the Court council, those over whom Amidei had held sway. "You have been led down dark paths," she said bravely. "Lord Amidei is our enemy. And we are the friends of God. Stay, m'lord Cardinals," she said sweetly, "but I sense deep conflict within each of you. When you see what God is about to do through Lady de Capezzana, I ask that you search within, past the dark web Lord Amidei has spun, to the truth of Christ that remains there. I can see that as well. You are not his yet. You are God's own. Fight back against the darkness. Choose the light."

The men watched her, some glowering, some shaking in fear, others already looking repentant, caught in the truth of the young girl's words.

Tessa returned to the group and laid her hand beside the others, atop Roberto's head.

Daria waited for Roberto to look into her eyes. "Pray, Roberto," she whispered. "Pray with everything in you. And believe. See your leg restored, as it was meant to be. Know that the God who brought you into this world can see you healed. Do you believe?"

He nodded at her, eyes wide and earnest.

Daria bowed her head. "Lord God, shield him from the pain," she began praying. "Tear apart what is not right within his body. Tear loose the tendons and ligaments that are not where they should be. Break apart the bone that covers a break that should have been set differently. Align his bones before us, Father. Heal him, Lord God on High."

Piero, Josephine, Gaspare, and Gianni all spoke, echoing some of her words, adding their own. Slowly, reverently, all in the hall went to their knees, all except the Court, who leaned forward from their chairs. As the last went to their knees, Daria felt the Spirit draw near, and with him came his angels. She looked to Tessa, whose face was alight in joy. Tears slipped from her eyes, wide and unblinking as if she didn't wish to miss a moment of this, making tracks down her cheeks that reflected in the torchlight.

One look at the Gifted about Roberto, at Roberto himself, and she knew that all sensed that something mighty was about to occur. Bishop du Puy, mouth agape, slipped into Latin, reverently repeating, *Dignus est agnus!* "Worthy is the Lamb!" as he stared down at them, then all around them. Could he see the angels too?

Gaspare raised his hands. "You are Lord of the heavens and the earth," he said softly. "You command the sun and the moon to move. We humbly ask you, Father, to move the moon from the sun's path, just as you move this child's leg back into the place you meant it to be."

Daria nodded, smiling. It was the perfect prayer, the method majestic, fitting of her Lord, in this moment. "Proclaim your power here, Savior," she said. "Rule over darkness. Bring us life and healing. Place your hands upon Roberto and heal him, Lord Jesus. Heal him. Heal him. Heal him."

She felt the heat first, a rise in temperature beneath her hands. It was warm at first, then moved to the heat of a fevered brow. When it reached a searing heat, as if she had just touched a stone by a fire, she opened her eyes. "Hold, my friends," she said to them all. Some had fallen back, alarmed by the heat. "Hold. Yes, Father," she said again in prayer. "We know you are at work. Come, Jesus. Come, Holy Spirit. Come, Father God. Heal this child, your child. We beg you, Lord. Heal him. Heal him. Heal him," she said in a hushed whisper.

Two beings of white walked through the kneeling men and women, heading directly in their direction.

"M'lady," Tessa said in an awed whisper.

"I see," Daria said, joy washing through her heart.

"As do I," said Piero.

"And I," said Gianni.

"And I," said Gaspare.

"And even I," said Josephine, white eyes staring as if she could truly see. "They are here."

"Do not fear," Daria said to Roberto.

But the boy looked up at the angels with such peace, there was nothing but joy in his eyes.

The angels knelt, one on either side of Roberto, and placed a hand on either shoulder blade. Their features were difficult to make out, so bright were their faces, but Daria could see their wings spread wide, as if encircling their group around Roberto. One nodded toward her. She could see that much.

"Father God in heaven. We are your servants. We love and adore you. We praise your name! Come and heal this child now. We beg you, Father, we beg you, make his leg straight! Allow him to walk as he was created to walk!"

The heat intensified, and Daria pulled her hands away in alarm. But it was the scent then that caught her attention, the pervading aroma of cloves and orange blossoms and something else . . .

Roberto groaned, and then cried out as his leg trembled in the air before them. They could hear popping, and the awful crunch of bone cracking. "Sustain him, Lord Jesus, shield him, Father," Daria whispered. She wanted to look to the child's face, but her eyes could not leave his leg, hovering as if lifted by the angels, who still stood at the other end of the boy, nowhere near ankles or feet. But their faces, their shining faces, seemed to stare upon it.

The pope gasped. The leg was straightening, before their very eyes.

Toes came into line with ankle. Ankle in line with calf. Calf and thigh into place. Slowly Roberto bent the leg, and the knee moved as it should, a perfect hinge, restored. He shouted.

"Glory, Lord," Daria whispered. "Glory, glory, glory, glory, glory!" She cried out, each word gaining in strength. "Glory is the Lord's, and none other. Glory is the Lord's! And none other!"

The angels rose, watching her, looking upon them all.

Others in the hall picked up her refrain.

"Glory is the Lord's! And none other!"

Roberto was the first to rise. He stood up tentatively, and then slowly leaned on his healed leg.

"Glory is the Lord's! And none other!"

It was then that Daria realized that the sun had returned, streaming once again through high, narrow windows. And at the same time, she realized the angels were no longer visible in the hall. But she could still feel them . . .

Daria met Hasani's eyes, and he nodded at the bishop, who was rising to his feet, mouth hanging open in wonder as he circled the child.

"Your Holiness. M'lord Bishop," she said to the pope and du Puy.

They tore their eyes from Roberto, reluctantly turning them upon Daria. They were filled with wonder, awe. Truth.

"Look to the drawing, m'lord," Daria said softly to du Puy. "Hasani gave you his vision, before this began, and it has been in your hands the entire time."

The bishop looked upon the scroll as if it were foreign to him. He slowly unrolled it, and his mouth dropped a bit wider. He turned to the pope, and then to the men he had chosen from the Court, those he trusted most. All their faces reflected shock, fear. Then he turned it outward, showing it to everyone nearby.

It depicted Roberto, flanked by two angels, the Gifted all about him.

And Roberto's perfectly straight leg.

Chapter Thirty-six

A knock sounded at the door. Abramo ignored it, sitting in the dark library of Cardinal Morano's palace. After a moment, it sounded again. Abramo remained where he was, in the large chair, chin in hand, eyes on the wall.

"Lord Amidei?" Vincenzo asked.

"I left instruction for no one to disturb me."

"Yes." He entered and closed the library door behind him. Vincenzo tossed a sealed letter to the table and sat down in another chair across from him, ignoring his request. "I imagine it is similar to the one I just received."

Abramo picked it up, broke the wax seal, and opened up the missive. "What is it?" he asked, even as he began scanning the text.

"A summons. We are to stand trial for the deaths of five innocents, the kidnapping of three more, and destruction of property. I, of course, am the primary party named, but you, m'lord, are an accessory."

"To murder."

"And theft. And kidnapping." Was he imagining it, or did Vincenzo have a note of pleasure in his voice? Or was it simply fear?

"Impossible." Abramo rose and went to the window in order to read it for himself. But Vincenzo was correct. "You should have killed every one of them."

"You told me to bring back several alive, to use against Daria."

Abramo shook his head, staring through gauzy curtains to the streets below, as if he could see her there. "She dares much, in this."

"They all do. It is the children, the old woman, Ambrogio, who witnessed the murders, the fire set. But it is Daria who will see them all through."

Abramo tossed the letter back to the table. "Send a letter to Marco Adimari. You saw to his placement as one of the Nine. Now he can return the favor by seeing these charges dismissed."

"I believe Daria has beaten us to that play. She must have reached out to Marco, told him everything, and appealed to him to assist. None of the others would have dared to move against us. But Marco . . . he has always been more moved by love and loyalty. And he has always loved Daria."

"So it will be eight versus one in deciding our fate."

"Mayhap. Daria is extremely persuasive. The city loves the Duchess. People will turn out of the woodwork to defend her, sing her praises, much as they did at the Court of Apostolic Causes. And Marco may well already be trying to persuade the other eight to see the truth before them."

Abramo turned away, back to the window, seething. It was impossible. *Impossible.* How had they escaped his net? His perfect noose, slowly drawing shut, cutting off their collective airway?

Another knock sounded at the door. The men exchanged a glance and Vincenzo went to open it.

Ciro entered, another three letters in hand. "For you, m'lord," gesturing toward Abramo.

Abramo strode across the room and took them from the hulking knight. He tore the seal from one, scanned it, and shook his head. He went to the next and then the next. He trembled with rage.

"Lord Amidei?" Vincenzo asked.

He laughed without humor. "They are on the attack. And they are in league with the doge and other nobles. These three letters," he said, raising them to shoulder height, "are notices of dissolution of my business agreements with merchants in Venezia and Provence, based on criminal charges brought against me in Siena. Something tells me that there shall be others."

He paced back and forth, hands on his hips, head down, thinking. "They intend to bring me down financially," he said. "To sever key relationships between here and Roma. They know that if they go after merchants of this caliber, then others shall follow suit." He stopped abruptly, staring at the ground. He looked up at Vincenzo and Ciro, shaking his head and cocking a brow in wonder. "It was an astute move. They have struck where I am vulnerable, and the effect shall be crippling."

Ciro and Vincenzo stared at him, waiting for him to continue. Never had they witnessed him at rest, stupefied. Even after Daria had taken his eye and escaped the isle in Venezia, Abramo had had an immediate plan, knew his counterattack. And yet Abramo could not move, paralyzed by sudden fear. The Gifted were formidable spiritual opponents. But never had he imagined they might take him on in this arena.

He sat down on the edge of a chair, thinking. How would his master advise him?

"The master shall not be pleased," Vincenzo said.

"You think I am not aware of that?" Abramo roared, rising. "You have spent much time in my company, Baron del Buco. You have gained financially based on my own gains, so if I lose, so shall you. Think. What would be a wise course of action when every day counts?"

"We must hold our ground here. Now. Then move out, regaining territory we may indeed lose. We could appeal to the cardinals for assistance—"

"Our favor is slipping with every hour that the Court deliberates on the fate of the Gifted. They seek a method to release them, which means they must find just cause to bless them. Nay, we are already suspect. To say anything shall lift the veil further."

"Mayhap we should go to the nobles, persuade them to continue to ask questions that shall chafe at the cardinals. If the Gifted are allowed to minister freely—"

"After witnessing the child's healing, not a one of them has the stomach to hand them over to the authorities, advising death. You'd think that God himself entered the Court of the Rota."

"It sounds as if he did."

Abramo frowned at Vincenzo. He knew he despised any favorable mention of the Gifted's God. Seeing his glower, Ciro took a step away from the baron.

"We have no time for such games. They have reached for our jugular. We must do the same." He circled Vincenzo, staring hard at him. "Write back to the Nine of Siena. Tell them none of the witnesses live and we shall not be brought to court for claims based on hearsay and rumor. We will arrive at our convenience, but we prepare our own claims against the Nine for inconveniencing us, costing us valuable business relationships, and shall seek remuneration."

Vincenzo frowned, confusion in his eyes.

"You hesitate, friend?" Abramo asked, pausing in front of him. He reached up to lay a hand on his shoulder. "I have asked what our master would advise, and it is this. We are to hunt down the Gifted upon their release. And kill every last one of them. The old woman, the artist, and the children first. Then the rest. They must see the extreme cost of their folly before they die."

Vincenzo swallowed. "They shall be under guard."

"Through Provence, yes," Abramo said, nodding, returning to the window. "It would be foolhardy to address them here. But where do you suppose they shall go when they are released? They have reached the end of the prophesied map, by coming here. They shall sense victory, progress, in facing the pope and his courts, and emerging alive, possibly even with the tacit agreement to allow them to continue ministering to the faithful."

He turned and walked back to them, smiling wryly now. The smile faded and an intense look again entered his eyes. "Add to that the fact that they are summoned, as are we, to appear before the Nine."

"They shall return to Siena," Vincenzo said in a whisper.

"Yes," Abramo said, nodding with a smile. "And we shall be waiting for them."

ல் ல் ல்

"Why do they tarry?" Daria asked, going again to the cell door and resting her forehead against the cool, rusty bars. "It has been five days since Roberto was healed!" As potential criminals now, they were no longer allowed the freedom and luxuries of the Court of Familiars. But the guards treated them as royalty, in awe of the stories they had heard and wary that they might turn their holy powers upon them. Small gifts from noble and commoner alike continued to arrive—icons of the saints, food, wine, and rare herbs.

"Be at peace," Josephine said. "They shall soon come to the end of their deliberations. I could not see their faces, but I could hear the decision in the bishop's voice. Surely you saw the same on the pope's face. They can do none else than release us, bless us."

They had gone through it thirty times before, but the waiting chafed at Daria. It wearied her, having to constantly comfort Tessa when she herself fretted, as well as encourage Agata, who found it exceedingly difficult to sleep upon the stone floor.

She closed her eyes. She, too, longed for a decent bed and her husband, with his arms around her. He must be like a caged lion, pacing in his agitation of being far from her.

"Lady de Capezzana?"

Her eyes flew open. So lost had she been in her thoughts, she had not heard the guard approach. The man lifted a letter up and slipped it between the bars. "For you," he said. His eyes covered her in awe. All the guards treated them all as miracle workers, bringing them extra blankets, extra bread, fresh water. She hoped they did the same for the men.

"Thank you," she returned. Tessa and Agata rose to their feet, curious at this. A letter delivered to her in the papal dungeon?

She turned it over to see the red seal. She smiled hopefully at the women. "It is from the Nine," she said, for Josephine's benefit. She shook her head. Her messenger had made miraculous time, as had this letter in return. On God's wings, surely. And aided by the doge's fastest vessels.

"Open it, m'lady!" Tessa said excitedly.

But she had already slipped her finger beneath the flap, noting the broken seal. "It is a personal letter from Marco." She felt sudden heat at her neckline.

"Read it aloud," Josephine said softly. She had sensed her sudden discomfort. "The best way out from under a secret's shadow is fact's light."

Daria cleared her throat and moved over to the high, small window in order to better see.

26 February 1340,
Siena

Lady de Capezzana,
As you can imagine, I was both gladdened and saddened to receive your missive from Provence. In the interest of time and with the goal of aiding you and yours, I return this letter via special messenger and pray it reaches you before you move onward. By his calculations, he shall reach you inside the span of a week, utilizing the fastest routes and with prayer that no storm delays his progress.

Great was my dismay in hearing how Baron del Buco has betrayed us both, and used me in making you vulnerable to Lord Amidei's evil intent. Never could I have imagined how far he could fall, nor was I fully aware of Lord Amidei's stranglehold upon our beloved city. It took much, but I believe I have others of the Nine convinced that we can do nothing else but pursue your claims, loose the chains about our necks, and see justice done as soon as possible. I beg you to forgive me for my shortsightedness. I was purchased for a time by your enemy, but shall never be again.

I cannot reiterate enough the need for you to take the utmost care. As you are reading this, so Lord Amidei and Baron del Buco shall be reading their own summons to appear before the Nine. They will immediately understand that you and yours are the key to seeing the charges through to sentencing, and therefore you are all in grave danger. Take care as you journey, Daria.

We eagerly await our child's arrival, due any day now. As much as I long for a male heir, you have shown me what a woman of learning and grace can accomplish, and I shall raise a girl child to emulate you. I imagine word of your own blessed pregnancy has brought you to your knees in awe at the power of the Almighty. I do not profess to understand why he did not bless us with a child during the time of our handfasting, but I praise him for blessing each of us now. I wish you continued good health and a safe delivery here in Siena, where our own fine midwives may see to our most celebrated healer. We shall observe justice done and your estate restored before your child is born.

I shall keep an eye to the western road for you, Daria. Hasten home.

Fondly,
Marco Adimari

She looked up at the women and girl, a bit dazed, unaware of what she had just said, only of Marco's voice ringing through her ears. *Purchased for a time . . . utmost care . . . raise her to emulate you . . . power of the Almighty . . . hasten home.* Slowly her eyes focused on the women, every face pointed toward her.

Agata rose and neared. She had one hand to her mouth, and the other reached for Daria's belly, resting it there. "My lady, is it possible?" she asked in awe.

Daria smiled. "Indeed, it is."

"How? When?"

Daria gave her a wry smile. "Agata, must I really tell you how this happens?"

The older woman blushed and stammered. "I mean . . . Marco . . . you were . . ."

"It is a miracle, isn't it?" Josephine asked, coming closer and reaching out for her hand. Daria took it. "Great was your love, m'lady?"

"Marco had my heart since childhood, the love of an innocent," she said. "But it is Gianni who has captured my heart as a woman grown. I am his now."

"As he is most assuredly your own," Josephine said. "Never have I known a man to be so in love with his wife."

"He has been that way since the day she first brought him home," Agata said proudly.

"God has blessed us in many ways. The road has been hard. Much has been sacrificed. But I count it all as gain."

Josephine smiled. "When a woman can say that from inside a prison cell, it bears witness to God himself. You are the image of our blessed Saint Paul."

"When?" Tessa asked, no longer able to keep her tongue. "When shall your babe be born?"

"In the autumn," Daria said, looking to the window, longing to see Bormeo flying high above them, herself free to stand and watch. "When the leaves are fully turned upon the oaks and maples that line the forests of Toscana, and the harvest is brought in, and the tinge of winter's frost is in the evening air. That is when the child shall come to greet us."

Her hand moved to cover her belly. Well she knew of the dangers ahead, the very real threat of bringing Abramo Amidei and Vincenzo del Buco to justice. But God had seen them through so much. She would not borrow tomorrow's trouble. She only wished to see this day through and be freed of the pope's prison cell. Tomorrow was in God's hands alone.

"Guard!" she called.

The man hurried toward her. "Yes, m'lady?"

"Please, I beg you. Can you get this letter to my husband? He must know of this at once."

"As you wish, m'lady," he said, setting off at once.

She watched him disappear down the long, dark corridor. The seal had been broken. Had the guard already read Marco's words? She doubted it. So few knew how to read, let alone the Toscana dialect. So who had it been?

ぺ ぺ ぺ

CARDINAL Morano arrived that night. The Gifted were to be released immediately.

"You have done all you could to preserve the sanctity of the Church and her court, m'lord Cardinal," Abramo said with a slight bow. "You are to be commended." He turned and reached for his cape, his gloves. His satchels were already by the door.

"You . . . you plan to depart? Now?"

Was that a note of relief in his voice? Abramo assumed that housing the men who had been tossed from the Court of Apostolic Causes must be providing some discomfort for the cardinal. Yes, it was best to leave, immediately. To preserve some semblance of relationship, so that he might pick it up again when he returned.

"Yes, m'lord Cardinal. Our time with you has been most edifying. I shall await you and my bride at my residence in Firenze, come summer. You shall conduct the ceremony yourself. It will be a grand affair. And greatly shall your church prosper."

"Where do you travel now?"

"Baron del Buco and I must see to other matters at hand." He smiled at the cardinal. Was he seeking information? Might the cardinal have been turned against them? Sent in to spy upon them? "We shall travel throughout the spring, beginning now with a journey to Paris. But I shall see you in Firenze." He reached out to tap the cardinal lightly on the chest. "Yes?"

The cardinal paused and licked his lips. "Yes. Of course. I shall set out for Madrid in a month's time and prepare your bride for your vows. We shall be there no later than summer's end."

"Summer's end," Abramo said, nodding his head as if the deal were completed, knowing that the cleric lied. He had been breached. He no longer belonged to Amidei—in fact, suspected him. Had they all fallen? Every cardinal? Had all his hard work here been in vain?

He turned to go and paused by the door, thinking of the cardinal in the caves, stalactites above them. The exquisite taste of carnal appetites, just beyond his reach. It made Abramo salivate at the mere memory. "M'lord Cardinal, we have shared much these past weeks."

He looked over his shoulder and waited for the man to slowly bring his dark eyes to meet his. Ah yes, fear. He remembered. Remembered his sin, his failures. How one might construe what had transpired as rationale for defrockment, as easily as rationale for praise. The cardinal had denied the women—in fact, denied every sweet, tantalizing offering the master had brought before him, tightening his belt, crying out with each one. But that he had been there at all tied him to Abramo forever.

"Do not fail me," Abramo said.

The cardinal stared at him, lips set in a grim line. He saw the lines of his cage well. And recognized no door.

Abramo reached for his bags and passed Ciro and Vincenzo in the hallway.

"We shall lay a trap for them in Provence?" Ciro asked, once they all were astride horses.

"Nay. They are being released as we speak. They will tarry, saying good-bye to all their dear, newfound friends. Whether they travel over-land to Marseilles or down the Rhône, Countess Anette shall see them well guarded. Once they reach the sea, the doge shall escort them. They are not fools. They shall suspect our intent to come between them and Siena. But once they reach Pisa and begin their trek toward home, they shall relax, believing the lies that I have planted. They shall send the doge's guard home to Venezia once they reach Pisa."

"Which lies?" Vincenzo asked, following him toward the docks of the Rhône.

"That we head to Paris," Abramo said. And for the first time in days, he smiled.

CHAPTER THIRTY-SEVEN

THEY were summoned to appear before the Court again at sundown, and they left their cells, hearts beating fast at the mere thought of what might transpire. What was their verdict? Excommunication? Or worse, would they be passed to city authorities to carry out a more despicable means of justice—something the Court wished, but had no stomach to see through themselves?

They climbed the long stairs and wound their way up into the massive courtyard, then into the long, hallowed chambers of the Court. Daria brought a hand to her mouth at the sight of Gianni and the other men, looking as weary as she herself felt. He broke from them and ran to her, ignoring the guards' shouts, and took her into his arms, kissing the crown of her head and cradling her close. "Daria, thank God you are well."

"Well enough, husband. I am relieved to be with you again."

A steward announced the entrance of the Court. As the cardinals and bishops filed inward, taking their seats along the curved dais, Daria noted Countess Anette and the other nobles filing in behind them. How had they known?

From the left, six cardinals and the pope and his stewards arrived, but her attention returned to Bishop du Puy and the Court of the Rota, those who held their immediate fate in their collective hands. The bishop rose. None of the awe that had graced his face five nights prior remained; instead he looked nonplussed, unable to do anything but what he was about to do. Daria's brow furrowed in fear.

The entire hall became as silent as a forest with a tiger about.

Tessa took her hand, leaning in.

"This Court finds you blessed and highly favored by the God we serve," said the bishop without preamble. "We find your method unorthodox but your intent holy. None can argue with the proof of the child before us," he said, waving toward Roberto, "of the miracle that transpired before our very eyes. Each of us has been profoundly influenced by the occurrences of five days past. That said"—he raised his chin—"we stand behind the defrockment of Piero, in that he has not done as the Church prescribes and confesses he shall do no other. We ask you not to baptize or commune outside the Church, for to continue to do so will be to risk excommunication. This court had decided to give you each time to consider our request. Shall you persist, we shall undoubtedly meet again. But until that time, you are free to go."

They stared in silence at him. Nico spoke first. "They're letting us go?"

"Yes, Nico," Piero said. He reached for the boy's hand and he took it. "They are releasing us."

"Where do we go now?" said the child as they all walked out, breathing more freely for the first time in weeks.

"Home," Gianni said, smiling toward Daria, pulling her close.

The nobles followed them out, and Countess Anette hugged each of them close. The doge shook hands with the men and nodded at the women, a grin across his face. He leaned close to Daria and Gianni. "It has begun. Lord Amidei received the first letters today, declaring their business arrangements null and void."

Gianni's smile faded. "What was his response?"

"Reportedly he and del Buco are en route to Paris."

"Paris?" Gianni asked, now frowning. He eyed Piero, who joined them. "I was certain they would come after us. Do they intend to ignore the summons from the Nine?"

"Apparently," the doge said, clapping him on the shoulder. "My informant has told me that they went to the docks, but they did not travel in the direction of Marseilles. Ease your guard, man. It appears your enemy has fled. The Nine shall catch up with them eventually. Venezia shall aid them. For now, enjoy the respite from your enemy. You have endured much."

Gianni and Piero shared a look. "I do not believe it," Gianni said.

"It is wise to be wary when one such as Amidei is involved," the doge said. "But the pope has granted you safe passage, and the countess shall see you safely through Provence. My own ships shall see you safely ashore in Pisa. You will reach Siena, and the Nine shall see to your welfare from there. Surely your city," he said to Daria, "is less embroiled in intrigue than Avignon."

"Surely," she returned with a smile.

Vito neared them, Bormeo on his gloved arm. "M'lady," he said with a flourish. "I once again return your bird to you." He cocked a brow at Gianni, who shook his head and smiled.

"Oh!" Daria cried. She kissed the knight on the cheek and took the glove from him. The bird fluttered to her arm. She leaned in, nosing his soft, downy feathers. And as she closed her eyes, all she could think of was the falcon soaring over the high, green hills outside of Siena, of rebuilding her country estate, a home with Gianni and their child, of laughter. Singing. Peace. Joy.

ᚖ ᚖ ᚖ

DARIA moved beside her husband at the rail of the ship, threading her hand through the crook of his elbow. He smiled down at her and pulled her a bit closer. She welcomed the warmth of his body beside hers. The winter sun was bright upon the sea, but little warmth accompanied it. Together, they gazed out to the coastline of Italia. In another day, they would reach Pisa.

"You think I am unaware that you keep watch behind us?" she asked softly, eyes still on the teal waves before them.

He was silent for a long moment.

"Could it not be that he fled to Paris to avoid the Nine?"

"It makes no sense, Daria. We threaten everything he has worked to attain in the last decade. Stopping us is the logical course of action."

"He has made illogical decisions before."

"Very few. Most every decision Abramo Amidei has made, in retrospect, has been the decision of a strategist."

Her eyes shifted left, to the curve of the horizon, no ship in sight. "If he follows, he is far behind."

"There is another possibility."

She turned and looked up into his kind, green eyes. He looked like he was reluctant to tell her, but must. "Go on."

"He could be ahead of us."

She frowned. "Why can you not let me rest in the idea that we are free of him, even for a little while? Do you have any comprehension what it has been like for me, these last two nights, to sleep beside you and not fear that Amidei might attack at any moment? It's enough to keep me at sea forever."

Gianni moved his hands to her shoulders. "We need to be prepared. The stakes are high, Daria. Amidei does not intend to kidnap us this time. He intends to kill us, remove the threat and opposition. We cannot afford to relinquish our guard."

Daria sighed and wrapped her fingers in his hand, turning again to the deck rail, with his arm around her. "Piero says this shall be much of our life, taking on the enemy. For he shall hunt us always, wanting us to abandon our mission."

She could feel Gianni nod his agreement. "The final three pages of our letter speak of little else." A steward had given them a copy of the last three pages of the letter—written by Paul? Apollos?—courtesy of the pope. "The dark hunts those of the light. The greater our following, the more we accomplish on behalf of our God, the more he shall wish to stop us. It is a battle. Always and forever."

"What of my dreams? I had hoped to rebuild outside Siena, raise our child in the quiet of the countryside. To rest for a time."

"I do not think that is an impossible dream, Daria." He waited for her to look his way. "Truly. God knows that we need time to recover, regain our strength. Mayhap our ministry is best suited to the countryside anyway, a bit away from the hovering eyes of the Church who shall feel compelled to try to control us. Our time in Provence made me think of such things as well. But Daria . . ."

She turned to him, hearing the note of urgency in his voice.

"Until we know that Amidei, and even Vincenzo and Ciro, are dead, we cannot relinquish our guard. Promise me you shall keep your eyes on the horizon with me. As much as I intend to keep you safe, I cannot be everywhere. Please." He took her hands in his own and pulled them to his chest. "I beg you."

Daria nodded. His words were sound, of course. But it was not just a sense of the unknown that drove him; there was something more. Was it the letter that had unnerved him? What did he know that he was not sharing? She was about to ask, when he wrapped his arms around her, pulling her close, ignoring the others aboard ship who could see their embrace.

And it felt so good to be held, to be warm, to be with him, Daria said nothing more at all.

᪥ ᪥ ᪥

VINCENZO followed Abramo and Ciro, falling behind a bit. He was tired, so tired, and the voyage to Pisa had been particularly rough, the captain encouraged to adopt full sail and the shortest course, regardless of the wave and wind, by Abramo's heavy coin purse. The result was that they had made spectacular time, but few aboard had seen rougher seas outside a storm.

So it was that he saw a nobleman and his men, high and behind them, before Abramo did. They were well past Pisa by then, halfway to Volterra, where they planned to spend the night. Even with four of Abramo's archers and six mercenaries, Amidei's troops numbered only thirteen. Lord Puccini came down the hillside with more than thirty.

Vincenzo watched as Abramo's archers each drew an arrow across their bows, intending to defend their master, but Abramo raised a hand to keep them from shooting. Vincenzo edged closer in order to hear what was about to transpire.

"Lord Amidei," said Lord Puccini, circling his prancing horse, "in accordance with the Nine of Siena, I have agreed to keep you from crossing my lands."

"Lord Puccini," Abramo replied evenly. "We are on a public road, nowhere near your lands."

"Excellent point," said the young man, eyeing one of the archers. "Then we have no issue." He grinned and reached out an arm to Amidei, who took it and grinned back.

"It is well to see you again, my young friend."

"And I, you, m'lord. I received your missive. We received it only a day ago. You must have made good time from Marseilles."

"The gods favored our passage," Abramo said. He looked beyond the young lord. "These are the mercenaries I asked for?"

"Thirty in number, just as you had asked," he said.

"With no ties to either Siena or other nobles, now forsworn as my enemies?"

"Nay. Most are from Sicily. They shall only understand your most basic of commands. But they are solid men, one and all."

Abramo eyed him with some disdain, then nudged his horse in the flanks and rode before the men, speaking easily in the dialect of the Sicilians, shouting promises, collecting the men as he so easily collected others everywhere he went. Vincenzo sat back, a bit in amazement. He had thought he had seen the beginning of decline in Lord Amidei. Watching him here, now, only proved that nothing would stop him, short of death. The master had chosen his apprentice well.

Abramo spoke of intrigue, damage done to his reputation and businesses by a group soon to travel this way, who called themselves the Gifted. His tone lowered. "They appear as a group you might see on the street, a lady, knights, older women and men, even children. But they are charlatans. Magicians. And worse, liars, who have placed me and mine in grave danger.

"Now, I am a lover of peace, but I shall defend what is mine. Every one of them must die. Not a one can escape. If you do not have the stomach for such a task, please depart now. Our goal is to cut off their entry to Siena, drive them into the countryside, and take them there. We shall wear hoods so none can identify us. No flags or colors shall be worn. And if we accomplish this task, once I feel the deadened pulse of every one in their party, we shall dispose of their bodies and disband. And at that moment," he said, reaching under his cape to his belt and holding up a heavy sack of gold florins, "each of you shall depart with a king's ransom. Pledge your service to me, follow my every instruction, and great shall be your reward."

ↀↀ ↀↀ ↀↀ

THE Gifted put into harbor that evening, edging through narrow passageways constantly dredged by the harbormaster. Once Pisa had boasted a navy that rivaled Venezia's. But a swiftly silting tide and a change in noble fortunes had forced a decline. Still, there were fifty boats and ships in transit as they traveled toward land, fishermen and merchants, in addition to three naval vessels that stood sentry at the mouth of the harbor, and more than a hundred at dock or anchored just off shore.

They moved off the doge's ship, glad to be free of the wind and the waves, and said their farewells to the mariners. Vito and Ugo ushered four horses off the deck, prancing in their agitation to be free to move about after the three-day journey. Gianni, armed with the Devenues' loaned coin, would purchase additional horses for the group in order to make the fastest time to Siena.

He looked up. Daylight was fading quickly. It was good that they traveled light, with naught but satchels to tie atop the rumps of the horses. He eyed each person in the group as they walked down the gangplank and onto the dock. Their eyes were wary and weary. Only the children bounded about, as restless as the horses after being confined aboard ship. Roberto jumped up on a crate, then climbed to the next, a bit unstable still on his new leg, but unstoppable. He thought again of Daria's words, her hunger to rest and recuperate and rebuild. *Please Lord,* he prayed silently. *Let us find a way to do all three before the year is out.* He ached for the same—and to give his people, this raggedy family of his, what they all needed.

He walked down the gangplank after Piero. "You left this land a priest in robes. You come back a man in shirt and jerkin. How do you fare?"

Piero turned and smiled. "You can take the priest out of the robe, but you cannot take the priest out of the man."

Gianni returned his smile and then moved on to his wife. She had planned to get the Gifted to an old family friend's estate, in a small village to the east of Pisa. But they would not make it by nightfall, not with having to purchase supplies and horseflesh. And Gianni refused to travel in anything but full daylight.

She saw it in his eyes before he said anything. "Think we can obtain beds for the night in an inn?"

Gianni nodded. "If we do, and leave at daybreak and push hard, we might make it to Volterra on the morrow, and Siena the following day."

"All right," she said. "I'll take the women and children and find us lodging. You men can go and find supplies and horses."

"I'll send Hasani, Vito, and Ugo with you," he said. She was not going anywhere without guard.

"Gianni—"

"Daria."

She sighed. "Very well. I shall send one of the boys to await you here and tell you where we are."

"Thank you," he said. He leaned forward and kissed her brow. After so long on her own, and as a woman who commanded others, it still took a lot for her to trust his decisions, to know that he only had her best interests at heart. And when it came to safety with a dragon lurking, Gianni would brook no argument.

☜ ☜ ☜

THEY spent a restless night at a harbor inn, on dirty mattresses and disturbed by the raucous crowd in the tavern below, so that all were up and ready to go as the morning sun crested the hills to the east. As they had hoped, they made good time and rode hard and encountered no opposition, climbing the high plateau on which Volterra sat and entering her gates just as they prepared to close them for the night.

Volterra was a strong and ancient city, but was a minor force as compared to Siena and Firenze. Still, her walls were sturdy, and high towers guarded her perimeter. Even though they were but a few of thousands spending the night inside her walls, Daria felt safe and satisfied as they gained lodging at another inn, this one a quiet, more stately abode just off the Piazza San Giovanni. *One step closer to home*, she thought, trying to decide between her favorite inns within Siena the next night, or seeking lodging with friends still loyal to her memory. The sights and smells of Volterra made her want to climb back atop her horse—as saddle-sore as she was—and race through the night for home. Merchants with carts full of familiar vegetables, meats, and cheeses rolled by. Daria stopped a few and purchased foodstuffs for the night and morn. There was no telling if this innkeeper cared to feed her guests, and after their long ride, none felt like emerging until morning.

The next day saw them refreshed and their spirits buoyed, with only a day between them and safety, revenge for their slain loved ones, possible remuneration for lost property. In Siena, much might be made right again. At least Daria hoped it was so.

She made her way to the stables, several blocks from the inn, and watched Gianni saddle her horse, reaching under the mare's belly and pulling a strap tight with quick, practiced moves. The grim set of his mouth told her he was still on guard. He caught her eye and tried to smile.

Daria cocked her head and looked up to him. "You are still worried that Abramo and Vincenzo might try to intercept us?"

"The only thing worse than having them about is not having them about," he said, reaching to caress her cheek. "I do not like it that we have lost track of them."

"Again, might they not be in Paris as we speak?"

"They might. But I think there is a greater chance that they are nearby. They could have traveled up the Rhône to fool us and hopped the first ship back to Marseilles."

"Then shall we not purchase the services of several mercenaries to help aid our progress?"

Gianni smiled and turned aside, so she could see beyond him. Twelve knights, bearing the Adimari coat of arms, were mounting behind him. "Courtesy of the Nine," Gianni said, studying her face.

Marco. Marco had sent them aid.

"Shall I send them away out of jealousy?" he asked.

Daria caught his teasing eye. The captain in him would never allow him to send away men-at-arms when he was so ill at ease. But he asked as her husband. She laid a hand on his chest and looked into his eyes. "Husband, Marco was dear to me, for many years, and we must forge the ways of friendship now. But you are my one true love, the man I shall grow old beside, the man with whom I shall raise our child."

"Children," he said, with a sparkle in his eye.

She shot a grin up to him, but his smile was fading. Daria turned to follow his gaze and saw Tessa, moving toward them as if in a daze. "Tess . . ."

The girl looked up at her and shook her head, clearly troubled. "My lady, I loathe to be the bearer of bad news, but I believe Lord Amidei is about."

Daria turned toward her and took her hands. Surely not. Not when they were so close to home. "Tess, could it be something else?"

Tessa searched the ground before her, eyes going back and forth as if looking for a lost key. She swallowed hard and shook her head, drawing her eyes reluctantly upward to look Daria in the eye. Gianni edged closer, holding his breath. "Nay, it must be. Or one as evil as he. He is not here now, but he has been here recently."

"You are certain he is not here now," Gianni confirmed, waving the Gifted nearer. Vito and Ugo came at a trot, Gaspare led Josephine forward, and the rest followed.

Tessa was thinking, feeling, searching. "Nay. He is not here now," she repeated, "or anywhere close anyway. But he was here."

"Why did you not sense him last night?" Gianni asked softly.

"I wasn't here, in the stables. I felt the barest whisper of him, but told myself it was a dream, a concern, a memory, not truth."

Gianni stared at her for a long moment, then eyed the rest of them. "We have no choice but to treat this as God's own warning for us. If Amidei was here, then he is likely ahead of us. His intent shall be to cut us off from Siena, to keep us from reaching the Nine, from testifying against him." With a cut of his chin, he sent Vito to go and bring the other knights to join them.

In a short time, all were gathered with them. Daria felt as if she were moving through fog, trying to comprehend that there might be yet another encounter with Abramo Amidei ahead of them. *Surely not, Lord,* she cried. *Surely not! Save us, Father! Keep your enemy from our path and preserve us!*

Piero moved forward and turned in a slow circle to look each of them in the eye. He understood the collective panic of the women, the concern of the men. "The Lord has seen this day. He has *seen* it. He knows what is to come, and none of it is a surprise to him. Should he allow it, we shall trust it, always praising his name. We do the greatest damage to our enemy by keeping to this path, always praising our God, no matter what we face—trial, trauma, or even death. *Dulcius post tribulationes.*"

" 'Sweeter after difficulty,' " Daria translated.

"Sweeter after difficulty," Piero returned. "The greater the trial, the more our Lord can triumph. No matter what is ahead of us, we shall not abandon our faith."

Daria looked to her priest. "If we do not reach Siena, justice shall not be served. We must reach Siena."

He eyed her calmly. "If we do not reach Siena, God shall have other things for us to accomplish. We must leave justice to the Lord, trusting that when and if it is wise, he shall allow us to take part in his plan. Ultimately, our enemy's fate is in his hands, yes?"

Daria stubbornly said nothing. His words were truth, but she did not have to agree to them. Aloud, anyway.

Piero turned away from Daria and looked to the knights of the Nine. "Well are we thankful for your arrival, good knights. Please know that if our enemy obstructs our passage, if he engages us, his intent shall be to kill every one of us."

The captain of the twelve, Ruggero, took a step closer and eyed Tessa, the boys, Agata, blind Josephine. "Surely you overstate your case."

Piero raised his eyebrows and sighed heavily. "I assure you that is incorrect. If we are attacked, you must defend us as if we are all people about to die. There is good cause for the Nine to send twelve of you to watch over us. Our enemy is very real and his intent, deadly. Do you believe this?"

The captain stared at Piero, sizing him up. He undoubtedly saw what

Daria did—a small man, with the shaved head of a priest, no chin, small shoulders—but a wisdom behind his eyes that could not be denied. "You have my word that we shall defend you unto death," he said solemnly.

"I shall have your prayers," Piero returned, smiling at the captain. "Come, brothers and sisters. Let us huddle here together and ask for God to set his angels before, behind, and beside us, and to get us yet to safety."

They prayed together, no doubt drawing curious stares from passersby, but ignored them, aware of only their God, his cause, and his intent for their lives.

Afterward, Captain Ruggero drew a hasty map in the hardened mud of the street. "If Amidei is ahead of us, he shall hope to draw us into this valley here," he said, tapping a segment with his stick.

"Before we cross the pass," Daria said.

The knight looked up to her. "Indeed."

It was the main passageway, south of San Gimignano, and the fastest route to Siena. But it was true. From the hills that pervaded the region, it would be easy to lie in wait for them and ambush them. There were frequent patrols that made their way across the road, intent on ridding the area of robbers, but it was notoriously difficult, because of the terrain.

"We could follow the Cecine," Vito said. "My brother and I know those valleys well. We grew up hunting there."

Ugo nodded. "We might make Massa Maritima before nightfall."

"Then approach Siena from the southern route," said Gianni.

"It is a good plan," the captain said, cocking his head to one side. "Unless your enemy is aware that you have passed by and gives chase. A group with women and children will quickly be overtaken by men in that rough country."

Daria waited for Gaspare to notice her stare, the question in her eyes. He nodded.

"We shall pray that our enemy doesn't recognize people of the light, moving in shadow among the mountains. Or at least until we are well past them," she said with a grin. "And we shall pray that our steeds are fleet of foot, making up any difference in man versus woman or child. You, Ruggero, and your men, are in the company of the Gifted. That means that our God shall go before us, beside us, behind us, and never abandon us, no matter what enemy we face. Now let us be on our way. The sun gains on the horizon."

Chapter Thirty-eight

"It is not possible that they were more than three days behind us," Abramo said, standing beside Ciro and Vincenzo, looking out to a setting sun.

"Mayhap they tarried, celebrating with Les Baux before resuming their journey here."

"That would put them overland to Marseilles, adding another two days," Ciro said.

Abramo paced back and forth, hands behind his back, eyeing the horizon again and again. "Send two scouts. One back to Volterra, to Pisa, if necessary, to find out if they have been seen. The other to San Camano."

Vincenzo stared at him. "You do not believe they would go the southern route. That would add two days!"

Abramo cocked a brow. "If they knew we laid in wait for them, yes. I believe they would."

Vincenzo shook his head. "That is a treacherous road. Difficult for men, let alone women and children."

"Again, if it circumvented battle with said women and children, would you not take it yourself?" He paced back and forth, his frustration lessening as a plan formed in his mind. "It is what they have done. I am certain of it. If they passed us, they might have done so within hours. Vincenzo, take eight men and two of my archers and head out. If you find them, send back a rider to tell us, and find the means to get ahead of them, trap them, until we can join you. If they are still a day away, I shall send word to you when and if we encounter them here."

"But m'lord, darkness is soon upon us."

"Yes," Abramo grinned. "Which means they shall soon set up camp and light a fire, making them all the more simple to find." He stared hard at Vincenzo, daring him to question him further.

"As you wish, m'lord," Vincenzo said with a tip of his head. He immediately moved toward his horse, calling to eight of the men, two of the archers to make ready. He tied his satchel and bedroll to the saddle, then swung upward, feeling the pain in his hips, and slid his sword into the saddle sheath. He stared at it. So the moment was at hand. Abramo, and the master, had made it clear that Daria and everyone dear to her was to die. He had killed her loved ones before. But could he truly kill her?

"Baron?" Abramo asked, suddenly beside his horse, looking up at him as if he could hear his thoughts as dialogue in a play.

Vincenzo started and sat straight up in his saddle. "Yes, m'lord?"

"This will soon be at an end. I understand it is taxing. See it through, and we shall avoid the trauma of a trial and regain what we are already losing. With the Gifted out of the way, we will experience new heights. There shall be nothing to stand in our way. All, *all*, Vincenzo, shall be ours. The master wishes it."

"And we shall not disappoint him," Vincenzo said, trying to give him a smile. But his heart was not in it, nor was his mind. He looked to the west, to the setting sun, and tried to think about the task at hand, his mission.

But all he could think of was his younger days with Ermanno Adimari and Giulio d'Angelo, when all three men had new marriages, none of them older than twenty-two. That year Daria and Marco had been born, and the fields produced an unseen bounty and business moved at a frenetic pace, coming nearly faster than any of them could manage. Food had tasted well in those days, and wine flowed. There had been feasts and celebrations. He had known clerics and nobles as friends. He hadn't been wealthy. But life had been rich.

Vincenzo sighed and turned down the road that would lead them along the Cecina River and the numerous mountain villages. It was so long ago. All so very long ago.

⚹ ⚹ ⚹

GIANNI glanced back at Daria, seeing what she had seen. The children were hunched over, falling asleep in their saddles, nearly falling from their horses.

Dusk, so short this time of year, was soon gone, and they were miles yet from Massa Maritima. A recent flood had taken a high, narrow bridge, sending them on a circuitous route about a valley, costing them precious hours.

Her husband sighed and whistled using two fingers, bringing back the knights who were half a mile ahead of them, and bringing forward those who guarded their rear flank. When all had gathered, he said, "We shall make camp here."

He turned to eight of the Sienese knights. "Go in groups of four, and make camp on either ridge, to our west and to our east. If you see anything"—he paused to look intently at each of them—"anything at all, even if it's a horse without a rider, I want one of you to come and tell me. Take turns at rest, never allowing yourselves to sleep when it is you who must guard our flank through the watches of the night. It is imperative you not fail us. Understood?"

They agreed and set off, bushwhacking their way up the hillsides, with the agreement to return at sunup. "Captain Ruggero, I respectfully ask that you and the remaining three set up camp a quarter mile behind us. It is up that valley that I most fear we shall be pursued. I'll send Vito and Ugo ahead, to guard our southern flank."

"It shall be done."

Gianni reached out and clasped the captain, arm to arm, then with Vito and Ugo. Suddenly the Gifted were alone.

Daria got down off the horse, her thighs aching with the effort. Was it bad for the babe within her to be riding so much? Were her mother alive and with her, she knew any horseback riding would be banned. But as Piero had said, God had seen this day before them, and knew of her pregnancy as well. She would have to trust the child's life in the hands of her God, just as she did her own.

♔ ♔ ♔

THE guards to the east were strong and vigilant. Two nearly escaped them, undoubtedly intent on warning the others. Had it not been for a waxing moon and Abramo's deadly archers, they would have slipped into the dark forest and sounded the alarm, and the Gifted, slumbering below, might have been alerted. One had been crawling forward toward the edge of the cliff, as if he intended to hurl himself over the edge as a last, dire warning, when Vincenzo reached him and slit his throat.

Vincenzo edged forward on the cliff overlook to gaze down upon their quarry. A small fire sent smoke upward. Neither this group of guards, nor the one barely visible in the moonlight on the western ridge, had a fire, intending to blend into the landscape as all good scouts and guards should. But he had known they were there. Abramo had trained him how to smell them on the wind, close his eyes and sense the master's leading. The Gifted had been easy to find, their scent of oranges and cloves discernible. He had assumed they would have set up guards. He chastised himself for not expecting trained warriors.

On the far side, he thought he saw a knight pause and look their way.

"Walk back and forth, as if on guard," he hissed to one of the men behind him.

Immediately the man did as he bid, and from the far side of the valley, mayhap an eighth of a mile, he thought the other knight resumed his own pacing watch.

Vincenzo eased back from the cliff overlook, confident now that their presence had not been detected, and moved among the dead knights. Sienese. Marco Adimari's men. Sent to guard Daria de Capezzana and the others, all in an effort to bring him down. Take away all he had worked so hard to attain.

Try as he might to use this to muster his courage, his desire to kill every last one of them, all Vincenzo felt stirring was a deep and profound sense of weariness. It was as if his heart had ceased beating within his chest, and yet he still moved. He could feel nothing . . . not rage, not joy, not greed, not peace. No hope. No love. Nothing. Hollow. The abyss.

A shiver ran through him, shaking him out of his dark reverie, just as one of the archers moved toward him. "Shall we take them now? We can reach them and escape back up here before any of their guards can reach us."

Vincenzo turned away, as if to look downward again, but they were away from the edge, out of view.

"Baron? The master would be so pleased to arrive and find his task complete."

Why not? he asked himself. He cared not whether he lived or died now. Why not carry through this task and hold on to honor, if nothing else?

"Yes," he said. "We shall move in a few hours, when sleep calls most to them. But you leave the Duchess to me. I saw her the day she was born. I shall usher her into death myself."

ಈ ಈ ಈ

TESSA, who could only fall asleep directly beside Daria this night, stirred again and again, as if fighting someone in her dreams. As weary as Daria was, Tessa's constant movement finally awakened her, and she opened her eyes to study the girl, visible in the soft glow of the fire's embers. The child's eyebrows lifted high, as if she were staring at someone, then curved into a frown of terror. Tessa pushed back on the bedroll behind her head, as if she could sink into it, escape.

Daria knew that expression. Her heartbeat raced, and a wave of fear washed through her body, sending her upright.

She looked about madly.

Gianni glanced at her, sitting on a rock in the shadows, sword across his knees, and then nodded up the path.

Daria looked that way in confusion. That was where four guards lay in wait. All she could see was an inky nothingness, with the firelight behind them and the moon now gone. They were still an hour away from dawn.

Gianni motioned her away from the fire. Daria looked about. They had lain with their heads toward the fire, alternating men with women and children. But their warriors, other than Hasani and Gianni, were at their flanks. If a flank had been breached . . . how long would it take for aid to come? Hasani stood in the shadows at the far side of the fire, curved sword in hand. He returned her look. It would be a long hour before daybreak came.

Tessa groaned and then sat up screaming, eyes wide. Two arrows came through the forest, but Gianni had already rolled to his left and Hasani dodged right, barely avoiding its deadly track. Gianni whistled, high and shrill, calling in the knights at their flanks, hopefully in time. The sound blessedly echoed through the canyon walls, cresting even the river's rush.

Daria looked around madly for cover. She had seen, too often, how good these archers were. Surely they would not miss twice. She grabbed Tessa and pushed her to the ground, huddling over her as another arrow, intended for the girl, came whizzing over her shoulder blades. Piero's words of warning sang in her ears. These were not robbers or kidnappers. They were assassins.

She rolled over to Bormeo, freeing him from his leather hood and tie to the ground with a quick tug, urging him to take flight. She rose and pulled Tessa to a hunched-over standing position, hissing, "Follow me." Gianni and Hasani came together to face their attackers, now crashing through the brush above them. They raised their shields, cutting off four more arrows that came in quick succession.

"Go with them!" Gianni shouted to Gaspare. The fisherman had little fighting experience, but he had a shield, a sword, and, Daria hoped, an urge from God to protect them using his gift.

Daria grabbed Josephine's hand and pulled, making their way forward off the path and down over the bulky river rock in an agonizingly slow manner, hearing every sound of battle above and behind them as if they were inches away. But she could see nothing! Nothing! Only the sound of the river kept her moving in the right direction. If she knew they all could swim, she would drag them into the river's current to escape the archers. But she knew she might well be the only one.

"Here, m'lady, allow me," Josephine said, pulling her back. She put Tessa's hand in hers, and Daria felt back to find the boys and Agata, a donkey train of blind refugees. And then Josephine took her free hand again and led the way. Of course, Daria thought, feeling the first semblance of hope. The best way out was to allow the woman accustomed to darkness to lead the way.

Behind them, over the din of sword-to-sword battle, above his breathing coming in short, labored breaths, Daria could hear Gaspare whispering a prayer of covering, protection, escape.

They continued to move over the rocks, and again found the trail, moving faster now that the road was more smooth. Daria looked up, hearing someone coming their way, her heart in her throat, but it was Vito and Ugo. Relief washed through her as she saw the dim outline of their forms and knew the sun was coming. Ugo ran past them, never pausing, intent on aiding Hasani and Gianni.

Vito paused. "Keep moving," he whispered between pants, "up around the bend, move up into the trees. They will think you have continued on. But you cannot outrun them. You must hide and allow the trees to give you some cover. We shall come to your aid as soon as possible." Then he was off, not waiting for their response.

She could hear men making their way down the path across the river, having heard Tessa's scream and Gianni's whistle. Hopefully the other Sienese knights behind them were closing in as well.

A crack of a branch in the forest just above and behind them brought them all up short, deadly still. "Down. Flat on your bellies," Gaspare whispered. "Cover yourselves with your capes."

They all did as they were told. Gaspare prayed then, asking for the cover of night's remaining darkness to now cloud their enemies' eyes, to blind them to their presence, to save them. Piero looked at Daria and she thought she could detect a bit of a grin. *"Post tenebras, tenebras,"* he quipped.

After darkness, darkness. She smiled, trying not to wonder what it would feel like to have an arrow pierce her back or throat. She prayed for faith, to believe the impossible—that God would once again shield them from their enemy, so close, so very close! Light footfalls in the gravel were perilously near, running toward them.

She held her breath.

Then past them! They were running past them, as if their bodies were naught but river boulders, pushed from the trail's path. When they turned the corner and they could no longer hear them, only the battle ensuing behind them, now with more swords than ever, Gaspare rose and whispered, "Move! Move now!"

They ran forward, hunched over, still holding one another's hands to stay together, and as Vito had instructed, when they were past the bend, moved up into the trees. "Hide yourselves!" Gaspare whispered, his face turned toward the path ahead, as if he expected the archers to see their folly and turn back any moment. Light was coming now, fast.

"Here, under here," she said to Josephine. "Lie down upon your belly and move to your left. It is a large rock with a good overhang. If you can squeeze through, you will be fully hidden."

The woman moved quickly, as if she were half her age. There were other boulders about, and Daria urged the children to find good hiding places, fully out of sight. Gaspare and Agata moved around a thick stand of trees and over a small hill. Daria's heart pounded at the sudden stillness. She was alone.

But not quite. Above her, at the mouth of the rift of this valley, a figure appeared, cape waving as he stopped to look downward.

Vincenzo del Buco. The baron. Her enemy.

But the first word that came to her mind, her heart, was one: *Uncle.*

Two knights ran up behind Vincenzo, but he dispatched them, sending them on to find the others. He moved down the small valley, sword in hand, directly toward her. With what intent? To kill her?

She glanced left and right, but there was no escape. Either direction might betray the children, or Gaspare and Agata. She would not lead the dragon's minion to the peacock's beloved. She would not. If it was to end here, now, so be it. But her eyes dragged upward to meet Vincenzo with dread. Was it truly ending here?

Daria drew her dagger as Vincenzo jumped down the last five feet between them, his cape billowing about him.

"Come now, Daria, put that down. You never could best me sword to sword. You shall not best me with a dagger."

He moved to her level, beside her. Bormeo screeched high overhead, and he glanced upward. "Remember when I gave you that falcon?"

Daria shifted, frowning. "When I was sixteen. Back when you were human."

Vincenzo lifted his chin. "Human." He raised a brow. "Mortal. Nothing but man."

"A man with a hope and a future. A man with love in his heart."

"Before I knew that all was vain hope and deep disappointment ahead of me."

She stared at him. He was still tall, but she had become accustomed to the brute power of her husband, his broad shoulders, his square jaw. Vincenzo was elegant, but gray had overtaken his dark, thick hair. He was very thin, reminding her of the elderly who refused to eat because food no longer had taste. Again, sorrow cascaded through her, echoing through her ribs like a small bird caught in a cage, knocking up against one side and then the other.

Daria gasped, a sob forming around the lump in her throat. "Do you remember, Vincenzo? Do you remember? Family? Love? What . . ." She paused to swallow hard. "What we meant to each other?"

He looked to the ground and then slowly met her gaze, his face still deep in morning's shadow.

"Great has been my suffering on your account," she said softly. She lifted a hand as if to reach to him, and then covered her belly. "Vincenzo, I carry Gianni's child. A child, after all this time, all this waiting. A child."

He moved back, his eyes going back and forth as if to detect a lie in her. "It is true, then?"

"It is true."

His brows, riddled with gray, furrowed and then sank. "It is most unfortunate how your God moves. I had the task of killing one. Now I must kill two."

He raised his sword and Daria moved a step away. She shook her head. "You do not wish to kill me, Vincenzo. Somewhere, deep within you, God is calling you back to him. Grave have been your sins. Loathsome. You have already murdered innocents, taken part in Abramo's foul ceremonies. Undoubtedly you have done other unspeakable acts. But Vincenzo," she said, reaching up again, "you can return to God. He sees you here. Now. And he can do what I cannot."

"And what is that?"

She held his solemn gaze. "Love you. It is where the divine separates from humanity. I look upon you and can see only loss. God looks upon you and can see only gain. Return to him, Vincenzo. Return to him and be saved."

He scoffed at her suggestion, but did not move. "Dear Daria. Always trying to save me, heal me." He looked up, into the trees—as if searching for Bormeo? He sighed heavily and lowered his sword a bit.

"Baron del Buco!" a woman cried upward.

Daria backed up a step as Vincenzo whirled and faced those down below, on the road. One archer was on one knee, arrow drawn backward. The other was on her feet, her own arrow drawn. "Kill her," said the one on her feet. "Or we shall."

Vincenzo took a step toward them, arms raised. Daria realized he was edging between the archers and her. But he could not cover her fully. "I shall do so, but in my timing. Be away from here. Go back to the fray in the camp and make short work of the knights who continue to plague Lord Amidei."

But the women did not move. "Turn and kill her now. We shall not wait more than another few breaths."

Vincenzo turned and raised his sword as if he were about to strike, and Daria raised her arms as if to fend off the blow. But then she could see that his face held no malice, only emptiness, grief.

"I am ready to greet my God," Daria said, slowly dropping her arms, seeing her last opportunity, a door opening within him. "Are you?"

"*Baron!*"

But still he paused, arms trembling now with an ache to release the swing of the heavy sword. His eyes searched hers.

Oh, Daria breathed, understanding his sorrow, the slow pivot within him, almost as if she could see him physically turning from his dark road . . .

The arrow came through him with such force that it almost pierced her as well, when he waved forward from the impact. The sword came down at his side, not slicing into her, but clanking to the rocks and moss and dirt beside them. Another arrow pierced him, this time high and to the right on his chest.

Still, he kept his feet, staring at her. "Live. Prosper, Daria. I have fallen far, but . . ." He tried to reach for her face, as if to caress her cheek, when a third arrow pierced his belly.

Daria cried out, falling to her knees as he went to his, holding him upright as a shield, knowing he was the only thing between the archers and her, weeping at the cowardice, the injustice of it. Her uncle. Once her warden. The shield her father had left behind for her, shielding her again, in the end.

An arrow sang over his shoulder as she stared into his eyes, weeping. The archers were making their way up the hill. She and Vincenzo would die here, in this valley so close to home. "Look to Jesus," she whispered through her tears, ignoring the sound of the archers perilously gaining ground behind him, coming fast. "Look to Jesus," she said again. "He shall save you when I could not."

Vincenzo gasped and then fell in a dead slump toward her, covering her, trapping her.

She fell backward and wept as the sharp points of the bloody arrows that had pierced her friend's body now sought to pierce her own. She cried for Vincenzo, for all he had lost in life, for all he had cost her, for all he had given her, looking up through the trees to Bormeo, sailing in a high circle above them, his wings catching the golden gloss of daybreak, wondering who would care for him when she was dead.

More arrows flew through the trees. A woman cried out, and dimly Daria wondered if Agata or Josephine had been discovered, praying they would not feel pain as they died. With each breath she expected an archer to arrive, to draw back an arrow upon her bow and pierce her heart. It would be over, over soon. *Oh, Gianni. Forgive me. Forgive me for dying. Father God, protect the others. Protect . . .*

But it was Gianni, Gianni's face then, blocking her view of Bormeo, pulling Vincenzo's body from her, then pulling her up and into his arms. "Daria," he whispered. "Are you injured? Are you all right?"

"I . . . I am . . ." she began, searching her body from head to toe as he was, taking mental inventory, certain she had suffered a grave wound.

But it was only her grief.

She pushed her way out of his arms and turned to Vincenzo. She moved to go to him, but Gianni held her back.

"He is dead, Daria," he said, no victory in his voice. "Killed by his own before we could kill them."

He wrapped his arms across her chest as she shook with sobs, staring down into her uncle's face. He nestled his face in the crook of her neck and shoulder. "I am sorry," he whispered.

ᑯ ᑯ ᑯ

"WE have to move, Daria," he said, after allowing her to weep for a few minutes. "Either Vincenzo's absence or a scout's return will undoubtedly tell Amidei we are here. We must move as if they are directly behind us."

Piero arrived and reluctantly prayed over Vincenzo's body, reaching out to lay a reassuring hand upon Daria's shoulder, then easing it under her armpit to assist her to her feet and away.

She followed him down the hill, where the rest had gathered. "How many did we lose?" she asked dully, her mind clearly on Vincenzo's body, abandoned behind them. What sort of funeral would he have had, had he never walked Amidei's dark path? Daria would have celebrated his life, honored his memory, as he had once done for Tatiana. Gianni supposed that was when his feet had begun to turn in Amidei's direction. The enemy, using grief for his own gain, he thought. Death was his weapon of choice.

"Six, plus two injured," he said. Leaving them only four more of the Sienese knights. Ruggero, the captain, had been taken down by the archers as he and his knights entered the sword fight.

Daria's eyes scanned the group for Vito and Ugo and Hasani, breathing a sigh of relief when she spotted them.

"Did any of Vincenzo's knights get away?"

"Not that we saw," he said. He helped her mount up and followed her gaze up the narrow valley.

"Will we do nothing about the bodies?"

"Other than Vincenzo, the others are back at the campsite. We shall retrieve them and give them proper burial, once we reach Siena. For now, we need to make for Siena." He left the rest unspoken. Because if they did not reach Siena, someone else might have to see to their own bodies as well.

Gianni mounted up, feeling echoes of another death scene, many months ago now, when his knights de Vaticana had been cut down in the forest outside Roma. The Sorcerer. He shook his head, fighting back the bile in his throat at the thought of him. *How long, Lord? How long until we are free of him? How long until he knows your victory in death, and his own eternal condemnation?*

He gave the order to move out, and the group of knights, men, women, and children did so, with Gianni and Hasani in the lead, and Vito and Ugo bringing up the rear. All scanned the ridges above them, watching for any sign of Amidei's presence.

Chapter Thirty-nine

"Lord Amidei," said the knight.

He rose from inspecting the dead Sienese knights bearing the crest of Marco Adimari, wondering how many more rode at the Gifted's side, and stared as the men dragged Vincenzo's body forward. Seeing their lord's expression, they laid Vincenzo gently to the ground, on his side. Four more brought the women, the two archers, laying them down on either side of his dead comrade.

"We found them in the next valley, downriver."

Abramo walked over to Vincenzo's lifeless body and studied his face a moment, wondering what his last thoughts had been. Had he given up all the ground Abramo had helped him win? Gone running, cowering, to the Gifted's God? His eyes went to the arrows.

It was as he had suspected, feared. His archers had been forced to kill him in an effort to get to the Gifted. It had to have been Daria he had protected. Only his familial love for the woman could have turned him at this late hour.

Abramo sighed and let Vincenzo's face roll into the dust. The master would be most displeased. Vincenzo's sacrifice had obviously greatly aided the Gifted. Not one of them, not even an old woman or child, were among the dead. And he had lost two archers and eight men. Nine, counting Vincenzo.

He eyed the remaining troops. Ciro clomped to a stop beside him, awaiting orders. "Take eight men. Make your way over this steep ridge, to Montalcinello and then southeast. It will be too difficult for the women and children. We shall close in behind them, but you must cut them off on the other side of San Galgano." He rose and looked into the knight's eyes. "Ciro, be certain that the Gifted do not ride through Siena's gates."

"They shall not get through, m'lord," said the man, ever eager. Abramo could read the greed within him, the desire to step into Vincenzo's position, a position he had always considered rightfully his own. That was fine. *Let him earn it. Show me at last that he is worthy.*

Although Vincenzo's failure stung, there were others ahead, others who would fully embrace the master's teaching and never look back. They were whom he sought. And if he was to be victorious, he could not pause over temporary losses. His master would not.

ॐ ॐ ॐ

By late afternoon, they were nearly out of the Cecina Valley and discussed making their way over a lesser pass, in order to cut some hours from their journey. It was after their noon meal, nothing more than bread and a bit of cheese, that the scout came galloping up behind them. "Lord Amidei and his men are coming hard, not far behind me."

Gianni ran to grab the reins of several horses and tossed Tessa and Nico atop theirs; Roberto was already astride his own. "Follow Vito!" Gianni cried to the children, pointing to the knight, already atop his horse and several paces ahead. "If we get separated, head to San Galgano and ask the monks for sanctuary. They are old friends of the d'Angelos."

He hit the horses' flanks, sending them scurrying forward. Vito turned and urged his mare up the steep path that led to what he and Ugo remembered as a little-known pass eastward, and Gianni ran to help Ambrogio with Josephine. Gaspare already had Agata astride a horse, and Daria's horse pranced, waiting on them. "Go! Go!" he cried, waving his arms.

Daria was off before he could say farewell, leading Josephine's horse by the reins, but he was relieved to see her departing. They shared a meaningful glance, saying their farewells silently. Ugo and Hasani rode off behind her.

"How many?" he asked, turning to the scout.

"Twelve, plus Lord Amidei."

Gianni placed a foot in his stirrup and mounted. "Was there a large knight beside him? Broad in shoulder, sandy haired? Bigger than I?"

The scout frowned. "No one of note. The nobleman was the largest of them."

Ciro. If not with Amidei, where was he? Again, the memory of Hasani's drawing waved through his mind. The trees, so like the conical cypress planted as windbreaks throughout Toscana. Was it this day he would face the knight again? That Daria would be caught by Abramo?

He kicked his horse in the side and snapped the reins, moving into a gallop to catch up with his wife.

ᏮᏮ ᏮᏮ ᏮᏮ

THEY had just passed San Galgano, the children eyeing the old abbey with eyes full of longing, when Ciro and the other eight knights emerged on the ridge ahead.

"We can take them," Vito said. "Let us be done with it, here, now."

Gianni rested his hands on the saddle horn before him, then looked over his shoulder to the rising dust of thirteen other men coming fast. They might be able to take Ciro and his knights, but if they tarried, Amidei and his men would arrive, just as they wearied. They would all be cut down.

"Look behind us, to the road," he said to Vito.

The knight turned in his saddle and then eyed the captain. "We cannot battle so many and keep the women and children safe."

"To San Galgano," Gianni said, wheeling his horse around. "Daria, you gain us entrance and persuade the monks to lock up the abbey. We shall head off the knights."

They took off, running madly toward their enemy for a time before arcing left, toward the old abbey rising from an ancient forest. Abramo and Ciro met and joined together, a thundering stampede of horses giving chase. Green hills surrounded them, and Gianni grimly again noted the conical cypress trees. Hasani eyed him over his shoulder, recognizing the landscape, too. So it would end here, now, as Vito wished. But in the manner he wanted?

Gianni looked over his shoulder, watching as Abramo and Ciro gained on them. Then he glanced toward Daria, moving slowly with Josephine. She was afraid to urge the horses past a trot, fearful she might send the older, blind woman sailing behind them. Agata and Gaspare moved at a similar pace.

"Go!" he cried to Daria, encouraging her onward, the children riding hard behind her.

"Stay with her, Hasani!" he cried, and the black man leaned down over his horse's neck, becoming as one with the mare, all muscle and sinew and strength.

ᚙ ᚙ ᚙ

DARIA clattered into the abbey courtyard, jumping from her horse even before the mare came to a full stop, and running toward the men in robes who looked to her in surprise.

"Lady d'Angelo," said one, rushing toward her.

"Enemies behind us," she panted, not bothering to tell the man of her name change. "Please, we need sanctuary! Ask the brothers to bring me and mine in and bar the doors!"

The monk frowned, hesitating over her unorthodox request. His eyes slid to Hasani, tall and silent, menacing in his own right, then to Piero, with the hair of a brother but the clothing of a commoner.

She glanced down, saw his stained fingertips, and grabbed his hand. "Long have the d'Angelos been a friend to this abbey. You are a scribe, entrusted to copy the Holy Writ. Well you know of our common, ancient enemy. I tell you, he lurks. He comes now, behind us."

He stared at her, then turned and barked orders. "Quickly! Inside, all of you! Prepare to bar the gates as if barbarians are at our door!"

"Oh, and if they were only barbarians," she whispered, following behind him. She glanced over her shoulder as she helped Josephine and the children from their horses and ushered them inside, with Agata and Gaspare. If they all had made it this far, what were the men behind them encountering?

ᚙ ᚙ ᚙ

THE men divided into two separate forces, forcing Amidei and Ciro to separate as well. Their plan was to fight off the marauders, then get back to the others inside the abbey, as soon as possible. *With whoever was left* was more like it, thought Gianni.

Gianni led Ambrogio and five of the Sienese knights forward, shouting warning to avoid a straight line, even as an archer took one of them down.

To his right, Vito and Ugo and three other knights rounded a mill and disappeared. Shelter, he thought. With a shield about them, they could avoid being picked off by the archers, and given the opportunity, strike back when possible. Wise, he decided, as he leaned deep into his right stirrup to avoid another arrow. Where could they go?

They rounded a corner and discovered the abbey, with none but riderless horses ambling about. Could they make it inside as well? He looked over his shoulder and saw two knights fall behind him. A third took an arrow to the shoulder but kept his saddle. To remain here, pursued by Abramo and the archers, could only be suicide.

"Stay with me," he said to Ambrogio, wheeling hard to the right, surprising his pursuers, who took a greater turn. They rode hard for the courtyard.

꧁ ꧁ ꧁

"Let them in!" Daria cried from the second-floor window. "Quickly, let those men in and lock the door behind them!"

Two monks scurried at the bottom of the stair to do as she bid. Gianni, Ambrogio, and one other knight came charging in, turning to slam the heavy wooden doors behind them, even as arrows came singing inward, slicing into the ancient wood. They managed to shut it and bar it even as the men outside came charging against it, falling heavily away.

Gianni reached for her, panting heavily. "Where are the weaknesses?"

She searched her memory of the abbey, a place she had been coming to from the time she was a small child in the company of her grandfather. "It is well fortified. The monks never wished to be held hostage in a nobleman's war."

"Are there weapons?"

She again thought back. "San Galgano's hall. Where many a nobleman relinquishes his weapons as the blessed saint once did."

Gianni met Hasani's glance. "Show me," he said.

They set off at a run, ignoring the impact sound at the back door, the rattling of fortified shutters. The enemy sought to instill fear, wild panic. They would not give him such satisfaction.

Four monks, younger men, ran behind Ambrogio, Piero, Hasani and the knight. Nico, Roberto, and Tessa followed.

They reached the hall and Gianni paused, amazed at the weapons that lined the walls, above those that were amassed in piles below. "It is a tradition of the abbey," Daria said, nodding toward the chapel ahead. In the center was a large, rounded granite rock with the hilt of a sword sticking out the top. "The younger nobles arrive here and relinquish their weapons in order to serve the Lord."

"The sword of the saint?" Gianni asked in wonder, staring forward. It was legendary, but many thought it more myth than truth.

She nodded.

A crashing sound drew their attention backward.

"Quickly," Gianni said, handing a sword to Piero. Hasani was already tucking daggers in his belt as the children gathered bows and arrows. The man grabbed the boys by the nape of their shirts, hauling them up a staircase, presumably to lay siege to the enemy outside.

Gianni hesitated before handing a sword to one of the monks. "Are you certain, brother?"

"I pledged my life to God," he said, grabbing it from him, "not my death to an enemy who would dare lay siege to a house of God."

"You fight for God in fighting for us," Gianni said, holding the sword still. "Know that before you enter the fray."

The priest nodded soberly, seeming to fully understand, inexplicably, and the others grabbed weapons of choice from the walls and ran to join the others upstairs.

Suddenly Gianni and Daria were alone in the hall.

"We take our stand, here," he said to her softly, as another boom was heard and monks cried out in fear. Prayer in Latin rose up to the rafters.

"Yes," she said. Quietly she eased the tattered shield from his shoulder and laid it on the ground. She moved to the side and returned with a sheath of chain mail in her arms. She eased it over his shoulders and settled it around his waist, looking deeply into his eyes. Did he know how much she loved him? How much she longed to see him live?

Daria turned away and lifted metal leg armor, judging the size in her hands. Deciding upon the larger, she turned and knelt before his feet, fastening the plates around his calves, then moving to fasten two others about his thighs.

He stood deadly still, watching her, transfixed. She moved again to the piles and chose a fine breastplate, handing it to him to hold, then moving behind him to fasten it. On his back she placed another, praying all the while. "Father God, protect the man within this armor. Keep him safe. Give him strength. Help him see what he cannot. Hear what he cannot. Make him your warrior, Lord Jesus. Fight off your enemy through this man, Father."

She reached for the arm plates, but Gianni grabbed her and pulled her to him, kissing her with such fervor that she could do nothing else but kiss him back in equal measure.

A boom sounded against the front door, and all the windows rattled in quick succession. He pulled her away from him, his eyes still closed. Slowly he opened them to stare upon her. "I have always loved you, Daria. Since the first day I saw you, and even more with each day. The loving of you threatens to undo me now."

"No greater is the love you bear for me than the love I bear for you," she said softly, turning to lay hold of arm plates. She fastened them on his forearms, then turned to take a belt full of daggers and wrap them around his waist. As she circled him again, she took a sturdy shield from the wall and placed it in his hands.

Daria edged up on her tiptoes and kissed him lightly on the lips. "Return to me," she said.

A terrible cracking sounded behind him, the sound of splintering wood.

The door had been breached.

"Until my last breath," he said. Then he turned and ran headlong toward battle.

Hasani emerged then behind her, on a dead run with the other young priests, so recently returned to arms, behind him. They filtered past on either side, running to join the knights who fought off the attackers below. The children trailed behind. At the last moment, Daria reached out and held Tessa back.

Nico and Roberto paused, looking over their shoulders, but kept running forward, emulating the ways of men and women beyond their years.

Daria caught sight of Abramo and edged backward into the shadows, even though his attention was solely on Gianni, who struck in savage fashion. She turned to grab a dagger and handed it to Tessa, telling her to hide it in the folds of her dress. Then she took the bow from the girl's shoulder and placed it in her hands, showing her how to aim.

She took another, larger bow and a quiver full of arrows, wishing she had spent more time practicing. They were surprisingly light, and Daria reached for another quiver, stepping slightly ahead of Tessa in an effort to be her shield. The men battled on, shouting and grunting and crying out. Soon, more of Amidei's men poured through the entrance, driving Gianni and his men backward, half toward the chapel, half up the stairs on the far end, where she supposed Agata and Josephine had sought shelter.

Ciro edged through the chapel door, panting and about to turn, when he caught sight of Daria and Tessa at the far end. He grinned and rubbed his glove across his sweaty lip, swinging his sword as if in idle exercise as he moved forward.

Tessa let an arrow fly, and it skittered across the cobblestone floor.

Daria let her own arrow loose, and it sang across the space. But Ciro deflected it with a lazy lift of his shield. "You could well use some lessons from Lord Amidei's archers, ladies," he said.

Daria let another fly, but he again deflected it. Tessa's arrow went high and to the right. He moved to the windows at the far side of the hall and opened a few as he advanced. "Your men," he said, "fought valiantly. That is, until we locked them in and set fire to their lair. They roast alive even as we speak. Shh. Do you hear them screaming?"

Nay, Daria thought. Not Vito and Ugo! Not the others sent from the Nine! Not them! It was not even their fight, their cause . . . She caught herself. But it *was* their cause. The cause of all who battled for light, for truth, for God, and against evil. Memory of Gianni, standing right here, filled her mind. *We stand here.*

Still, her eyes traveled to the window. Vito and Ugo, their music, their laughter . . . their hearts, loyal and true. So much had the brothers seen the Gifted through!

Ciro paused by the last window. "Come and see, m'lady. Come and say your farewells."

She centered another arrow on her bow and took aim, refusing to take the bait. But was that smoke she smelled upon the wind? Is that why Vito and Ugo did not burst through the doors behind Ciro, coming to their aid?

Chapter Forty

"M'LADY," Tessa said in a high whine behind her as Ciro advanced.

Daria's eyes cut to the door when Abramo rammed against the door-frame, then whirled inward. As Ciro had done before him, he paused upon seeing Daria and Tessa, but turned to slice the throat of a monk, complete his rotation, and gain such momentum that he decapitated a knight.

"Oh!" Tessa cried, and Daria pulled her dagger out from her belt at the same time she pulled the girl to her, hiding her face in the bodice of her dress. *Please Lord, intervene! Save us!*

Abramo turned and advanced behind Ciro, the two of them making Daria feel very small indeed.

They circled her, one taking either side, and Daria tried to shield the moaning child, rendered almost paralyzed in the face of the Sorcerer and his man. "They are legion, m'lady," she moaned.

"Yes, we are," responded Abramo, grinning. He reached for the girl, and Daria sliced at his arm with the dagger, drawing blood.

He eyed her in fury. "Take her," he said to Ciro.

The man lunged, and Tessa screamed, but Daria was too late. The massive knight had the child, held her by the hair, eyeing her as if she were a tasty bit of meat atop a skewer.

Piero entered the hall, crying out in rage.

"Ah, the defrocked priest," Abramo said, circling him. "Put down that child's plaything and die with some dignity," he said, jabbing at Piero's short sword.

The little man glared at him. "God intends for us to *live*." He lunged forward and surprised Abramo, who narrowly avoided the tip slicing his throat. Surprise turned to anger, and he moved upon the priest, driving him backward with one fierce blow after another. Daria watched in mute fear, then realized she was succumbing, succumbing to exactly what the enemy wished to instill.

"Holy, holy, holy is the Lord God Almighty," she repeated, advancing behind Abramo even as he advanced on her priest, driving him nearer the rock of San Galgano. Amidei lifted his head, distracted from the priest by her words, the same words that had fought him off on his own dark isle. "The angels sing in the heavens at the mere sound of his name, our Savior, our King," she said.

"Cease," he spat over his shoulder at her, striking with more fury than ever at Piero. But she was distracting him. Piero bravely lunged forward, then turned away, bleeding at the cheek.

"We fight in the name of the One who was, and is, and is to come," she said.

He tried to ignore her.

"We fight in the name of the One who was, and is, and is to come!" she cried, grabbing a sword from the wall and ramming it down toward Abramo's right clavicle.

He whirled as her stroke came downward, but Ciro lunged forward, narrowly blocking Daria's stroke. He tossed Tessa to his lord.

Abramo pulled the girl to him, his sword edging into her throat.

Daria stilled.

"Ahh. At last the women are silent," he said.

Ciro turned and rammed his sword down upon Piero behind him, who just barely managed to block it.

Daria let her sword tip fall to the ground, staring into Tessa's eyes. "Forgive me," she whispered.

"It is not necessary," the girl whispered back. "We fight in the name of the One who was, and is, and is to come," she shouted. "Jesus! Jesus! Jesus!"

Abramo, enraged at the sound of the Name above all names, whipped her away from him, hurling her in an arc toward the stone of San Galgano.

The child sailed through the air and struck the rock, seeming to hover there for a moment, and then slid down the side of it, limp as if lifeless.

"Nay!" cried Daria, watching with wide eyes stinging with tears as the girl landed in a slump at the base of the rock.

But Abramo had turned back to her.

cb cb cb

GIANNI could see Daria, Tessa, and Piero in the chapel, but could not get to them, no matter how hard he tried. No sooner had he dispatched one knight than another took his place. They seemed endless, tireless, and his armor had begun to feel heavy upon him.

He turned and saw that Hasani had suffered a chest wound and yet labored on in the fray, refusing to give up. But he was on the other side of the entrance hall.

Gianni fought off another knight, turned to see Abramo fling Tessa through the air, but then a Sicilian with a wicked sword was back at him, narrowly missing his jugular with a strike, then his belly with a thrust of a dagger. He whirled and swung his sword wide, hoping to catch him and did, but even as the enemy fell, another advanced. He glanced into the chapel and saw Father Piero receive a terrible blow from Ciro, a strike with such force and momentum from his shield—an unexpected blow—that the priest's head snapped backward and he slumped to the ground beside Tessa.

Now both men moved upon his wife. He had to get to her. Had to. But how, with three knights between him and the entrance?

cb cb cb

SHE could not reach Piero and Tessa. Abramo advanced fast upon her, wiping his upper lip with the back of his hand. Daria saw no other recourse. She turned and ran, lifting the bar from the huge, ornately carved doors of the sanctuary and tearing down the hill outside. Were Vito and Ugo truly dead? Might she reach them in time? Could someone yet come to her aid?

She could hear Abramo running after her, his footfalls louder and louder. There was the smell of smoke upon the wind. *Nay, Lord, nay . . .* she cried out. But Abramo was impossibly close. At last she turned and whirled, facing him, panting.

He laughed and circled her, saying nothing, breathing nearly as hard as she did. She had to prolong this encounter, as much as she wanted to see its end. It was her only hope. *Please Lord,* she cried out silently. She reached out her hands, as if in surrender.

"You think you and yours can best me?" he whispered, his breath still coming in a hot pant. "That the house of men purporting to be *holy* could protect you?" He took a step away and held the tip of his sword out toward her, tracing her shoulder, her breast, her arm, her back, up the nape of her neck, as he circled her, stopping behind her. With a quick slice he cut apart her hairnet and her hair tumbled down around her shoulders, reaching her waist.

Daria whirled around to face him again, and he swore under his breath, shaking his head in naked admiration.

"By the stars, Daria de Capezzana, you are beautiful. Despite all, I confess to still desiring you. No woman has denied me. No woman has dared bring me bodily harm. But it builds inside me, this need for you. Fall, fall to your knees and I shall yet spare you. Walk beside me, and I shall raise your brat as my own."

She laughed without mirth and shook her head. "Never."

He sighed heavily and advanced upon her even as she backed away. "I shall bring your beloved Gifted in chains, so you can watch them die before you give in to death. I shall not leave a one of you alive." He took another step. "And you shall suffer much before death relieves you."

ↄ ↄ ↄ

PIERO looked to the child, who yet lived but was blissfully unaware of what was transpiring about her. He looked for his short sword, now beyond Ciro and Gianni, who battled fiercely. The armory was similarily out of reach. He knew Daria had run outside, with Abramo in pursuit. He had to go to her and do what, fight off Abramo alone? Nay, better to try to distract Ciro so Gianni could save his wife.

His eyes moved about the sanctuary for a weapon. A brass torch? The chalice on the altar? His eyes moved over the saint's sword in the stone and onward, then abruptly back. Could it be? He searched his heart as the urge overtook him. Nay. It was impossible. Had not many a man tried and come up short?

But then he felt that this was what he was called to do, and there was no time to argue with the Holy. He gently set Tessa to the ground, said a prayer of protection over her, and crossed around the rock. He eased over the ornate fence that circled the stone and climbed atop the smooth granite on all fours, until he was atop the boulder. Placing one foot on either side of the sword, sunk deep within the rock, he said a prayer. For blessing. For favor.

For the same numinous power that allowed Galgano to sink the sword, to now allow him to release it.

He looked to Gianni. He had just suffered a torturous blow to the chin, sending him reeling. Ciro advanced upon him.

"Ciro!" he called, staring at the knight. "Ciro!"

Reluctantly the hulking knight turned, panting as he glanced his way.

But Piero had already reached for the sword.

Slowly it eased from the stone as simply as from a sheath. "Surely a sword that God took from Galgano and housed here for two hundred years was meant for you and no other," Piero said, raising the heavy sword with both hands and jumping the four feet down from the rock.

Ciro smiled down at him. "Should such a small priest be carrying such a mighty sword?"

Piero returned the grin. "I am no priest."

Ciro's smile faded. "Here. Give it to a man who can handle such metal." He lifted his chin, daring Piero near.

Behind him, Gianni rose and rammed the flat of his sword into the side of his head. Ciro fell heavily and then closed his eyes.

"If God chooses to spare him, I want to see him on trial before the Nine," Gianni said.

Piero raised Galgano's sword in victory. And then both remembered at once.

Daria.

♔ ♔ ♔

Daria backed up, aware that the light of day was quickly fading. Her eyes cast desperately left and right, seeking aid, weapon, escape. But there was nothing but towering juniper and cypress and Bormeo, sailing overhead, screeching in agitation.

Abramo lunged, and she narrowly avoided his grasp. He lunged again, and caught her hair this time. He wound it in his hand, pulling her toward him, even as she reached out to scratch him.

He took her right arm and pinned it against her side, reaching around for the other as well, easily holding both behind her. "Easy, kitten. Easy. I have but one eye left to scratch out."

He let her struggle against him, seeming to enjoy it, so she ceased, motionless except for her breaths, which came in quick succession.

"Ahh, yes. 'Tis a pity you and yours must die. But there is nothing for it. Our battle ends here."

"They shall find you. You shall stand trial before the Nine."

"With whom to accuse us? My men and archers have certainly killed the others by now."

"Marco had my letter," she said.

"Letters are lost at times." He pretended to grimace. "Even poor Vincenzo, who is most culpable for the acts accused, is now dead behind us. And Marco may come to an unfortunate end as well, should he not see the error of his ways."

"You shall spend eternity in hell," Daria said, aghast to again face such utter depravity. She panted now, not in fear, but at the harrowing chasm she sensed between them. She closed her eyes, wanting to block the utter terror, the sheer sense of *void* that was Abramo's future. "The abyss, Abramo. The devil lays no claim other than upon those who are willing."

It was then she saw it, the hovering shadow, just behind him. Cold, so cold.

Tessa would be screaming in terror by now. *The enemy! The enemy of old!* Her heart screamed at her to be away.

Abramo saw her take note of his master and smiled. "Ah. But m'lady, you continue to think I am a begrudging servant." He looked over his shoulder and let her go. But before she took a step, he pinched her throat in his right hand and lifted her up off the ground. "I serve the dark and no other. Your light, m'lady," he said through clenched teeth, as he lifted her higher, "is about to be . . . extinguished."

CHAPTER FORTY-ONE

GIANNI ran down the hill, watching as Abramo lifted Daria to her tiptoes and then into the air. He let out a roar, intending to distract his enemy, but Abramo did not so much as turn, so focused was he upon Daria.

A sting ran through the back of Gianni's knee, and he stumbled, wondering what had torn into him. As he rolled to the ground, Piero rumbled past him, grunting Ciro's name even as he ran toward Daria and Abramo.

Gianni rolled and with each turn, took excruciating note of the cause of the tearing within his knee. An arrow. He had taken yet another of Amidei's archer's arrows.

He moved to try to rise, had to get to Daria, to cut away Amidei's arm, when what felt like a boulder ran over him, driving him to the ground.

Ciro. Impossible.

But the man was above him, atop him, cruelly twisting the arrow at his knee, making him scream in pain.

Unable to reach the man's neck nor kick him from his torso, Gianni reached for one of the daggers at his belt, digging through the dirt and grass beneath him, even as Ciro again moved the arrow at his knee, laughing as Gianni cried out.

ॐ ॐ ॐ

"JESUS," Daria said, fighting for breath, pulling at his fingers.

Bormeo screeched and swooped past, narrowly missing Abramo with his talons.

"What did you say?" Abramo asked, lifting her higher.

He was distracted, by her bird and her words.

"Je-sus!" she cried. "Christ! Liv-ing! Lord!"

With a cry of fury, he cast her down to the side.

His master moved behind him, and gasping for breath, Daria tried to keep her vision from swimming. Bormeo swooped by again.

"Behind me?" Abramo muttered, as if the master had warned him.

And so it was that he was perfectly in place.

Piero, charging down the hillside with the sword of San Galgano, roared as he struck the Sorcerer, driving the sword through his belly with such momentum that he fell atop Abramo Amidei, even as the man at last toppled to the ground.

ঌ ঌ ঌ

GIANNI reached the dagger and swung it upward, driving it into Ciro's head, just above his temple. But it was at an awkward angle and glanced off the bone, so it did nothing more than enrage him. He stood up and kicked at the arrow shaft, broken now but still lodged through Gianni's leg, making Gianni roll away, swallowing a scream. Ciro lifted his sword and straddled the knight, holding it with both hands with the clear intent to drive it into Gianni's neck.

ঌ ঌ ঌ

ABRAMO, sitting halfway up on account of the sword through his belly, touched the blood that spread up his jerkin and lifted his fingers, as if seeing odd paint atop the tips.

"Killing a man," he said to Piero, "shall land you with me in hell."

"Killing you," Piero said, pushing harder on the shaft of the ancient sword, panting, "shall save other souls from the abyss. I shall leave my fate to God's judgment."

Abramo looked down as if in odd amusement at the sword and the priest, and then paused, as if struggling for breath.

Daria moved to her knees, still struggling for breath of her own.

Hasani raced past them, leaping over a boulder as he moved toward Ciro, just then pulling his sword in a downward thrust. Ambrogio was right behind him.

Daria turned and screamed, but little sound came out of her wounded throat.

But Piero's attention remained on Lord Abramo Amidei, who at that moment took the last breath he would ever take.

ずる ずる ずる

HASANI cried out and whipped his arm across, driving his curved sword down toward Ciro even as Gianni sank yet another dagger into his leg. Hasani's blow abruptly stopped Ciro's downward momentum and Gianni pushed the sword, hovering just inches from his chest, away. Ambrogio struck next, plunging his sword into Ciro's chest.

The hulking knight wavered above Gianni, still looking down upon the wound at his chest as if in wonder, then down to his leg, gushing blood as Gianni pulled the dagger back out.

Vito and Ugo arrived then, soot-covered but alive, with five remaining Sienese knights behind them. Vito leaned forward and pushed with the tip of his sword at Ciro. The man toppled off Gianni, to the side, dead.

Daria stumbled over to them, reaching for Gianni.

Vito eyed Abramo, clearly dead beside Daria and Piero, and then looked back to the dead, hulking form of Ciro. "Well then," he said. "My work here is done." He sheathed his sword, feigning self-satisfaction.

Gianni laughed, still trying to gain his breath, comfort his wife, and battle the pain. He rose to a sitting position and took Daria in his arms, holding her close. "We made it, Daria. God has seen us through."

Piero came, dragging the heavy sword of Saint Galgano that now seemed impossible to lift. Agata, Ambrogio, Gaspare, and the children ran down the hill toward them, the monks filtering out behind them, apparently having waylaid or vanquished any remaining knights inside.

A fierce, cold wind, sudden and strong, ran across the fields and forest, blowing past them, lifting their hair and causing them to shield their faces. And then it was gone, leaving naught but a quiet heat of the early spring sun, setting on the horizon.

Piero rose, dragging Galgano's sword above his head, up to the skies, praising their God for deliverance. Then he looked to each of them. "Steep has been the cost. Great has been the battle. But greater still, God's victory."

EPILOGUE

Nine months later

HASANI and Ambrogio worked side by side in the magnificent Santo Paulo Chapel of the fortified mansion de Capezzana, just outside Siena and north of San Galgano.

They stood back and silently looked upon faces from their past, of their future. At the chapel entrance were images of Scripture, of Saint Paul's conversion, of him speaking to the masses and in small rooms, as dark storm forces raged outside, and others of him alongside his scribe, dictating missives to the faithful far from him.

Farther into the chapel were knights and ladies, images of Basilio and Rune, Vito and Ugo, Hasani and Gianni. Of ladies in finery, of Daria and Tessa and Josephine. The others were there as well . . . Count Armand, Anette and Dimitri, Ambrogio, Lucan, Agata, Beata, Aldo, Nico, Roberto, even some of the Sienese knights whose faces they could still well remember. They bathed the walls in memory, of people lost and people healed, from the farmer's wife nearby to the lepers of Venezia to the pope in Avignon.

But in the front of the chapel, on either side of the nave and behind the cross, the walls were reserved solely for Christ and his men, those who had begun what the Gifted had merely hoped to continue.

Daria entered, her baby boy in her arms, with Gianni right behind her. The others followed, never far from their mistress and their lord. Father Piero entered at the rear, still their priest and leading them in ministry among the villagers and people of the hills, regardless of whether the Vaticana approved or not. Of late, people were traveling as far as from the city to listen to them preach and move among them on Sundays.

Daria paused over the images of Basilio, Rune, and Armand, a hand going to her nose as quick tears rose in her eyes. Ambrogio moved aside as she caressed the men's images, remembering, and on to the others they had lost, remembering, remembering.

The rest exclaimed with delight and dismay, doing the same behind their lady, moving forward, touching, praying, making the chapel fully theirs. At last they made it to the cross, embedded into the plaster. A Christ figure seemed to alight from it, half hanging, half rising, so lively that it was as if they witnessed the resurrection. They stood in silence.

Daria picked up her chin and glanced over her left shoulder, as if sensing a call from far off.

Gianni shook his head. "I know that look . . ."

Piero grinned and gazed into each of their faces. "Let us be about it, then. The letter was clear. We have witnessed just the beginning of this grand adventure. There is much ahead of us, brothers and sisters. Much." He placed his hand in the center of their circle, and the others moved in to add their own hand. "With God ever before us and beside us, my friends. We shall never be alone. And in the darkness we shall sow . . ."

"Light," they said.

AUTHOR'S NOTE

MANY in the Church did lobby to bring the papacy home to Roma and away from Frankish influence. They came close with Pope Benedict XII, but then never again, through the reigns of five more popes. Roma was considered unstable, and in fact, was rather scary in this era, with constant shifts of power and the very real threat of murder in order to usurp papal authority.

I fused aspects of the more austere and restrained Pope Benedict XII, who actually imposed a firm rule against wayward priests and bishops and cardinals abusing their power, with aspects of his more flamboyant and off-base successor, Clement VI, as well as their palaces (Clement added on yet three other grand wings to the imposing palace), for creative effect. Obviously my characterization of Benedict/Clement, who became the fictionally named Cornelius II, is a figment of my imagination, only loosely based on fact, but meant to represent an eighteen-year span of papal authority and impact.

If you are a language scholar, you probably noticed I translated the Latin Vulgate into NIV; as gifted as these people are, it would have been miraculous indeed for them to be reading a modern translation in 1340. However, for the sake of readability, clarity, and flow—and to avoid making any inadvertent errors with Scripture—I elected to use a modern translation for modern readers.

Bernard of Clairvaux predated the Gifted and espoused many Protestant-leaning beliefs. Soon after the years of our fabled Gifted, a man in England (John Wycliffe) and another in Prague (John Hus) and still another in Germany (Martin Luther) would see the Reformation become a growing reality. God moved through the world, calling his people forth and into real, vital relationship with him. And no force of the dark could stop it.

Petrarch, Dante, Simone Martini, and Cardinal Stefani were historical figures but are largely a figment of my imagination in terms of characterization, dialogue, etc. Petrarch was a vociferous critic of the papal court and spent quite a bit of time away from his native Italia and in and around the pope. Martini and Stefani were Sienese, like our fictional Daria d'Angelo, and truly resided in Avignon at this time. As you undoubtedly know, Dante wrote the famous *Inferno,* and rumor has it that he based the caves of hell on the eerie cliffs that face the real Les Baux of Provence. Burning deceased nobles upon funerary pyres was a fictional device of my own, not fact.

The Cathars had been defined as heretics and stamped out of existence by the Church, a precursor to the Spanish Inquisition by a couple of centuries. The Cathars' widespread influence and the threat of a resurgence—or something similar—would have set the papacy against our Gifted had they actually appeared in this era.

In 1252, the antiheretical movement came to a head with Innocent IV's papal bull *Ad extirpanda.* Two years later the pope formed districts in which the Dominican or Franciscan inquisitors could be active. Most punishments involved pilgrimages or imprisonment. Those unwilling to recant might have been transferred to a secular court and executed, but this was rarely done until later. Still, it did occur on occasion, and the desire to rout out heretical groups was even backed by military engagements at times, for instance with the Cathars of Sirmione near Verona (1277) and the Apostles (1307). Since heretical thought seemed to gain a toehold in southern France, it follows that our fictional Cornelius and his cardinals would have indeed been on the watch for prowling heretics. And the Court of the Rota beneath the Palais de le Pape, as described, was very real. But it was in 1478, with the backing of the Spanish monarchy, that the Inquisition became most fearsome and powerful.

San Galgano truly houses the sword of the saint, reportedly encased in stone, and Galgano, a crusader, truly did relinquish his sword after returning home from battle, in order to serve his God. The abbey arose around the stone and became a powerful force in the region, supplying Siena with her clergy. This legend of the sword in the stone may have served as inspiration for the Arthurian legend of Excalibur. Alas, when I went to tour the ancient abbey, now roofless but still standing, much of it was closed, so I could only walk the sanctuary itself, never laying eyes on the sword and the stone. As I type this, a few new videos have appeared on YouTube. Just type in "San Galgano" to see them for yourself.

The Catholic Church, and the Protestant Church, and now the nondenominational Church, our Christian Body as a whole, have all seen their share of corruption, sin—many, many things that would make the Lord either cry out in dismay or shout in fury—and will undoubtedly continue to suffer and fall before Satan's attack. But that is because the Church is peopled by people—people like you and me, fallible, imperfect, given to follow our more base nature, even when the Lord on High calls to us to something more. The siren call of Satan is powerful and insidious, weaving in and out of all our lives, pulling us away from the Father of life. Beware the dragon, who lurks even as our Savior abides and calls us forward. He is nonfictional.

It is my most fervent hope that this series might have called you to examine your own life, your own ways, the paths you have taken and those ahead of you where the path forks, forcing you to a decision. God calls to each of us, beckoning us toward something higher, something deeper, toward *life at its most rich*, in and out of every day, every hour. Can you hear him? I believe there is a whisper on the wind, or in our hearts, right now, if we all only have ears to hear.

I wish you every blessing upon the journey.

Lisa T. Bergren
January 2008

READERS GUIDE FOR

The Blessed

DISCUSSION QUESTIONS

1. In this novel, Daria emphasizes to those the Lord is about to heal that they must believe, hope, trust (Dimitri Devenue, the nobles, the blind boy at the river, Roberto). What effect, if any, do you believe positive thinking and faith play in modern healings?

2. Have you known anyone who was "healed"? If so, what was their attitude and faith life like?

3. Hasani knows what is about to transpire on the Pont du Gard and at San Galgano—that his dearest friends are on the edge of disaster, even death. Have you ever known that people you loved were in danger—could see the "train wreck" ahead—and been powerless to stop it? What was that like? What did you do? Did you wish you could've done something different?

4. Cardinal Morano enters Abramo Amidei's cave and the ceremony as a test of faith. Do you believe that testing your faith/beliefs is important? When does testing strengthen faith? Does it ever weaken faith?

5. Amidei approaches each of the powerful cardinals he wishes to influence, by appealing to their unique weaknesses. His master says, "What is right for him, shall be right for him." If you believe in Satan, do you believe he works in such individually targeted ways? Why or why not?

6. Consider the modern saying "Whatever works for them" and the philosophy that there is no absolute truth, absolute good, absolute right. Could that leave one vulnerable to corruption? Why or why not?

7. Daria and Gianni both fall for Amidei's tactics involving confusion. Do you believe Satan uses "mind games" with us today?

8. Vincenzo del Buco—Daria's "uncle" and favored friend who has fallen so far under the tutelage of Amidei—ultimately saves her. What do you think got through to him at last?

9. Vincenzo had done many horrible things. In *The Betrayed*, he was involved in kidnapping, torture, and even murder. Do you think he went to hell or heaven? Why?

10. Some key characters die in this book—Rune and Basilio, and Count Armand. Do you believe that pursuit of a goal is ever worth the cost of a life? Why or why not?

11. This series ends with *The Blessed*, but in the end, Daria is hearing the call to heal another. Do you think it ended there? What do you think happened with our characters in the years that followed?